Countdown Zero

COUNTDOWN ZERO

Thomas H. Saffer
and
Orville E. Kelly

Introduction by Stewart L. Udall

G. P. Putnam's Sons
New York

The text of this book is set in 11 point Electra.

Library of Congress Cataloging in Publication Data

Saffer, Thomas H.
Countdown zero.

Bibliography: p.
Includes index.
1. Atomic weapons—Testing. 2. United States—Armed Forces—History—20th century. 3. Veterans—Diseases—United States. 4. Atomic bomb—Physiological effect. 5. Ionizing radiation—Physiological effect. I. Kelly, Orville E., 1930-1980 II. Title.
UF767.S218 363.1'79 81-22659
ISBN 0-399-12685-6 AACR2

PRINTED IN THE UNITED STATES OF AMERICA

This book is dedicated to the National Association of Atomic Veterans and those who took part in and suffered from the effects of the seventeen-year undeclared war from 1945 to 1962.

Special Acknowledgments

The author is eternally grateful to:

Barbara Paris, editorial assistant, who unselfishly committed herself to assuring that *Countdown Zero* was historically and journalistically accurate.

Robert T. Cochran, Jr., who analyzed the manuscript and provided literary insight and journalistic balance.

Wanda Kelly, who provided invaluable information about Orville Kelly's life.

Sally Wecksler, literary agent, who, motivated by the strength of her convictions, saw to it that the book would be published.

Faith Sale, a senior editor at Putnam's, who worked diligently with the author to prepare the manuscript for publication. Every author should be fortunate enough to work with an eager editor of Faith's caliber.

—T.H.S.

Contents

The author wishes to thank:

Glenn Alcalay, John Alder, Bob Alvarez, Donald Baker, Larry Barber, Albert Bates, Eddie Becker, Penny Bernstein, Rosalie Bertell, Bob Bonney, Glenn Bouck, "Cuzk" Brumett, Irwin Bross, Pat Broudy, Bob Burton, Glynn Caldwell, Tim Lee Carter, Elizabeth Catalan, Jess Clark, Nancy Cooper, Alan Cranston, Gene Curbow, Russell Jack Dann, Nancy Dobies, Joel Donn, Jim Dugan, Bob Eckhardt, James Elliott, Richard Elliott, Carl Engstrom, Anne Fadiman, Allan Favish, Gaelen Felt, Anne Firestone, Charles Fleming, Morris Frieberg, Betty Fronterhouse, Connie Gallaudet, Ellis Gaspard, Jeanne Gerson, John Gofman, Lew Golinker, Andy Hawkinson, Dee Dee Helmick, Jack Holl, Karen Jackovich, Gerry Johnson, Giff Johnson, Lillian Johnson, Cloyd Jones, Lisa Kadam, Hideo Kasai, Tom Kelleher, Eugene King, Gary King, Sheila King, KUTV–Salt Lake City, Susan Lambert, Gene LaRoche, Cathy Lawhon, Sue Lee, Bennie Levy, John Loveridge, Shelley Madden, Tom Mancuso, Ed Martell, Bill McGee, Eddie McKinnon, Nancy McKracken, Molly Milligan, Karl Z. Morgan, Maryanne Mott, Bernie Mracek, Jim O'Connor, Bill Ogle, Greg Pagunson, Larry Pray, Richard Ray, James Reeves, Barbara Reynolds, Thornton Saffer, Wynne Saffer, Gay Santelli, Johanna Schrambling, Sam Scione, Mark Sennett, Frank Silvestri, Pat Smith, J. Arthur Solomon, Norman Solomon, Jacque Souadjain, Jonathan Steinberg, Al Taylor, Charles Trent, Harvey Tschirgi, Frank von Hipple, Henry Vyner, Bill Wagner, Herman Warsh, Dee Watts, Michael Wayne, Eric "Rip" Wieler.

Introduction

By Stewart L. Udall
Former Secretary of Interior

This is an alarming book, composed in quiet anger by two atomic veterans. The man who started the book, one-time Army Sergeant Major, Orville Kelly, is dead, his body riddled with cancer. Former Marine Captain Thomas Saffer, who wrote the book, is another casualty who has dedicated his life to obtaining fair play for the unsuspecting soldiers who were put in "front-line trenches" during the years this country was testing its new family of nuclear weapons.

This book is an indictment, an accusation lodged against the rash scientists and macho military men who ignored common-sense precautions in their headlong pursuit of nuclear superiority. It is also an exposé of a systematic thirty-year coverup by high officials in the U.S. government of the plague of cancer and other illnesses they needlessly inflicted on the soldiers and civilians who were unwitting participants in their experiments.

After Hiroshima snd Nagasaki the United States created two outdoor laboratories for its nuclear testing programs, one in the Marshall Islands in the Pacific and one in Nevada. However, unlike France or Britain, this country elected to expose its civilians to the fallout from the bombs and to conduct "war games" with its soldiers in the penumbra of these nuclear explosions. But even if one chooses to argue that such actions were defensible in the Cold War environment of the 1950s, the appalling truth is that our government is still stonewalling in the 1980s, still turning its back on the human guinea pigs who were forced to take part in ionizing-radiation experiments.

This book is part of a search for justice which Orville Kelly started in 1977, a search which now includes not only the atomic veterans who were sacrificed, but the Marshallese and the civilians who were downwind from the Nevada tests, the test-site employees whose workplace was the poisoned pit at Yucca Flat in Nevada, and the early uranium miners who were allowed to work underground in air impregnated with long-lived radiation emanations.

I salute Orville Kelly and Thomas Saffer for firing this rifle shot at the nuclear establishment, for I am convinced that our country has not yet come to terms with the nuclear age. It remains for our leaders to admit that supposed "low level" radiation causes cancer and other degenerative diseases and then for the nation to make restitution to all of those innocent citizens who, in the name of national security, bore the burdens of these reckless experiments.

The splitting of the atom has changed everything save our mode of thinking, and thus we drift towards unparalleled catastrophe.

—Albert Einstein

Prologue

On July 15, 1945, at Trinity, a site in the New Mexico desert, the first atomic bomb was detonated. Military personnel who were present at the test and at others conducted subsequently were exposed to ionizing radiation without their knowledge or consent. Because of this exposure, they have become known as atomic veterans. Today, these atomic veterans are living and dying examples of humans who were treated with less precaution than was taken with the laboratory animals. Demands for the advancement of nuclear technology have left them with a haunted past and an uncertain future.

It took nearly thirty-five years for the American people to become fully aware of the dangers of radiation. In 1977, news articles about veterans who were contracting cancer and other chronic and debilitating diseases in larger-than-expected numbers and at earlier-than-usual ages triggered responses from others who were suffering from similar medical problems: residents of the Marshall Islands, those living downwind from the Nevada Test Site, test site workers, uranium miners, nuclear submarine workers, and employees of the Rocky Flats nuclear weapons facility. Gradually, these civilians recognized their relationship to the military men who were on the islands in the Pacific and in the trenches in Nevada during the seventeen-year atmospheric nuclear weapons testing program. The civilians and the military men had one thing in common: repeated and excessive exposure to radiation.

Since 1978, congressional investigations have revealed that the U.S. nuclear weapons development program may have created a human health legacy of major proportions. A total of 235 announced atmospheric tests were conducted between 1945 and 1962, primarily in the Pacific and in Nevada. A total of 626 U.S. nuclear detonations, including underground blasts, were announced through the year 1979. Approximately 250,000 military personnel and 150,000 civilians participated in the seventeen-year testing program. Additionally, unknown thousands have been exposed to radiation from the nuclear weapons' fuel and manufacturing cycles and the continued underground testing of weapons.

All wars leave scars on both the battlefields and the participants; but after the end of most wars, scars of the conflict heal as the years pass. Yet today, some twenty years after the cessation of atmospheric testing, many of the Cold War veterans who had been ordered to assist in the U.S. development of nuclear weapons are convinced that they were attacked by an insidious killer. Unwarned, they were unprepared to ward off their assailant. Unlike conventional military opponents, this invisible adversary could not be defeated. A report released in September 1980, by the Center for Disease Control in Atlanta, Georgia, shows that instead, this adversary has returned again and again to attack and torture its victims. The report, a result of the only epidemiological study performed on atomic veterans, disclosed that the incidence of leukemia among the 2,595 veterans included in the study was nearly three times the level expected.

When countries send combatants into war, they are reasonably sure that the nation they are defending will care for them if they are wounded, disfigured, or disabled. During the Cold War years, soldiers, sailors, airmen, and marines were sent into test areas where they were exposed to ionizing radiation. Yet when the latent effects of their exposure became undeniably apparent, the government refused to recognize them as radiation victims or in many instances to acknowledge that they had ever been at the proving grounds where nuclear devices were detonated. Rather than being cared for, they were denied assistance. They could only conclude that they had been pawns in one of the deadliest games ever played with American citizens.

Thomas Saffer and Orville Kelly were two among tens of thousands who discovered that they were suffering from radiation-induced illnesses, that they were victims of a swiftly developing technology that outran moral responsibility. Orville Kelly was commander of Japtan Island at Eniwetok Atoll in the Marshall Islands in 1958. At twenty-two, he was promoted to sergeant major in the U.S. Army, one of the youngest men to ever hold that prestigious rank. In four months, he witnessed twenty-two nuclear blasts. Thomas Saffer was a newly commissioned twenty-two-year-old lieutenant in the Marine Corps when he was ordered to the Nevada Test Site. He participated in three nuclear detonations in June and July 1957, including a test of the largest experimental device ever exploded within the continental limits of the United States. *Countdown Zero* is their story and the story of many others like them who were trampled in the mindless race toward nuclear superiority.

1.

Land of the Giant Mushrooms

> *. . . troops successfully attacked directly toward ground zero immediately following the atomic explosion. You can hereafter remember with a sense of pleasure and accomplishment that you were one of those troops, a real pioneer in experimentation . . .*
>
> —Brigadier General H. P. Storke
> Camp Desert Rock Exercise Director
> June 2, 1952

"Good morning, gentlemen. Welcome to Frenchman Flat, the land where the giant mushrooms grow. You will see exactly what the survivors of Hiroshima saw. You will be closer to a nuclear explosion than any American troops have ever been. You may be injured if you do not obey orders." An unseen loudspeaker carried the voice. It droned on: "Today, you marine officers will witness a nuclear explosion scheduled for detonation at 0630 hours. This shot has been named Priscilla, and you are here to become acquainted with the effects of nuclear weapons." There was a pause, and the still desert dawn was empty of sound except for the crackling of the loudspeaker. Then the voice continued, "The trench lines to your immediate front are two miles from ground zero. It is now H minus fifty-five minutes."

As the disembodied announcer finished delivering his message, the tension among us grew. My own anxiety increased as I realized that in less than one hour I, Thomas H. Saffer, second lieutenant in the U.S. Marine Corps, would be exposed for the first time to the physical and emotional effects of a nuclear explosion. What little conversation there was ceased when we saw the balloon from which Priscilla was suspended being raised slowly into place, seven hundred feet above the desert floor. The apparatus seemed terrifyingly close.

As H hour approached, we reviewed our instructions to ourselves. Fifteen minutes before the countdown began, we were to enter the trenches. Two minutes before the detonation, we were to kneel on one knee with our right sides toward Priscilla and shield our tightly closed eyes with our left forearms. We had been issued gas masks to prevent us from inhaling the dust that would be raised when Priscilla's shock wave passed over the trench. After the detonation, we would be taken to within a few hundred yards of ground zero to inspect the effects of the blast on the equipment that had been placed at calculated distances outward from the hypocenter.

The only potential risk, we were told, would be from gamma rays. One of the natural products of a nuclear explosion, these rays would travel at the speed of light in a horizontal plane and would pass harmlessly over us if we knelt down in the trenches, as we had been told to do. Film badges clipped to the breast pockets of our field uniforms—under our field jackets—would measure our exposure to these rays.

It was 5:30 a.m., June 24, 1957, four days before my twenty-third birthday. The faint light of early dawn picked out the hills and the vast desert wasteland surrounding us. It was a stark contrast, I remember thinking, to the lush green of the northern Virginia countryside, where I lived before I had been sent to the Nevada Test Site. Virginia bloomed with life. My new surroundings looked like a good place to get rid of used razor blades. How did I happen to be at America's Outdoor Nuclear Explosives Laboratory only two short months after saying goodbye to my family and friends in beautiful Virginia?

Getting There

You may be whatever you resolve to be.

—Stonewall Jackson

I was trained and educated to become a citizen-soldier—a citizen who would contribute something worthwhile to mankind, and an officer who would command the respect and admiration of his men. I had graduated from VMI, the Virginia Military Institute, the only school in the country beside Annapolis, West Point, and the Air Force Academy that requires its graduates to serve for a period in a branch of the armed forces. VMI is often called "the West Point of the South," and each day spent there as a cadet instills discipline, obedience, and development of a sense of honor, all needed to transform young men into capable commissioned officers. I learned to follow the orders of my superiors without question.

VMI is steeped in the traditions and history of the South. "You may be whatever you resolve to be"—words of Confederate General Thomas Jonathan "Stonewall" Jackson—are cut into the stone archway over the entrance to the barracks. I had resolved to become a commissioned officer in the United States Marine Corps. VMI had graduated three Marine Corps Commandants and an untold number of senior officers.

Becoming a Marine Corps officer was not easy in 1956. I was rejected twice because my five-foot-six-and-a-half-inch stature was one half inch under the prescribed height for officers. Disappointed but undaunted, I applied for a third time and finally was accepted. In June of that year, I was awarded the bars of a second lieutenant and the globe-and-anchor emblem of a marine. I raised my right hand and promised "to bear true faith and allegiance to the United States of America . . . and obey the orders . . . of the Marine Corps." It was the culmination of my life's ambition at age twenty-one. I signed up for three years. I was obligated both by my oath and by a written contract, in which my responsibility to my country and my service were clearly spelled out. Conspicuously absent from this contract was any mention of the corps' or my country's obligation to me. Graduation over and the contract signed, my next destination was basic school in Quantico, Virginia.

Basic school lasted eight long and often boring months. The newly commissioned officers were indoctrinated daily in leadership and combat tactics. An attitude of gung-ho guts and glory prevailed. One instructor began every lecture by saying: "The greatest honor I could ever achieve would be to die on the battlefield defending my country as a Marine Corps officer, and I am going to teach you how to defend our country."

Next, we were assigned to duty stations in the Fleet Marine Force. All of us were weary of training, and each of us looked forward to assuming his first command.

Some assignments, of course, were better than others. I felt I was one of the fortunate few because I was being sent to California. I yearned to leave the East Coast, where I had spent all my life, and to travel. Guests at a farewell party in my hometown of Middleburg, Virginia, joined their voices in a rousing chorus of "California, Here I Come." The words still echoed in my head as I reported to Camp Pendleton, the home of the First Marine Division, on April 18, 1957.

The corporal at the main gate glanced at my orders and directed me to the base adjutant's office. Once there, I introduced myself to a first lieutenant in charge of assignments. After thoughtfully studying a large chart on the wall, he said, "Looks like we'll put you in the Seventh Marines."

Hesitantly, I asked, "Could you please assign me to the Fifth Marines? My two roommates are in the First Battalion and I would like to be with them."

"Um, let's see. The Second Battalion needs an officer. I can assign you there."

Another officer who overheard our conversation said, "That's the group that's going to Nevada to participate in the atomic exercises." His comment made no impression on me. I was simply relieved that my request had been so readily granted.

That same day, wearing my gabardine summer dress uniform and carrying my swagger stick, I rode from the base adjutant's office to Camp Santa Marguerita, home of the Fifth Marine Regiment, known as the Fighting Fifth. The regiment was one of the most tradition-steeped and decorated units in the corps and had distinguished itself in two World Wars and Korea. The Fifth had been awarded the French Fourragère in 1918 for outstanding valor in combat, and its officers and men wore the distinctive red-and-green striped cord beneath the left epaulet of their dress uniforms. I was assigned to F Company, one of the five companies that comprised the Second Battalion. When I arrived, F Company was out on a field exercise. First Sergeant Mike Esperanza acknowledged my arrival and asked me to sit down.

Within an hour, I heard the company returning to the barracks area. The men were chanting and running in formation as they approached. After they had been dismissed, I was introduced to the company commander, First Lieutenant George Ballard. Following a brief indoctrination, I was assigned to the second platoon as platoon leader. Before I met with my platoon sergeant and my men, Ballard began discussing the forthcoming exercise. Our battalion had been selected as the nucleus of the Fourth Marine Corps Provisional Atomic Exercise Brigade, and we were going to Nevada to practice combat maneuvers using atomic bombs as offensive weapons. I felt a small knot in the pit of my stomach when he said the word "atomic," but I still was excited to be participating in such an exercise. After all, I was only one month out of basic school and anxious to prove myself as a leader. The more adverse the conditions, the greater the challenge. And I was a highly motivated, confident, physically fit Marine Officer.

My first two months in the Fleet Marine Force were ones of major readjustment. It was clear to me early on that each lieutenant was judged carefully on his performance, and I was not only the junior officer in the company but the junior officer in the entire battalion. Ballard was distant in his dealings with me. The other two lieutenants in the company tolerated me but did not accept me as their buddy. I sought rapport with my platoon sergeant, Ray English, a senior noncommissioned officer. English, veteran of World War II and of the Korean conflict, had fourteen years of service to his credit. He had been the platoon leader for six months before I arrived. The men in my platoon held him in highest regard. Suddenly, *I* was *his* leader. I sensed that he could either make me or break me. Realizing I could teach him little, I concentrated instead on gaining his respect.

While I was making my own adjustments to the company

and becoming imbued with its history and tradition, important plans were being developed in an off-the-beaten-path building on another part of the base. Because the wooden frame structure had no identification, a passer-by would not have known that inside it the brigade staff was planning a dress rehearsal for nuclear war.

A newly promoted senior officer, Brigadier General Harvey C. Tschirgi, had received orders in January notifying him that he was to become commander of the brigade, 2,100 strong, made up of units drawn from many different parts of the corps. The laconic Iowan, an experienced planner, was enthusiastic about being picked to lead the largest group of marines ever to participate in nuclear field exercises.

Tschirgi was no hell-bent-for-leather type, but he certainly was capable. He was reputed to be a tactician who could assemble and motivate a staff and get things done. His nearly three-year tour of duty as a logistics specialist with the Joint Chiefs of Staff in Washington had prepared him well for his current assignment. A decorated veteran of the Okinawa, Peleliu, and Korean campaigns, he believed, like many of his fellow senior officers, that nuclear war was inevitable. His mission was to create a proficient team of nuclear warriors to prevail in such a holocaust.

Detailed planning carried out under tight security was essential. Marine officers reviewed the after-action reports of the three previous brigades that had gone to the Nevada Test Site. They analyzed the missions and objectives of the field maneuvers and developed an operations plan for the Fourth Brigade. Completed and issued on May 27 as Brigade Order 003121.2, it stated that the mission of the brigade was to "employ all means available by use of atomic fires and troop participation to detect, delay, and destroy enemy mechanized forces in the zone of action." The execution section of the order included the words, "employ atomic munitions as required and directed."

The brigade would execute field maneuvers after the detonation of a shot named Diablo. This device, a product of the University of California Radiation Laboratory at Livermore, was expected to have a yield approximately equal to that of the bomb dropped on Hiroshima. It was scheduled to be detonated June 26 from the top of a five-hundred-foot steel tower.

When the brigade order was received by the Second Battalion, troop preparation began in earnest. For nearly a month, we readied ourselves to show off the country's finest fighting force at its absolute best. In the field at Camp Pendleton we practiced launching a coordinated assault, pursuing a fleeing enemy. When we had pushed our adversary to his last line of defense, we would stop and lie quietly, awaiting deployment of "the bomb." A one-ton TNT explosion was set off, the blast echoing through the nearby hills. A column of black smoke rising in the distance signaled us to renew the attack. En masse, we rushed toward the objective in vertical envelopment fashion, attacking from three sides simultaneously, while planes strafed overhead and tanks advanced from the flanks. Parts of the battalion were lifted by helicopter to the final objective; others were transported by armored personnel carriers. My platoon pursued on foot. The execution of the maneuver was an impressive sight. Each time we rehearsed the battle plan our timing improved. I could not imagine any enemy force surviving such an onslaught. We always defeated the "foreign" adversary. We were *totally* prepared. Yes, we marines would demonstrate to the world that "Semper Fi" and "gung ho" were not empty words. We young, Cold War marines could uphold the proud tradition of the corps on the hot new battlefields of the atomic age.

We were assured repeatedly that no harm would come to us because the 1957 test series marked the advent of the "clean" bomb—in contrast to a "dirty" bomb, it would produce only an insignificant amount of radioactive fallout. A few months before our arrival in Nevada, the question of the clean bomb had been the subject of a protracted debate within the nuclear community.

On February 11, 1957, the Atomic Energy Commission held meeting number 1265. The directors of the nation's two nuclear weapons centers, Los Alamos and the University of California Radiation Laboratory at Livermore, were there and made a presentation to the commissioners about the laboratories' objectives during the Plumbbob series. Norris Bradbury, director of Los Alamos, told AEC Chairman Lewis Strauss, "There has been no specific effort to develop clean weapons for the current series. This phase of weapons development is difficult to pursue except for a full-scale thermonuclear test series." In other words, nuclear weapons technology had not progressed to the point where clean weapons could be produced without thermonuclear tests. "Thermonuclear" was synonymous with "hydrogen," and no hydrogen tests were supposed to be conducted in Nevada. An executive order limited tests in the continental desert to small-yield atomic devices.

Yet four months later, on June 23, Chairman Strauss, Dr. Edward Teller, and his colleague from Livermore, Dr. E. O. Lawrence, met with President Eisenhower for forty-five minutes at the White House. That afternoon, Eisenhower emerged with an official statement for the media. Beaming, Ike said, "We will produce an absolutely clean bomb, and the current series is designed to see how clean we can make them."

National and international concern over the damaging effects of contaminated fallout had led the Atomic Energy Commission and the nuclear laboratories to attempt to reduce the radioactivity in atomic and thermonuclear clouds. In 1955, Chairman Strauss released a document that described the nature of contamination from shot Bravo, which had been fired in the Pacific the previous year: "About 7,000 square miles of territory downwind was so contaminated that survival might have depended upon prompt evacuation or upon taking shelter and other protective measures."

The Supreme Allied Commander of NATO, General Alfred Gruenther, read the report and quickly sent a top-secret message to the Joint Chiefs of Staff requesting information about protective measures for troops in the field during a nuclear attack. The NATO commander and his subordinates were concerned that American soldiers would be endangered by the fallout from U.S. bombs during a nuclear battle. Shortly after the inquiry, the NATO commander received a reply from the JCS: "Although a great deal is unknown about fallout, the problem is a manageable one." The method of management, however, was not spelled out. The AEC in 1955 had its own theory about fallout. Forever sensitive to criticism and staunchly defending its role in the development of nuclear weapons, Commissioner Willard F. Libby, during a February 1955 AEC meeting, angrily declared, "People have got to learn to live with the facts of life, and part of the facts of life are fallout!"

News from the outside world rarely reached us at the test site, and we were unaware of the statements made in official circles. In an attempt to dispel any fear we might have, our superiors assured us that our nuclear test experience would be comparable to observing the explosion of a large conventional weapon. There was nothing to worry about, they promised, but we were cautioned again and again not to discuss our activities with anyone.

In earlier testing years, particularly in the North Pacific region of the Marshall Islands, military participants were required to sign agreements in which they promised not to discuss their mission. Violators were subject to a ten-thousand-dollar fine and/or a ten-year prison sentence. It was not uncommon for armed personnel to be present during the signing. One of the participants recalls being warned that if he violated the agreement he would never live to see the world outside Leavenworth. Fearing retaliation, men went to their graves without revealing, even to their families, that they had participated in nuclear weapons tests.

By 1957 nuclear weapons test participants no longer had to sign security agreements. It was difficult to conceal the fact that nuclear weapons were being detonated. The flash from the explosion could be seen for hundreds of miles across the flat, southwestern desert, and the nuclear clouds were easily tracked. Maintaining nuclear supremacy was the prime U.S. objective, and openly demonstrating nuclear weapons capability was one way to establish and maintain that supremacy. The 1957 Plumbbob series was publicized, and we marines assisted with the publicity. Three weeks before our departure for the test site, each marine in the brigade was photographed. We posed in our field dungarees and steel helmets in front of an artificial desert scene of rocks, shrubs, cactus, brown sand, and a yucca tree. The pictures were sent to our hometown newspapers with a press release that told of our participation in the atomic exercises. The caption under my photograph read, "At Test Site—Lieutenant Thomas H. Saffer, USMC, will participate in the first extensive troop exercises in the current series of atomic tests at Camp Desert Rock, Nevada."

I had been at Camp Pendleton for sixty days when our brigade was sent to the Nevada desert. We arrived at Camp Desert Rock on June 18, 1957, flying from Marine Corps Air Station El Toro in California to Indian Springs Air Force Base in Nevada and then proceeding by truck to our temporary home—tents that had been set up by an advance party.

One of the first things to greet us was a bulletin entitled *Camp Desert Rock Information Book*, wherein we read, "The sun, not the bomb, is your worst enemy at Camp Desert Rock."

The living conditions in that wasteland were the most miserable I had ever known. Daily temperatures reached 120°F, and the heat in our canvas tent once hit 130°F, the upper limit of our thermometer. We never put our tent flaps down, and we awoke daily to find ourselves covered with a layer of dust blown in by the hot desert winds. Our miserable quarters were only fourteen miles from the site of the atomic detonations. Much of our food was laden with dust and small particles of sand. At times, gusts of wind reduced visibility to less than twenty-five feet.

In contrast, two miles away stood Camp Mercury, where Atomic Energy Commission and nuclear laboratory personnel were comfortably quartered in ventilated tin buildings protected from the blowing desert dust and sand. (They even had recreation provided by "Poker Joe," a professional gambler, and many an AEC employee left the test site with less cash than when he arrived.)

Like all marines, we learned to adjust to conditions, and I felt a surge of pride in the knowledge that my platoon and I would have an opportunity to perform in exemplary Marine Corps fashion. We had been led to believe that we would represent the cutting edge of tactical deployment in the new age of atomic warfare. We believed that the use of an atomic bomb as an assault weapon would contribute dramatically to combat readiness for any form of warfare. We were frequently reminded that it was an honor to have been chosen for this mission.

We actually knew very little about the test site or why we were picked to be placed only a few miles from a nuclear blast. In 1950, the Atomic Energy Commission and Los Alamos Laboratory wanted to test nuclear weapons closer to the point of manufacture. Pacific tests were prohibitively expensive and security posed a problem. President Truman approved a series of tests of low-yield atomic devices in

Nevada. The remote desert area was selected because it was virtually uninhabited, had no substantial population within nearly seventy miles, was next to an existing air force gunnery range, and afforded maximum security. Although no mention was made of the wind direction, the prevailing winds blew east over southern Utah. The desert testing area grew to encompass 1,350 square miles. The operations area at Camp Mercury was approximately sixty-five miles north of Las Vegas and thirty-five miles south of Beatty, Nevada.

When Nevada was selected as a Continental Test Site, the AEC's Division of Biology and Medicine cautioned that fallout from the site could become a health hazard and recommended that only underground tests be conducted. The Joint Chiefs of Staff and the Department of Defense disagreed, arguing that only aboveground tests could provide realistic assessments of military effects. The Defense Department also believed that there was an urgent and pressing need for all the armed services to obtain practical field experience with nuclear weapons.

In 1952, the Defense Department attempted to gain control of troop maneuvers at the test site. The AEC balked, maintaining that the agency's rigid safety precautions would have to be altered substantially if military personnel were allowed to maneuver freely at the site.

The Department of Defense and the Pentagon grumbled about the AEC requirement that troops be seven miles from ground zero during a nuclear blast. Foot soldiers, the Pentagon reasoned, should have realistic combat training during atomic testing. The Marine Corps was particularly adamant about close-range troop participation. The corps maintained that its well-trained, disciplined troops could maneuver much closer to ground zero than the distance specified by the AEC.

The AEC's Division of Biology and Medicine warned, "the

nuclear explosion is experimental in type, and its yield cannot be predicted with accuracy. Any injury or death during the explosion might well have serious effects."

Undaunted and ignoring the AEC's warnings, the Defense Department persisted and sent a letter to the AEC's Division of Military Applications, which was directed by Brigadier General K. E. Fields. "The Department of Defense wishes to assume full responsibility for the physical and radiological safety of troops and troop observers while in the Nevada Proving Grounds."

The director of the Division of Military Applications forwarded the message to the AEC, recommending that the Defense Department's request be granted. On December 23, 1952, the AEC yielded to the military's demands. Radiological-safety responsibility for military participants at the test site was transferred from experts to amateurs.

The 1952 tests in Nevada were the first to have troops in trenches as close as four miles to ground zero. Shortly after the detonation the men attacked toward ground zero in mock assaults.

The military's maximum allowable radiation dosage was raised to 6 roentgens—almost double the dosage allowed Atomic Energy Commission personnel. AEC employees wore protective clothing in the field; military personnel wore their field dungarees and a steel helmet.

Military radiological safety officers were taught that troops could withstand as much as 300 roentgens and continue to function. The Army's official *Infantry School Quarterly*, in an apparent attempt to allay fears of radiation exposure, reported:

> The facts are:
>
> Your troops can move into or leave an exposed area a few minutes after an air burst. A soldier is not a casualty until he requires treatment. Even though

> he has been exposed to a lethal dose of radiation, he can perform his combat mission until symptoms appear.
>
> Radioactivity does not permanently affect sexual potency. Men exposed to radiation can have normal children. Radiation sufficient to produce permanent sterility or impotency would also be lethal.

Regardless of the accuracy of the standard of the day as far as radiological safety was concerned, we never were enlightened; we did not once have a lecture by a radiological-safety officer. We, the foot soldiers, trained to fight on a nuclear battlefield, were told only that a trench was our best friend and our protector.

Because no one wanted a group of marines at a nuclear test site worrying about the potential life-threatening experiences they might be subjected to, we were purposely kept ignorant and never had contact with anyone but other military personnel at Desert Rock. We were totally unaware of the activities of the Atomic Energy Commission and the laboratory personnel. We were warned not to talk with media representatives. During rare moments of levity, I rehearsed how *not* to divulge information with members of my platoon. I put a white sock over a pear, and acting as though I were a reporter, I would call one of my men over to me and pretend I was interviewing him for a major network. My men always answered with, "I'm sorry, mister, but I don't know anything about anything." None of us was going to be guilty of violating national security! We were like the three classic monkeys: we saw nothing, we heard nothing, and we spoke of nothing.

I had no thoughts about the number of tests conducted before my arrival, and only years later—twenty-three years later—did I learn that I was participating in the series known as Plumbbob. The series ultimately involved 20,103 military personnel and two large contingents of civil-defense people. During the years 1951–1962, 80,000 military personnel trooped the desert sands of the most radioactively contaminated place in the United States.

The 1957 continental series began with the first atmospheric detonation, known as shot Boltzman, which was exploded from a five-hundred-foot tower on May 28. The term "shot" was used by the AEC instead of "bomb," because the nuclear devices of 1957 were detonated from towers or balloons and not dropped from airplanes: the marines used "shot" and "bomb" interchangeably. Plumbbob ended with shot Morgan, detonated on October 7. Military personnel from the U.S. Army, Navy, Air Force, and Marine Corps and from the Canadian armed forces performed maneuvers in connection with the series.

We marines were prepared for our field exercises, but we were not prepared for the dangers of the blast or for the thermal effects and radiation exposure we were about to experience. During our free time, we speculated about the forthcoming test. We all knew that the detonation would be different from the TNT explosions we had seen at Camp Pendleton, but we had no concept of the extent of the difference. No one in our group had ever seen an atomic explosion, and no one who had witnessed an atmospheric test briefed us. We were told again at the site that we would not be harmed; that the bombs were "clean," with little radioactivity; and that there was nothing to fear because the trenches would protect us. Alpha and beta rays, neutrons, americium, uranium, plutonium, strontium 90, and cesium—terms vaguely familiar to us—were never mentioned.

With each succeeding series of tests between 1952 and 1957, marines were moved closer and closer to the actual detonation, tentatively at first, but later without caution.

Beginning in 1955, the test site manager reported directly to the AEC's manager of the Division of Military Applications; since the applications manager was an army major general, he told his subordinates not to interfere with the military's plans at the site.

When a marine unit goes into the field to conduct a maneuver, the exercise is referred to as a "problem." My brigade actually had a series of problems to complete in Nevada. The first problem was named Priscilla.

38 Kilotons

With 38 kilotons, what do you get?
Nausea, red face, and a frenzied sweat.

—T.H.S.

Sunday, June 23, 1957, began like any other Sunday at the site, with religious services conducted by the brigade's chaplain. However, after services something unexpected happened: we officers and noncommissioned officers of staff sergeant rank and higher were placed on "stand by"; liberty was canceled. Toward the end of the day, after our allotted evening shower and before supper, our company commander summoned the staff noncommissioned officers and us three lieutenant platoon leaders to the company command post. We helped ourselves to ice water or coffee and sat down.

George Ballard, our commanding officer, had been attending a briefing most of the afternoon. He told us we were going to witness the detonation of a bomb named Priscilla. The company commander went on to explain that we would be observers and would get the "feel" of an actual atomic explosion. We would then brief our troops on what to expect during the field exercise on June 26 in connection with shot Diablo. We were told that Priscilla would have an explosive force of 14,000 tons of TNT; Diablo would be larger.

Ballard said that we officers would observe the blast from the trench lines two miles from ground zero at a location called Frenchman Flat, one of many dry lakes in the area. The sergeants would see the blast from a vantage point eight miles away. We would perform a postdetonation inspection to determine the bomb's effects. Departure was scheduled for 0230 hours. The only equipment we would have, besides our usual field uniforms, would be gas masks. These masks would be worn by those of us who were going into the trenches. Ballard concluded his briefing: "There are no other additions to the uniform. You will be wearing utilities [field uniforms], web gear [cartridge belts], and steel pots [helmets] with brown side out. Any questions?"

There were none.

That same evening at Camp Mercury, Al Taylor from Pocatello, Idaho, was lying in his bunk thinking about the next day's activities. He was the assistant training officer of the Idaho Civil Defense Department and had come to the test site on June 17 to participate in civil-defense training. He had observed shot Wilson five miles from ground zero on June 18 and thought the 10-kiloton device was possibly the most striking event he had ever witnessed. Taylor was impressed by the scientific project officers' concern for his safety. When Taylor went into the field, he wore specially designed protective clothing. He had been given seventy-seven handouts containing information about radiation. Some of the titles were: "Clothing for Protection Against Nuclear and Thermal Radiation," "Blast Damage from Nuclear Weapons," "What You Should Know About Radioactive Fallout," "Questions and Answers on Fallout," and "Radiation Hazards."

Priscilla was going to be interesting to Taylor because he would have an opportunity to study bomb shelters that had been designed to withstand the force of the blast. He would observe the shot from the Fire Direction Control Center. He felt he would be safe because he would be ten miles from ground zero at the time of the actual detonation. He would not make the trip to Frenchman Flat to examine the effect on shelters until three days after the detonation, and not even then if measured radioactivity in the area made it inadvisable.

At Indian Springs Air Force Base, First Lieutenant John Alder was playing cards. His squadron, the 4926 Test Squadron, had been moved to Nevada from Kirkland Air Force Base in Albuquerque, New Mexico. Alder was an air force officer in his third year of cloud sampling for the AEC. Flying a modified F-84 jet fighter, he had two missions to perform after each nuclear shot: to collect particulate matter on specially designed metal grids attached to the fuel tanks on the wings of his aircraft and to record the prompt gamma radiation dosage readings from instruments designed to measure radiation intentionally allowed to seep into the aircraft. As soon as Alder and his fellow pilots made their first pass into the radioactive clouds, they radioed the readings to the base. Many times a scientific adviser from the AEC accompanied Alder or one of the other pilots on a cloud-sampling mission; and he, like the pilot, wore a lead-lined suit and breathed 100 percent pure oxygen through a mask.

Alder had total faith in his equipment. Between missions, his aircraft was thoroughly checked and serviced by a crack ground crew. These technicians also wore special clothing and respirators. They submitted daily urine and fecal specimens to determine if they had ingested or inhaled any plutonium.

Alder, like the other pilots, wore a film badge but complained that there was often a discernible difference between the dosage the instruments inside the aircraft recorded and what his film badge registered. Because of this discrepancy, he and the other pilots did not consider their film badge readings accurate. Tests to determine the cause of the divergent readings were inconclusive.

Alder recalled the 1955 Nevada series as being extremely "dirty." The explosive nuclear devices were in large metal canisters and were detonated from steel towers. Because both the canisters and the towers were vaporized by the explosions and then mixed with sucked-up ground debris and dirt, a large amount of radioactive material was blown into the atmosphere. An extremely radioactive cloud was formed, and the pilots were unable to perform their missions for five or six hours after a shot.

Following the 1955 continental series, Alder was among pilots sampling the large detonations of Operation Redwing at the two Pacific atolls of Bikini and Eniwetok. Although the Pacific was beautiful and the pilots' leisure time was spent skin diving and swimming, Alder and his buddies were pleased to be back on the mainland. Sampling the smaller clouds of Nevada allowed the pilots to develop a special loop method of maneuvering, and Alder was especially proud of his skills. He would fly directly at the intersection of the stem and base of a mushrooming cloud. When he was within a few yards of his target, he would pull the stick back, accelerate, and literally shoot up through the top of the cloud. He would repeat the maneuver until he had fulfilled his mission. The pilots referred to particulate matter as "dog" and to prompt gamma radiation as "rascal." When the dog and rascal readings were within the expected range, Alder radioed the code words "red, white, and blue" to base. When the radioactivity readings indicated an especially hot cloud, he used the code words "chili pepper."

Alder's squadron had returned to the Nevada test site in 1957, knowing that the package size of the nuclear devices had been reduced considerably. Those devices with larger yields would be suspended from balloons. A promise of cleaner bombs meant that the cloud-sampling flights would not be delayed.

Seven miles from Frenchman Flat, ten AEC field men were preparing to spend the night in a reinforced-concrete bunker below ground level. One of the men would watch the detonation of the shot through a shielded periscope while the others either rested or took turns peering at the ascending fireball through the periscope. After the detonation, they would don protective clothing and retrieve recording instruments placed near ground zero.

In the Fire Direction Control Center, ten miles away from where Priscilla was hanging from a helium-filled balloon, Dr. Gerald Johnson and his men busily completed their check-out procedures before the detonation, scheduled for 6:30 a.m. Dr. Johnson had joined Livermore Laboratory in 1953 and had managed to weather the storms of criticism that had resulted from the California laboratory's early failures and miscalculations. The bespectacled physicist experienced a particularly difficult relationship with Los Alamos management during the Pacific tests of 1956. After he returned to California he insisted on better treatment for Livermore personnel. His pleas were answered when the AEC appointed him the scientific technical test director of the Plumbbob series. The appointment was significant in that it was the first time a scientist from the California laboratory was placed in charge of a nuclear test series. Johnson was in charge in the control center, and only he could issue the order to fire the shot. The electrical impulses flowing through the cable to the terminals affixed to Priscilla would be carefully monitored. Standing next to Johnson were the bomb's designer and a representative from the Department of Defense.

The two-story control center where the scientists worked was specially constructed into the side of a hill. It was made of concrete reinforced with steel and was designed both to withstand blast effects and to repel radiation. The scientists entered through one of four doors. On the upper floor was the control room. On the lower floor, protected by the hill, were quarters for laboratory personnel. Briefing rooms were next to the living quarters.

The control center was always the hub of activity before a nuclear detonation. During the evening of June 23 and the early morning of June 24, it was particularly active. Priscilla, the fifth planned detonation of the Plumbbob series, was a joint project of the Department of Defense and the Los Alamos Laboratory. Unlike other experiments, this one was designed to test thermal and blast effects, and it was the largest thus far detonated in the series. A successful explosion was critical to the nuclear weapons planning of the Defense Department. Although Priscilla was designed by Los Alamos and Scientific Test Director Johnson was associated with Livermore Laboratory—and the rivalry between the two nuclear laboratories at times was bitter—on this June morning the detonation of the nuclear device was all that mattered.

Test Site Manager James Reeves conferred with meteorologists for assurance that the perfect weather conditions would hold. The light on the top of the flagpole at Camp Desert Rock was green, indicating that conditions were "go." Reeves alone had the authority to make the final decision as to whether conditions were right for a shot to be ordered. A few minutes before the scheduled firing, Reeves would join

Johnson in the control room and nod his approval for the test to proceed.

At 2:30 on the morning of June 24, we marines boarded trucks. The desert had cooled noticeably, and we were wearing field jackets over our combat dungarees. I thought to myself, "Well, I guess this is why we came out here. In a few hours, I'll know what an atomic bomb looks like." We left tent city, drove past Camp Mercury, and headed for Frenchman Flat. About an hour later we reached the trench area and filed out of the trucks.

It was a crystal-clear desert night, and the stars were exceptionally bright. A slight breeze brought a pleasant change from the oppressive heat of the day. When the trucks departed, there was no sound except for the distant purring of the generator used to power the searchlight illuminating our new girl friend: two miles ahead of us, she hung suspended from a parabola-shaped, helium-filled balloon seventy-five feet in diameter. We lay down behind the trenches in the dust and dirt and napped.

As day broke over the bleak Nevada desert, I could see various types of equipment scattered about. Tanks and trucks were positioned beneath the balloon and extended outward from ground zero toward us. A few hundred yards in front of us were mannequins standing like scarecrows in a long-barren field. Directly behind my trench was the mannequin of half a soldier. His upper torso wore a utility jacket, and a helmet covered his head. Because Priscilla was a weapons effects test, the equipment and the mannequins were being exposed to evaluate the effects of the bomb on them.

I did not know that there were dogs, monkeys, burros, and pigs positioned at various distances from the bomb's hypocenter. The pigs had been dressed in military uniforms and placed behind glass shields. Officials from the Defense Department wanted to use the pigs in a simulated test of blast effect on a uniformed man standing erect, but for months their determined efforts to train the pigs to stand on their hind legs had met with only disinterested grunts. When the bomb was detonated, the problem was solved. A moment of terror accomplished what months of training could not. The pigs not only stood erect but leaped over the enclosure fences as particles of glass drove deep into their bodies.

At about 5:30 a.m. there was an explosion. A cloud of black smoke was instantly visible five hundred yards to Priscilla's right. At the sound, one of the lieutenants sprang to his feet and ran toward the trench kicking up puffs of dust. We all laughed out loud. When he was ten feet from the trench, he stopped, realizing that *the bomb* had not exploded after all. The noise was from some TNT detonated by AEC personnel to check wind velocity and direction.

At 6:15 the disembodied voice we had heard earlier over an unseen loudspeaker boomed again. "Gentlemen, proceed to the trenches." In the soft light of the desert dawn, we filed silently toward the narrow enclosure that would hold us captive for what would seem an interminable period. Entering through a cut in the trench wall nearest us, we walked down a slight dirt incline to the powdery bottom. The trenches resembled those used during World War I except that there were no ledges for footing or seating. They were two and one-half feet wide with vertical walls five and one-half feet high.

After moving down the dusty incline, I turned right, walked a few yards, and stopped. I stood there, awaiting further instructions.

The loudspeaker barked an order, "Face left, put your gas masks on, and replace your helmets. Kneel on your left knee, and remain in this position. Do not stand. I repeat, do not stand." I obediently followed the command and placed my left knee on the powdery desert dust that lined the bottom of the trench. The coolness of the earth penetrated the thin layer of cloth between my knee and the desert floor.

"Place your left forearm over your eyes. Close your eyes tightly, and do not open them. It is now H minus five." I felt my eyelashes brushing the plexiglass lens of the gas mask as I followed the brusque order of the voice.

In the control tower, Johnson and the young designer of the weapon scanned the lighted panel and watched carefully as the color of each individual light changed from red to green. Everything was proceeding as scheduled. Priscilla would soon fill the sky above Frenchman Flat with a kaleidoscope of nuclear colors.

We remained kneeling in the trench, bent low to the ground, filled with anxiety and anticipation, not knowing exactly what to expect.

"It is now H minus thirty seconds and counting."

The only sound was my own breathing and the humming of the loudspeaker. I began to perspire and felt the moisture collecting on my cheeks inside my gas mask. I nervously stroked the stubble on my chin with my right hand and then felt beneath my field jacket to assure myself that the film badge was still there. It was clipped to the flap on my left breast pocket on my utility jacket. I strained to keep my eyes closed tightly.

The loudspeaker started the countdown. "Ten . . . five, four, three, two, one."

At zero, I heard a loud click. Immediately, I felt an intense heat on the back of my neck. A brilliant flash accompanied the heat, and I was shocked when, with my eyes tightly closed, I could see the bones in my forearm as though I were examining a red x-ray. I learned many years later that I had been x-rayed by a force many times greater than a normal medical x-ray.

Within seconds, a thunderous rumble like the sound of

thousands of stampeding cattle passed directly overhead, pounding the trench line. Accompanying the roar was an intense pressure that pushed me downward. The shock wave was traveling at nearly four hundred miles per hour, pushed toward us by the immense energy of the explosion. The sound and the pressure were both frightening and deafening. The earth began to gyrate violently, and I could not control my body. I was thrown repeatedly from side to side and bounced helplessly off one trench wall and then off the other. Overcome by fear, I opened my eyes. I saw that I was being showered with dust, dirt, rocks, and debris so thick that I could not see four feet in front of me. I could not locate the person who had been nearest to me in the trench. A light many times brighter than the sun penetrated the thick dust, and I imagined that some evil force was attempting to swallow my body and soul. I thought the world was coming to an end. I was certain that, with the raging, angry shaking of the earth, the very ground beneath me would be rent asunder. If what I was experiencing was an example of nuclear war, I wanted no part of it. I saw no way that friend or foe, marine or foreign adversary could survive such an experience.

As the initial sound wave bounced off the surrounding mountains and returned, we were struck by a second shock wave. A loud noise comparable to a tremendous clap of thunder made me cringe. The trembling of the earth mercifully ended at last.

I had been bounced helplessly around in the trench for ten to twelve seconds that seemed like an eternity. I felt as though I had been attacked and savagely beaten by a gang of toughs who hammered on my helmet and tore at my clothing from all sides. I was alive but dazed. No one had prepared me for what I had experienced. Had something gone wrong or was my encounter typical of a nuclear explosion?

Priscilla had not been the 14-kiloton lady we had been promised. She had erupted with the overwhelming force of a

38-kiloton monster. Whose decision was it to place us only two miles from such a vengeful creature?

On the ridge line eight miles away with the staff noncommissioned officers from our battalion was First Lieutenant Eric "Rip" Wieler. He recalls,

> We had to turn our backs to the flash. The heat at eight miles stung and singed the backs of our necks. We were allowed to turn around after five seconds. After twenty-five seconds, the shock wave hit. Several people who were looking up at the mushroom and not expecting the shock wave were knocked off their feet and thrown against a bus with such intensity that the sides of the vehicle were dented in a number of places. It [the shock wave] blew the helmets off the heads of half a dozen people. I saw the wave coming because it was advancing rapidly in a cloud of dust and, unlike the other marines, I hit the deck and hugged the ground as the force passed. Altogether, it was quite impressive, and none of us will ever forget it.

In the control center, Johnson and his associates rushed to the thickly paned glass window and watched the bomb's beautiful display of colors. A ring of gaseous fire was visible near the top of the double-tiered mushroom cloud. Even veterans of many detonations found the sight ethereal. The scientists could not watch for long, however, as the shock wave was racing menacingly toward the control center. Although the center had been designed to withstand its force, these men backed away from the window when they saw the dust approaching. They were startled by a loud noise. After the shock wave had passed, they rushed to the lower level of the building to find out what had happened. There, embedded in the far wall of the room, was a steel door. Someone had neglected to close one of the four doors, and the steel panel had been blown off its hinges. Four miles beyond the control center, the walls of a thick concrete blockhouse had been cracked. Clearly, the men who had designed this weapon had not accurately predicted its terrifying, cataclysmic force.

On the hill next to the control center, Al Taylor and his civil defense companions were knocked down when the shock wave reached them. As he struggled to his feet and brushed himself off, Taylor nonetheless thought that Priscilla was the most wondrous sight he had ever seen. The changing colors of the fireball mesmerized him as the mushroom top of the cloud rose rapidly to forty thousand feet. While Taylor was captivated by what he saw, he was thankful to be viewing it from ten miles away. He had been trained to respect and fear the radioactivity released by a nuclear explosion.

After the vicious shaking subsided, we marines filed out of the trenches in ghostly silence. We watched the multicolored fireball ascend rapidly. Nearly twenty thousand feet high, it was red, white, gray, and beige and looked like a double-tiered mushroom. The stem was wide at the base, where it touched the ground, and became narrow as it merged with the main mass. As it rose, burning gases roared like a mammoth forest fire.

I glanced at the mannequin directly behind me, and I noticed that the stake to which the lifeless form had been attached was bent at an angle. The face was aflame, the uniform was smoldering, and the helmet lay on the ground about thirty yards away. We removed our gas masks and stood transfixed, watching the cloud ascend higher and higher until it was practically overhead. My neck ached from the strain of leaning back to peer up at such a sharp angle.

My first participation in an atomic bomb explosion had

lasted less than five minutes, but more happened in that short time than in any other like period of my life. Never had I experienced such anticipation, anxiety, suspense, fear, and awe. The event left an indelible impression on me; and to this day, I shudder and perspire when I recall my experience in that trench.

I could now see the other marines who shared my trench and my fate, and I was reassured to discover that there were no discernible injuries among us. I was immediately conscious of an offensively strong smell and taste. The odor reminded me of that of an overheated electrical unit and the metallic taste in my mouth was foul and would not go away.

My attention was diverted from the fireball to emergency vehicles with flashing red lights that came rushing across the desert, sirens blaring. They stopped abruptly at one of the trenches some yards in front of us. Men carrying picks and shovels leaped from the vehicles and ran toward the trench. The marines and Canadians in that trench had been partly buried by debris from the bomb's blast, and the emergency crew was hastily digging them free.

I heard a plane overhead.

As John Alder approached the gaseous mass, he pulled back hard on the stick and headed upward through the atomic cloud. Despite the gravitational pull on his body, he remembers he held his eyes open and stared intently at the radiological recorder mounted on the outside of his aircraft. From past experience and his preflight briefing, he expected to find no more than 50 roentgens of gamma radiation at H plus ten minutes, but the instrument was showing a much higher reading. He completed his first backward loop and returned to the rising cloud for another pass. Heading nearly straight up at almost a ninety-degree angle, he fixed his attention again on the externally mounted instrument. Five hundred roentgens! He quickly depressed the button on his radio transmitter and dispatched his frantic message to the base, "Chili pepper! Chili pepper!" His transmission was equivalent to the international distress call of "May Day!" The bomb had not been "clean" after all, and the pilot was startled to find ten times the expected contamination. Without waiting for a reply from Indian Springs, Alder left at once.

Ordinarily when Alder landed on the airstrip, the ground crew met his aircraft and decontaminated it. This landing was met by no one, and the pilot was instructed to taxi the aircraft to the far end of the strip and leave it there. He slid the canopy back, released his seat belt, stood, stepped out on the wing, and jumped to the ground. From a megaphone mounted on top of a vehicle one hundred yards away, a voice instructed him to remove all of his clothing except his undershorts and leave all his belongings next to the aircraft. He followed the instructions and walked barefoot on the runway, knowing that all his clothing would be burned. Never again would he slip his feet into that expensive pair of kangaroo flight boots he had purchased only a few weeks before. He was thankful he had worn lead-lined clothing and wondered how the lead would be destroyed. The asphalt felt rough and warm against the tender soles of his feet as he slowly made his way to the portable shower that had been left on the runway for him. For five weeks, no one went near Alder's F-84, the "hottest" aircraft in the air force.

After the plane disappeared from the vicinity of the cloud, I walked over to my battalion commander, who was standing about twenty yards to my left. His face was bright red, as though he had been sunburned, and he had the stunned look of a combat marine with a thousand-yard stare. "What do you think, sir?" I asked sheepishly. The major continued to stare blankly. I repeated the question, "What do you think, sir?"

He muttered without looking at me, "Incredible. Absolutely incredible."

Obviously this combat-toughened man had never lived through an experience like the one in the Nevada trench line.

Within minutes, the brilliant, sunlit day became gray-black, as though clouds were gathering from some cataclysmic storm. A column of dark, powdery dust from the vicinity of ground zero had been sucked up several hundred feet by the force of the blast. As this ugly mass spread like a dark pall over the entire area, I felt as though some ominous force were enveloping me.

I glanced at my right sleeve and noticed a white-gray ash about the size of a small button. No one was smoking. The ash had to be coming from the low cloud overhead. Noticing the ash, the major remarked, "We're receiving fallout, and I'm worried." Fear showed unmistakably in the lines of his face. I thought to myself, "If this professional marine, fifteen years my senior, is alarmed, then my own fears are justified." The ash continued to fall, and we had nowhere to go for shelter. I flicked an ash away with my finger and saw a burn spot where it had been.

By the time we boarded the armored personnel carriers, our green utilities looked as though they had been splattered with beige paint. We were covered with desert dirt and dust. We were to inspect the equipment that had been placed in front of us, three hundred yards from ground zero. After an extremely rough ride, we stopped. The rear ramp was lowered, and we filed out onto the desert floor. Looking at the area between us and ground zero was as unsettling as returning to a place where time had begun or ended. I was flabbergasted by the totally unexpected sight. Where trucks and tanks had stood before the detonation, there was nothing. Everything had been vaporized or tossed hundreds of yards from its original position. Dust devils, small desert twisters, swirled near the hypocenter and blew past us. The ground felt hot beneath my feet.

One of the ten AEC field men who had witnessed the detonation from the safety of the steel-reinforced concrete bunker had driven the seven miles from his position to near ground zero. Dispatched there to recover an instrument used to record certain effects at the time of detonation, he was attired in special radex protective clothing. All his skin was covered, and he was wearing a hooded respirator. He observed the devastation from behind a tinted glass shield that protected his eyes and face. He planned to retrieve the instrument, place it in a lead box, and leave the area within three minutes. In his right hand he carried a portable monitoring device with which he checked the ground as he moved purposefully over it. He picked up the instrument he had come to retrieve, placed it in the container, and was preparing to leave when he was distracted by movement nearly a hundred yards to his right. To his surprise, he saw a group of marines, dressed as though they were taking a casual stroll in the desert, standing in the contaminated area. Even though the marines were not his responsibility and he was uncomfortable about remaining in the area longer than planned, he decided to postpone his exit long enough to order the intruders to leave.

Standing there with the other marine officers, dumfounded by what I was seeing, I became aware of a figure in white approaching us from the left. With swift and deliberate movements, he glided toward us over the powdery desert floor. He moved to within a few yards, looked at us, and then pointed to the instrument he held in his right hand. Without uttering a word, he gestured for us to leave at once. We all looked at one another, wondering what to do. Finally, our major said, "All right, men, let's go. We've seen enough."

As we left the eerie scene at Frenchman Flat, members of the Reynolds Electric and Engineering Company helicopter team were preparing to circle the area and record radioactive readings at twenty-five, fifty, and one hundred feet in the vicinity of ground zero. Their departure was scheduled for 11:15 a.m., four hours and fifteen minutes after the detonation of Priscilla. At that time, however, the air was still saturated with dust, and the crew had to postpone the mission. Early in the afternoon, when members of the helicopter team again attempted to perform their mission, poor visibility prevented them from getting any closer to ground zero than 710 yards. On the following morning, at an altitude of five hundred feet, the team took readings of 100 roentgens, a level much higher than expected.

Alder recorded 500 roentgens at H plus ten minutes; members of the helicopter team recorded 100 roentgens at H plus twenty-seven hours. No doubt about it, Priscilla had been one hot shot!

Decontamination

If you get rid of the dust, you get rid of the radiation.
—Assistant Chief of Staff
U.S. Army *Armed Forces Talk*
September 1952

We military personnel were "decontaminated" after each nuclear detonation. I never thought of myself as having been contaminated, but I was. The extent of my contamination never will be known, and those who thought that they were decontaminating us were as unsure about what they were doing as we were about the exposure to which we had been subjected.

Our decontamination began immediately after we arrived at Camp Desert Rock. All 349 of us lined up in a column of twos and were inspected by men dressed in fatigues. The Geiger counter made a clicking sound as it passed over my body. My film badge was taken away, and no one bothered to tell me how much prompt gamma radiation I had received. Two men with brooms brushed at me from either side. The dislodged dust stung my eyes and burned my nostrils.

Up the road at the Reynolds Electric decontamination center, the experimental animals that had survived the explosion were faring better than we humans. They were carefully monitored. If they were found to be contaminated, they were vacuumed to remove the dust and then washed thoroughly with soap and water. After being brushed, I washed my hands and face and hurried over to the officer's mess. It was almost noon, and I did not want to miss a well-deserved hot meal. It had been a long time since the last one, and my stomach was growling. A shower would have to wait, because the showers were available to us only in the late afternoon. I had no fears. I had survived the terrifying experiences of the morning and felt an overwhelming sense of relief as I neared the mess tent. For a moment I stopped, turned, and looked into the eastern sky. The atomic cloud from the morning's explosion was white and gray now and barely visible as it drifted toward the east and off the site.

At that same moment, Dr. Gerald Johnson was leaving the control center, a pleased individual. He had successfully detonated Plumbbob's largest nuclear test to date.

2.

The Cobra Strikes

Friday's device was a creation of the University of California Livermore Labs, where development of the hydrogen bomb is believed to be centered. However, it has been officially stated that hydrogen bombs are tested only in the Pacific.

—Gladwin Hill
New York Times
July 6, 1957

The Misfire

The devil made me do it.

—Flip Wilson (as Geraldine)

It was eleven o'clock on the evening of June 27 when the brigade assembled at Camp Desert Rock. The nuclear field exercise would be conducted in a few hours. The marines had been at the test site for ten days and were eager to complete the planned maneuvers and return to Camp Pendleton. Roll was called: all hands present and accounted for. There was excitement as we boarded the waiting trucks for the thirty-five-mile ride to Yucca Flat. Shot Diablo (Spanish for "devil") was scheduled for detonation at 4:30 the following morning, four days after Priscilla had been exploded. We had been told that the bomb would be exploded from a five-hundred-foot tower and that its size would be approximately 17 kilotons.

I was no stranger to Yucca Flat. Two days before the brigade's departure, I had been placed in charge of a work party assigned to refurbish the trenches. The steady desert winds had filled the narrow openings with dirt and debris. The thirty-three marines who comprised the work detail were as unhappy about the temporary assignment as I was. They had looked forward to spending a few leisurely hours in Las Vegas gambling, drinking, or chasing girls. Instead our liberty was canceled, and we spent the day choking on dust we shoveled from the bottoms of the trenches.

Yucca Flat was nearly as barren as Frenchman Flat. The desert monotony was unrelieved by anything pleasant or interesting. We could see the tower, but every area except the trench lines was strictly off limits. Because of the oppressive heat, we worked in our undershirts.

After we had been digging for several hours, a jeep drove across the sand toward us and stopped. Its occupants, two army captains who identified themselves as radiological-safety officers, berated me for allowing my men to work without dust masks. I explained that no one had issued masks or advised us to wear them. One officer insisted that we cover our noses and mouths, and his adamant tone persuaded me to follow his order. He provided us with brown, surgical-style masks, which we wore during the remainder of the afternoon.

Although a marine radiological-safety team was attached to the brigade, these specialists never briefed us. The team was trained in atomic, biological, and chemical warfare, and was taught never to go into a dusty area after a nuclear blast without a gas mask (field protective mask). However, what they knew was not passed on to the troops. Perhaps the Marine Corps and the Department of Defense did not want photographs released that showed troops wearing gas masks during a mock assault at a nuclear test site, on the chance that this might alarm the public.

At five o'clock, my detail and I returned to Desert Rock.

The trenches were ready to receive the marines. I considered the outing disagreeable and insignificant, but beyond that I had an uneasy feeling that the two army radiological-safety officers possessed a knowledge about those trenches that we did not.

While the brigade was en route to Yucca Flat on the evening of June 27, a six-man party in two automobiles escorted by an army security guard stopped at the base of the five-hundred-foot tower a little more than two miles from the trenches. Led by Robert Burton, an experienced engineer, the men reached the tower at midnight and took the elevator to the top. Burton attached the terminals at the ends of the connecting cables to the nuclear device and tightened the lugs. The bomb was armed and ready. Using a phone in the small room at the top of the tower, Burton notified Gerald Johnson, the scientific test director, that the arming process was complete. The arming party took the elevator down from the top of the tower, climbed back into their cars, and drove to the control center, where they would witness the detonation.

While the arming party went cautiously about its business, trucks carrying marines rolled noisily across the desert to the trenches. When the vehicles lurched to a stop, we marines filed out of the trucks and down the shallow dirt ramps into the trenches. The shot itself is best described by First Lieutenant Eric "Rip" Wieler, who noted in his diary:

> We got to our places about two in the morning. Then all the trucks and vehicles left the area. Diablo was in a five-hundred-foot tower about four thousand yards to our direct front. It was announced over a loudspeaker when there were sixty minutes to go; then thirty, twenty, ten, five, four, three. At

> this point we put on our protective gas masks so that we would be prevented from breathing in all the dust that would be stirred up from the desert floor. At H minus two, we turned ninety degrees to the left and kneeled down in our trenches. We closed our eyes and put one arm across our faces. At the one-minute mark, the loudspeaker began to drone out the number of seconds.
>
> It seemed like years waiting there, stooped over, pressing against the side of the trench, less than six feet down, our backs only a couple of feet below the surface. Suddenly the count was "four, three, two, one . . ." and then nothing. For perhaps five seconds that seemed eternal there was a deathly silence. Then someone in front of me cursed. Others began to wisecrack. The loudspeaker began again. "Remain in your places; do not move. There has been a misfire." We couldn't believe it! The devil was playing tricks. After thirty minutes, we were allowed to stand up. Half an hour later, we got out of the trenches and into the trucks for the return trip to Camp Desert Rock.

Our training was behind us. Now we only needed a bomb to go off so we could carry out our mission. Diablo's failure was, in a sense, a disappointment.

In the control center, Gerald Johnson, James Reeves, and five other men were staring at the changing colors of the lights on the control panel. All seven were anxiously awaiting the signal indicating that the electrical impulse was en route to the terminals connecting the bomb to the detonation source. In the last forty seconds, an uneasiness permeated the room, prompting Johnson to declare, "It's not going to fire.

It's not going to fire." The men did not want to believe what they were hearing and seeing. They waited for what they hoped would happen, but there was no explosion. The cameras recording the event photographed only darkness.

Johnson hurriedly called a meeting of the men most familiar with the weapon's design. That day's heroics were displayed not by the marines but by three scientists. The three men in the arming party who had been primarily responsible for arming the bomb were now responsible for disarming it. They would have to climb to the top of the tower, enter the cab housing the bomb, and detach the cable terminals so carefully attached only a few hours before. The bespectacled Johnson looked at the trio in front of him and declared, "You men are probably going to have to climb the tower." Then he asked, "Is that all right with you?" Each replied affirmatively, and Johnson said he would accompany them to the tower.

After Johnson had thrown the switch in the control center to shut off all power, he, Robert Burton, Bernard Rubin, and Forrest Fairbrother left for the Diablo tower. Rubin and Fairbrother were engineers from the University of California Radiation Laboratory at Livermore and had worked on Diablo since its inception. Burton was an electrical engineer from Sandia Corporation, the manufacturer of the triggering mechanisms for the Plumbbob series. All four men were in their mid-thirties.

On the way to the steel tower, the quartet stopped at the first electrical checkpoint, a relay substation. Everything was normal. Three miles from the tower they stopped again, this time at a blockhouse where they checked the instruments and discovered there had been an electrical failure somewhere between the blockhouse and the nuclear device. But where? Could Diablo be slowly simmering atop its steel perch?

The men sped down the dusty desert road at sixty miles an hour. As they neared the derricklike tower, Burton recalled that he had recently given his wife a book, *Teach Your Wife to Be a Widow*. Fairbrother hoped his wife and family, back in Livermore, had not learned of the misfire. Rubin remembered afterward that his only thoughts were of the sensitivity of the weapon and the task's urgency.

The team arrived at the base of the thin steel tower at 7:30 a.m. Johnson knew that none of these men had ever disarmed a potentially live nuclear device—nobody had—but the test director had faith in their combined knowledge and ability. Standing at the base of the thirty-six-story tower, Johnson looked up at the cab; then he fixed his gaze on the disarming party. He reviewed the disarming procedure with them one last time and concluded tersely, "You know what you have to do. Good luck."

As Johnson got into his car and drove back to the control center, Burton, Fairbrother, and Rubin strapped metal instrument boxes to their shoulders. Because the flow of electricity to the tower had been shut off, the elevator was dead. The men would have to climb; they would carry all needed equipment on their backs.

They began their ascent. Burton led, and Fairbrother and Rubin followed. Not a word was exchanged as they methodically threaded their way to the top. It took the trio thirty-five exhausting minutes to reach the platform seven feet below the cab. They stopped and looked anxiously at one another, then up toward the inexplicably undetonated bomb.

As planned, Rubin was the first to enter the cab. The designer from Livermore climbed the remaining seven feet, stood erect, and opened the door of the enclosure. Wasting no time, he loosened the straps holding the instrument box to his shoulders and set his burden down gently. He opened the lid and took out a voltmeter and a Geiger counter. Two quick checks indicated that no current was flowing from the power source to the bomb and that the cab had not been contaminated. Rubin called to Burton to come in.

Burton entered and moved directly to the cable connections. Without hesitation, he loosened the lugs that held the terminals to the bomb. With a steady, even tug, he pulled until the first cable came free. He then turned his attention to the other cable. After he had loosened the lug, he pulled once again until the second cable had been disconnected from the weapon. Relieved, Burton sighed, "It's done." Fairbrother and Rubin performed their tasks in the disarming process, and Burton called the control center from a phone in the cab to report to Johnson that they had successfully completed their mission. As he hung up the receiver, he remarked to his associates, "Gerry Johnson just told me that some reporter from London is on the phone wanting a story about the heroes who disarmed the bomb." In the control center, Johnson threw the switch that restored power to the tower, and the three "heroes" took the elevator down.

It had been an uneventful day for the marines and an anxious and disappointing one for the scientific community. But Diablo wasn't finished with us. Within a week, this devil's trick would place 2,100 marines within three miles of the largest nuclear explosion in the history of the Nevada tests.

Hood

What you are about to do is very special and for the benefit of all mankind. Marines, historically, have always been the first to fight and have remained unafraid. No marine has ever backed down from danger. Your country will be proud of you.

*—Brigade Chief of Staff
to the Fourth Marine Corps
Provisional Atomic Exercise Brigade
before the Hood detonation*

It was June 28, and Johnson had not slept in twenty-four hours. He had spent most of that time in the control center reviewing each step in the elaborate procedure that preceded a nuclear shot and trying to decide what had gone wrong with Diablo. The next six days promised to be the most important in his life. A highly experimental device was scheduled for detonation within the week, and Gerry Johnson could not afford another misfire. Not only would the directors of Livermore be present to witness the explosion, but AEC chairman Strauss would immediately relay the results to an anxious Dwight Eisenhower.

Named after the volcanic peak in northern Oregon, Hood was designed to demonstrate that the United States could produce weapons that would not contaminate the environment.

By spring 1957, widespread national and international criticism of the Atomic Energy Commission and growing concern about fallout made an immediate change in policy necessary if weapons testing was to continue.

Analysis of the catches of the Japanese tuna fleet revealed that 580 metric tons had been irradiated by earlier Pacific tests. Sheep and goats in Nevada and Utah were dying from mysterious diseases, and their offspring were frequently born without wool or hair. Sheep ranchers had never encountered this before atomic testing and insisted that the AEC determine whether fallout was the cause of the problems. The first AEC team to test the sheep found that internal radioactivity readings and the appearance of the animals were strikingly similar to results from experimental radiation damage to laboratory animals. These findings were documented in a report, but the report was classified "top secret." Under no circumstances could the AEC allow a claim to be substantiated, thereby establishing a precedent.

Public alarm peaked in the early summer. The editors of *Time* devoted an entire section of their June 3 issue to the fallout debate and quoted Nobel laureate Linus Pauling as having declared, "The bomb tests will ultimately have caused the death of about 1,000,000 people in the world . . . who will have died ten to thirty years earlier than their normal life span." Other scientists and health physicists not connected with the testing program supported Pauling.

Eisenhower, the Atomic Energy Commission, and the design laboratories were caught in a dilemma. The president wanted the United States to maintain nuclear supremacy, the Atomic Energy Commission adamantly supported continuance of the tests, and Los Alamos and Livermore and their subcontractors wanted no cutbacks in an industry that yielded annual revenues in the billions of dollars.

The media was used to defuse public pressure. Avoiding shutting down or cutting back the industry became the primary task of the president and the nuclear weapons community.

They escaped their dilemma with the help of a Hungarian scientist, the bellicose, vituperative Dr. Edward Teller. This shrewd and able nuclear physicist had fled Europe during the Nazi years. An early student of molecular phenomena, he claimed to have an ingenious method to hurriedly produce the so-called clean bomb. In 1943, he had worked diligently at Los Alamos on the Manhattan Project and made a significant contribution to the development of the country's first atomic bombs. After the war, Teller had moved to the University of Chicago, where he taught at the Institute for Nuclear Studies. Believing fervently that the continued development of nuclear weapons was essential to the defense of the United States, he made frequent trips to Washington to enlist support for a special project, the development of a "super" or hydrogen bomb. This bomb could have a thousand times the killing power of an atomic bomb.

There was considerable controversy within the political and scientific communities regarding advanced nuclear weaponry. Many eminent scientists—among them Albert Einstein and Albert Schweitzer—spoke publicly of dangers inherent in the proliferation of nuclear weapons. Robert Oppenheimer, the scientific genius of the Manhattan Project, saw no need to produce more weapons and said that weapons tests should have ended the day after Trinity. Pictures and accounts of Japanese men, women, and children dying by the thousands in Hiroshima and Nagasaki were etched indelibly in the minds of scientists who had designed the bombs and on the consciences of government officials who had made the decision to drop them. Many of the scientists felt betrayed. A group of nuclear physicists who had worked on the Manhattan Project were so enraged that they resigned from weapons production and vowed never to return to the program.

In September 1949, world events swung the pendulum of public opinion toward Teller and other nuclear weapons proponents. A U.S. weather observation plane recorded an increase in radioactivity in Eastern Europe. Scientists pieced together fragments of information that led unmistakably to a conclusion that the U.S.S.R. had detonated a nuclear device. The United States was no longer the exclusive possessor of nuclear weapons technology.

North Korea invaded South Korea in June 1950, and within a few months, the U.S.S.R. conducted two more nuclear tests. War hysteria mounted, and with it, fear of a global nuclear confrontation. In the interest of national security, once-reluctant scientists and politicians openly advocated U.S. nuclear superiority and the research and testing needed to achieve and maintain it.

Activity at Los Alamos increased. Scientists returned to New Mexico. When Teller rejoined them in 1950, he found that weapons development was progressing rapidly but not in the direction he wished. The primary concern was mass production of existing designs. Experimentation with new techniques had a low priority. Teller was obsessed with the urgency of developing a hydrogen bomb. In 1951 he achieved a theoretical breakthrough and announced that a hydrogen bomb could be produced and tested within two years. Because senior scientists at Los Alamos were not willing to redirect the program and change priorities at the New Mexico laboratory, the persuasive physicist took his argument to Washington. There he not only urged immediate development of a thermonuclear weapon but also advocated setting up another laboratory to design and manufacture this super bomb. He found a willing listener in Senator Brien McMahon, former chairman of the Special Committee on Atomic Energy. McMahon declared, "War with Russia is inevitable. We must blow them off the face of the earth quick, before they do the same to us—we haven't much time." Retired Admiral Lewis Strauss, then one of the five members of the Atomic Energy Commission of which he later became chairman, also supported Teller.

In Berkeley, California, Ernest O. Lawrence had developed a method for producing tritium, a component essential to the manufacture of hydrogen bombs. Lawrence and Teller had met at Los Alamos in 1949 and found they were theoretically and philosophically in accord. Both believed that the future security of the United States depended upon developing a hydrogen bomb.

President Truman created an executive committee to investigate the controversy surrounding the H-bomb. The committee dispatched a team from Washington to assess the mood of scientists in New Mexico and California. The evaluation team reported that there was a kind of "bloodthirstiness" among these weapons specialists. Many of them, including Lawrence, were eager to produce a super bomb, which they referred to simply as the "super." Members of the advisory committee presented their findings to the president.

AEC chairman David E. Lilienthal advised the commander-in-chief that "things were rapidly coming to a showdown stage and fast."

During the protracted discussion, the "super" acquired a code name: "Campbells" ("super" equals "soup"). Truman decided Campbells would be built. Once the decision had been made, the need for a second weapons laboratory was apparent. On July 1, 1952, the Atomic Energy Commission approved the formation of a radiation laboratory at Livermore, California. Lawrence became the director of the new facility and was responsible for gathering a staff. Teller was the associate director and the scientific authority. Eager, young, inexperienced designers were selected to fill the Livermore ranks. One of the supervisors of this unproven group was Harold Brown, who was to become director of Livermore and later Secretary of Defense.

When the new laboratory was formed, Teller was ecstatic, but his former associates at Los Alamos were not. In their eyes, he was taking knowledge acquired in their laboratory and using it to outdo them at another facility. About the same time, Teller became publicly critical of Oppenheimer, which contributed to widening the gap between the two laboratories. Even though Oppenheimer had not returned to Los Alamos, many of the men at Los Alamos were still loyal to "Oppy."

From its inception, Livermore differed from Los Alamos in procedure and organization. While scientists at Los Alamos used existing designs to create and stockpile weapons, those at Livermore experimented with radical new designs that put larger and more destructive weapons into smaller packages. Los Alamos personnel branded Livermore's approach to weapons design as reckless and predicted mass failures.

While Los Alamos was characterized by a well-defined structure in which each level of management was clearly identified, Livermore's trademark was nonorganization.

There were no bosses. Emphasis was on allowing young designers to find their own levels of achievement.

A third area in which the two laboratories differed was their relationship with Washington and the rest of the world. Livermore's scientific community established a rapport with the Washington political community. Realizing the support that Washington could provide, Livermore spent considerable time and effort lobbying members of the AEC, Congress, and the Joint Chiefs of Staff. Livermore promoted frequent visits from those in Washington who held top-secret clearances. Scientists at Los Alamos saw no need to cultivate the friendship and good will of politicians, however. They kept to themselves, seldom ventured outside their New Mexico hilltop community, and discouraged visitors from coming in.

During the early 1950s, competition between the two laboratories was intense. Both laboratories, particularly Livermore, assigned top priority to tests at the test sites. As the years progressed, more atmospheric tests were incorporated in each series to accommodate the outdoor experiments of the two laboratories.

By 1957, nuclear weapons technology had developed to the point where both laboratories had the capability to produce larger weapons in smaller packages. Livermore, in particular, had demonstrated the capacity to transform theoretical weapons designs to the practical application of field-tested hydrogen devices. As technology progressed, the need for testing increased—and with it came controversy. Nuclear scientists were accused of poisoning the world in the course of their atomic adventures. When Los Alamos director Norris Bradbury told the AEC in February that no effort had been made to develop clean weapons for the Plumbbob series, Edward Teller saw an immediate opportunity to repay his old friend and loyal supporter, AEC chairman Lewis Strauss. Strauss was on the hot seat because Eisenhower was reacting to public criticism of the testing program. When it was announced that thirty-four tests were to be conducted during the forthcoming series, the residents of Utah who lived downwind from the test site were furious. Congressional representatives of the downwind residents were deluged with calls and letters from constituents. Western journalists wrote article after article critical of the AEC's plans.

On June 23, 1957, Strauss, Teller, and Lawrence met at the White House and briefed President Eisenhower about Livermore's special nuclear devices that were designed to reduce radioactive fallout. The forty-five-minute meeting concluded with a statement from the president: "We have reduced fallout from bombs by nine-tenths, and the current Nevada tests are designed to see how clean we can make them." Teller, Lawrence, and Livermore Laboratory ostensibly had achieved a breakthrough that still eluded Los Alamos. While Strauss and Eisenhower were relieved, the announcement served to exacerbate the bad blood between Los Alamos and Livermore. Bradbury and his crew had been outdone once again by Teller.

Teller and Lawrence rushed to incorporate into the program the design and testing of this new type of weapon. The Rand Corporation, a large nuclear weapons subcontractor, had conceived a cost-effective people killer—highly efficient, in that it destroyed individuals, not structures and property. An agonizing death usually occurred within six days to six weeks after prompt exposure to a lethal dose of radiation from this device.

This bomb may have been incorporated in the 1957 series because it was unique in that it spread substantially less fallout. A high-energy thermonuclear fusion reaction was necessary to its success. When detonated, the hydrogen reaction would release cell-damaging high-energy neutrons. Most of the radiation would be contained onsite.

Select representatives of the news media were invited to

the Nevada Test Site to witness the explosion of the country's first "clean" bomb.

The person critical to the success of Eisenhower's hoped-for clean bomb was the Plumbbob scientific test director Dr. Gerald Johnson. A Livermore man would detonate one of Livermore's greatest achievements: code name, Hood. The test was not only important to the Plumbbob series, but Hood was to herald the advent of tests of much larger similar bombs at Eniwetok and Bikini, the Pacific Proving Grounds.

Johnson, well aware of the special significance of the Hood shot, took extra precautions to assure that the detonation would occur. The innovative physicist devised a new procedure for arming nuclear devices that would, it was hoped, eliminate the possibility of an electrical failure during countdown. Johnson's mission was to ensure success and maintain utmost secrecy.

The military, on the other hand, was concerned with a different problem. Members of the Fourth Marine Corps Provisional Atomic Exercise Brigade had yet to execute the field exercise for which they had been brought to the Nevada Test Site. The misfire and postponement of shot Diablo had increased the number of days the troops had to remain at Camp Desert Rock, and there was mounting anxiety that the budget, always a Marine Corps concern, would be exceeded. General Tschirgi and his staff decided to request that the brigade be allowed to participate in the next scheduled shot, rather than wait for the rescheduling of Diablo.

When Johnson was told of the brigade's decision, he immediately conferred with Test Site Manager Reeves. At first, these men were hesitant to approve the brigade's request because the next scheduled detonation was Hood. Only Johnson, Reeves, some of the members of the Nevada Test Group, and the Atomic Energy Commission knew what kind of nuclear package Hood was. It was highly unlikely that such a weapon would ever be used in combat, because the device had not been designed as a tactical or strategic weapon. Personally, Reeves was anxious to have the brigade leave the test site. As test site manager, he had the overall responsibility for all personnel at the site except the military. He had no control over their maneuvers in the field, and this fact made him uneasy. The brigade operations plan, submitted to Reeves, was stamped, "For Information Only." The test site manager could review the plan but was prohibited by his boss, the director of the Division of Military Applications, from interfering with a military exercise. After much discussion, the two senior managers agreed to grant the marines' request. Actually, the participation of the brigade in shot Hood would work to the Nevada Test Organizations' advantage, because if the marines could survive the detonation and conduct the field exercise without incident, the special nature of the bomb would be cleverly concealed. In effect, foreign powers would be led to believe that the explosion was nothing more than a continuation of the regular testing of atomic bombs.

On Friday, June 28, at 8:00 p.m., the test information director issued the following release:

> A conference between the Fourth Marine Corps Provisional Atomic Exercise Brigade and the Nevada Test organization has resulted in the decision that the Brigade will conduct its exercise on shot Hood, the open shot, scheduled for July 3.

Thus news correspondents learned about the marines and Hood.

Before Hood could be detonated, it had to be assembled. Bomb components arrived both by surface and air and were put together under the tightest security in a building at the test site.

New trenches had to be dug because none suitable for the forthcoming blast existed. The Desert Rock commander, an

Army general, was responsible for selecting the trench location. Using a chart that set out criteria for positioning troops, he decided to place the trenches fifty-five hundred yards, or about three miles, from ground zero. According to his chart, troops that far away should be able to withstand the effects of a 100-kiloton explosion.

By July 1, all preparations were complete. The bomb was mounted on a wooden platform at the balloon lift-off station in Yucca Flat Area Nine. The balloon, with Hood in a gondola below it, would be raised into position, provided conditions were favorable for a July 3 detonation. Test Director Johnson secretly hoped for a one-day postponement because he wanted to explode this special nuclear firecracker on July 4, Independence Day.

While Hood was being readied, a so-called safety experiment weapon was detonated at Frenchman Flat. The code name for the experiment was Coulomb A. The test's ostensible purpose was to prove that a nuclear explosion would *not* occur in the event of an accidental detonation of the conventional high explosives used as part of the triggering mechanism. In fact, the test was an experiment that scattered deadly radioactive elements liberally across the desert floor.

On July 2, the day after the safety experiment, a special meeting took place at the United Nations in New York. Addressing an international disarmament conference, the U.S. representative made an impassioned plea for an *immediate* moratorium on atmospheric nuclear testing. Unfortunately, his pleas were not heard thirty-two hundred miles away at the Nevada Test Site. They rang hollow when, scarcely three days later, the United States detonated the largest and most highly experimental weapon tested during that period.

The officers at my level learned of the change in plans on June 29, but I was away on a one-day pass to Las Vegas and did not get the news about the brigade's participation in

Hood until the following day. I was told the name of the bomb and that it was going to be a large explosion—probably in the 60-kiloton range. No mention was made of possible radiation exposure, and our administrative and operational plan remained unchanged.

As the detonation date approached, my apprehension mounted. I still had vivid recollections of Priscilla's force and fury and of the mental and physical beating I had taken in that trench line. How could I survive a bomb almost *five times* larger when I was going to be only one mile farther away? (At that time, I was still under the impression that the nuclear explosion I had experienced was, in fact, the 14-kiloton one its planners had predicted. I was unaware that the blast had far exceeded the expectations of the bomb's designers.) Participation in Hood's colossal explosion was supposed to be an honor, but I did not feel honored. For the first time in my life, I was beginning to doubt the wisdom of those in command.

Hood was postponed twice. Finally, on the evening of July 4, the persistent desert winds stopped blowing, and the green light on the flagpole went on. There was a palpable air of excitement among members of the battalion. Anticipation had replaced ennui. It was difficult to tell how much of the change in mood was attributable to the approaching test and how much to the knowledge that, after three long weeks, we were finally going to leave that desolate desert hellhole and return to California.

At 10:00 p.m., the green light still shone atop the flagpole; I was certain we would be going to Yucca Flat in a few hours. I called a platoon meeting. As I looked at the faces of my young men, I somehow summoned courage to project a confidence I could no longer share. I told them that our forthcoming experience would be an enriching one for us all. I reminded them that we were living in an atomic age and that, if war should occur, in all probability it would be fought with nuclear weapons. We were here in the Nevada desert to become familiar with the use and effect of these weapons. I emphasized the importance of our mission and reviewed the procedures we were to follow. Then I assured them that, if they obeyed orders and performed as I knew they were capable of performing, we would be successful. In the past I had often joked and kidded when talking to the men, but this time I was deadly serious because I had survived one nuclear experiment and knew personally what the experience was like. My platoon could only imagine the effects, but for them the unknown would soon become known. I left the briefing tent feeling fearful for them and for myself.

We were scheduled to depart from Camp Desert Rock at 11:00 p.m. As the hour approached, I went to the noncommissioned officers' tent to find my platoon sergeant and tell him to muster the platoon and call roll. When I went into the tent, I saw Gunnery Sergeant Tall Bear, a full-blooded Cherokee, taking a long swig from a bottle of bourbon that he had partially hidden in a pack hanging from the center pole of the tent. Tall Bear, a veteran of Guadalcanal, Iwo Jima, and Korea, had witnessed Priscilla from the ridge line. He disliked officers in general and young lieutenants in particular. Surprised to see him so blatantly violating regulations, I said, "Sergeant, put that bottle away. It's time to move out."

He stared at me contemptuously with sunken, piercing eyes and declared defiantly, "Lieutenant, Chesty Puller [the Marine general who commanded the First Marine Division in Korea and who had endeared himself to his men] said that a good marine always takes a drink before he goes into combat."

"Well, Sergeant, this isn't Korea, and it isn't even combat. It's an exercise," I snapped.

He took another swallow and fixed his gaze on me. "Mister, out there," he said, as he gestured toward Yucca Flat, "hanging from a balloon is the most powerful *enemy* you or me is ever going to face." Silently, I left the tent and joined my platoon.

A battalion formation was held, and someone on the brigade staff gave us a rousing speech about the importance of our mission and how it was an honor to have been selected to participate in this test. Like all the marines there, I was moved by the senior officer's words, but while we were en route to the trenches, my uneasiness returned. Just before we left Desert Rock, we were told that Hood was to be about five times larger than the bomb dropped on Hiroshima. The size estimate was revised upward from 60 to 80 kilotons. I asked myself, "If a much smaller bomb detonated at nearly the same height killed one hundred fifty thousand Japanese, then why or how are twenty-one hundred of us expected to survive?" Were we leathernecks supposed to be immortal?

Around 1:30 a.m. on July 5, we arrived at the trenches. The night was pitch black. The half moon had set at midnight while we were en route to the trench area. The stars twinkled brightly against the dark sky. In front of us, we could see the illuminated balloon holding aloft the canister that contained the nuclear weapon. As soon as the sound of departing trucks faded away in the distance, most of the men went to sleep, but some paced anxiously behind the trenches.

Burton and his six-man crew were already at ground zero arming the shot. Within four hours, the device that had been approved by the president in April for detonation would be fired.

I shall never forget my feelings and sensations during the countdown. As I entered the trench at 4:20 a.m. I recalled Priscilla. I remembered all too vividly the violent rending of the earth, the boom of the shock wave, the collapse of nearby trenches, the grotesquely twisted and burned mannequin, the severe dust storm, and the omnipresent fallout. When the last ten seconds of the countdown began and we assumed the kneeling position, I wondered, "Why is my very own government intent on killing me?" My body shook uncontrollably. Perspiration streamed down my palms, and my eyes filled with tears. I began to hyperventilate and was convinced I would die of a heart attack if not as a result of the bomb's devastation. I could neither control nor conceal my body's bizarre behavior, and I feared the men nearest me in the trench would notice it. I felt we were there to be sacrificed and was certain we would all perish. I wanted to stand and yell, "Stop! Stop! You must not explode that bomb! We don't deserve to die this way!" Instead, I prayed harder than I had at any other time in my life and asked to be spared.

After the count reached "one," I heard a click. Then as before, I felt I would be melted by that unbearable heat. Once again, the intense brightness allowed me to see the bones in my forearm through my tightly closed eyes. But all similarity to Priscilla ended there. Within a second after the detonation, the ground started to tremble violently. After about seven or eight seconds, the trench wall near me collapsed. It was another five seconds before the shock wave hit with a sound comparable to that of a cannon being fired directly overhead. The earth oscillated back and forth. I gritted my teeth and braced myself against the near wall of the trench to avoid falling over. The second shock wave hit with a sharp crack, and the ground was still.

In the control center twenty miles away, Gerry Johnson, Ernest O. Lawrence, and their associates watched the console as, one after another, the lights changed from red to green, indicating that the electrical impulse was on its way to the triggering device. Detonation occurred, and the fireball churned rapidly skyward, pushed by the tremendous heat and energy released by the explosion. The ominous swirling mass resembled a giant cobra poised to strike.

The scientists in the control center rushed to the reinforced window to watch their successful thermonuclear experiment. Within thirty seconds, they felt the heat generated by the explosion through the thick walls of the building and saw the pall of dust that extended for miles, totally obscuring vision. The failure of Diablo had been followed by an overwhelming success.

Veteran nuclear watchers had never seen anything comparable to the Hood detonation. One reporter, Colin McKinley of U.P.I., who observed Hood from a peak fifty-five air miles from ground zero, described the flash that accompanied the explosion of this 77-kiloton giant as "500 times brighter than the sun." That flash created a false dawn in Los Angeles, three hundred miles to the west, and was seen by an airline pilot twelve hundred miles away. Another reporter likened the bomb's effects to a man-made hell. He wrote, "The fireball had a temperature of nearly one million degrees Centigrade. The blast was the most violent ever felt at the location [News Knob, eight miles from ground zero] by veterans of atomic tests. The explosion ignited the entire floor of Yucca Flat and most of the small yucca trees on a mountain range several miles north of ground zero." A Salt Lake City resident mistakenly identified the shock wave that rattled her home thirty minutes after the detonation as an earthquake.

On a ridge line eight miles from Yucca Flat Area Nine, site of the Hood explosion, members of the Second Motor Transport Company milled around in the darkness before nuclear dawn. These marines, who had driven us to the trenches, had been ordered to watch the explosion from the ridge. They had heard of the intense heat produced by nuclear weapon detonations, and five minutes before the countdown, several of them put on their military ponchos. Intended primarily for foul weather, these plasticized rubber garments protected their heads and the sides of their faces and enveloped their bodies like small tents. Wearing these hooded ponchos with drawstrings tied, members of the motor transport unit sat with their hands over their eyes and their backs to ground zero. In the flash that followed the detonation, these men saw the bones of their hands through closed eyelids. The thermal radiation from Hood transformed their once-solid ponchos into sticky masses which they had to peel from their bodies.

My prayers had been answered. I had *not* been killed. Engulfed by a ring of fire, I left the trench quickly. My men, who were conditioned by training to react as instructed and by instinct to survive, moved quickly also. Everything about us was aflame, and we had to be careful not to step on or stumble into a flaming bush. The acrid smoke and thick dust made breathing extremely difficult. Still, despite the conditions, we were determined to fulfill our mission.

Only 900 of the 2,100 of us had been assigned to secure the objective, a hill to the left of ground zero. Fifteen miles to our rear, a skeleton company of 150 men waited aboard helicopters used in the vertical envelopment tactical exercise. Their lift-off was delayed one hour and fifteen minutes because conditions in the area made flying unsafe. We were supposed to board amphibious tractors and advance on the "enemy," but the dust hanging over our heads made it impossible to find the vehicles. And, rather than stand around waiting for the choking dust to settle, we decided to attack on foot.

As we left the area, I glanced back at the members of the brigade who remained behind. I could discern the vague outline of heads above the leading wall of a trench, and thought to myself that those marines resembled groundhogs cautiously poking their heads out of their holes to decide whether it was safe to venture forth. I turned toward our objective and led my men into the dust storm.

One of the units of our battalion, Echo Company, was to follow the radiological-safety team and the pathfinders to within four hundred yards of ground zero, where they were to clear and secure a landing zone for the helicopters. At that distance, it would have been incredible to find so much as a bush left standing or a jackrabbit that had survived.

The safety personnel moved toward ground zero. The pathfinders were delayed because the weapons platoon leader and his men were among those hardest hit by the blast. Sergeant Israel Torres, the weapons platoon leader, remembered:

> Directly after the countdown stopped, there was a big, loud blast and a very bright light appeared. The ground began shaking violently. My trench began to cave in, and I got scared. In my attempt to get out of the trench, I lost my sunglasses. I tried to avoid getting buried, and I had moved about a foot when the space around me began filling with dirt very quickly, and suddenly I was buried up to my chest. The air was intensely hot as it blew into our trenches. There was a thick layer of dust all around me, and I could not see more than a few feet. The ground gyrated savagely as the shock wave hit following the big blast. A strong wind [estimated to be moving at well over one hundred miles per hour] hit me in the face and knocked me backward, even though I was partly buried. My head snapped back, and my helmet went flying off behind me. I was fighting to get out of the trench, but I could not move. I looked up to my front and saw a big mushroom cloud forming. I managed to free my arms, and using both hands I

wiped away the thick layer of dust and dirt that covered my face and eyes and looked down. As I opened my eyes I could see the blinding light through my hands. I shook all over and began to vomit.

The scene was chaotic. Something unexpected had happened. I could hear my men moaning and yelling: "Where are you?" "I can't move." "I can't see you." "Please help me." Grown men were crying. Even though I had survived some tight experiences in Korea, I had never been through anything like this, and I had never been so frightened. Many men could not free themselves from the trenches, and we had to wait at least thirty minutes for a special emergency force to get us out. Part of the problem was that, because of the thick dust, the team had difficulty finding us. The strong wind did not stop blowing, and it was not easy to see very far. When I was finally free, I was shaking, nauseated, and my vision was still blurred. I held a quick roll call of my platoon, and two men were unaccounted for. The remainder of my men and I conducted a search for the two missing marines, but we could not locate them. They had gone into the trenches with us, but now we were unable to find them. I never saw the two young marines again.

My platoon had been delayed in its mission, and we had to conduct our field exercise. We began to sweep the area [perform a tactical maneuver]. As we approached ground zero, I saw tanks melted down, and other heavy equipment burned to cinders. We continued sweeping for about two hours, cleared a helicopter landing zone, and formed a tight perimeter while a company of marines landed in the area we had cleared. The company that arrived attacked a hill and joined other elements of the battalion that

> were attacking from different directions. Later we were force marched to a place where trucks were waiting for us. Before boarding the vehicles, we were checked with some type of an instrument that I think was a Geiger counter. When I was checked, the thing ticked loudly, and the man who monitored me told me something that I have never forgotten. He said, "Marine, you have had it. You get in that truck over there with the other men." Before I got in the truck, my badge was taken away by a young lieutenant. About half of my platoon was with me. We were then transported to a special place where we stripped down, were hosed off, and were given some special type of soap to shower with. All our clothes were burned. We were issued new clothing and weapons. I was still shaking. I felt nauseated and had a splitting headache. My vision had not returned to normal.

Bill Starbuck had been transferred to Desert Rock specifically for the Hood exercise. He was a recruiting officer sent to the test site to experience atomic deployment firsthand. His superiors felt that his becoming an atomic veteran would make him more effective in his recruiting. While he was kneeling in the trench, dirt and sand collected around him like sugar poured from a large sack. Partly buried, he felt fortunate at being able to pull himself from the trench alive after the shock wave passed.

The thermonuclear detonation left a lasting impression on Jim Kleinschmidt. He was assigned to an 81-millimeter mortar platoon as a communications operator. He and other members of the platoon were partly buried beneath loose soil from the trench walls but managed to dig out and move off into the desert as planned to lay down a base of fire for the attacking troops. When the exercise was over, they boarded trucks and were driven close enough to ground zero to see the hypocenter. Kleinschmidt saw the remains of equipment and structures around him—tanks and trucks and buildings—that had been destroyed by the blast. From his experience, he knew that thousands of mortar shells hitting directly on target could not cause the kind of damage he saw all around. He was awed by the degree and extent of the devastation. None of the other men spoke. They, too, were in shock.

Following the blast, First Sergeant Charles Trent, assigned to the brigade staff during the actual detonation, grabbed men by the arms and pulled them from a certain grave in the collapsing trenches. Once out of the trenches, members of his group groped through the thick dust in search of one another. When a semblance of military order had been restored, Trent's small group formed a column of twos and began their forced march toward ground zero. A radiological-safety expert who accompanied them halted the sergeant far short of his objective. Trent was evacuated by helicopter. As he was being whisked away from the contaminated area, he looked down at the desert floor through holes in the dust cloud and saw marines scattered over the earth below.

The Reynolds Electric helicopter survey team, as after Priscilla, had to delay its mission. Because a heavy layer of dust obscured the ground checkpoints, the aerial survey at twenty-five to one hundred feet in altitude began six hours later than planned.

Hood's awesome fireball quickly became an ominous radioactive cloud. Within a few minutes, the gaseous mass had ascended forty-five thousand feet—eight and one-half miles—into the atmosphere. High winds aloft scattered it in three directions at altitudes of fifteen thousand, twenty-five thousand, and forty-five thousand feet. As was AEC practice, Hood was detonated during a calm before an approaching front accompanied by high-velocity winds. The highest layer disappeared among the other clouds in the troposphere. The mission of Air Force Lieutenants Merl Kimball and John Alder was no longer to *sample* the cloud, but to *find* it. They were told that the blast would have to be repeated if they could not locate the top layer of the nuclear cloud. It took the two experienced pilots more than an hour to find the cloud, fifty miles offsite and camouflaged by surrounding natural clouds, so that they could collect radioactive particulate matter on the specially designed grids attached to the fuel tanks of their aircraft.

Seven hours after the countdown had ended in a click, the brigade of blast-weary marine veterans completed its mission and left the test site.

Aftermath

> *A series of military effects experiments [have been] designed to increase knowledge of the effects of atomic detonations upon military equipment, material and personnel.*
>
> —Department of Defense memo, April 15, 1957
> addressed to Major General A.D. Starbird
> Director, AEC Division of Military Applications

Until 1978, most of the marine participants in the Hood shot viewed it as an experience of the past and saw in it little cause for alarm. But some of them died prematurely, and others began to develop unusual degenerative diseases.

On January 24, 1978, the Subcommittee on Health and the Environment of the U.S. House of Representatives International and Foreign Commerce Committee began hearings into the matter of participation by military personnel in nuclear weapons tests. Chaired by Representative Paul Rogers of Florida, the hearings were held over a period of two months. One member of the subcommittee, Representative Tim Lee Carter of Kentucky, was particularly concerned. Two of his constituents had been nuclear weapons test participants; one had died and the other had leukemia.

During the second day of the hearings, Army Major Alan Skerker, a Department of Defense nuclear weapons officer, appeared before the subcommittee. Representative Rogers questioned Skerker about Hood. The major confirmed that the blast had in fact been 77 kilotons. Rogers queried further, "There was heavy exposure in Hood?"

"Yes, sir," Skerker replied.

Rogers then asked Skerker if the major knew the identity of the marines involved in the test. Skerker replied that he could not very readily identify the Hood participants, and Carter said, "It would be easier for us to find the members of Quantrill's guerrillas than it would be to find the men who were at Desert Rock. I think, if you have no more organization and no more knowledge of what you are doing, that a dozen good men with some willow switches could whip the Pentagon."

Skerker did tell Carter that two marine companies moved to "within safe distance—four hundred yards—of ground zero" after the explosion of Hood. Carter then asked Skerker to reveal the message on a card handed to him by a senior officer before he testified. "Which card is that, sir?" Skerker asked.

Undeterred by the witness's apparently feigned ignorance, Carter made his question precise: "The one in your left breast pocket."

A sheepish Skerker pulled the card from his pocket and read, "Do not volunteer any information. Make them get it out of you." Shortly after the close of the hearings, Major Skerker was transferred to Germany.

Hood was mentioned specifically again when Rogers called Frank Putnam of the National Academy of Sciences as a witness. Questioning Putnam, Carter said, "I believe the *dirtiest* [emphasis added] explosion in the United States was at Hood in 1957 [involving] 2,100 marines."

Putnam replied, "Oh yes!"

How could the bomb described before the fact as *clean* by President Eisenhower and others have become known as the *dirtiest*? Was Hood a neutron bomb? Only the designers and the planners know. The information is classified and unobtainable, but all the ingredients were there. A "clean" bomb test was officially announced. The neutron bomb as it was designed certainly reduced offsite radioactive fallout considerably. But what occurred onsite after the July 5 test?

Test Director Gerald Johnson's report on the Plumbbob series dated November 15, 1957, provides a possible answer. With regard to the radiation accompanying the balloon shots, Johnson explained, "The activity induced by neutron absorption in the soil was as high as several hundred roentgens per hour at one hour [after detonation]. The neutrons were absorbed in a relatively thick layer . . . of one to two feet of soil." The soil within seven hundred and fifty or more yards of the hypocenter was made dangerously radioactive to a depth of two feet by each bomb's blast. Residual radiation remained in the soil and was carried into the air by the force of each successive detonation and blown about by the continual and capricious desert winds.

Thus, while our film badges recorded only small amounts of *gamma* radiation, many of us were exposed each hour to as many as several hundred roentgens of *neutron* radiation, which our film badges were not designed to record. Yet one government bulletin states, "Very few, if any, of the nuclear weapons test participants were exposed to neutron radiation."

When questioned about Hood, representatives of government agencies and high-ranking officers in the Marine Corps have offered only a standard, vague response: "Very little is know about Hood," or, "We know less about Hood than about any other shot in which troops were involved." There has never been an official admission that a thermonuclear or hydrogen weapon has ever been detonated within the continental limits of the United States.

All efforts by Congress, veterans, and others to discover the type and composition of Hood have been repeatedly thwarted. I had sent Freedom of Information Act requests to Livermore Laboratory and the Department of Energy. Both replied with statements that indicated the information was not to be released. But I uncovered the truth in a letter—which came as a complete surprise—written to me by Lieutenant Colonel William J. McGee of the Defense Nuclear Agency. Dated July 7, 1980, the letter revealed that, "Hood was the largest device detonated in the United States. It was a thermonuclear device and a prototype of some thermonuclear weapons currently in the national stockpile. The neutron output was comparable to that produced in some other tests. . . ." Thus, Colonel McGee gave away one of the best kept secrets of nuclear testing. A hydrogen bomb had been exploded in Nevada, and marines had been exposed to a blast with many times the killing force of an atomic bomb!

The Atomic Energy Commission and the nuclear scientific community were well aware that a hydrogen experiment would be conducted in the United States. Gerry Johnson's "top secret" operations order, which has since been declassified, read:

> Plumbbob is designed to conduct experiments advancing technical understanding of nuclear and thermonuclear weapons, to test prototypes and

develop further information on their military and civil effects.

On that fateful day in July 1957, we eager young marines were unaware of the memo Major General A. D. Starbird had received three months before: "A series of military effects experiments [have been] designed to increase knowledge of the effects of nuclear detonations upon military equipment, material and personnel." That dreadful flash in the western sky at 4:40 on the morning of July 5, 1957, did not enrich anyone's existence. The bomb's designers congratulated each other on their success because the hydrogen trigger mechanism employed in the Hood event would be used in the large megaton explosions planned for subsequent tests in the Pacific.

While the nuclear gang was overly pleased with the results of the July 5 test, we members of the Fourth Marine Corps Provisional Atomic Exercise Brigade were becoming heirs to a grim and insidious legacy of genetic mutation, delayed radiation illness, and premature death. Far from being proud and willing participants in necessary combat maneuvers, we were, instead, unwitting subjects of nuclear experimentation, initiated by our exposure to radiation into eternal membership in the "neutron brigade."

Beyond the Blue Horizons

If I were asked . . . I would say . . . go back to Eniwetok . . . put them on a raft and set them off.

—Lewis Strauss, Chairman
Atomic Energy Commission

The 1957 Plumbbob series ended in Nevada on December 12 with a small safety experiment exploded in an underground shaft. Dr. Gerald Johnson urged the switch to underground testing in Nevada because he believed the atmospheric tests were "a scene resembling some giant floor show with all types of persons running around as though they were at a carnival." Johnson argued, "The tests should be conducted in an environment where there is maximum security and secrecy and where there is *no* resultant fallout."

The thirty-four nuclear experiments of the Plumbbob series were a record for Nevada. The next atmospheric tests would be carried out at the Pacific Proving Grounds.

Beginning in 1954, the Atomic Energy Commission tested during even-numbered years at Bikini, Eniwetok, and Johnston atolls. There were military tasks, but no mock attacks.

The 1958 Pacific series was Hardtack I. Much larger versions of the Plumbbob experiments were scheduled, with some tests in the megaton range. A task force supported by four task groups was formed. Altogether, 20,704 air force, army, navy, marine and scientific-community people were involved in Hardtack I. These men arrived at the proving grounds by air and sea. Few except the planners of the tests knew that during the course of five months, between April and August, the Pacific skies would be filled with the fires from thirty-five nuclear explosions.

One of the men assigned to the task force was U.S. Army Sergeant First Class Orville E. Kelly of Burlington, Iowa.

3.

Destination Unknown— Mission Uncertain, Nevada to the Pacific

When you reach those Pearly Gates,
You will hear St. Peter yell;
Fall in, men from 'Wetok;
You've served your hitch in Hell!

—A Lonesome GI
Eniwetok

Orville E. Kelly, co-founder of the National Association of Atomic Veterans, recalled his hitch in hell:

> Fourteen of us, communications specialists from the Air Force, Army and Navy, stood on a quiet beach on Japtan Island at Eniwetok in the North Pacific listening to the voice from a portable countdown receiver on the sand beside us. It was Monday, May 5, 1958, and we were about to observe our first nuclear detonation, as members of Task Group 7.2; Joint Task Force Seven. We were participants in phase one of Operation Hardtack.
>
> Each of us was lost in our own thoughts in the predawn silence, as we reluctantly faced toward ground zero across the calm lagoon. The blast was

to be a surface shot, called Cactus, and it would be detonated from a site on Runit Island approximately seven miles from our island. Cactus was expected to be 18 kilotons in size. It would be more powerful than the bomb dropped over Hiroshima, but none of us knew exactly what to expect.

As a sergeant first class in the U.S. Army, I was the enlisted noncommissioned officer in command of Japtan Island. The thirteen other servicemen at the beach site worked in the radio receiver station on the island or as cooks in the mess hall. In addition to the fourteen servicemen on the island at the time, there were four employees of Holmes and Narver, a civilian contracting firm. These four men operated the power and distillation plants on Japtan Island.

All of us, except for the civilians, were at the beach site because my commanding officer had ordered us to be there. No one seemed to know why we had to stand on the beach and face toward the blast, but as a member of the armed forces I had learned to follow orders without questioning them.

I detested the sound of the voice coming from the countdown receiver on the beach. Its tone was so calm, while we were all fearful of what we were about to see. We had heard rumors of how a nuclear device, when detonated, might set off a chain reaction in the atmosphere. There had been some talk about an earlier blast that had wiped an entire island from the atoll.

It was just ten seconds away from H-hour and the countdown continued: "Ten, . . . five, four, three, two, one."

Suddenly the world in front of me exploded into one big frenzy of light, heat and sound. Gigantic

> flames shot upward. Shortly after the blast a shock wave swept across the lagoon, startling us as it almost knocked us over. My eyes saw what was happening, but it seemed as though my brain was unable to record all the sensations I was experiencing.
>
> Not one of us who watched that nuclear blast signaling the start of Operation Hardtack could ever describe accurately what we saw. I could only imagine the devastation at ground zero as Runit Island was completely obliterated by an intense, blinding light, many times brighter than the sun. We stood there mesmerized by the brilliance of the fireball that we viewed through the clouded lenses of our special goggles. There had been rumors that people in Hawaii, 2,380 nautical miles away, could see flashes of light from some of the larger predawn detonations of previous tests in 1954 and 1956. I thought about all the people who had no idea of the terrible force I was seeing. I wondered how many more of these shots I would have to watch.

Cloyd Jones, another army sergeant, was standing next to Kelly that May morning. He tells his story:

> We were grouped together on the side of the island facing the blast, and we had to look toward the ground zero area. Our eyes were covered with tinted glasses. We wore khaki shirts and shorts, and our clothing was covered by our military ponchos. Nonetheless, we still felt the heat and the shock wave from the blast. When the force reached our island, the land beneath our feet began to tremble and shake, and I thought we were having an earthquake.
>
> As we continued watching the Cactus shot, we

> observed that the cloud from the blast reached its maximum height in about ten minutes. Then, the cloud began to spread out and for about two hours after the blast the sky above us was pink. Because the explosion created a huge crater on Runit Island, dirt and debris were carried skyward with the cloud.

Kelly picks up the story:

> After about twenty minutes of watching the awe-inspiring phenomenon, I dismissed my men and returned to the barracks. Later, as I sat in the recreation building on the island, drinking cognac and Coca-Cola in the stifling, tropical heat, I thought about what I had seen. It frightened me to think that I was participating in the testing of weapons so terrible that just one of them could destroy a large city and kill tens of thousands of innocent men, women and children. It would not be conventional warfare as we know it, but rather a crime against humanity, if an atomic weapon were to be dropped again on any city in the world.
>
> What was I, a twenty-seven-year-old sergeant first class in the United States Army, doing on an isolated island in the Pacific in 1958, watching the first in a series of twenty-two nuclear weapons tests at the Eniwetok Proving Grounds?

A Home at Last

I am pleased to announce that Orville E. Kelly has been promoted to Battalion Sergeant Major.

—William F. Long
Colonel, U.S. Army

Kelly was born in Columbus Junction, Iowa, the son of an unwed teenage girl. As she was unable to care for him, he was passed on to her parents. His grandfather was an itinerant farm laborer and the family led a nomadic life. Their longest stop in any one place was Farmington, Iowa, when Kelly was nine. A dilapidated, unpainted, two-story wood house became their home for a time.

One evening Orville was surprised by a discovery that would heighten his awareness of the world outside Iowa. He found the entrance to the attic, and, carrying a kerosene lamp, he climbed a wooden ladder to the storage place. Lifting the light into the darkness, he saw books and magazines stacked neatly in a corner. Orville's excitement mounted as he approached the dusty cornucopia. He brushed off the cache and picked out books that intrigued him.

He began to read. He read stories of faraway places and imagined himself as the central character. *Swiss Family Robinson* became a favorite story. The young farmboy pictured himself as a member of a family living in a tree house on a tropical island and dreamed of the day his fantasy would become real. Using a dog-eared dictionary, Orville found the meaning of words he did not know. In three months he read all the books and magazines stored in the attic of the farmhouse. The peace Orville found reading in the attic ended when his grandparents began to quarrel frequently. Their arguments led to the end of the marriage, and Orville was not able to live with either grandparent.

* * *

Orville was sent to an aunt and uncle. There was not much happiness in his new home, and during his senior year in high school, when an army recruiter visited the town, Orville enlisted without a moment's hesitation. He had heard stories of the opportunities in the army, and he wanted to travel to some of those places he had read about. In his seventeen years, Orville had yet to leave the state of Iowa.

In July 1948, Kelly went into the army. He felt the service would become his home and expected the men in the service to become his family. Reading and writing appealed to him, and he chose administration as a specialty. Kelly completed a four-month course and reported to his first duty station. His newly acquired skills prepared him to carry out administrative tasks with great competence. His promise was recognized by his superiors and he rapidly acquired the three stripes of a buck sergeant. Tours of duty in Japan and Korea provided some of the travel he longed for.

After his tours in Asia, he was assigned to duty in France. He had been involved in operations and staff work, but now he had a desire to lead men. He mentioned to his buddies that he wanted to be in the infantry and they thought he was insane. France was pleasant, easy duty. Germany, where he wanted to go, meant associating with "dog-faces who drink and fight."

Kelly did go to Germany and in the bitter cold led his men as they patrolled near the Czechoslovakian border. In spring 1954, he was assigned to the Third Battalion of the Twelfth U.S. Infantry in Hanau, Germany. The Third Battalion was on continuous Cold War alert, and the operations staff of the unit was its nerve center. Kelly's superb performance had been noted, and when a temporary position of sergeant-major opened up, his superior officer recommended him to Colonel William F. Long, Jr., the battalion commander, for the increase in rank.

"Sergeant Kelly was my personal choice for sergeant-major

of the battalion," says Colonel Long. "When it developed that I had appointed the youngest sergeant-major in the Fourth Infantry Division, and perhaps in the United States Army, it was a tribute to his professional reputation and personal modesty that there were no complaints by his fellow noncommissioned officers."

At the age of twenty-two, Kelly had become the highest ranking noncommissioned officer in his battalion. His friends admiringly speculated that he probably would be a general before he was thirty.

Kelly knew differently, however. He was not interested in becoming an officer. He had been to Officer Candidate School in 1951 and, although he was a good student, he did not like the attitudes of superiority and elitism he observed in future officers. Kelly was proud of his ability to work with those above and below him in rank. This was a considerable achievement, given the rigidly adhered-to stratification of duty and social relationships within the service.

The sergeant-major rank was temporary, but Kelly received another promotion from his permanent rank of staff sergeant and left Germany with the rank of sergeant first class. With eight years of life devoted to the military, he reenlisted for another six years on December 31, 1956. After completing Signal and Communications School in Fort Monmouth, New Jersey, he was transferred to a top-secret army transmitter site in Woodbridge, Virginia.

While Kelly was in Virginia, an opportunity arose to volunteer for duty in the Pacific. His childhood fascination for the tropics had been recently heightened by reading James Michener's *Tales of the South Pacific.* He dreamed of idyllic settings with swaying coconut palms and unspoiled, sunny beaches. These visions led him to look forward to his twelve-month tour of duty.

A few months later Kelly was told that he would be joining Pacific Task Group Seven. When he inquired where the group was going, his immediate superior, a captain, mentioned a foreign-sounding name, "Eniwetok Atoll, a part of the Marshall Island chain."

The Marshalls lie nearly midway between Hawaii and the Philippines and consist of a large group of small coral islands clustered around the lagoons of thirty-two separate atolls. The atolls are scattered across six hundred and fifty nautical miles; Eniwetok Atoll is the most northwesterly. It is a ring-shaped coral reef circling a lagoon twenty miles long and eighteen miles across at its widest point. A chain of islands rises above the shallow reef.

During World War II the Marshalls were of strategic importance to both Japan and the United States. The island chain was directly in the path of the United States' progress across the Central Pacific, and as long as the Japanese occupied the Marshalls, the U.S. was denied a direct route to both the Philippines and mainland Japan. In February 1945, there were an estimated 24,000 Japanese troops in the Marshalls. On February 12, American marines and infantry launched an offensive which swept across the Marshalls and culminated twenty-one days later with the capture of Eniwetok Atoll. With the words, "The last atoll is secure," marines hoisted the Stars and Stripes to the top of the flagpole on Eniwetok.

Many of the islands of Eniwetok were almost leveled to their coral bases by naval bombardments and repeated air attacks. After the near destruction of much of their homeland, many of the Marshallese, including the Eniwetokians, became the Pacific orphans of World War II.

Two years after the surrender of Japan, the Marshall Islands became a U.S. Trust Territory. The trusteeship arrangement allowed the United States to use Eniwetok for military purposes, while denying entry to outsiders. In

December 1946, Washington officials announced that Eniwetok would be used for a series of nuclear tests. The inhabitants met the same fate that had earlier befallen the Bikinians and were moved to other atolls south of their homeland. Bewildered and confused, the one hundred forty-two islanders wept when they left. The U.S. Navy, which relocated the natives, concealed their misery when it issued a statement: "The natives are delighted about the atomic bomb which has already brought them prosperity and a promising new future."

In April 1948, nuclear tests began at Eniwetok, and during the next ten years, forty-six announced atmospheric detonations were exploded on the islands and in the tranquil lagoon. Prior to 1952, there were forty-one islands in the Eniwetok Atoll. Upon the detonation of the United States' first announced thermonuclear device, shot Mike, 10.5 megatons in size, one of the islands was vaporized.

Hardtack I—1958

> *I do not understand why, with all the land in the United States, the government chose to blow up my country and destroy our homeland.*
>
> —Chief Johannes Peter
> Eniwetok

Planning for the 1958 atmospheric tests at the Pacific Proving Grounds began as early as December 1956. In October 1957, plans took a long step forward when directors of Los Alamos and Livermore met with AEC commissioners, and representatives from the Department of Defense, the State Department, and the Sandia Corporation, which made triggering mechanisms for nuclear devices, to outline plans for the forthcoming Pacific tests.

Hardtack I was the name given to the Pacific operation. A total of thirty-five nuclear events was planned: twenty-two at Eniwetok, eleven at Bikini, and two missile firings at Johnston Island. AEC Commissioner Willard Libby expressed concern about the large number of tests, but the director of Military Applications pointed out that the Department of Defense insisted that a multitude of tests was necessary to develop nuclear warheads for missiles. As a result of discussions concerning the nature of the weapons to be tested, the AEC redefined the "danger" area in the Pacific. A 375,000-square-nautical-mile area was declared off-limits to all civilian and foreign ships.

During the meeting the possibility of a test moratorium was discussed. The American nuclear weapons testing program was under assault from an alarmed national and international community. Winds carrying radioactive fallout moved steadily across national boundaries, and governments of the world were clamoring for an end to atmospheric testing. In order to continue testing there was an immediate demand for the nuclear labs to produce a clean bomb, but they seemed unable to do it. The point was made by Commissioner Libby that President Eisenhower had "talked repeatedly of the need to develop clean weapons and has based his defense of continued weapons testing on the fact that more tests are needed to achieve such weapons." In response to worldwide concern about fallout, a group of United Nations personnel was scheduled to observe an attempted clean shot. Those attending the meeting were reluctant to allow UN observers because, as General Starbird, director of the AEC Division of Military Applications, said, "The program of nuclear weapons testing would suffer a serious setback if a weapon which was claimed to be clean proved not to be." This was a legitimate concern, for although the Plumbbob series in Nevada in 1957 was supposed to test clean bombs, the results, as demonstrated by several of the shots, had been quite the opposite. Shot Smoky, for example, had contaminated the area around ground zero to such an extent that AEC scientists, unable to return to the site, were forced to leave their measuring instruments there.

Commissioner Libby, recalling those events, said, "The test of a clean weapon for UN observers should be canceled."

The meeting adjourned with some of the commission members convinced that there was no cause for concern about a possible test moratorium. However, others did not share this optimism.

The hot desert sands of the Nevada Test Site, laden with contamination from the Plumbbob series, had barely cooled when the thirty-five atmospheric nuclear events of Hardtack I were approved.

One AEC executive was relieved to see the tests leave the continental limits. The contamination, fallout, misfires, excessively high yields, and rescheduling had been taxing. The harried official remembers:

> We were happy to see that bunch from Livermore leave Nevada, because it seemed that every time we had a problem shot it was caused by them. Those shots might have been referred to as prototypes, but let me tell you, when Livermore was involved, the word prototype was a misnomer. Livermore tests were experiments where the unexpected happened frequently. After the Plumbbob series, Livermore went out to Eniwetok and really blew the hell out of the Pacific.

Eniwetok, Eniwetok

I wish I could tell you about the sweating jungle, the full moon rising behind the volcanoes, and the waiting. The waiting. The timeless, repetitive waiting.

—James Michener
Tales of the South Pacific

At Travis Air Force Base, Orville Kelly and other military personnel boarded a military air transport plane that would fly to Hawaii, Johnston Island, and finally to Eniwetok. Kelly was approaching what he had always wanted—tropical duty. The day after Thanksgiving, which was spent on Oahu, the contingent left Hawaii to complete the nearly twenty-four-hundred-mile trip to Eniwetok. The aircraft refueled at Johnston Island, eight hundred miles west of Honolulu. Some hours after crossing the International Date Line, Eniwetok Atoll came into view. Kelly thought it looked like a sparkling jewel gleaming on the sea. The blue-green waters were interspersed with islands. One island appeared to be heavily covered with coconut trees.

After circling the atoll, the plane landed, and Kelly stepped out into the heat of Micronesia. He reported to the headquarters building and was briefed by a Signal Corps lieutenant, who explained that three islands in the southern part of the atoll—Eniwetok, Parry, and Japtan—were occupied by members of Joint Task Force Seven. After examining Kelly's service record, the lieutenant recommended him as commander of Japtan Island—the Army Signal Corps receiver site. Japtan Island would receive all incoming messages for the army task force and relay the information to the main island of Eniwetok.

During the briefing Orville was surprised to learn that he was at the Pacific Proving Grounds where nuclear tests were conducted. Orville's ignorance about his eventual mission was not unusual. Because of the secrecy surrounding activity at the Pacific Proving Grounds, information about the nuclear testing rarely became public.

Security had high priority. One memo distributed to all military personnel said, "When in your entire life have you ever been in an area so classified that everyone is cleared to handle secret information? Even our superiors, including the Task Force Commander, are prohibited from releasing *any* information for publication. They may neither confirm nor deny any articles appearing in the press."

Troops participating in the exercises were instructed: "When you write home tell them what you miss the most, and you will never violate security regulations. Do not discuss your job or the jobs out here. If you violate security regulations, appropriate disciplinary action will be taken."

The prospect of commanding an island appealed to Orville, and he gladly accepted the responsibility. The Japtan Island commander's primary task was to maintain the receiver site. He was also responsible for the discipline and morale of the military personnel. The thirteen men who reported to Kelly were communications specialists drawn from different branches of the services. Orville worried that members of the navy and the air force might resent taking orders from an army sergeant. However, he was eager to demonstrate again his ability. He had yet to receive any instruction as to what his responsibilities would be once the testing began.

The next morning, Kelly slung his duffel bag over his shoulder and boarded an M-boat, a small launch used for interisland traffic, and began his trip to Japtan. The boat stopped at Parry Island, five miles from Eniwetok, and discharged a group of civilian scientists. Parry Island, like Eniwetok Island, was a mostly barren stretch of coral and sand.

Japtan was across Oget Channel, and the ocean swells, surging through the narrow, deep-water channel, meant rough seas for the three-quarter-mile journey. Kelly was not a swimmer, and the boat's heaving and pitching frightened him.

The M-boat finally crossed the channel and made the lee side of Japtan. The island appeared to be about two miles long and less than a mile wide. In contrast to Parry and Eniwetok, Japtan was covered with lush, tropical vegetation and groves of coconut palms planted by German settlers in the early 1900s. At first Kelly could see only a thatched roof shelter near the beach, but as the M-boat approached the small dock, three other buldings on the far tip of the island came into view. He looked down into the clear water and saw an assortment of brightly colored fish swimming near the surface. In the Pacific sunlight the beaches of the island, lined with palms, were the most beautiful Orville had ever seen. He thought his teenage dreams of a tropical paradise had come true.

The M-boat idled up to the small dock and Kelly jumped out. The lieutenant who had accompanied him tossed out his duffel bag and said, "Take care of the men, Sergeant Kelly." Orville helped them cast off, and the boat headed back out into the channel.

Orville recalls his first day on Japtan:

> In the tropical heat of the November day, I stood and looked down the sandy beach that was shimmering in the morning sun. This is my island, I thought. How lucky I am to be assigned to the most beautiful island of the atoll.
>
> I walked up the beach toward the cluster of buildings I had seen from the dock. The three Quonset huts, made of corrugated metal, stood under palm trees which afforded some shade from the intense heat of the day. The largest building was the barracks, and its metal sides could be swung out to allow the breeze to pass through. Near the barracks was the mess hall and a recreation building.

> I entered one of the Quonset huts and introduced myself to two of the men. An easygoing West Virginian with a Southern accent stuck out his hand and smiled. His name was Cloyd Jones, and I felt we would get along well. The other man, an immense two-hundred-sixty-pound cook, nicknamed Tiny, reluctantly acknowledged me, and I immediately sensed he might cause me trouble.
>
> While we were talking, a small dog ran up to me and barked for attention. When I looked down I saw he was missing part of his upper lip. Jones told me that the dog's name was Smiley because his lip had been torn into a permanent smile by a sand shark he tried to catch. I reached down and patted Smiley, and the little dog followed me into my quarters, where I placed my duffel bag on my bunk. With Smiley as my escort, I went out to meet the other personnel on the island.

The men under Orville's command had come to Japtan as a result of various circumstances. Some, like Kelly, had volunteered, while others had been assigned to duty in the Pacific. A few of his men had been sent to Eniwetok Atoll for disciplinary reasons. One army corporal under Kelly's command had threatened to burn down his stateside barracks if he was refused a transfer. It was Orville's task to organize these men into an efficient team.

Orville thought he had found his island paradise. At first the men gave him few problems, the receiving station was manned and operating, and his mission went well. As the weeks passed, he came to know his island more intimately. The coast facing the lagoon had long expanses of white beaches that extended into warm, turquoise waters. On the ocean side of the island the rusted remains of a Japanese freighter, run aground during the Japanese occupation of the Marshall Islands, jutted from the water.

Orville found Japtan to be a curious mixture of idyllic beauty and hidden danger. Sometimes the men swam in a netted area of the lagoon that protected them from sharks and from the deadly lion fish and stone fish, whose poisonous barbs could end a man's life. Some of the more venturesome swimmers snorkeled the reef, where they collected beautiful sea shells. A few Java lizards remained on the island. Hunted nearly to extinction, they were rarely seen. Kelly was shocked when he first saw one. Eight feet long with a huge head and flicking tongue, it dragged itself across the ground like a prehistoric monster. Coconut crabs, with one huge claw strong enough to break open a coconut, scuttled across the sand. Like many tropical islands, Japtan was infested with large rats. Stray dogs, left behind by the evacuated Eniwetokians, roamed the jungle perimeter of the small military camp.

Although the men enjoyed the waters of the lagoon, there were many hours during the day when they had nothing to do. They amused themselves by playing practical jokes on one another, drinking, gambling, and watching an occasional movie in the recreation hall. There was no female companionship. Activities yielded little satisfaction, and the men became bored and restless in their tropical paradise.

Orville tells what they did to overcome boredom:

> The men had their projects and I had mine. On Japtan the senior person was in charge of managing the recreation hall and the beer concession. We did not have liquor on our island, and on one of my trips to Eniwetok Island I learned that the personnel on Parry could not obtain beer except from a dispenser in their club. On the return trip to Japtan I stopped by Parry Island and negotiated an exchange program. I traded them one case of beer for one bottle of liquor.
>
> A deciding factor for the men in choosing a pastime was its deviation from military regulations. If it

> was against military rules, they wanted to do it. I ignored these infractions because there simply was not enough activity during nonduty hours to keep them busy.

Morris Friberg was one of Kelly's exuberant young men. An army reservist who had been in his third year of college studying to be a mining engineer, Friberg had married one of his classmates. At age twenty-one, he chose to volunteer for active duty in order to provide his wife with the means to complete her education. He respected the Japtan commander and felt that Orville was a cut above the other men. Friberg tells about his special project:

> I made a brilliant discovery one day that allowed me to tinker with explosives. I had studied and worked with high explosives in school, and when I discovered that our Army bleach would explode when mixed with sugar, I started experimenting. I began making pipe bombs for no other purpose than to see if they would explode. At first I had numerous failures because I could never control the timing of a bomb's detonation. Once I mixed what I considered to be a safe proportion, screwed the cap on the pipe, and without warning sugar and bleach spewed all over me and the guys who were watching me. It ruined our clothing. Later though, I was *sure* I had the right chemistry. I screwed the cap on the pipe and placed the bomb in a steel wash basin in the kitchen. I moved to the other side of the room to talk with some friends who were watching the operation when, in mid-sentence, the thing exploded, sending a scorching fireball up to the ceiling. Our cook nearly panicked because he thought the mess hall was going to disappear in flames. After that episode, I decided not to make any more pipe bombs.

Friberg tells of another project:

> On Japtan men were always doing something different and unique. We had two men who made a glass-bottom boat. Somehow they acquired a bulldozer engine and the frame of an old Army truck and used it for the boat. Amazingly, they found a glass pane big enough to insert in the frame and started to construct the craft. The project took much of their time, and as the boat took shape the guys became excited by the prospect of cruising in the lagoon and being able to look down into the water at the varieties of sea life.
>
> Finally, the boat was finished. The engine was mounted, and the small vessel was launched amid much cheering and celebration. The two boatwrights floated out on the water, fired up the old diesel and jammed it in gear. Instead of going forward, the boat went backward. Amid jeers and catcalls, the two skippers struggled with the engine and its gears, but when they turned on the power the glass-bottom boat only traveled in reverse.
>
> One night I was awakened by a loud noise. I stumbled outside in the darkness to see the two men dragging the boat behind the jeep. They went around the coral perimeter road over and over again. The men didn't stop until there was nothing left of the glass-bottom boat but splinters, twisted metal and broken glass.

Kelly remembered the boat incident well:

> When those men finally launched their contraption I cheered along with the other men. When they got out in the lagoon and couldn't get the boat to go forward they cursed and yelled as they tried every-

thing to get that creation of theirs to go forward, but nothing worked. I was amused most of the time, but when they destroyed the boat in the middle of the night I was angry. I made them clean up the mess, and for the moment I forgot about the whole episode.

One afternoon, not long after the boat was demolished, a group of us were sitting around drinking. Cloyd Jones was really miffed. When I asked him why, he said because he had been on the island six months and had never had a ride on the cruiser. Puzzled, I asked him what he was talking about. He smiled and said, "Oh, you know, the Japtan Cruiser—the glass-bottom boat." We all laughed heartily, and the Navy chief proposed a toast. He raised his glass and spurted, "Here's to the boat built by the U.S. Army—the glass-bottom boat that forever dragged its ass backwards."

I guess we should have stopped drinking right then because later that night things got ugly. The afternoon sun slid behind the tops of the palm trees. As darkness descended on the island the tropical breezes brought relief from the day's heat and we drank well into the night.

The three sergeants, the Navy chief and I began to talk about the women we had known in the past, and it became impossible to separate truth from fantasy. Some stories were told repeatedly, and the men who told them began to believe them. Tiny carried around this picture of a cheerleader he said was his girl. He confessed to me once that he had found the picture on a barroom floor. I did not reveal his secret and usually went along with his story of how he happened to meet her.

This night, as he described her, his huge hands

formed the contours of her body in the air. Each time he told the story his imagination created a more beautiful and appealing woman. I was amused but the chief became indignant and allowed that if the girl in Tiny's photograph was a cheerleader then the chief's wife was a movie star.

Tiny paused a few seconds, his face turned beet-red, and he called the chief a goddamn son-of-a-bitch for making such a statement. The huge cook rose to his feet and told the chief that he was not going to take that kind of crap from him. Tiny ordered the Navy noncom to stand up because he intended to break the guy in two. Our cook had a wild, outraged look in his eyes, and as the chief rose I stepped between them to stop a potentially violent confrontation. Tiny pushed me aside and yelled that he was not in the infantry any more and that I had better leave them alone because they were going to settle the matter.

There was only one thing to do. I told Tiny that if he wanted to fight so badly, then he should take me on. He turned, faced me, grabbed his bottle by the neck and broke it over the side of the table. He started moving toward me and said that he was going to get me. I then smashed my bottle over a table and thrust the jagged edge in his direction and told him that if he took one more step I would kill him. I meant it too, because at that moment I hated that giant of a man. I was fed up with the constant brawling and bickering. Tiny stopped no more than three feet in front of me. We stood glowering at one another, breathing heavily, our faces set in hard lines. The other men in the room had moved away and were watching silently. I did not back down; I stood my ground.

Finally, the cook dropped his arm to his side and released the neck of his broken bottle. He mumbled something about how the isolation and boredom made him act strangely. As an act of reconciliation he invited me to the kitchen to have a steak with him. Later, we sat there eating our meal and chatting amicably. It was hard to believe that we had been intent on killing one another less than an hour ago.

I was the authority on the small coconut cay. I intended to enforce military discipline as I always had with men under my command. In an attempt to maintain a semblance of military order, I sometimes had the men form a small platoon, and I would conduct close-order drill. The men did this with varying degrees of cooperation. However, as the days passed into weeks, and then into months, with no change in the listless routine, general conduct among the men began to deteriorate. If the men misbehaved, I reproached them. But the absence of military police and a brig made it difficult for me to do more than severely reprimand anyone for even the most severe violation of military regulations.

By spring 1958, six months after Orville's arrival, nearly all the men on Japtan had developed serious drinking problems. Isolation, boredom, loneliness, and frustration were all taking their toll. Discipline was breaking down alarmingly. Disagreements among the men were frequent, and the island's small population was becoming increasingly hostile. Kelly found himself trapped in his role as island commander. It was Kelly who broke up the fights, and he was singled out as the symbol of resented authority. He knew the contempt his men felt for him and their loathing of this tropical assignment, and he slowly began to lose control of them. He had already caught some of them engaged in homosexual acts, and he felt powerless to reverse the degradation that was overtaking the personnel on Japtan Island.

He became withdrawn and began to find solace in a constant companion—a fifth of cognac. While taking long walks along the beach, he damned himself for volunteering for this duty. The pleasure he had felt when he first received the news of his command many months ago had turned to disgust and hatred. Why were they here? It was impossible to make these men behave like soldiers. He hated himself for succumbing to the bottle like so many of them, but he was powerless to stop it. When he was not drunk or breaking up fights or sleeping, he attempted to maintain peace of mind by reading and keeping to himself. He tried to convince himself that he would not be overcome by the same malaise that affected many of the men.

Some of them seemed to revel in malice and cruelty. Their pranks became increasingly harmful and dangerous. One day Kelly noticed black smoke billowing from the southern shore of the island. He joined others running toward the fire and when he broke through to the beach, he found the palm trees facing Parry Island ablaze. The men worked frantically to extinguish the fire and were only just able to put it out before it spread to other groves and on across the entire island. After asking some questions, Kelly found out that two of his men had conceived the idea of setting the fire as a joke to make the civilians on Parry Island believe that Japtan was burning.

It was in this state of mind that Kelly and his men finally learned the details of their mission at Eniwetok Atoll. They were to be among the witnesses to the nuclear fires of Operation Hardtack.

No Place to Hide

We has met the enemy, and it is us.
—*Pogo*, Walt Kelly

I have seen men do things I don't ever want to discuss.
—Orville E. Kelly

With the advent of nuclear testing during the 1958 series, the problems that Kelly had faced on Japtan would seem minor by comparison. He recalled his instructions:

> On April 28, 1958, I went to Eniwetok Island to meet with my immediate superior. The Lieutenant told me that nuclear tests would begin the next week, and that it was mandatory that all the men on Japtan under my command witness the tests. I was told that the men would be issued tinted goggles and were to wear their ponchos during the actual detonations. We were to march to the lagoon's edge, sit with our heads lowered, and face the blasts. After the explosion we were not to look at the fireball until we had counted to ten. Then the men were to stand and observe the fireball and the cloud until I dismissed them. I was given an instrument that would monitor radioactivity with instructions how to use it and was to report any unusual activity. There was no indoctrination, there were no lectures about the hazards of radiation, and no warnings about airborne radionuclides or fallout. I was issued film badges and instructed to have each man wear one during the day of the explosion.

Orville Kelly had been at Eniwetok nearly seven months when he was notified the nuclear tests of Hardtack were to begin. He called his men into the recreation hall and briefed them, as sketchily as he had been briefed, on what was going to happen and what was required of them. He issued the goggles and the film badges, and answered what questions he could. For the most part, he had no answers.

Some days later the men found themselves marching down to the beach that faced the lagoon. In the predawn darkness they stood on the sand, each with his own thoughts, doubts, and fears. Kelly placed the radio receiver that broadcast the countdown on the beach by his side. The men waited in the dark, on the threshold of their initiation into the atomic age.

Morris Friberg recalls the effects the testing had on him:

> I was on Japtan because I had applied for foreign service feeling I should take every opportunity to see the world before I settled down into my career. Therefore, when I was notified of the testing, I anticipated the events as something that would broaden my life experiences.
>
> Although not a spiritual person then, I changed. I was totally unprepared for the first bomb explosion I witnessed. The real thing was a frightful experience. The moment I stared at the violet ionized air, my conscience said, "Does God really want this?" Then as I watched the orange tongues of flame moving up and down in the smoke cloud, a shock wave hit that nearly knocked me down.
>
> I only watched a couple more of the predawn tests before I became very disquieted with the whole business. After one of the blasts my entire body turned bright red and burned for three days. It was then that I decided those who were reassuring us that everything was fine and that it was perfectly safe standing on the lagoon's edge watching the explosions, did not know what they were talking about. After my third nuclear experience, I spent

> the remainder of my time sheltered beneath a bed in a building whenever there was a detonation.

During the next sixteen weeks, Kelly and his men walked to the lagoon shore twenty-one more times to witness Armageddon. They endured the penetrating light that, for one long moment was all that existed, felt the searing heat, heard the long, rolling thunder, steadied themselves on the trembling island, braced themselves for the shock waves and winds, were awed by the ascending fireball of colors and flames, experienced the dwarfing scale of the blasts and their own feelings of insignificance, and they knew a penetrating horror. But they could not sense the radiation. They witnessed Butternut, and Koa, and Wahoo, and Holly, and Yellowwood, and Magnolia, and Tobacco, and Rose, and Umbrella, and Walnut. The men went to the dark shores of Japtan and saw the rising suns of Linden, and Elder, and Oak, and Sequoia, and Dogwood, and Scaevola, and Pisonia, and Olive, and Pine, and Quince, and Fig. The men watched a nuclear blast about every three days. Once there were two shots in a day. The longest period of respite from the bombs was eight days. On an average, the men were six miles from the blasts.

By the sixth week of testing, the men of Japtan were showing signs of the stress from both their previous isolation and the effects of the continuous nuclear blasts. Whatever margin of control Kelly had over the men eroded until they were only a loosely bound group sharing an island. They seemed to have only the bombs in common. Only the bombs brought them together.

While the military men at the Nevada Test Site were closer to ground zero than the men on Japtan Island, no one in the continental United States had to withstand the awesome effects of explosions in the megaton range. A new megaton weapon created by Livermore Laboratory was tested during the Hardtack series on May 12, one day after two smaller shots had been fired. Code-named Koa, it was exploded no more than fifteen miles from Japtan. The blast was the equivalent of more than 1,000,000 tons of dynamite.

The colossal force of the megaton shot seemed to produce new stress on the men who witnessed it. Orville, in particular, was aware of the inner turmoil he was experiencing. He became excessively nervous and rarely had a restful night. In his sleep he saw the flames of nuclear explosions engulfing the atmosphere. He became afraid of the ocean and dreamed that the island would be submerged as the angry sea took retribution against those who disturbed its tranquility. He drank most of the day and began to gain weight and lose muscle tone.

The effects of the blasts on Kelly and his men had to be dealt with by them alone. The colonel in command of Joint Task Group 7.2 made only infrequent visits to Japtan Island, solely for the purpose of troop inspection. On one occasion he ordered Kelly to muster his men for inspection. Because the number of men on Japtan fluctuated from the initial thirteen to as many as forty, it often was difficult to account for their whereabouts. During roll call one of the men was discovered missing.

Orville recalls the incident:

> I'll never forget the most embarrassing day of my life on Japtan. The colonel arrived and wanted to address the men. I held a muster and all answered "here" except for Hooker. I repeated his name three times but there was no response. I sent one of the men to search the buildings as I thought the missing man was asleep, but when the searcher returned and reported that he could not find Hooker I could only conclude that something had happened to him. The

> colonel admonished me rather severely and told me to contact him when I found the missing man. For two days we searched the island and the lagoon. Hooker was nowhere to be found. I thought he must have drowned. On the third day, to my total surprise, the missing soldier wandered into camp as breakfast was being served. I asked him where the hell he had been and explained that we thought he was dead.
>
> Hooker looked at me sheepishly and asked me to go with him. I left the mess hall and followed him into the jungle. We proceeded deeper and deeper into the tangled undergrowth until the man stopped and pointed to a tree. I looked up into the tree and saw a platform. Hooker explained that it was a treehouse he had built and was living in. He showed me a power line that he had rigged from the communications room. The line provided electricity for a small radio and light in the treehouse. Standing there, staring at the house in the tree, reminded me of *Swiss Family Robinson,* and I could no longer be upset with this man because he had achieved what I had always dreamed of doing.

Shortly afterward Orville reported that all of his men were now present and accounted for, and a member of the colonel's staff came to the island to verify the report. A warrant officer, who was an overzealous disciplinarian, arrived on the afternoon M-boat. The officer had been to Japtan before, and his presence was not appreciated by Kelly's men.

Morris Friberg remembers the incident:

> That evening, those of us not on duty and the warrant officer sat down in the recreation hall to watch a movie. The warrant officer sat erect; his uniform was clean, pressed, and starched. The house lights went down and the movie began. The male lead

> appeared on screen, and one of the men made a suggestive comment about the actor in a manner that made the warrant officer stiffen. Each time the actor appeared in a scene the men whistled and groaned their approval. When the movie ended, the visiting officer jumped up from his seat and yelled that it was obvious we were depraved. He insisted that we needed discipline. Several of the men agreed with him and remarked that all of us should be sent to a remote island where we could be disciplined. The warrant officer then stormed out into the night, and we broke into laughter that lasted long after he was gone.

For Kelly the remainder of his Pacific tour was a continuous nightmare. As time passed, the behavior of the men became still uglier. He received complaints from the sailors who ran the M-boats. They accused Kelly's men of trying to poison them. After investigating the charge, Orville found that some of his more sadistic people were injecting formaldehyde into stuffed coconut crabs and selling the crabs to the navy men.

One evening, on a walk around the island, Kelly saw a sudden movement in the jungle. He was able to make out the form of one of his men. The man had caught one of the island's dogs and was having intercourse with it. Kelly was sickened and returned to his room and wept. He knew that he and his men were dangerously close to a psychological breaking point. Some had already disintegrated. He felt he would lose his mind if he did not escape from the island to a place with normal patterns of behavior.

Kelly went to Eniwetok Island to see an army medic and confided to him that his anxiety and nervousness were leading to unbearable psychological problems. He requested psychiatric help. The medic examined him, asked a few questions, and gave him a bottle of phenobarbital. Kelly was instructed to take two teaspoons a day and get some rest.

More disturbed than ever, Kelly then went to his commanding officer and requested to be relieved of his command. He asked for a transfer from Japtan to the main island of Eniwetok. The officer told Kelly that he was invaluable; that he was doing an outstanding job and was probably the only non-commissioned officer in the army who had ever commanded an island. After praising Kelly for several minutes, the officer presented the sergeant with a three-day pass to Guam.

En route to Guam, Orville reflected on the turmoil and unhappiness that had consumed his life since the testing began. He felt small and insignificant watching the world being blown apart in front of him. Each blast seemed to be a small glimpse of hell. He recalled Dante's *Inferno* and, in his unstable state, was convinced that he had been sentenced to purgatory on Japtan—condemned to suffer for the sins he had committed during his life.

Once he reached Guam, he found a room in one of the few hotels there. The island was far from luxurious, but he had the opportunity to bathe in fresh water, eat a meal in a restaurant, and read, undisturbed by his querulous men. For those three days he lived without the anticipation of the bomb.

The second evening on Guam he decided to sample local ladies of the night. He was desperate for the warmth and release that sex would bring. He arranged to have a woman visit him in his room. At the appointed time there was a knock on his door, and he opened it to see a woman with greasy black hair, wearing a faded cotton dress that was much too tight for her bulk. With disgust, he noticed that her bare feet were filthy. Regaining his composure he told the woman she was in the wrong room. The prostitute insisted she was not mistaken. Her words came to him with a strong smell of garlic. Orville reached in his pocket, pulled out a ten-dollar bill, and told the woman to get out. He slept fitfully that night.

While on Guam, he read an Associated Press story about an unexplained atmospheric phenomenon in the vicinity of the Hawaiian Islands. A bright red ball of fire had appeared in the sky over Waikiki Beach that sent people screaming into the streets. Thousands of hysterical residents had called the Honolulu police department to report the frightening event.

Although Kelly did not know it, at the Hardtack I planning session in October 1957, the Defense Department had referred to two planned missile launchings from Johnston Island whose purpose was to determine if nuclear detonations in the upper atmosphere could be detected. It so happened that Kelly's three day leave coincided with one of these launchings. In the predawn hours of August 1, 1958, a megaton-range nuclear missile was fired from the vicinity of Johnston Island and exploded at an altitude of two hundred fifty thousand feet. This was the ball of flame that caused the terror in Hawaii eight hundred miles away.

One of the men associated with the missile shot, Walt Fitzpatrick, a rocket propulsion engineer at the time, recalls, "I remember the light from the blast was so bright I was able to read a newspaper on the deck on my ship. The scientists told us they really didn't know what would happen. The results were more astonishing than anyone had expected."

By the time Orville returned to Japtan he had decided there was no escape from the explosions and the bomb's aftermath of psychological turmoil. He received some relief when personnel from the other islands visited Japtan, and he saw how the lush, tropical foliage of the coconut cay was a welcome change for them.

One weekend the M-boat brought John Loveridge to Japtan. Loveridge, a witty, amiable air force sergeant manned the Armed Forces radio station on Eniwetok. He and Kelly struck up a friendship, and Loveridge visited Japtan more than once.

Loveridge recalls one of those meetings:

> I enjoyed my visits with Orville. I shared news with him from the outside world and Eniwetok Atoll. I remember telling him about the evening I received a teletype marked "cleared for release." The news item stated that Eniwetok was surrounded by Russian submarines that were patrolling and observing the nuclear tests. I read the message on the air and then dedicated the next song to "Ivan, who I know is listening."
>
> Within minutes my tiny broadcast booth was swarming with military officers demanding to know who gave me authority to broadcast such a statement. I showed them the teletype copy with its "cleared for release" notation. One of the officers reminded me that Eniwetok was a top secret area and soldiers were not to repeat things that could jeopardize national security. The officer said to me, "Remember, Loveridge, the infirmary in Hawaii is filled with people who couldn't keep their mouths shut!"
>
> Frightened and ashamed, I handed the teletype copy to the officer, apologized, and assured the man that I would forget I ever received it.
>
> I also told Kelly the news of a former AEC physician who, opposed to the testing, had sailed his boat *Phoenix* into the forbidden zone. When told to turn back, he refused, was apprehended by a destroyer and escorted to Kwajalein. Dr. Earle Reynolds and his wife Barbara had been placed under arrest and

flown to Honolulu where the doctor was sentenced to six months in jail for violating the laws of the U.S. trusteeship. I told Kelly that I hoped the doctor was not one of those guys who ended up in the Honolulu hospital.

Before I arrived on Japtan, I had stopped at Parry Island. The scientists there had just caught a fish from the lagoon, and, to show me how radioactive it was, we went into a darkroom and they held the fish against some unexposed photographic film. I was astounded when the fish actually photographed itself. There was a perfect image of the fish on the film.

I cautioned Kelly about eating fish from the lagoon. Kelly reassured me that his men did not eat fish although they did eat the coconut crabs. Kelly said that all the water from the lagoon was used for was showering and drinking purposes. He then asked me if radiation could be filtered from the water and I said that I had no idea.

After more drinks and a good dinner we went to the recreation hall and watched the current movie. It was about atomic radiation and monsters. The acting was awful, and the special effects were Hollywood at its most transparent. We thought it strange to see monsters destroyed by radiation when all the men at Eniwetok were exposed to it every day.

The atomic detonations continued. When he was not on the beach observing the nuclear fires, Kelly spent most of his time with Smiley, driving around the island in the jeep or walking in the surf. There seemed to be no end to the brilliant days which lapsed one into the other, punctuated by the nuclear blasts.

An atmosphere of unreality pervaded Japtan. Many of the men resented being made to watch the blasts because they could see no military purpose in what they were forced to do. In an attempt to provide variety in the routine, they devised a game. Shortly after a detonation they stood and waited for the shock wave to reach the island. They could see the lagoon churning as the force moved toward them. At the last possible moment the men threw themselves to the sand before they were knocked off their feet.

After one of these shots there was a heavy rain. When it ended Kelly took the instrument he had been issued and passed the probe over the puddles. Making a rapid, sputtering noise, the instrument recorded 10 roentgens, which, according to the information given Kelly during his briefing, was high enough to demand an evacuation of the island. Alarmed at the radioactivity, he reported the readings to his superior officer on Eniwetok. Kelly was told that the unsafe limit for radioactivity had recently been raised to 20 roentgens and that there was no cause for alarm.

Kelly sent one of his men, Jack Fisher, to Eniwetok Island for a few days to work at the transmitter site because there was a temporary shortage of communications personnel. Fisher, an expert in advanced communications, recalls:

> On the eve of a test, we were told to shut all the transmitters down and make no move to key them. I then went off duty because I had worked two consecutive shifts. I went to the tent where I was billeted and fell asleep. I was in the tent alone, dead tired and sleeping soundly when someone rushed in and told me to get my fatigues on and line up on the beach to watch an explosion. I got up, dressed, and, half asleep, followed the rest of the men to the edge of the beach. I turned my back to the blast, closed

> my eyes tightly and waited. There it was—a million bright suns at once—and then the heat and shock wave hit. We turned around and looked at the glow. It started to drizzle and then rain lightly, but I stumbled back to my tent and fell asleep again in my wet fatigues. The next morning I was told that we had been doused with radiation fallout. Every one else had been told to strip and shower, but no one told me until the next day. I had slept in my wet clothes for several hours. I went to the radiological-safety people and had them take the crystal out of my dosimeter and check it. They said it [the radioactivity reading] was high; higher than anyone else's, but I was assured that I was okay.

The largest detonation of the Hardtack I series was shot Oak, which was exploded from a barge in the Eniwetok lagoon. In fact, Oak was the third largest device of the two hundred and thirty-five announced detonations during the seventeen years of United States atmospheric testing. Shot Oak, in excess of 10 megatons, created a blast equivalent to more than 10,000,000 tons of dynamite.

George Mace, a twenty-two-year-old air force teletype specialist on Eniwetok Island, had watched many blasts from the shoreline. The men were never told that a shot was going to occur until the day of the event. However, the men knew that when the island's water tower was anchored with cables connected to bulldozers, another explosion was sure to follow. When Mace inquired about the distance from the blasts, his supervisors always told him the range was roughly fifty miles. In actuality, Mace's distance from ground zero varied from seven to ten miles.

When the water tower on Eniwetok was secured one day, Mace expected the usual. However, the men were ordered to place their footlockers on top of the metal lockers that lined the sides of the tents. They were also told to sandbag the shoreline against a possible change in water levels following the imminent blast. On Japtan, Kelly only knew that another nuclear blast would soon be history, and he moved his surly troops down to the water's edge.

Fifteen miles from Oak's hypocenter, on Eniwetok Island, George Mace had a substantially different reaction:

> After it went off we could not turn and watch the fireball for several minutes. When our backs were to the blast, it felt as though the sun was coming out and the heat on my back became unbearable. As I turned, I saw a column of water rising rapidly from the center of the lagoon. The sight of the tremendous mass of ascending water was so startling that no one spoke. You could hear the shock waves bouncing off the islands as they came down the chain—boom! boom! boom! As the column rose, it was surrounded by ragged halos of white waves that seemed to produce an electrical field. There was a crackling sensation that swept through my body which I felt as much as heard. For several seconds the hair on my body bristled and my knees became weak. The column of water climbed and then mushroomed out until the lagoon was covered with a giant umbrella of water.
>
> A silence returned to the beachhead. Thinking that the effects of the blast were over, we began to move about and discussed our reactions and thoughts. Perhaps twenty minutes passed.
>
> Some subtle motion at the shoreline caught my attention. There was a change in the beach; somehow it looked larger. I walked down to the sandbags and looked at the lagoon. It was receding. The water in the lagoon was moving away from the island at a steadily increasing rate. I had never seen anything like it. Then a totally unexpected phenomenon

occurred. The shock wave had been accompanied by winds of staggering magnitude and had boomed past us. Without warning, the calm was broken as the high-velocity winds returned, roaring back toward the hypocenter. We were mesmerized by the activity in the lagoon and were caught by surprise. The wind struck us in the back and knocked many of the men to the sand, blew our hats into the lagoon, and sharply bent the palm trees lining the beach.

The water in the lagoon continued to move out, revealing the coral, the sand, and the sea creatures of the bottom. I watched as the sunken PT boats, listing at crooked angles on the sandy bottom, were exposed. How many times have I held my breath and dove into those wrecks, I thought. They were deep enough that the water pressure hurt my ears, and now I could walk right out to them. I felt as if the bottom of the lagoon had been cracked and the water was draining into the crevice. In a moment of terror I thought that the island, being a honeycomb of coral, might break off and crumble like a sinking ship.

The water continued to recede for several hundred yards, building itself into a huge wall. There was a pause in its outward motion, a moment of changing dynamics, and then a wall of water began to move slowly toward the island. The water gained tremendous momentum, and the tidal wave bore down on the coral island where my companions and I stood awestruck on the beach.

The lagoon water had swept out in a gradual, almost graceful manner. On its return it churned and roiled, and we ran up the beach for cover, not knowing if the sandbags would hold against the huge wave.

> The wave hit the shallows near the shore, reared higher and broke with tremendous force against the beach. It surged up against the sandbags and threw a voluminous plume of water and spray into the air. Thankfully, the sandbags held, and the successive waves, which diminished in size, were also contained by the abutment. For hours the water in the lagoon continued to slosh like disturbed water in a basin, and for the rest of the day the lagoon water was muddy and treacherous with crosscurrents.

On Japtan Island, Kelly's men had also prepared for a tidal wave, but the waters of the lagoon did not recede as noticeably as had the waters facing Eniwetok Island. However, the intensity of the blast shattered most of the light bulbs in the buildings and blew large holes in the screens on the window frames.

Kelly recollects the Oak blast aftermath:

> My men were much quieter than usual following the big shot when the island rocked like a swing. As the day progressed they became less subdued and prepared for the party we held after every shot. In the evening the men held the party in the newly constructed recreation hall made from driftwood. There was much laughter and boisterousness and several of the men danced with one another to the old records that were playing.
>
> Most of the men had been drinking for an hour or more by the time I arrived. I sat alone, feeling detached, in a corner of the room with my bottle of cognac. A group of men nearby were talking loudly. The loud chatter turned into an argument and then a fight.
>
> As had happened many times before, I moved to separate the men—an Army sergeant and a Navy petty officer. When I grabbed the petty officer he

> jumped aside, pulled a knife and held it menacingly with the point a few inches from my nose. He told me that before I awoke the next morning that knife would be embedded somewhere in my body.
>
> The entire group stopped and stared at us. Even the record player was turned off. Hard teasing and fights were commonplace, but this time my life had been threatened. I walked slowly from the hall and took my bottle with me. I could not be sure whether or not the drunk and belligerent man would assault me as I slept. Since there were no doors on the rooms, I felt very unprotected. I sat up all night with the light on. Fortunately, the man did not enter my room, and I had him transferred off the island within two days. But the situation on Japtan had become unbearable for me.

The nuclear testing ended at Eniwetok with shot Fig, fired on August 18. On October 30, 1958, President Eisenhower declared a moratorium on U.S. atmospheric nuclear testing that lasted four years.

The second phase of Operation Hardtack began at the Nevada Test Site, but the tests were conducted underground. The military men of Task Force Seven remained in the Pacific. Orville Kelly did not leave Eniwetok until the middle of November, when his twelve-month assignment ended.

In the military air transport plane en route to the United States, Kelly reflected on the past year:

> I knew I had changed and sensed that I would have a difficult time readjusting. It was unclear to me what my problem was, but I could feel some disturbing force erupting inside me. I had seen terrifying destructiveness in numbing repetition. Each nuclear explosion had been comparable to looking into hell. When I closed my eyes to rest, I had terrifying

visions of blinding bright flashes and water cascading into the air.

I attempted to unravel the real purpose of my presence on Japtan Island. I could understand the reasons for maintaining the receiver station, but not why my men and I were ordered to witness all twenty-two Hardtack explosions. Watching one test would have been enough, because after the first shot I had become fearful of nuclear might.

That men were placed in such a remote environment, exposed to repeated nuclear blasts, and then expected to perform as soldiers was ludicrous. I had seen soldiers turn into animals as they lost touch with reality. I was virtually powerless to discipline these men as they underwent a metamorphosis that transformed them into strange, indolent creatures capable of destructive and absurd behavior.

During the last month and a half of the nuclear tests I excused some of my more hypertensive and nervous men from watching the blasts, but I continued to set an example by returning to the small area on the sandy beach to hear the countdown intoned by the recorded voice I had come to loathe. The blasts, the intense heat, the shock wave, and the violent disturbance of the placid lagoon caused such an angry reaction in me that I was not surprised to discover that I carried much hostility. But my anger was directed primarily toward myself. "If I'd been a better noncom . . . ," I thought.

Perhaps Kelly had been too complete a soldier. He had followed orders and accepted official statements. Now he was headed back to the United States with some kind of emotional poison inside him.

He was deeply troubled. He brooded. The career army sergeant felt shame and guilt. Despite his attempts to repress his emotions, he could not overcome his conviction that he had contributed to the development of something so intolerably hideous that mankind would forever be sentenced to live in a nuclear shadow.

The residual effects of Eniwetok were still with him; they were coming home with him.

4.

Deathblow and New Life

I do not consider myself dying of cancer, but living despite it.

—Orville E. Kelly

There was tragedy ahead for this talented young man, but at the time we served together there was only admiration and respect for his performance as a soldier.

—Colonel William F. Long, Jr.
U.S. Army Infantry, Retired

When Kelly arrived in Oakland, California, on November 21, 1958, he had been out of the country exactly one year and three days. Travis Air Force Base, Kelly's first stop upon his return to the States, hadn't changed much during his absence. There had, however, been a major transformation in Sergeant First Class Orville E. Kelly. Years later, he tried to put the last months of his year in the Pacific in perspective:

> I do not remember much about the end of my tour of duty at Eniwetok. My mind is a blank when I try to recall events from that period. I requested psychiatric help on numerous occasions while I was still at Eniwetok but got instead just one more bottle of phenobarbital, and some encouraging words from my superiors about my outstanding performance of duty and my critical assignment.
>
> After I served my tour of duty I was given a thir-

ty-day leave when I came back to the United States before reporting to my new post at Fort Monmouth, New Jersey. I don't remember much about that leave but I know that I was drunk most of the time. I know that I had no control over myself. I reported to Fort Monmouth, but immediately asked for a seven-day leave which was granted, and I returned to Burlington, Iowa, my home area.

I stayed in Burlington, and I did not report back to duty. I was listed as an AWOL soldier. Once I called the military police and asked them to come get me, but nothing happened.

Then one night three men and I had been drinking pretty heavily and we stopped by a house where one of my aunts had worked taking care of an elderly couple. I wanted to get some clothes I had left there. One of the men I had just met that night broke a window on the back porch and we entered the house. While I got my clothes he grabbed an old iron and an adding machine. He gave them to me in the car and I took them with me to the apartment where I was staying. Twenty minutes later the police came and arrested me. I later learned the man who had given me the iron and the adding machine was a police informer, and he had turned me in for whatever good it did him. I was the only person charged. I was tried and convicted and served one hundred and twenty days in the Des Moines County Jail in Burlington for misdemeanor larceny.

While in custody I worked as a clerk in the sheriff's office and rode on patrol with them. The sheriff wrote a letter to the United States Army saying that if they would release me from service he would be willing to hire me as a deputy sheriff. I even helped interrogate the prisoners since I knew shorthand.

> The country attorneys also wrote a letter to the Army telling of the extenuating circumstances of my case, and that even though charges were pressed, the lady who owned the house had asked that there be no charges, only that I pay for her broken window.
>
> Looking back I suppose that 120-day term in jail probably saved my life, because I wanted to destroy myself. I had visions of the entire world being destroyed by nuclear bombs. Lightning scared me to death. I couldn't bear an electrical storm. One night I drove fifty miles to get out of one. All I could see were flames shooting ten miles into the air, as they did in my dreams and nightmares—reminding me of Eniwetok.

When he got out of jail, Kelly went back to Fort Monmouth to face a court martial for unauthorized absence, since he had been absent without leave because of the jail sentence. He realized he had committed a serious offense and could expect a stiff sentence. When he didn't get one he believed he knew why:

> Several members of the court martial board felt that there were entirely too many unanswered questions as to why I had not received psychiatric help when I asked for it, both at Eniwetok and at Fort Monmouth. I had asked for assistance there too, and gotten none. I remember one psychiatrist who interviewed me. He didn't treat me, mind you, just interviewed me, and he said, "Well, you have problems." For God's sake, I knew that. I never did receive any psychiatric help. None at all.

Although the board never said why it decided Kelly's case as it did, he got off lightly for a man who had been AWOL for one hundred and sixty-two days. He was fined fifty dollars, lost two stripes, and was given a suspended six-month prison sentence. Kelly knew that his future at Fort Monmouth was not promising because officer friends told him that the commanding general was outraged by his lenient sentence. Kelly volunteered for overseas duty and was ordered to Korea. He had a brief leave which he spent in Burlington.

The first evening of Orville's furlough, he stopped for dinner in a downtown cafe. It was an unpretentious place, clean and quiet, not a customer to be seen. He sat and stared out of the window, feeling lonely and discouraged. He felt ashamed that he'd lost his stripes and that his twelve years in the army had left him with so little. The empty restaurant seemed to fit with the emptiness Orville felt within himself.

It was then that Orville heard a soft voice ask, "May I help you, sir?" He looked up to see a small, slender young girl in a waitress's uniform. She couldn't have been more than seventeen, with long, curly hair and large green eyes.

He discovered that her name was Wanda Klossing, she was a senior in the local high school and had been born in Tuscaloosa, Alabama. Despite her initial nervousness, Orville persuaded her to chat. His loneliness had suddenly become insufferable. He reeled off the names of foreign places he had visited during his twelve years with the military. She told him she had always wanted to travel.

That evening Orville walked Wanda home and he elaborated about the countries he had seen. She was fascinated by his travels, but didn't say much about herself.

The next evening he was back at the restaurant. As he walked in Wanda saw him and beamed. He walked her home again. This time Wanda talked a little more about herself. She told him she was glad to be finishing school, and couldn't wait to graduate; that she wanted to do something new and interesting, but didn't know what. Orville knew how she felt—he had felt the same way when he was in high school.

What Orville did not know at the time was that he had fallen in love. But he was sure that he needed this young, fragile and trusting girl. And he knew he could not leave for Korea without being sure of her.

The next day Orville called her when she got home from school. She sounded uneasy. Orville paused, took a deep breath, and asked Wanda to marry him. She thought he was joking. He finally succeeded in persuading her that he was absolutely serious.

Four days later on October 24, 1959, Wanda and Orville were married. Their honeymoon was over almost before it began. They had two weeks together in Burlington and then Orville was off to Korea. Orville had hoped to be able to make arrangements for her to follow, but the army rules were rigid and inflexible.

Orville arrived in Korea in November 1959 and was assigned as operations non-commissioned officer to the Armed Forces Korea radio and television network. Later, he was promoted to senior radio announcer. He recalled those days:

> I was elated that the Army had given me another chance, that the members of the court martial board had said this man should be returned to duty. Several officers I had worked for in the past, including generals, requested that I be sent to serve under their command, but I was happy with my job. I was determined to become a good soldier and earn my sergeant's stripes back again. I wanted to have a family and some roots.
>
> Then something happened. I was informed that the Finance Section had discovered a number of errors in my pay records, many of which they had made. I had been overpaid, according to them, and I owed money for the expenses incurred by the mili-

tary police who came to Burlington. The Army decided I should get no pay whatsoever. They cut off my Class Q allotment to my wife who was now pregnant. I lived on money that I borrowed from my friends and from Army Emergency Relief funds.

I couldn't exist without pay, and my wife had no income. No one seemed to know what to do. The commanding officer couldn't discharge me without a reason, and I was doing an outstanding job he said. Finally it was decided that I should receive a discharge based on my financial problems and bills which I could not pay.

The commander had me draft my own recommendation for an honorable discharge, and he signed the document. It was sent to the states. When the final discharge papers came back, however, they had been changed to an undesirable discharge—one step away from dishonorable! I was trapped. My commanding officer could only say, "I just don't know what to do. You're doing an outstanding job, but you're getting the undesirable discharge, and because of that I can't give you a good rating on your discharge papers."

So I was discharged with an undesirable discharge. I went along with it. I didn't fight it. What could I do? They weren't going to pay me. They would not take out so much each month, even though they knew they had me for quite a few years to come. But no, they would not do this. I was caught in a web of red tape. I didn't have any income and I couldn't continue as a soldier. They had given me another chance, but then they took it away. Here I was doing my job, not a disciplinary problem, not one mark against me in Korea, not one single mark, but I was given an undesirable discharge because they didn't know what else to do with me!

From Specialist E-4, after taking away all my other stripes, they reduced me on down to recruit E-1. That's the lowest you can get in the Army. That's what you are the day you enter. I will never forget my return trip home from Korea. I was sent to a processing center. I was with the lowest ranking soldiers ordered to report in front of the barracks each morning to be assigned to such details as "kitchen police." The top ranking sergeant in that unit happened to be a soldier who served under me when I was a sergeant major. We had been friends, but I was too embarrassed to confront him. One day he heard the platoon sergeant call my name and out of curiosity, came up to me while I was standing in ranks. I'll tell you, I won't ever forget that moment. He took me to his room. I told him what had happened. He cried and so did I. That night he gave me one of his uniforms and we went to the NCO Club.

A Painful Transition

Orville tried hard to make it as a civilian, but the circumstances were far from cheerful.

—Wanda S. Kelly

Orville left the army on May 13, 1960. A routine physical examination before he was discharged gave him a clean bill of health. Back in Iowa, he joined Wanda, and they tried to begin a normal married life. It wasn't easy. Orville describes best what followed:

> Now you might think that my problems would have ended when I left the Army, but I cannot tell you how many jobs I applied for, was qualified for but was turned down—all because of the undesirable discharge. None of the prospective employers would hire me. Finally I moved to California. I was hired and promoted. But when I had to become bonded, there it was again—my discharge record surfaced and another job disappeared.
>
> My family suffered terribly because I did not get that psychiatric help I asked for on numerous occasions after Eniwetok. I settled for second-rate jobs which included mowing yards or working in factories when I was qualified to do much more. I was sure qualified to run that island for the army, for the United States government, but I wasn't qualified to hold a decent job.

Orville drifted from job to job. Finally he tried journalism, and was successful—for a while. He was beginning to have health problems, and was finding it hard to keep up with the rigorous demands of a weekly publication schedule. He began to look for easier work. But even when he found such work, at times he would find himself so exhausted and in such pain that he literally could not get out of bed in the morning. Part of the problem, according to the doctors, was a high uric acid count. One doctor suggested to Wanda, however, that most of Orville's problems were psychosomatic.

By September 1972, Orville's physical problems had become so acute that he could not hold any kind of steady job, no matter how simple. Destitute, he decided to move his family, which now included four children, back to Burlington.

For a while things seemed better. The three oldest children were in school and Orville found an occasional job. Wanda found work in an electronics factory, which made Orville feel bad about not being the breadwinner. But they were still together as a family, and for that he was grateful.

Then in early 1973, Orville decided to attend an office managers' school in Des Moines, Iowa, about two hundred miles away. He lived at the YMCA and came home to be with his family in Burlington on weekends. Things did seem to be improving. The morning of his graduation, however, he awoke with severe pain in his legs and he could not get out of bed. It wasn't until several days later that, with the help of a friend, Orville was able to get to the bus station for the trip back to Burlington. Orville describes the events that changed his entire life:

> One morning in April of 1973, while shaving, I felt a lump under my left arm. A second one appeared a few days later, and then a third appeared, in my groin. The third one really frightened me, and I went to a doctor.
>
> The doctor told me there was no cause for alarm. The growths were just harmless fatty tumors, he said. This diagnosis was encouraging, but it wasn't all that convincing. I was exhausted constantly and weak, and getting more so every day.
>
> By June it was impossible not to worry. Things were getting worse, not better. I saw a second doctor. He was far less optimistic than the previous physician had been and he suggested I have one of the tumors removed and examined. He urged me not to delay.
>
> I remember distinctly the day I went to the hospital. I finally crawled out of bed and, as I dressed, Wanda, her mother, and my thirteen-year-old son, Mark, waited for me downstairs. The four of us

drove to the Burlington Memorial Hospital. None of us spoke.

Needless to say, I was quite apprehensive about this operation. I specifically asked that only a local anesthetic be used. The fear of death had been with me for a long time now, and I was terrified that death would come to me during the operation if I wasn't awake and conscious the entire time.

The doctor removed the tumor and I waited. Half an hour later, he came back with the laboratory report in his hand. "Mr. Kelly," he said "it's a malignant lymphoma—cancer of the lymph glands. We'll have to run more tests to see how advanced it is." Finally I managed to get some words out. I asked him to please tell Wanda. After all we had been through, I just didn't have the courage to add this to her burdens. I had known something was wrong with me, and almost resigned myself to needing a wheelchair. But cancer! Never in my remotest imagination did I think I had cancer.

The doctor was mercifully quick in delivering the news to Wanda. "Mrs. Kelly," he told her behind the closed doors of his office, "your husband has lymphoma." "Can-cer?" she stammered. She could hardly bring herself to say the word. Numbly she stumbled out of the doctor's office. Her eyes began to burn and she knew she was about to cry, but she bit her lip and drove a fingernail into her palm. "Not here, Wanda, not here," she told herself. Straightening, she marched down the hall to the office to await my arrival.

Gathering my courage together, I slowly walked out to join Wanda. My eyes were beginning to brim with tears. I couldn't look at Wanda for fear I would cry. With my eyes glued to the floor, all I could mumble was, "Don't worry, I'm O.K."

> I waited outside the door as the others walked to the car and brought it around for me. When the car pulled up, I could see that Wanda had been crying. I was afraid that if I talked to her, I would start crying too.
>
> The trip home was even more quiet than the trip to the hospital. As soon as we got home, I headed straight for the den, closed the door, and lay down on the couch. I wanted to be alone. I wanted to know why God was treating me so unfairly. I had waited until I was twenty-nine years old to marry, and now I had been chosen at the age of forty-two to die, leaving my family—Wanda, Mark, Tammy, Lori and Britty—behind.

Was there a chance for a cure? Kelly couldn't go on without knowing. He went to the Iowa City University Hospital for more tests. He was there for a month, going home on the weekends. When he was home, friends didn't know how to treat him; in a way, he was more comfortable at the hospital. Soon they stopped coming by. His doctors avoided answering his most important question: "How much time do I have left?" He began to think of the many ways he might end it all—pills, driving off a cliff into the Mississippi River, shooting himself in the head. He decided to wait. He wanted to spend one last Christmas with his family. He could commit suicide next year.

> I began to brood about the past. I cursed myself for joining the army. I cursed the army for sending me to Eniwetok. I even cursed all the awards I had won both as a soldier and as an editor. None of them mattered now. And the more I brooded about my past, the more bitter I became.
>
> Finally, the doctors proposed chemotherapy. Neither surgery nor radiation would help, they had decided. For my treatment, we travelled to Iowa

City. I'll never forget that first return trip. Despite the treatment, I had felt good enough to drive home. The car was as silent as the grave. Wanda and I still could not bring ourselves to talk about my cancer. As I drove, I thought of what I was doing to myself and my family. Without really knowing it, all of us had been designing a funeral—mine. Yet, I realized suddenly, I am still alive! I'm not dead yet. Moreover, I had a beautiful family who loved me.

"What have you got to lose by living?" I asked myself. For the first time in months, I noticed the beauty of the sunshine, of the leaves in the trees, the birds, and the rolling Iowa countryside. Suddenly I blurted out, "Wanda, you know, I'm not dead yet!" Just as suddenly, I pulled the car to the side of the road and stopped. "Cancer," I said. "I've got cancer. I'll probably die from it. But I'm not dead yet. We've got to talk about it." Wanda reached over and touched my hand.

"We've got to face it together. I know you haven't told me the way you really feel. I don't know how we can help each other if we don't talk about it. I've just been moping around the house making everyone miserable. Let's go home and have a barbecue and tell the kids. I don't want to waste any more time living like we have." Part of a great burden had suddenly been lifted from both of us.

That evening I told the kids. It was not one of the easier things I had ever done in my life. "The doctors have told me that I have cancer," I began. "That's why I've been sick so much. The doctors say that I'll probably die from this."

The girls began to cry. Mark sat motionless, staring into the darkness of the backyard as we sat on the porch.

"I'm not dead yet though," I continued. "I'm going to stay alive as long as I can. There will be bad days for us, but there will be good days, too. We don't have to like death, but we don't have to be terrified by it, either." And then we held each other.

The last thing I did that night before going to bed was to take a piece of paper from the desk in my studio, and write the word DEATH on it. There! I had spelled out my own death, and now I faced it. That night, for the first time in a very long time, Wanda and I slept in the same bed together.

Make Today Count

We walked the land together, you and I
And never knew what future days would bring.
—Orville E. Kelly

Orville began to write again. He wrote an article for the local paper, the Burlington *Hawkeye*, about the struggles of a cancer patient. The thought had come to him that there should be some kind of organization of people with incurable diseases who could share ideas and help each other.

After publication of the article in early January, Orville received a number of phone calls from local people suggesting a meeting. Two weeks later, eighteen cancer patients and members of their families met with Orville and Wanda. They decided upon one thing they all had to do consciously: derive the most from every day. Orville suggested they call their fledgling organization Make Today Count. All agreed.

The local paper reported that first meeting. The wire services picked up the story. Accounts of the organization and its purpose appeared in newspapers everywhere. Within days, Orville had received hundreds of phone calls. He subsequently appeared on "Tomorrow," "Good Morning America," "60 Minutes," and "Phil Donahue." Make Today Count snowballed, and suddenly the two Kelly's were so busy that they decided to devote all of their time to the effort. Orville commented about this time in his life and this new organization:

> Our purpose was to teach people to be frank, honest and open about their illnesses and to teach others to show compassion. My attitude towards my illness was that I did not consider myself dying of cancer, but living despite it. I did not look upon each day as another day closer to death, but as another day of life, to be appreciated and enjoyed.

With Make Today Count well on its way, Orville now turned his attention to certain matters he was determined to accomplish before he died. First and foremost, he wanted to clear his name with the army because he felt he had been released unjustly from active duty with the less than honorable discharge. Secondly, he was reasonably sure that his cancer had been caused by his exposure to radiation while at Eniwetok. He was determined to prove that connection by obtaining from the Veterans Administration the same benefits as any other veteran injured during military service. Finally, he wanted to write and publish a book, or books, which would help others, by sharing his life's experiences.

Absolved

When I asked God, "Why me?", I may have found the answer.

—Orville E. Kelly

The achievement of Orville's first goal was not long in coming. After two unsuccessful attempts to change his discharge status, he finally received the letter he had anxiously been awaiting for months. He nervously slit the envelope and read the letter from the Department of the Army dated April 25, 1974:

Memorandum for the Adjutant General:

1. It is directed that all the Department of the Army records of Orville E. Kelly be corrected to show that he was separated with a certificate of General Discharge on 13 May 1960.
2. That the Department of the Army issue to Orville E. Kelly a certificate of General Discharge from the Army of the United States dated 13 May 1960, in lieu of the Undesirable Discharge of the same date now held by him.

Herman R. Staudt
Under Secretary of the Army

The fourteen-year stigma had finally been removed. Orville E. Kelly, age forty-four, terminally ill with cancer, had been vindicated. Orville reread the letter, and then set it aside, reflecting on the years of embarrassment and hardship that first discharge label had caused both him and his family. He also felt gratitude for the friends who had believed in him enough to help make this moment possible: Colonel William F. Long, Orville's former commanding officer in Germany, Congressman Thomas Railsback of Illinois, and friends in the

American Legion who had written letters to the Army Board of Corrections in support of Orville's request.

Orville now went after his second goal. It would turn out to be the most difficult and frustrating undertaking of his life.

Since he was convinced that he had become ill as a consequence of military nuclear testing, he reasoned that he was entitled to service-connected benefits for his family and himself. The only way to get such benefits was to petition the Veterans Administration.

> I don't care what the odds are. I'm going to stay alive long enough to see that the injustice done to me is set right. I'm going to file for service connected disability, and I'm going to win. When I do, I know that my award will help thousands of other people too. Maybe I've been chosen to break down the bureaucratic barriers. I've been helping terminally ill cancer patients and now it's time to help the veterans who were involved in those tests. The best way I can achieve my objective is to file with the VA, become an expert, and bring national attention to the issue. In the end I want to see a world free from the menace of nuclear warfare. If people learn what a supposedly harmless level of radiation did to servicemen like me, perhaps they will begin to understand the urgency of uniting to stop senseless nuclear weapons proliferation. After all, except for those megaton explosions, the nuclear blasts I saw were nothing more than firecrackers by today's standards. People must realize that an eighteen-kiloton bomb the size of the Cactus shot destroyed an entire city and killed nearly 200,000 Japanese at Hiroshima.

Neither Kelly nor his physicians knew how much longer he had to live. But he did know that as long as he was able he would work to prove that government negligence was responsible for his cancer.

He recalled all too vividly the effects of having to watch twenty-two nuclear explosions. What he had witnessed could easily destroy mankind, and he had been part of it. He knew that the effects of what he had seen were destroying him and probably many others who had been involved in the tests. The life that had been only unbearable in the Pacific was about to end altogether.

> Neither the government nor the army did anything to help me. In all the years since those tests, I never had been warned even to have a physical. Now I have cancer. Had I been warned, perhaps my illness could have been discovered in its early stages and treated. I'm certain someone out there on Eniwetok knew the dangers and the potential consequences. Today I have difficulty understanding why the government is so brutal. It's hard to believe that what happened really happened. I was a very dedicated military man once, and now I am a victim of a soulless technology. I am a disabled veteran and I'm going to get the same relief as any other veteran who has been injured. The government should not ignore those who are ill because they were forced to take part in nuclear experiments.

Orville decided to file a claim for service-connected disability with the Veterans Administration. He knew that he could not sue the government in the courts for negligence. A 1950 U.S. Supreme Court decision, *Feres vs. U.S. Government*, had interpreted the Federal Tort Claims Act, which allows U.S. citizens to sue the government, to specifically prohibit servicemen from suing for injuries that occur as an incident to military service.

What he was not aware of, however, was that the Veterans

Administration awards disability compensation only if a veteran contracts a disease while on active duty, or if the illness is diagnosed within one year following release from military service. Otherwise, it is extremely difficult to obtain a favorable ruling.

As if that wasn't enough of a problem for someone in Orville's situation, the Veterans Administration also places the burden of proving one's illness squarely upon the claimant. For Orville this created a seemingly no-win situation. It was virtually impossible to prove that his cancer had been caused by radiation exposure, because radiogenic cancers do not differ from those caused by other carcinogens.

After studying Japanese survivors of Hiroshima and Nagasaki, the AEC-appointed Atomic Bomb Casualty Commission determined that lymphocytic lymphoma, which Orville had, is the second most frequently occurring form of cancer that results from radiation exposure. The commission also found that there was a latency period.

As Orville collected information to support his claim, he discovered that a law enacted after the Civil War limited attorneys' fees in Veterans Administration cases to ten dollars. Orville mentioned this fact to a friend who was experienced in legal matters. "That law is archaic," his friend said with a snort. "It will cost you more than ten dollars just to have a lawyer tell you to get out of his office after you have insulted him with that ridiculous fee offer. No attorney is ever going to take a case for such a paltry sum. No wonder veterans lose the majority of their cases."

During the next seven years Kelly would be ridiculed, harassed, vilified, and embarrassed as he fought to obtain the benefits he deserved. He would realize that he had uncovered a national horror story. He would find others who also were enraged at the bureaucratic coverup. These men, their widows, and their families would join him in a crusade to correct one of the greatest injustices ever perpetrated on

American citizens. Kelly no longer would be able to live in the comfortable anonymity that most people enjoy. He would become the representative and the spokesman for this country's veterans of nuclear testing. During his crusade he would be near death twice, but as though looked after by some supernatural force he would recover enough to continue the fight. Both the Veterans Administration and the Department of Defense would learn that they were dealing with a zealous crusader of tough farm stock. Despite seemingly insurmountable obstacles, he would not quit.

Orville was fortunate in one matter, however. He had spent nearly a year collecting the required military personnel and medical records as part of his efforts to upgrade his discharge status. He had them in his possession before the July 12, 1973, fire which raged out of control on the top floor of a federal records storage building in St. Louis, Missouri. That fire destroyed over seventeen million records—85 percent of the army and air force files which were kept there.

Before a veteran can file a claim with the Veterans Administration for nuclear weapons radiation-related disability, he must first prove that he was a nuclear weapons test participant. For those who would follow in Orville's footsteps the obliteration of their records during the St. Louis fire would mean that they or their widows would spend years trying to prove that the veteran was involved in a nuclear test.

Orville's first encounter with the Veterans Administration—it considers itself "the country's most compassionate agency"—came one month after his change in discharge status. In May of 1974, he received the forms he would need to file his claim for service connected disability.

The patient Iowan carefully answered all the VA questions. Under the section entitled "Issue," Orville wrote, "I contend that my cancer was caused by my exposure to ionizing radiation during the nuclear tests at Eniwetok Atoll where I was the commander of Japtan Island also known as site David." He described his tour of duty during Operation Hardtack, including dates, and named others who were on the island with him. He specified his film badge reading of 3.54 roentgens, knowing he had been exposed to higher levels. He remembered the instrument readings on Japtan after the rains, but there was no record of those radiation levels. Kelly completed the forms and mailed them to the VA regional office in Des Moines, Iowa.

On August 13, four months after he filed, the VA ruled on his claim:

> We have carefully reviewed your claim of service connection for your lymphoma condition based upon all the evidence of record, including your service records. There were no abnormalities noted at discharge. There is no evidence in file to indicate there is any relationship between your service and your current condition. Therefore, service connection is denied.

That evening Orville and Wanda sat on their porch overlooking the Mississippi River. Kelly puffed his pipe, put his arm around his wife's shoulders, and thought aloud:

> I don't intend to give up. I won't leave you with nothing. I'm going to learn all I can about what radiation can do to the human body. I know that if I hadn't been exposed to that radiation out there in the Pacific, I wouldn't be dying now. The government did it and the least they can do is help us now. I promise you, honey, I won't stop fighting until I get what I'm entitled to.

Kelly began to accumulate information about radiation and cancer. It wasn't easy because the local library had little on its shelves. There was nothing about nuclear weapons tests and servicemen who took part. This lack of information was unsettling. He began to wonder what had become of the other military men who were involved in the tests. How many were there? Were many of them ill? How could he find them? He intended to ask questions while he traveled.

Orville plunged headlong into public appearances for Make Today Count. The organization attracted national attention, and chapters were started in nearly every major city. Between public appearances he wrote his first book entitled *Make Today Count*. The dedicated patriot was becoming nationally known as a humanitarian who was helping the terminally ill.

On August 2, 1974, he received a telegram that read, "My personal wishes to you for a pleasant and memorable birthday. Richard M. Nixon." Orville received another birthday greeting from a U.S. President. This time it was Gerald Ford. Orville framed both telegrams and hung them in his studio.

After almost three years of chemotherapy treatment, Orville's cancer had gone into remission. It was, at least for the time being, under control. He would, during the remainder of his life, continue to receive Presidential salutations and honors from organizations and people across the country. The American Legion would honor him as their "Man of the Year." He would be honored by the U.S. Army, the Air Force, and the Navy for recruiting efforts. At the request of Representative Edward Mezvinsky of Iowa, a flag was flown over the U.S. Capitol on September 9, 1976, to pay tribute to Orville for the work he had done with the terminally ill.

Orville's greatest honor, however, was the fulfillment of a dream he had carried with him ever since he left the army. Around Thanksgiving of 1975, Orville heard from an old friend, Colonel William F. Long, Jr., the officer who had promoted him to the rank of sergeant major. Long was sympathetic and concerned about Orville's condition. The conversation ended with Long asking, "Is there anything I can do for you?"

"Well," Orville later remembered saying, "I certainly miss the army, and I sure would like to drill troops again."

Orville said it half-jokingly, but Long took him seriously. The colonel contacted the army Chief of Staff, General Wyatt, who personally authorized orders making Orville E. Kelly an honorary sergeant and allowing him to once again drill troops. Orville describes those two most exceptional and important days in his life:

> I returned to Fort Knox, Kentucky, where I went through basic training in 1948. I brought my family with me, and we lived in the general officers' quarters. I was given the red carpet treatment and everyone called me "Sergeant Major Kelly" for two days. I enjoyed that. I appreciated what the army had done.
>
> I remember drilling the troops, and one of the sergeants presented me with his hat, which meant a lot to him. And then, at the very end of the ceremonies, one of the companies I drilled presented their flag to me.
>
> I went to a party at the Officer's Club, and to a special party at the NCO Club where I visited with all the top ranking noncommissioned officers. They all knew what had happened to me. A reporter from the Louisville *Times*, however, asked me, "Mr. Kelly, there is one thing I don't quite understand. Why were you a specialist fourth class when you were a sergeant major?" And I replied, "Well, it's a long, long story."

5.

The Path of Truth

Truth, crushed to earth, shall rise again.
—William Cullen Bryant

For two years Kelly researched material dealing with the health effects of ionizing radiation exposure and wondered if other veterans were ill from radiation poisoning. His answer came one March evening during a network television program in which a veteran told of his experience at the Nevada Test Site.

Paul Cooper was a career army noncommissioned officer who could have stepped out of a recruiting poster. An enlisted man he commanded in Vietnam once said, "I owe my life to Sergeant Cooper. Without his leadership and courage I doubt I would have survived." Paul Cooper's fellow noncommissioned officers admired him, and the men he commanded loved him. His officers praised his dedication and ability. Six feet one, one hundred ninety pounds and handsome, the highly decorated sergeant first class was a quintessential noncom. Nobody asked questions when Paul ordered, "Follow me!"

Cooper retired from the army at age thirty-nine, after serving twenty years and six months, a veteran of Korea and two tours in Vietnam. A member of the elite Green Beret Special

Forces, he led missions that were among the most daring in the Southeast Asia war.

Once Cooper was nearly killed when he was sent to confirm whether the Viet Cong were using Cambodia as an operations base. Leading his platoon through heavy jungle, he suddenly raised his hand, stopping his men. He had heard the distinctive click, click of bamboo sticks striking together ahead of his column. Then he heard clicks to the right and left. This told Cooper that his patrol was menaced from three sides. Quietly he passed the word to retreat. When the platoon had moved back about two hundred yards, he calmly radioed for helicopter evacuation.

When the helicopters arrived, they could not land because there were no clearings. The copters lowered cables and lifted the men out one by one. Firing at both evacuees and the helicopters, the Viet Cong wounded a number of men. "I could hear bullets whizzing by," Cooper wrote to his wife, Nancy, "and it was a miracle I wasn't hit. The man right next to me took a round in the armpit and died before we could get him to a hospital."

Cooper came home from Vietnam on emergency leave to visit his father, who was gravely ill. While at his father's home in Vallejo, California, he heard on a newscast that his former outfit had nearly been annihilated by the Viet Cong. Stunned, Cooper exclaimed, "My God, those were the men I was with until I left." Nancy Cooper remembers that Paul felt he had been spared more than once for a reason.

When he went back to Vietnam, he was on the scene when a helicopter collided with an airplane fifty feet in the air and crashed to the ground. Without thinking of himself, Cooper ran to the wrecked and burning copter and freed the pilot, copilot and a crew member who were wedged inside, injured and not able to move. The helicopter was in danger of exploding. Cooper got the men out, administered first aid and returned to the helicopter. Cooper turned off the fuel lines and prevented an explosion. This heroism earned him the army's second highest award, the Soldier's Medal.

He survived Vietnam and was decorated with the Bronze Star, the Air Medal, and the Republic of Vietnam Medal, in addition to the Soldier's Medal. He was recommended for promotion "ahead of his contemporaries."

Cooper decided to go into law enforcement after he retired. He enrolled in the Lewis and Clark College of Law Enforcement in Lewiston, Idaho . While he was in college, he worked as a deputy sheriff on weekends. Once he had completed the one-year course, Cooper became the chief of police in Middleton, Idaho. Later he decided to join the Idaho State Police.

Paul Cooper, his wife, two sons, and a daughter were extremely happy. Suddenly, he began to suffer from dizziness, fatigue, and pain on his left side. The symptoms persisted. He checked into a local hospital for two weeks of tests. They were inconclusive, and he went home without a diagnosis.

Within two more weeks Cooper felt much worse. He had trouble standing for very long. His vision dimmed and he saw everything through an orange haze. Finally, when the pain was almost unbearable, he drove a hundred miles to a Veterans Administration hospital in Boise. Two hours after being admitted in February 1976, he was told he had leukemia.

Shortly afterward, Cooper was transferred to a hospital in Salt Lake City. Dr. Thomas Cosgriff, who examined him, asked if he had ever been exposed to radiation. Cosgriff, formerly a U.S. Center for Disease Control physician, knew about the leukemias caused by radiation exposure, and Cooper had the same kind of leukemia as the Japanese survivors of Hiroshima and Nagasaki.

Cooper told Dr. Cosgriff about his 1957 experience at the Nevada Test Site during the Plumbbob series. He and 1,104 soldiers had been assigned to special task forces named Big

Bang and Warrior. His superior told him he was participating in a new military concept known as the Pentomic Army.

His unit, part of the Eighty-second Airborne Division, was sent to the test site to learn how to perform combat maneuvers on a nuclear battlefield: "To show the army at its best."

In the early morning hours of August 31, Cooper and the rest of the task force were trucked to trenches forty-four hundred yards from the seven-hundred-foot tower where Smoky was to be detonated. Smoky was the fifteenth planned atmospheric shot during the "clean" bomb series.

At 4 A.M. the soldiers were moved from the trenches to a hillside position less than three miles from the Smoky tower at Jackass Flats. An unexpected wind shift made the move necessary, since officials feared fallout from the blast would contaminate the trenches. At 5:30 A.M., after a thirty-minute postponement, the 44-kiloton bomb was fired. Cooper, with his back to the blast, shielded his closed eyes with his hands. The blinding light from the explosion startled him. Like other atmospheric test veterans, he saw the bones in his hands.

The men, on command, turned and looked at the fireball. Within seconds they heard the rumbling thunder of the approaching shock wave, traveling at nearly one hundred miles per hour. A huge mass of compressed energy carrying dirt, dust, and desert debris hit the troops, and tossed many of them ten to fifteen feet from where they stood.

After the shock wave passed, the men got to their feet and began the planned maneuvers that would take them dangerously close to ground zero. Cooper said that he and the other 250 men in his group went to within one hundred yards of the twenty-foot melted remnants of the tower. The heat was so intense, he said, "I felt as though my uniform was going to catch on fire!"

Cooper and his companions had no idea the area was contaminated. Scientists who approached from a different direction had to abandon their attempt to retrieve instruments because of intense radioactivity. The instruments were left in the field for several days until the radiation dissipated.

The army trucks that had taken the troops to the trenches came back on schedule to pick them up for the return trip to Camp Desert Rock. The drivers had not been told that the task force had moved from the trenches to the hillside.

One of the drivers has recalled the event:

> We went out there to Yucca Flat to the trenches to get the men but they weren't there. [Radioactive readings at the trenches were 100 roentgens one hour after the blast.] We had no idea where they were.
>
> There was a blinding dust storm. We had to turn the headlights of the trucks on because visibility was about twenty feet, and it was late morning.
>
> We wandered all over Yucca Flat looking for those men. Because of the intense dust storm, I am positive they became disoriented. We couldn't see them, and they couldn't find us.
>
> We finally found them. Many had wandered to within a few hundred feet of ground zero. You could see the tower or what was left of it. The ground around it was fused, molten sand.

Once Paul Cooper told his physicians about his Smoky experience, one of them called the Center for Disease Control in Atlanta, Georgia, and reported that he had examined a man who had been exposed to ionizing radiation at the Nevada Test Site. He explained that his patient had acute myelogenous leukemia. Eventually this information reached Dr. Glyn Caldwell at the Center, who launched an investigation to determine if there were leukemia clusters among the former Smoky soldiers. Caldwell knew the task would be enormous, but he was determined to investigate any carcinogen that caused cancer. "I was very interested in this study and pigheaded enough to see it through," said Caldwell.

Cooper's physicians also filed with the VA for service-connected disability for their patient. At the time, Cooper didn't know that the claim had been filed.

In the disablity application, Dr. Cosgriff wrote, "The duration since Mr. Cooper's exposure is well within those limits observed for previous cases of radiation-induced leukemias. Even if Mr. Cooper had stayed at the observation point the estimated risk of leukemia is sixty percent above the expected."

J. C. Peckarsky, a layman and the VA compensation officer in the central office in Washington, denied the claim, saying, "The likelihood that the veteran (Cooper) developed leukemia as a result of radiation in 1957 is remote to the vanishing point."

Cooper learned about the claim when it was denied. He then wrote the Department of the Army and obtained his personnel and medical records. Armed with this new information, he filed a second claim. It also was turned down. Annoyed but undaunted, Cooper filed a third. When it was denied, he was indeed disappointed and dejected. Cooper then solicited the aid of the Disabled American Veterans to have the VA reverse its decision.

Paul told Nancy he was going to tell his story to the media, "because there must be a full-scale investigation into this matter. It is wrong for the army to have exposed me and not warned me and to turn their backs on me now when I am asking for help. I gave them twenty years' service and was a good soldier."

Cooper called a local television station, KUTV, in Salt Lake City. He reached a secretary in the news department, and he told her his story. She laughed and replied, "If you were that close to ground zero why weren't you disintegrated?" The young lady did, however, transfer the call to a

TV reporter, Sandy Gilmore, who found Cooper's experience considerably less than amusing. He interviewed Paul in his hospital room and found his story utterly believable. Gilmore then aired the interview on KUTV.

Newspapers carried versions of it, and the terminally ill patient was deluged with interview requests. His story gained national and international attention, and he heard from many veterans who were with him at shot Smoky. One of the people who reached him was another leukemia victim, Donald L. Coe of Tomkinsville, Kentucky, who had been a member of Task Force Warrior.

U.S. Representative Tim Lee Carter of Kentucky saw a Paul Cooper interview and read an Associated Press story about what had happened to him. A former country doctor, Carter was particularly interested when he read about Coe in the same A.P. story, because Coe was from Dr. Carter's home town. The U.S. representative was a member of the House Interstate and Foreign Commerce Subcommittee on Health and the Environment, and was keenly interested when he read Cooper's statement in the newspaper: "I am mad as hell about the way the government has treated veterans who were exposed to nuclear radiation. Congress should investigate, and I am going to do my best to see that it is done!"

In Washington, Representative Carter said, "We in government must not let the nuclear veterans' faith in their country be destroyed by letting them down now that they are ill and dying." Then he promised, "I intend to see the work Paul Cooper helped begin continue, and to see that justice is done for all our veterans who served their country honorably and well."

After a long struggle, the DAV was able to convince the Board of Veterans' Appeals to reverse Cooper's third claim denial and awarded him service-connected disability benefits of $820 per month, without admitting his disease was radiation related.

Paul Cooper and several shot Smoky companions were featured in the 1958 "Big Picture" television series titled "Atomic Battlefield." Narration by an army master sergeant said, "The battlefield of the future may well be an atomic battlefield. That brutal fact has forced upon the army the absolute necessity of testing both men and tactical concepts under atomic conditions." Cooper and other leukemia victims of shot Smoky then discussed how and why they were tested.

After fighting his disease for two years, Paul Cooper died in February 1978, three days after his forty-fourth birthday. He is remembered as a gentle, proud, and able man, stung to anger when those who exposed him refused to help him. A few days before Cooper died, Dr. Cosgriff said to a reporter, "We ask ourselves what possible justification could there be for so wanton a disregard of human welfare, and for what small purpose? We have no answer."

Just before Cooper died, he said, "I have been cheated out of half my life, but I only hope that the government will admit its responsibility to the thousands of men like me who were used in those atomic tests." He was the first serviceman who had been at the Nevada Test Site to say publicly that it had been a terrible mistake to expose troops to potentially lethal levels of ionizing radiation. His courage and determination in telling his story resulted in both a congressional investigation and an epidemiological study of radiation and disease by the Center for Disease Control. Had Cooper remained silent, countless veterans of nuclear testing might have gone to their graves without linking premature disease and subsequent death to their forced involvement in ionizing radiation experiments.

The cork was out of the bottle. Many veterans who had been at the test sites began to go public with their experiences. Some remained silent because they feared retribution, but many decided to follow Paul Cooper's example and talk to both the media and their elected representatives.

In Beverly Hills, California, Dorothy Jones, the chairperson of Another Mother for Peace, was moved by a Paul Cooper appearance on "Good Morning America." Ms. Jones was researching radiation monitoring, and she had begun to think about how she might help radiation veterans to find each other in order to compare health problems. One day her phone rang, and it was a widow whose husband had been with a Marine brigade at the Nevada Test Site. After a long conversation, the two women decided to launch Project Searchlight, to locate other veterans who had taken part in nuclear testing. Within a few weeks, two hundred men, widows, and families of veterans had called or written to Another Mother for Peace. One was Orville Kelly, who happened to be in Los Angeles. Kelly thus learned of another source of help as he planned an appeal of his 1974 VA claim denial. He identified the recognized authorities in the field of radiation health effects and solicited their opinions to support his case.

While Another Mother for Peace was collecting case histories of former nuclear test participants, Representative Carter interviewed Donald Coe. The veteran related his Nevada Test Site experience and told Dr. Carter how he had conducted a military maneuver practically next to the remnants of the seven-hundred foot tower. Years later Coe developed leukemia and applied to the Veterans Administration for service-connected disability. His claim was denied because the agency informed Coe that there was no proof that his radiation exposure and his illness were related. Their conversation disturbed Dr. Carter.

As Dr. Carter evaluated his information, Representative Paul Rogers, chairman of the House Subcommittee on Health and the Environment, had a visitor. Robert Alvarez, a Washington environmental lobbyist, urged him to open hearings on the effects of low-level ionizing radiation on human health. Alvarez, dedicated to protecting the environment, had made a brief study of the incidences of premature diseases among military men who had been involved in nuclear tests. Rogers was sufficiently impressed to discuss the matter with other members of the subcommittee. One was Tim Lee Carter. The two legislators persuaded their subcommittee colleagues to schedule hearings.

On January 24, 1978, Rogers opened the hearings before a large audience in Room 2322 in the Rayburn House Office Building.

The next day, Dorothy Jones appeared as a witness:

> Mr. Chairman, I am a social scientist trained at the University of Chicago. Our organization, Another Mother for Peace, launched Project Searchlight, a nationwide effort to try to locate men who were used as human guinea pigs by the Department of Defense in their testing of nuclear weapons in Nevada and in the Pacific.
>
> The victims of nuclear testing and their families express shock and outrage at the way they have been treated. We charge the Department of Defense and the AEC with criminal disregard for the life and health of the men for whom they were responsible. There was casualness and extreme carelessness in the exposure of our men.
>
> Another Mother for Peace also charges the medical doctors of the Department of Defense and the Veterans Administration with deceit and medical malpractice. No serviceman was ever notified of the fact that he should check with his doctor for symptoms of the many possible radiation-induced and radiation-connected illnesses which might beset him. By 1964, the biomedical effects of ionizing radiation exposure were well known to scientists and medical men in the military.

> Regardless of where the fault lies—with the top administration decision maker—with the military officials—with the AEC—or with the medical doctors themselves, the fact remains that what was done, and what was not done, was inexcusable.
>
> Another Mother for Peace charges that there is, and has been for years, a coverup by the Department of Defense, the AEC and the Veterans Administration—a consistent attempt to hide from the public the facts about experimentation with servicemen in nuclear testing.

Many eyebrows were raised among the committee members as she told Orville Kelly's story and then went on to the cases of other military men. One had described the questionable mission of Artie Duvall, who was involved in a top secret project called Operation Greenhouse in 1951:

> During the months of April and May, he was involved in four events in which he and three other members of his boat crew were ordered to go to the atoll where a bomb had been detonated. Each time these men performed their mission they were exposed to high levels of radiation. The third time—May 8, 1951—they conducted well-protected scientists to the test site. Mr. Duvall was on the island for an entire day.
>
> A Board of Inquiry was held in connection with this third event. Duvall was told that he had been exposed to lethal radiation and that he could not reveal any of the facts regarding this event for 10 years, or a penalty of 10 years in prison and/or a $10,000 fine would be imposed. Then Mr. Duvall was sent on a fourth mission back to the irradiated atoll again. The purpose of his return visit was to test the capacity of the men to withstand very high doses of radiation. Mr. Duvall was later hospital-

> ized. He nearly died. His exposure had been recorded at 15,720 millirem [3,000 was considered maximum allowable exposure]. Artie kept his oath of secrecy for 10 years and lived in constant fear of death. He then applied for service-connected disability, but was told that he was being denied on the grounds that he had waited too long to apply. When he asked for his hospital records for the period following his exposure, he was told they were not available because they were classified top secret!

She concluded her testimony. "We are not going to rest until those surviving men and their families have been found and paid the service-connected benefits they are entitled to."

The room grew silent. A stunned, bewildered panel looked at Dorothy Jones. Finally, Tim Lee Carter's voice broke the quiet:

> Mrs. Jones, the wonderful paper and testimony you have presented here today was tremendous. You have brought out the names of men who have diseases which were the result of the radiation exposure which they received.
>
> One of the most deplorable things I noted in your testimony was that some of the scientists went on an atoll completely dressed in protective clothing, and at the same time they took our servicemen in without any protection. I think that act constitutes a heinous crime.

Dorothy Jones had told the committee startling stories of military men who had been subjected to government experiments. She had also introduced the name of Orville Kelly to members of Congress. During the next two years, Kelly would be a frequent topic of conversation in Washington—

among members of Congress, the VA, and the Defense Department.

In Burlington, Kelly received daily reports of the hearings and was encouraged by the increased awareness on the part of Congress and the media that service people had been exposed to potentially dangerous levels of radiation during government experiments. He could not participate in the hearings because he was preparing to present a new claim on April 3 at the Veterans Administration Regional Office in Des Moines. Kelly had never devoted as much energy and research to an undertaking before. He had requested and received opinions from outstanding medical experts. Dr. Alice Stewart, Director of the Regional Cancer Registry in Birmingham, England, and an officer of the International Commission on Radiation Protection, assured Kelly that his illness could easily have been caused by his recorded roentgen exposure. Dr. Thomas F. Mancuso, Research Professor of Occupational Health at the University of Pittsburgh, had published seventy-eight articles, many of which dealt with the health effects of radiation exposure. Dr. Mancuso, in a seven-page letter, concluded: "In my opinion, your lymphoma cancer was induced beyond a reasonable doubt by a combination of radiation exposure that you sustained . . . during a span of thirteen months in 1957 to 1958." Dr. Karl Z. Morgan, a professor and research scientist in nuclear engineering at the Georgia Institute of Technology, had been in charge of conducting radioactivity readings at Eniwetok when Kelly was there. Dr. Morgan wrote, "There is no question about the fact that your exposure to ionizing radiation at Eniwetok could be the cause of your cancer. We had problems during the tests in the Pacific, and at that time I pointed out the inadequacy of the film badges and portable survey meters used by the military to evaluate the radiation dose."

William S. Gray of the National Cancer Institute expressed his opinion, "Repeated exposures to very low doses of radiation have the same hazardous potential as exposure to one larger dose." Dr. John Gofman, former director of the Biomedical Research Division of Livermore Laboratory, said, "Your recorded exposure is far above the level of that which can produce cancer." To further substantiate his claim, Kelly had gathered a mass of medical literature showing that the Japanese survivors of Hiroshima and Nagasaki developed far more lymphomas than leukemias.

At 10 a.m. on April 3, the regional VA hearing opened before a three-person panel in Des Moines, comprised of two VA employees and a physician employed by the VA. Several representatives of the press and television whom Orville had invited were present. Kelly chose Val Likens of the American Legion as his authorized representative, but decided to present his own case.

The hearing opened with a review of Kelly's circumstances. "The issue in this case is service-connection for lymphocytic lymphoma. Service-connected was denied, and Mr. Kelly was informed on August 13, 1974. No appeal was taken. Mr. Kelly has recently reopened his claim and requested a personal hearing. He indicated that he has additional evidence to present."

After Val Likens's opening remarks, Orville Kelly, the fifty-fourth U.S. military claimant for radiation-related illness, offered his new evidence. He presented the opinions of physicians Stewart, Mancuso, Morgan, and Gofman, and of Gray. He cited the studies of the National Cancer Institute and the Atomic Bomb Casualty Commission. Kelly recounted his Japtan Island experience and cited the high radioactivity readings on the island. The former island commander was concise, eloquent, and said repeatedly that his illness was radiation-related not only in his opinion, but also in the opinions of some of the most eminent cancer-radiation-research specialists in the world. Kelly had carefully prepared a notebook for each board member, condensing his presentation so that the review panel could follow his argument.

He was highly persuasive and his statements became increasingly moving. At the end he said:

> Maybe some people would think that we were guinea pigs. I wish we had been guinea pigs because there would have been a medical follow-up which may have saved me from having advanced lymphocytic lymphoma, but there was no follow-up. Therefore, I asked a Pentagon spokesman why we were ordered to do what we did. He told me it was a part of the Army's plan to introduce soldiers to this age of nuclear warfare. It was a sort of public relations introduction to the nuclear age, and I bring this up again because I want to tell you something. I still have nightmares about those blasts I saw out there. I have cancer now, and I am living with the realization that my time statistically is limited, according to my physicians. I can think of no worse hell unless it's the hell created during those nuclear tests at Eniwetok, because always on my conscience will be the fact that I participated in nuclear testing conducted to perfect thermonuclear weapons capable of killing millions of human beings and capable of destroying our country and other countries and entire economies.
>
> I have talked with one representative from the Defense Nuclear Agency who told me, "Well, someday the government is going to do something about you servicemen with cancer who were exposed to nuclear weapons tests!"

Someday, well, to me, someday is now. I can't wait for someday to come. Have I not created for you properly a reasonable doubt with testimony from experts as required by your own Veterans Administration? Doesn't the evidence I have presented indicate more than just a remote possibility that my cancer could have been caused by my exposure to radiation, and who, once again, who can say whether that's accurate or not? Who can say whether that exposure record is accurate? The answer is no one! They can't tell me at the Pentagon, the Defense Nuclear Agency or at the Atomic Energy Commission. They can't tell me at the Department of Energy. Someday one of these agencies might be able to tell me what my total exposure was, but no one will tell me now.

I presented testimony from an expert witness, Dr. Karl Z. Morgan, who personally recorded the measurements when I was at Eniwetok. He stated that the film badges were inaccurate and did not measure beta radiation or alpha or neutron radiation. The inhalation problem was never taken into consideration. I have established from experts that cancer effects from radiation can be delayed. I have shown through a statement from the National Cancer Institute and other authoritative testimony that inhalation of various airborne isotopes can affect the bone marrow or lymphoid tissues.

Today I want to point out that radiation workers employed by the Department of Energy as well as those employed by the department's contractors are subject to medical surveillance during their employment in radiation work regardless of the levels of radiation exposure. For individuals who have received radiation exposure from nuclear testing sub-

> sequent to October 4, 1971, there has been a medical follow-up. What about the men prior to that time who were exposed to nuclear weapons testing? Why has there been no medical follow-up on these persons? Why?

Kelly summarized his presentation:

> I cannot sue the United States Government because of what happened to me. You know that the government is protected by sovereign immunity. The only justice I can obtain is here in this room, so ladies and gentlemen, justice is in *your* hands!
>
> Had I been wounded by shrapnel or a bullet, there would be no doubt about my disability if the possibility of death existed. Radiation is just as deadly as bullets and hand grenades. You just don't die as quickly.
>
> In conclusion, I think that a reasonable doubt has already been established for you, and I trust that you will render a decision based solely on the fact that I have created a reasonable doubt. As you make your decision, ask yourselves if you, each of you, would be willing to stand out there on that island where I was and witness that series of tests, secure in the feeling that there would be no danger at all, and that the U.S. Government protected you properly from excessive radiation.

When Kelly finished, the VA panel asked a few questions about his radiation exposure and protection on Japtan Island, which he answered. The VA physician who was on the review board asked his questions and the chairwoman asked the third member of the panel, "Do you have any questions?" The woman replied, "No, I think you have presented your case superbly, Mr. Kelly." Kelly said, "But I'm not through yet. I know it's getting late, but there is one more thing I have to present." The first part of Kelly's presentation was but a preamble. The regional board in Des Moines, whose members had never reviewed a radiation-related claim, was to hear one of the most complete descriptions of the effects of nuclear weapons tests on a person's life that had ever been delivered.

> What I am about to say is very sensitive. I would appreciate no press coverage of this. But I do want it made a matter of record because what I have to impart is important. And I want to tell you that what I'm about to present to you—and please remember that I am under oath to tell the truth—what I am going to tell you is harder to present than my case about cancer.
>
> Please do not get the idea that I am a disgruntled serviceman as I tell you about something that happened that never should have occurred. I am not here as a man who is bitter toward his country. I am here as a man who misses the U.S. Army. I really look back with nostalgia on that period of my life.

Kelly reviewed his distinguished career before his assignment to Eniwetok. He told about his many awards and achievements while on duty. He read a letter from a former commanding officer who had promoted him to the high position of battalion sergeant major when he was barely old enough to vote. Kelly said that he undoubtedly had been the youngest sergeant major in the army. He said the colonel who had promoted him ahead of many older and more senior noncommissioned officers had complimented him as an individual "whose performance was remarkable; a young man for whom I had the highest admiration and respect." He took his audience through the years of his army career when promotions had been frequent, commendations plentiful, and all his ratings "excellent" and "superior."

Kelly paused, took a sip of water, and cleared his throat. A sad look came over his face as he continued. He told the board in harrowing detail of his eleven months on Japtan Island. How he and his men looked upon their isolated Pacific post as a prison; how gradually they became animals; how, as island commander, he agonized over the almost total erosion of discipline; how he had come back to the United States a psychological wreck because of what had happened to him in the Pacific; how the nuclear horrors he had been ordered to take part in still haunted him.

All this contributed to his endless difficulties in adjusting to life as a civilian, he explained. An uncaring army had ignored his pleas for help and tossed him aside with a black mark beside his name. Inch by inch, Kelly fought his way back to respectability. When he finally had rehabilitated himself, with little help from anyone except his wife, he discovered that the radiation the Pacific nuclear tests had poured into his body had left him with terminal cancer. Still, he said, a heartless government was deaf and blind to the misery and ruin of Orville Kelly. The Veterans Administration, charged by law with helping servicemen whose service had disabled them, twisted its regulations to deny the help that was his right. Kelly finished his passionate plea: "Now the reason I have wanted to help desperate cancer patients is that I can tell you the truth of knowing what it's like to suffer and not receive help from anyone."

When his testimony ended, the young woman who was recording his testimony looked at him across the room and, with tears streaming down her cheeks, put his final words into her machine. The chairwoman cleared her throat, blew her nose, and said,

> Mr. Kelly, I'd like to assure you that the fact that your military record may not be as blemish free as you wish will have no effect on any decision we will make.

> The VA has been doing intensive research in conjunction with the Department of Defense on the issue of radiation exposure. We will notify you of the decision made on your reopened claim.

After the board members and media people left, Kelly and Val Likens walked outside. Likens recalls their conversation:

> Orville asked me what I thought of his presentation. I told him he had made an excellent showing. It was apparent to everyone that he had researched the facts as well as any person could have. The expert testimony of eminent physicians on Kelly's behalf would add credence to his claim.
>
> I told him that all the board members had been in tears when he finished, but Kelly hadn't noticed and confessed that he had been close to breaking down as he painfully recalled the events that had virtually ruined his life. It took a lot of courage to bare your soul as he had in that room.
>
> Kelly told me that he had forgotten to tell the board about the bureaucratic gauntlet he had run trying to get government records to support his claim. The only compassionate man he found was Major Alan Skerker at the Pentagon. Kelly kept being referred to the Defense Department by the buck-passing agencies that would not help him, and the major took the time to tell him which agency had which documents. He talked to Skerker so many times that the two built a kind of rapport. But during one of their meetings Orville really bristled. The major said, "Mr. Kelly, I am sorry about your cancer, but you should not be so upset. In every war there are casualties." Orville replied, "But, Major, what I was involved in was not war, it was nuclear

testing in a time of peace, and there should have been no casualties."

Kelly said that if he had difficulty obtaining documents, then other veterans must be going through the same discouraging process. He wondered aloud how many other claims like his had been filed. I told him that I had no idea and there was no easy way to get the answer. I said I felt he was a pioneer in the field of service-connected disability that was radiation-related and that his efforts eventually were going to help many others.

Kelly was concerned that Washington would take months to get to his claim, and he had no idea how long he had to live. He decided to ask his congressional representative to help expedite his claim.

Right before we parted I told him to keep a positive attitude. If he was denied again, we would appeal. I told him that both the American Legion and I were committed to the end. We would not stop fighting for him. Orville thanked me and left for Burlington.

A week later Kelly wrote Iowa Senator Richard Clark and asked him to help expedite his claim:

> I do not feel my case should be delayed any longer than is necessary, because statistically, I do not feel I have enough time left to fight my case much longer. My physicians say that there is no way to predict my future.
>
> During my presentation of new evidence, I proved that my film badge reading of exposure to radiation was not accurate and that no readings were ever taken on what I may have inhaled. I wonder how much longer I must endure the problems caused by mistakes on the part of the U.S. Govern-

> ment agencies responsible for monitoring the radiation levels, not warning the servicemen of dangers from exposure to radiation and not conducting a medical follow-up after exposure occurred?

Senator Clark wrote to the Veterans Administration and, on May 11, received a reply from the VA's Congressional Liaison Service: "The Chief Medical Director here in Washington has been asked to give this matter every consideration."

Clouds of Doubt

> *To care for him who shall have borne the battle, and for his widow and his orphan*
>
> —Abraham Lincoln

Kelly's claim was denied on June 13. Dr. James J. Smith, director of nuclear medicine at the VA, sent a memo to the Chief Benefits Director:

> Mr. Kelly was exposed to 3.445 rems (roentgen equivalent man) during the period from April 10, 1958, to August 31, 1958. His exposure is far below the dose level at which leukemia is considered to develop from radiation exposure. There is a remote rather than a reasonable probability that Mr. Kelly's exposure to ionizing radiation in 1958 could have caused lymphoma, diagnosed in 1974. The veteran's 3.44 exposure is well below the Federally established 5 rem safety level established for today's radiation workers.

On June 28, Kelly got a letter from the VA's Des Moines

regional office telling him of his second denial. Understandably, Kelly was dejected and ready to give up. He called Val Likens and told him the depressing news. Likens said he should not think for a moment of quitting: they would file again. Orville agreed reluctantly, dreading having to repeat the entire process. Veterans Administration rules allowed another hearing, provided the claimant could present new evidence. Kelly began to think about what that evidence would be.

After the Fourth of July weekend, he wrote Iowa Senator John Culver, a member of the Senate Armed Services Committee:

> I was denied compensation, even though I presented evidence which I feel established a reasonable doubt. The last decision was reached at the VA's central office in Washington, D.C. I appeared before a regional rating board that was supposed to reach a decision only after they received an advisory opinion from the central office. However, it is quite apparent that the Chief Medical Director of the VA reached that decision for the board in Des Moines before they even had a chance to meet.
>
> I feel this is quite apparently an unjust decision. I also feel the Chief Medical Director completely ignored evidence from experts in the field of radiation exposure and from the National Cancer Institute with regard to the health effects of low-level radiation.
>
> I cannot help but feel, as many other veterans do, that the VA is an adversary instead of an agency that follows the creed at the bottom of their letterhead, "To care for him who shall have borne the battle, and for his widow and his orphan."

Kelly had learned that the VA regional board in Des

Moines, although it was moved by his testimony, had no authority where radiation claims were concerned. That issue was the VA's hot potato, and it did not intend to admit officially that American servicemen had been exposed to harmful levels of ionizing radiation during nuclear tests.

Kelly was right on another point in his letter to Senator Culver. The VA totally ignored the opinions of doctors Gofman, Mancuso, Morgan, and Stewart. As far as it was concerned, the nation's only authority on the heath effects of ionizing radiation was the agency's director of nuclear medicine.

Dr. John Gofman, the noted medical authority on the health effects of radiation exposure, was extremely angry about the VA's reason for denial. Gofman was well qualified to state an opinion. A professor emeritus of medical physics at the University of California, he had been involved in the nuclear industry since the Manhattan Project. He co-discovered uranium 233 and formerly was an associate director of Lawrence Livermore Laboratory and director of the laboratory's Biomedical Research Division.

Gofman's reaction to Kelly's claim denial:

> Nothing in this VA statement is correct and their findings are totally contrary to the existing scientific evidence of the world! To say the 5 rem limit is *safe* is absolutely false. No one can make the statement that 5 rem is a safe level when there is *no known* safe level of radiation exposure. Further, the decision made against your claim is clearly erroneous. Anyone conversant with the facts would know that there is a long silent period between radiation exposure and cancer becoming clinically evident. The absence of an abnormality at the time of your discharge would be expected since the development takes place over a period of time.

Kelly felt deceived and betrayed. The opinions of recognized experts had been ignored. His new evidence had not been evaluated, and his personal account of pain, suffering, and emotional distress had been delivered in vain. It seemed as though nothing he said to the VA mattered. But he was determined to win despite overwhelming odds. He found new courage in the face of his newest adversity.

Kelly reflected on his two denials and analyzed the situation. He marshaled his thoughts carefully. He concluded someone had to help the men, widows, and families who were being denied government assistance. Before a veteran could receive help, he had to know the obstacles. The roadblocks seemed virtually insurmountable. Kelly wrote out his conclusions to help all veterans who were exposed to ionizing radiation experiments and sent them to Senator Richard Clark of Iowa:

1. There is no absolute assurance that proper monitoring of radiation was done for each soldier.

2. The veteran has to use information provided by the Department of Defense, and it is apparent that the DOD does not want adverse publicity about exposure to ionizing radiation since the department created many of the tests and ordered servicemen to participate in them.

3. The Veterans Administration ignores the opinions of a claimant's medical and scientific representatives.

4. In the VA's eyes, they, and only they, have the experts in the field of radiation health effects.

5. The veteran is caught in the middle of a controversy centering around the safety threshold of radiation exposure. There is *no* known safe level of radiation exposure.

6. The veteran must appear before ratings boards on a regional basis with members of the VA who are not qualified to hear the case and evaluate the evidence.
7. The veteran exposed to ionizing radiation has discovered that the VA has become his adversary as he attempts to establish a legitimate disability claim.

In mid-July Orville Kelly received a personal letter with the presidential seal. It said, "Rosalynn and I were very sorry to learn of your illness. We hope you will be strengthened knowing that the thoughts and prayers of your family and friends are with you." The letter was signed by Jimmy Carter.

Orville looked at Wanda and said:

> This is really something. Last month I was called a liar by the VA; a nut by the Defense Department, and here I receive a personal letter from President Carter, who is sad because I am ill. I appreciate the sentiment, but I wish he had the same concern for the sickness at the VA.

Kelly opened another letter. With a laugh, he said to Wanda:

> Honey, look here. It's an article sent by a friend in Washington. Dr. Smith, the same VA doctor who denied my claim, was interviewed by a medical magazine. He was asked about veterans' radiation exposure claims. He said there have been so few claims that the veterans obviously don't think that they are ill from radiation exposure. He also says that the Department of Defense is reconstructing all the nuclear tests and evaluating them in detail,

and that it appears that the average exposure was .5 rem. Smith says that the VA plans studies if the claims increase, because "We [the VA] are pilgrims on the path of truth"! What a statement! My God, I have just proved that the VA ignored all my evidence. It didn't even weigh the statements from eminent experts that I gave them. And the very VA physician who ruled against me and didn't take the time to read the opinions of recognized radiation health physicists and physicians has the audacity to say he's a pilgrim on the path of truth!

6.

The Atomic Veteran and a Landmark Decision

We will call ourselves atomic veterans.

—Orville E. Kelly

By spring 1979, Congress and the media had discovered that thousands of veterans had been needlessly exposed to ionizing radiation during atmospheric nuclear testing in Nevada and the Pacific.

Paul Cooper's widely publicized account of his Nevada Test Site experiences had encouraged other veterans to tell of their own exposure and subsequent medical problems.

The 1978 hearings of the House Subcommittee on Health and the Environment revealed for the first time incidences of morbidity and mortality among nuclear test veterans. The hearings aroused the press and the public, embarrassed the government, and gave a strong boost to the Center for Disease Control's epidemiological study of nuclear veterans.

After the CDC learned of Cooper's case, it decided to study the frequency of leukemia and other cancers in servicemen who had been exposed to shot Smoky. The CDC tried to get a list of their names from the Armed Forces Radio-Biology Research Institute, the surgeon general of the army, the Department of Defense, the Department of Energy, and the Veterans Administration. These agencies either denied the existence of a list or refused to provide any individual names, taking refuge in the Privacy Act—a law to prevent invasion of privacy.

In June 1977, *Parade* magazine published an article about the study, with a photograph showing soldiers watching shot Smoky. "Were you there?" the caption asked. "If you were, contact the Center for Disease Control in Atlanta, Georgia." Within a week, over two thousand letters and phone calls flooded the CDC. Of the two thousand, more than four hundred came from Smoky veterans, and there were five leukemia cases among them—nearly five times the expected number for the forty-to-forty-five age group responding.

Reaction to the *Parade* article gave the center a toehold. The formerly lethargic Department of Defense came to attention. When it and the AEC's successor agency, the Department of Energy, learned that the CDC's study was actually underway, both departments refused categorically to provide a list of Smoky veterans. This government stonewalling came to the attention of Representative Tim Lee Carter. One month after the *Parade* article, he introduced a resolution of inquiry in Congress to force Secretary of Defense Harold Brown, formerly director of Livermore Laboratory, to release the list of Smoky veterans. Within a few days, the army's surgeon general produced the list. Methodically, the CDC began to get in touch with each person.

Although the CDC study was well on its way, the Defense Department commissioned a parallel study by the National Academy of Sciences. The department's nuclear arm, the Defense Nuclear Agency, announced in December 1977 that the tests would be reconstructed and the exposure of veterans studied. From six to ten million dollars annually were allocated to the project. One of the first study contracts went to Science Applications, Inc., of McLean, Virginia. This company employs what they call "oral historians" whose purpose is to re-create military exercises and radiation exposure during the nuclear tests. The personnel who prepare the reports use old, incomplete, sketchy information of military troop maneuvers and have refrained from interviewing participants who were present at the exercises. The reports prepared by Science Applications are submitted to the Defense Nuclear Agency and eventually become part of the official record. The first report published for the Defense Nuclear Agency by Science Applications described the circumstances of shot Smoky.

The information about Smoky veterans that had been denied to the Center for Disease Control was instantly available to the National Academy of Sciences, once it began the Defense Nuclear Agency's study. The academy got names, ranks, serial numbers, unit designations, participation dates, current addresses, and other basic information.

Orville Kelly was one of the veterans who contacted the Center for Disease Control after the *Parade* article appeared, but he was not included in the CDC's epidemiological study because it was limited to Smoky veterans. Kelly then tried to reach the Defense Nuclear Agency by calling a toll-free number that had been established for nuclear veterans. An outreach program was set up by the Defense Nuclear Agency because a U.S. district court in New Jersey ruled that the Defense Department had to warn nuclear veterans of possible medical risks. The agency published the toll-free number in some newspapers, but the notice usually amounted to a small paragraph buried on a back page. It didn't even mention medical risks, simply saying that the Defense Department wanted nuclear veterans to contact the agency. For five days Kelly tried to call the agency without success. Frustrated, he called the Army Chief of Staff's office at the Pentagon and asked how he was supposed to reach the agency when the line was always busy. The sergeant Kelly spoke to said he had had more than a hundred such complaints.

Kelly, more determined than ever, finally reached an officer at the agency:

> I asked the Officer of the Day if he was surprised by the number of ex-servicemen who were calling. He replied, "It's been a very interesting situation." Then I asked what the Defense Department was going to do about the problem of veterans who were ill. The man said, "Well, I think they're certainly going to do something."
>
> Later that night I finally got through on the toll-free number and reached an Army PFC. I gave her the basic information including my service at Eniwetok. Her last question was, "How is your health?" I said I had cancer. She paused and said, "Well, I'm sorry to say that about three-fourths of the calls I've taken tonight have come from servicemen who have cancer. I've also heard from many, many widows. I was even crying right along with one lady who told me that her husband had just died. I can't believe all this happened!" I reminded her that it *did* happen, and that someone had to help the veterans who were suffering as a result of radiation exposure.

Before Kelly and the young private first class ended their conversation, she told him the people on duty at the agency had received over two thousand calls during the brief time the toll-free number had been in operation. Kelly reflected:

> I know that number will be busy for a long, long time. There are thousands of former servicemen and civilians who were involved in nuclear testing, and many probably have cancer. I suspect other diseases are cropping up, too. I continually ask myself, how could this have happened in America? I don't know. But the sad fact remains that it did.

Kelly had good rapport with the media, and many journalists who had interviewed him when he organized Make Today Count interviewed him again when he announced publicly that he was convinced his cancer was radiation-related. Kelly was in the process of filing his third disability claim with the Veterans Administration when Dorothy Jones, who was terminally ill, sent him nearly two hundred veterans' files gathered by Another Mother for Peace. She wrote:

> Orville, I can no longer carry on this work because of my depleted finances and my health. I am sending you the information because I know you will do your best to help these poor veterans. What happened to them and to you is a tragedy that must be corrected.

Soon after Kelly received these files from Dorothy he called Bob Alvarez at the Environmental Policy Institute in Washington to say that he wanted to form an organization to help nuclear test veterans. Alvarez invited him to Washington to discuss his ideas and promised a press conference.

Kelly arrived in Washington on March 6 and that day met with Bob Alvarez and Howard Rosenberg—an investigative journalist on the staff of Jack Anderson—to discuss the forming of a new veterans' organization. Alvarez explained that Kelly was organizing nuclear test veterans. Rosenberg had written several articles about nuclear veterans and found the concept interesting and timely. He believed the only way these men would be helped was to help themselves.

Alvarez recalls the meeting:

> We discussed a name for the organization. Orville said it should be a national association. Howard said all these men took part in atomic experiments, and Orville agreed but said there had been thermonu-

> clear or hydrogen tests too. However, we all agreed that the name had to be something the public could relate to. We knew everyone could identify with the word "atomic" and Howard said, "Why don't you call the group the National Association of Atomic Veterans?" Orville thought Howard's suggestion was terrific and said the members would be called atomic veterans. In effect, Kelly created a new class of veteran. One of the first things he intended to do was publish a newsletter to keep the veterans informed and in touch with one another. He realized one of the most frustrating things about being an atomic veteran was not being able to find other men who were at the tests. The Department of Defense certainly wasn't going to help these men find one another. I promised to help Orville get some financial backing. The three of us left that lunch knowing that these men, widows and families would at last have an organization that would do its utmost to help them.

Kelly went back to Burlington, and he and Wanda designed stationery for the new organization. Kelly busied himself by planning the association's first newsletter, which would be sent to veterans and members of Congress.

On April 11, 1979, a few weeks after the Washington trip, a letter arrived from the Veterans Administration: "The evidence does not support a reasonable probability . . . therefore, the doctrine of reasonable doubt is not appropriate in this case. Service connection for your lymphoma is denied." This third turndown of his claim stunned Kelly.

Despondent, he told his wife he was going to take his case to the Board of Veterans' Appeals in Washington and appear in person to argue it. Since the VA obviously did not seem to be interested in helping atomic veterans, Kelly decided to try to enlist the Senate Committee on Veterans' Affairs in his cause.

Two weeks later Kelly left for Washington to see Bob Alvarez again. Alvarez had arranged for him to meet with fifty representatives of foundations and philanthropies. Kelly spoke to this group, explaining why the National Association of Atomic Veterans had been formed. He summed up his own case, saying that his denials were typical of those of all atomic veterans.

> None of the veterans were warned of the possible health consequences of their exposure during the tests, and there has never been any medical follow-up. Our relief can come only through the Veterans Administration, and it won't admit the possibility of debilitating disease resulting from radiation exposure during the tests.
>
> It is not only the VA that frustrates us. The Defense Nuclear Agency, which is reconstructing nuclear tests involving military personnel, is releasing false and misleading information. Of the 250,000 military participants in the tests, only about thirty percent wore film badges, but the agency is saying that the average exposure was approximately one-half rem using the film badge as a form of exposure record.

Kelly told the group that there were four forms of radiation exposure from nuclear blasts but that the agency was basing its entire study on gamma exposure. Inhalation, ingestion, and residual radiation from previous tests were all important factors not measured by the film badges.

He said it had been ridiculous to expose troops to nuclear explosions and explained that when he asked the Pentagon why he had to watch twenty-two nuclear tests, he was told that it was a matter of public relations to show each service at its military best. One of Kelly's favorite examples of the pointless tasks soldiers had to perform was to field strip their rifles immediately following a blast, for no other purpose than to determine whether a nuclear explosion would affect their ability to assemble or disassemble a rifle. Kelly said:

> Can you imagine that? A young soldier a few miles from one of those horrible explosions, on his knees in the dirt and sand in the shadow of an atomic cloud, disassembling his rifle, while dust, debris and fallout covers him.
>
> The fact is, ladies and gentlemen, not one government agency has helped these men who followed orders and were not aware of the dangers. The Japanese, the Marshallese and downwind residents from the Nevada Test Site have been studied and many of them helped. Nothing has been done for the veteran.
>
> Our association will have an outreach program to work with atomic veterans. We'll help them document their test participation, we'll provide legal, medical and political assistance, and we'll help file claims with the VA.
>
> If we accomplish nothing else, atomic veterans will know that there is a self-help organization whose founders and fellow members care about them.

When Kelly finished, everyone applauded—something unusual for reserved foundation and philanthropy people. There were many questions. One woman wanted to know, "Are members of your organization antinuclear activists?"

Orville said:

> I am glad you asked that. I want to explain that we are veterans representing the cross-section of Amer-

> ica, and we are seeking restitution and assistance for our problems that are radiation related. We are not activists, and we have no position either pro or con on nuclear power. I can tell you, though, that we are definitely against human experimentation and nuclear weapons proliferation. Which brings me to the point: today you certainly would not see those proponents of more nuclear weapons standing on a beach or kneeling in a trench two or three miles from a nuclear explosion.

After Kelly finished talking and answering questions, he went across town to see Shelley Madden, a young, energetic caseworker on the staff of the Senate Committee on Veterans' Affairs. Shelley had been in touch with both Kelly and Senator Richard Clark's office. She knew about Kelly's problems with the VA, and his file had been sent from Senator Clark's office in Des Moines.

She remembers their first encounter:

> When Orville contacted me and started talking about radiation, I had no idea what he meant. I knew absolutely nothing about radiation. I was a caseworker who spent most of my time trying to help people who were in VA hospitals who were objecting to the stuff VA physicians were prescribing for them. I asked Senator Clark's office to send me a letter describing what they were talking about. When I read that letter, I asked myself, "What the hell is this—twenty-two nuclear blasts—cancer—aaah." It all sounded unreal, but Orville was totally sincere and his genuineness convinced me I should try to help him. It was a big decision for me because the committee had never done anything like that. I discussed the situation with the health counsel and the general counsel, who referred me to the chief

> counsel. No one knew anything about radiation. All of them felt it was a new issue and a potentially political one. No agencies had done any research, and we had no attorneys to help us. But I was convinced that there was something to this radiation exposure and resulting cancer. There could be a connection, and I didn't want our ignorance of the health effects of radiation exposure to keep a man from obtaining the benefits that were due him. I became obsessed and wouldn't be denied and finally, after two months of persuading, the chief counsel gave me permission to get involved and do what I could to help Orville with his claim. Meeting Orville that first time in April 1979 convinced me I had made the correct decision.

One month after Kelly met Shelley Madden, he returned to Washington. This time he also met her associate, legislative correspondent, Molly Milligan. He was in the capital to speak at a rally that drew an audience of nearly a hundred thousand.

Kelly knew that his illness was progressive and he had periods of intense discomfort. On this day he was in severe pain as he stood on the steps of the Capitol and gazed out across Constitution Avenue. Shelley Madden and Molly Milligan watched from the Senate wing. As far as he could see, there were people sitting and standing in the humid, ninety-two-degree heat. The master of ceremonies introduced him.

In his speech, Kelly reviewed his Japtan Island experiences of being ordered to witness twenty-two nuclear blasts and later being released from the army without ever being advised to have periodic physicals. He related how he learned that he had cancer and then applied to the Veterans Administration, which was founded to take care of veterans like Kelly:

> Well, my friends, I am the perfect example of a man whom the VA is taking care of. They are just waiting for me to die so I'll shut up, but let me assure you, I refuse to give up.
>
> You, each one of you, can do something about tomorrow—today. I do not want my children, nor your children, to grow up with the fear that their world will be destroyed in a nuclear holocaust. We must work to create a world living in harmony without finding more efficient ways to kill people.
>
> I am but one of America's Forgotten Brigade of Radiation Fodder—a victim of my own government's nuclear weapons testing. My insistence that justice must prevail is keeping me alive. I do not intend to die until my job is done.

Loud and continuous applause echoed off the Capitol after Kelly finished his speech. This crusader for America's atomic veterans had lifted the emotions of the huge crowd.

When Kelly returned to Burlington, he worked ceaselessly helping other veterans with their claims, while he planned his own presentation before the Board of Veterans' Appeals.

In Washington, Shelley Madden went often to the VA to study Kelly's case file. She noticed that the file was not being reviewed by anyone at the agency and there seemed to be no urgency about digging into the files' masses of information. The VA had no clear definition of policy on radiation claims, and there was no formal procedure to review them.

From time to time, the chief counsel of the Committee on Veterans' Affairs would ask Shelley what she was learning about Kelly's case. Once she retorted: "Plenty!"

A Denial and Recovery

I cannot, in good conscience, allow such a violation of justice to go unchallenged.

—Dr. John Gofman

On June 8, Kelly had a relapse and was taken to the Burlington hospital in an ambulance. New tests indicated the need for intensive treatment. Wanda was with him constantly, spending many nights at the hospital. She recalls that her husband was having serious difficulties. For days he was confined to his room, unable to leave his bed. He read letters from veterans and dictated answers to the association secretary, Jeannie Kuster. Those closest to him were deeply concerned that this relapse might mean the end. Kelly had no intention of giving in, however. His job was not finished.

He awoke early one July morning determined to somehow get himself across the room to a chair next to the window. Against his doctors' orders, he struggled to navigate the twenty-foot distance. It took him nearly fifteen minutes to reach the chair. Dizzy and weak, he gazed out the window at the scene below. He saw the green grass of the hospital lawn and the hills in the distance. He thought about the things he was seeing, reached for a pad and pen, and wrote:

I watched a parade this morning
From way up in the sky.
I saw it from my hospital window,
And watched the clouds go marching by.

On earth, the trees applauded,
And the birds sang merrily.
I watched a parade this morning,
And it was just for me.

On July 10, Kelly had recovered enough to be released from the hospital. Within six days he and Wanda were on their way to Iowa City, where he would begin a new series of chemotherapy treatments.

In Washington, Shelley Madden began to apply increasing pressure on the VA. She intended to stir interest in Kelly's file so that someone would review the case. She wanted to let the VA know that she knew the file was dormant. Possibly it was dormant because officials were annoyed by Dr. Gofman's review of Kelly's case. He spelled it out in a letter to Shelley:

> I am enclosing a copy of the letter I sent to Mr. Orville Kelly. In that letter I have made it clear that the Veterans Administration decisions are obviously erroneous and that his claim should be granted. I am hopeful that the error in the Veterans Administration decisions can be corrected, for it represents the most gross miscarriage of justice that I have ever encountered in my thirty-two years in medicine.
>
> I am so shocked by the errors of fact and opinion of the Veterans Administration that I cannot, in good conscience, allow such a violation of justice to go unchallenged. Unless this is rectified, I intend to contact my own senators and other senators I know to request a full-scale probe of the Veterans Administration's actions in such matters. If such a probe were held and if competent physician-scientists and other experts were brought in to testify, the results would represent the largest scandal of mishandling of our veterans that has ever occurred in this country.
>
> I have high respect for the men who serve their country in the armed services, and I do not believe the sort of shabby treatment I see here should be condoned. I cannot personally sit by and see this happen.

After Shelley Madden read the letter, she called the VA and insisted that an independent medical opinion be obtained in Kelly's case. At first the agency ignored her requests, but she called daily and became more insistent. She told the VA, "I will not stop, and if you want to get me off your backs, then do as I ask. My requests are not outlandish. I want an independent medical opinon, and this veteran deserves one!"

After a time, the VA relented:

> Finally, one day a congressional liaison representative from the VA called me and said, "All right, Miss Madden, we are prepared to send the Kelly case to an independent medical group, but *you* have to pick the medical examiner."
>
> I was furious. I said, "No way, no way. It's unethical for you to suggest such a thing. If I select the examiner and the results are in your favor, then you could use me to weasel out of making the disability award. You find the examiner, and he or she had better be a recognized pathologist!"

Shelley Madden's strong words to the representative accomplished what she wanted. The case was sent to the Armed Forces Institute of Pathology for review. Its comment:

> The veteran's dosimetry was available for only four and one half [months] of his twelve-month assignment. Beta radiation was not measured. Therefore, it appears that the veteran's exposure was probably much greater than listed for the twenty-two nuclear blasts. In summary, the staff believes that the radiation exposure in the service was a probable factor in the etiology of the veteran's neoplastic process [maligant tumor growths].

While the Institute was reviewing Kelly's case, Jonathan

Steinberg, chief counsel of the Senate Committee on Veterans' Affairs, stopped by Shelley's desk. Shelley got a large surprise:

> Steinberg, whom I consider a brilliant man, occasionally checked on my progress. He jokingly referred to me as the radiation lady. This one morning he asked me what I was working on, and before I could answer, he said, "Don't tell me, I bet it's the Kelly case." I said he was right and he continued, "Well, Shelley, because of all the furor you've created and what we've seen that a veteran has to go through to get compensation for an illness he feels is radiation induced, we've decided to hold hearings." I was astonished but very, very pleased. I remembered that six months before Steinberg's news, the committee had no idea of veterans' radiation-caused health problems, and that I had to beg and plead to be allowed to start work on Kelly's case. Now we were going to hold hearings. That was real progress! My entire face was aglow. I thought—fantastic!

At 9:34 a.m. on June 20, 1979, in Room 6226 of the Dirksen Office Building, California Senator Alan Cranston, chairman of the Senate Committee on Veterans' Affairs, opened the one-day hearings with a statement: "There can be no doubt that the federal government today has a compelling moral responsibility to do everything possible to facilitate Veterans Administration disability and death claims related to nuclear weapons testing."

Kelly, who was in the Burlington hospital again, could not be at the hearings but sent a statement to be presented by another atomic veteran, O. T. Weeks of Birmingham, Alabama. Cranston introduced Kelly as the founder and director of the National Association of Atomic Veterans and said that

Mr. Weeks was his spokesman. Weeks read Kelly's statement:

> The atomic veteran is a pawn caught in the middle of a raging controversy between those who feel there is and those who feel there isn't a safe level of exposure to low-level ionizing radiation At least the men who served in combat and were killed or injured received the benefits from a grateful country, benefits which I feel were earned and well deserved. We, the veterans of the nuclear age, who also served our country in a time of need, feel we are entitled to the same disability benefits as any other veteran—no more, no less.
>
> As a veteran of the U.S. Army who observed twenty-two nuclear detonations and presently is a cancer patient with no hope for recovery, I would like to tell you how I feel today after receiving my third VA denial. I believe that America is the only country where true justice can be obtained. As proof of this, I am reminded of the fact that even though my case has been denied several times, I still have the right to keep fighting.
>
> I am asking that the U.S. Government assume responsibility for the medical conditions of people like myself who just want the right to die in peace, knowing I earned the right to use these benefits for my family.
>
> Unfortunately, time is not on our side. The veterans are asking for action now. I feel each of you realize that a certain number of veterans have died and continue to die because of exposure to ionizing radiation. The question is not really whether or not the veterans be compensated, but rather how it should be done. Please make the decision as soon as

> possible and correct a grave injustice that has been simmering for years.

Kelly, as was his habit, said what he thought positively, firmly, and without rancor. It was clear that he wanted assistance for all atomic veterans, not only for himself.

Attending that day was Patricia Broudy, the widow of a veteran who had participated in shots Priscilla and Hood, accompanied by her attorney. Both had a laundry list of charges against the VA. Said the attorney:

> I am embarrassed that we have to hold these hearings. The time is for *action*, not for more hearings. The Marshallese, whom I represented on a pro bono basis, received lifetime guaranteed medical care, a $25,000 illness payment and/or a $100,000 death benefit. The veterans say, "We were at the test sites, we were exposed, and now we have cancer. Shouldn't we get at least what the Marshallese got?"
>
> My initial investigation of the problem confronted by these former servicemen revealed a shocking and disgraceful system which resulted routinely in their denial of veteran benefits. The problem lies in the fact that the Veterans Administration is guilty of both ignorance and incompetence concerning radiation claims.

Patricia Broudy let loose her feelings:

> The Veterans Administration has a quaint quotation from Abraham Lincoln which states, "To care for him who shall have borne the battle, and for his widow and orphan." How ironic! Instead of caring for these veterans, their widows and children, each case has become an adversary proceeding. We are guilty until proven innocent. We must prove that

> our husbands were at the tests, and we must prove cancer is a result of low-level ionizing radiation.
>
> While these hearings are going on, more men are dying, and more widows and orphans are going on welfare. These men were used as guinea pigs. We know the results of these tests from the horrible atrocities we inflicted upon the Japanese. Why did we have to do this to our own men?
>
> Now why do we have to be subjected to the humiliation of begging for what is rightfully ours?

The hearings lasted well into the day. There was testimony from advocates of the nuclear weapons tests and those who defended their policies: Vice Admiral Robert P. Monroe, director of the Defense Nuclear Agency; Mahlon E. Gates, manager of the Nevada operations office of the Department of Energy; Duane Sewell, assistant secretary of Defense Programs, the Department of Energy; and J. C. Peckarsky, the director of the VA Compensation and Pension Service. The party line was the same: the Defense Nuclear Agency and the Department of Energy insisted that every precaution had been taken at the test sites and that the exposure of troops to radiation was minimal. The VA maintained that it was following guidelines established by the Defense Nuclear Agency, and that atomic veterans could not prove that their diseases were radiation-related. Thus, most claims were denied.

When the hearings ended, a reporter from the Associated Press filed a report headed, "A-Test Veterans to Receive More Aid." The article, which appeared in major newspapers across the country, could easily have been headed, "Atomic Veterans Receive More False Hope." Through no fault of Chairman Cranston or Shelley Madden, whose initiative had brought about the hearings, the testimony that June day did little to ease the plight of atomic veterans.

When Shelley Madden realized that there had been no admission of mistakes by those successors to the men who had exposed the veterans to radiation, and that the VA had not altered its position, she analyzed the problem:

> The VA is simply not a thinking body. There is no manner in which the radiation claim can fit into any category that exists there. If a claim doesn't fit, then the veteran doesn't get the benefits. If the individual didn't have the symptoms while on active duty or within a year afterward, then he won't receive any benefits. The VA doesn't even know the meaning of the word "latency." The known period for radiation illness simply isn't a part of the VA medical doctrine.
>
> Well, I made a promise to Orville Kelly. I studied his files, and I was horrified. He had all the evidence and the best of medical opinions, yet he was denied three times. If the Board of Appeals denies him, that's it. There is no judicial review. The board's decision is final. I will work on this case until my dying day, and I will not stop until his claim is approved.
>
> Kelly is one of the most unbelievable people I have ever met. He helps others even when he is so ill. He never has turned anyone away. The VA and the Defense Nuclear Agency have seriously underestimated me. So what if I am only twenty-six and they think of me as a little girl? They're going to learn that I am obsessed, and once I'm obsessed, you'd better listen to me, because I'll fight you until I die. Money, money, money, that's all the DNA and the VA think about. No one considers the moral injustice that was done to those men. Kelly's going to die soon. He has no insurance. He has enor-

> mous medical bills that Wanda will spend the rest of her life paying off. His family will be destitute. John Gofman said that he would not sit by and allow this to happen. Well, neither will I!

During the months that followed, Shelley Madden called and visited the Veterans Administration often. Not only did she hound the VA; she also persuaded the chief counsel of her committee to add his pressure to hers. She believed a two-level attack might have a better chance of succeeding. In August, Shelley and Molly Milligan met with Orville Kelly for the last time before the VA appeals hearing in September. He was well prepared, but unfortunately, his illness forced him to become a hospital patient again. On September 10, very ill, he was admitted to the University of Iowa hospital. His case would have to be presented by his service representative, the American Legion. The evening before the hearing, Orville and Wanda prayed together for a favorable decision. All they could do was wait.

The afternoon before the hearing, Shelley made a final call to the VA. She was resigning from the committee staff soon to go to law school. This would be her last chance to talk to the agency before Kelly's hearing. She reached the person responsible for Kelly's case and made the point that Kelly was in the hospital, obviously without much time left to live. When he died, she went on, his family would have to use everything he left to pay his medical bills. Finally, "After seven years of denied claims, I hope that the VA will show some compassion during this final hearing."

Landmark Decision

Now I can die in peace.

—Orville E. Kelly

After spending nearly a month in the hospital, Kelly was released in October. Many of his friends were surprised, because they thought he would not recover. But he had a mission to complete. He spent the rest of the month working on association matters, returning often to the hospital as an outpatient. During the next month, Lew Golinker, a staff attorney from the National Veterans' Law Center in Washington, came to visit him. The center, a public interest project of American University's law school, wanted to help atomic veterans. Its attorneys were among the few who would represent a veteran at a VA hearing without a fee.

The meeting was useful to both men. Golinker had a keen, quick mind and wanted to help where he was needed. He understood the issues and promised the center would represent as many atomic veterans as it could.

November was a particularly anxious month for Kelly and his family. They were told the Appeals Board would decide his case by Thanksgiving. The day passed with no news. Kelly was depressed, convinced that he would be turned down again. On November 24, he and Wanda left for the West Coast for several appearances arranged by the publisher of his second book, *Until Tomorrow Comes.* Kelly planned to meet with atomic veterans in addition to discussing the book. He would stop first in San Francisco and then travel down to Los Angeles and San Diego.

On the evening of November 25, Kelly appeared on a three-hour live radio talk show in San Francisco, talking about his radiation exposure and his subsequent cancer. When the station opened the switchboard for call-ins, veterans and others who were involved in nuclear tests flooded the lines. One of the callers, who identified himself as Dr. Earle Reynolds, said, "Mr. Kelly, you may remember me as the person who sailed into the testing area in 1958 to protest the nuclear tests. I tried to warn everyone that the tests would have bad effects on the participants. Had you men listened and joined my protest, the tests could have been stopped, and you might not have cancer today. All this happened the year you were on Eniwetok. Do you remember?"

Kelly was stunned. He recalled his conversation with John Loveridge, the Armed Forces Radio announcer, twenty-one years before. Loveridge had told Kelly about Dr. Reynolds. He said, "Yes, Doctor, I do remember the incident. You were taken to Kwajalein, I believe. I should have listened, and now I am sorry I didn't."

Kelly wasn't feeling well. Exhausted, he fell into bed that night at the Fisherman's Wharf Holiday Inn. The number of calls to the radio station had surprised him, and the three hours he spent answering them had drained him. He told Wanda he was convinced that there were more people affected by the tests than they would ever know.

At 6:01 the next morning, the phone in Kelly's room rang. Groggy with sleep, he answered it. Molly Milligan in Washington was calling. "Orville, I was told just now by a caller from the VA that the decision is favorable. The Appeals Board allowed your claim!"

The news snapped Kelly awake. "I don't believe it, but we've won!" he shouted to Wanda. "We won our case!" Soon all three were crying.

When they concluded the conversation, Molly Milligan said to herself, "This is the most satisfying thing that's happened since I've been with the committee."

The next two days were among the busiest of Wanda and Orville's life. The media called constantly. Newspaper, television, and radio reporters wanted interviews. Atomic veterans and friends all over the country phoned or sent telegrams congratulating Kelly on his victory.

A *New York Times* story called the decision one of the most significant in the history of awards to former servicemen. The *Washington Post* reported, "A terminally ill veteran of the mid-Pacific atom bomb tests has finally won a six-year battle to get official government recognition of the cause-and-effect relationship between fallout more than twenty years ago and the cancer that is killing him today." U.P.I. said, "A former Army sergeant dying of cancer has won what experts say is a landmark victory."

The *Iowa Legionnaire*'s Tom Quinlan went into more detail:

> In seeking information, Orville Kelly received an unbelievable runaround by government bureaucrats. He was sent from one government agency to another, only to end up back at the original agency. Kelly's long fight to get his benefits was the most disgusting example of a government refusing to accept responsibility for its own actions I have ever seen. The Department of Defense, the Nuclear Regulatory Agency and the Department of Energy foot-dragged every step of the way. Not one of them would willingly cooperate. The information that Kelly needed to support his case became very hard to get. The word got around quickly about this "nut" who was seeking information. It was this "nut" who, twenty years earlier, had received a Certificate of Commendation for a job well done as a noncommissioned officer in charge of Japtan Island.

On San Francisco television, the day of the award, Kelly said:

> The award will allow me to die in peace. I won't lose my home now, and my children will be able to go to college. I don't think anybody thought I'd be around

> this long, especially the government. But I outwaited them. Maybe that's what kept me alive. Yes, I am elated. As a matter of fact, I am still kind of numb as a result of this morning's news. I hope and pray that my award will pave the way for other atomic veterans who are even worse off than I am.

When Kelly got back to Burlington after his trip to the West Coast, there was a twenty-two-page document from the Board of Veterans' Appeals. The last paragraph summarized it: "Decision: Entitlement to service connection disability for a malignant process is established. The benefit sought on appeal is allowed."

There had been a few claims approved for other atomic veterans, but Orville Kelly's was the only one that directly linked disability to radiation exposure where no symptoms had appeared while a veteran was on active duty.

7

And There Were Others

Until 1977 there was no indication that former test participants were experiencing any adverse health effects which might be attributable to exposure to ionizing radiation at the tests.

—Defense Nuclear Agency
Fact Sheet

There is no danger; there is no danger.

—AEC radio broadcast
to the residents of
St. George, Utah, 1953

When Orville Kelly was awarded his disability claim, he made a point of saying he hoped his breakthrough would help radiation victims everywhere. The nuclear tests had affected the lives of thousands of people in every area where the blasts took place, and wherever nuclear clouds deposited their radioactive fallout around the world.

1943: The Test Before the Test

You have claimed that you were present during bomb testing in November 1943. The first test of a nuclear bomb was not conducted until July 1945.

—Adjudication Officer
Veterans Administration

In 1943, Carl Mautte was a twenty-two-year-old airman stationed at Kearns Air Force Base in Salt Lake City. Carl, like many of his generation, joined the air force to help his country win the war.

In November of that year, something unexpected happened. Carl remembers it:

> One afternoon a convoy of army trucks arrived at the base, and the first fifteen men from every other barracks were told to board the vehicles. I was one of those men.
>
> We were briefed that we were going to take part in the testing of a Super Bomb that would end the war. The trucks took us to an area past the Great Salt Lake where there was a plateau of land. We were lined up at the base of a cliff and told to face the cliff and cover our eyes with our hands. When a whistle blew, we could drop our hands and open our eyes.
>
> We followed instructions, and after about ten minutes I heard a distant thud and felt a slight tremor of the earth. My skin felt funny—like an electrical shock.
>
> Then we returned to our barracks. None of us knew what had occurred, and we were never told. We were informed, however, that we would receive a Distinguished Service Medal for our bravery. It is a part of my service record. I never did receive the medal.
>
> Three months later I was temporarily assigned to Alamagordo, New Mexico. Tests of parts of the new bomb were conducted as a matter of routine every ten days or so. One day while we were returning from our mess hall after the noon meal, the public address system announced that all personnel were

to take shelter immediately. Four hours later we were given the "all clear" signal.

I was told later that tests of the new bomb had carried something over our area, and the testers had not wanted to conduct that day's test until the wind shifted, carrying whatever it was over the base and away from civilian-populated areas.

When I contracted leukemia, I filed for service-connected disability. The VA had the audacity to reply that I could not have been a radiation victim because my alleged exposure occurred before the Trinity test. The VA must think that bomb was built in a garage overnight. It took those scientists three years to develop it, and all kinds of tests of components had to happen before the finished product was exploded. Just about everybody knows that!

September 9, 1945

The purpose of today's visit, gentlemen, is to show you that the dangerous levels of radiation at the site have completely diminished.

—General Leslie R. Groves
Director, Manhattan Project

Patrick Stout had been assigned to army intelligence and now, at age twenty-nine, was a part of the Manhattan Project at Los Alamos. He was well aware that he was participating in something that could end the war. Sometimes Stout was assigned as General Leslie R. Groves's personal driver. It was not unusual for him to encounter the world's foremost nuclear scientists, such as Robert Oppenheimer.

On the day of the world's first atomic explosion, July 16, 1945, Patrick Stout had an excellent view of the experiment. Like most observers, he was overjoyed when it succeeded.

On the day of that nuclear success, Enrico Fermi, the Italian scientist who worked on the development of the bomb and who built the first successful nuclear reactor in 1938, cautiously approached ground zero in a Sherman tank lined with lead. Fermi surely knew there were dangerous radiation levels near the explosion's hypocenter. He saw the explosion had made a sizable crater nearly fifteen feet deep in the desert floor and reported that the sand surrounding ground zero was fused into a milky-green glass. Only a molten metal stump was left where the one-hundred-foot tower on which the bomb was mounted had stood. Despite Fermi's massive protection, the radiation was so intense that he had to leave the area.

On September 9, General Groves, Robert Oppenheimer, and other scientists escorted media representatives close to ground zero. Groves wanted to show the reporters that the area was free of harmful levels of radioactivity. He was driven to ground zero by Patrick Stout. Stout was encouraged to go into the crater, which he did. He stayed there for thirty minutes and was photographed—a smiling, happy soldier.

A scientist later told him he had been exposed to dangerous levels of radioactivity.

In April 1967, Patrick Stout became ill. Leukemia was diagnosed, and two years later he died. He told his wife he was certain that his exposure at site Trinity had caused his cancer.

Pilot with a Conscience

> *One has only one life, and if the experiences of my life can be used for the benefit of the human race, then that is the way it will be used.*
>
> —Claude R. Eatherly

Claude Robert Eatherly flew his plane, a B-29 named *Straight Flush*, over Hiroshima looking for a hole in the clouds so the bombardier of the *Enola Gay* could find his target and drop the first bomb used in anger. Once Eatherly found a hole he radioed the information to the *Enola Gay* and flew back to Tinian Island in the Marianas. He was not aware of the type of bomb to be dropped that August morning. When he learned what had happened, Eatherly had mixed emotions. He was elated that the war would very likely be shortened, but he was also concerned about the thousands of lives that had been sacrificed.

After the war, Eatherly stayed in the air force. He was assigned to Operation Crossroads in the Pacific at Bikini Atoll in 1946. The United States had in its arsenal two atomic bombs that originally were intended for Japan had the Japanese not surrendered after Nagasaki. Officials decided to use the bombs in tests to discover their effect on seventy-four ships anchored in Bikini lagoon. Test Able was an airburst, while the second test, Baker, was underwater. Some 42,000 civilians and servicemen took part in the test.

Eatherly saw Able explode from the cockpit of his B-29 flying at twenty-five thousand feet:

> I can see it—brilliant, brilliant colors; every color you can imagine. Then these ships, huge ships, being tossed way, way up in the air. Then the shock wave, a dark wall of spray coming right at us like a huge fist, pushing us sideways. Then our plane, shuddering and tossing like an insignificant leaf. I

realized at last what power mankind was trifling with.

After the detonation, he flew directly into the dense mushroom to measure airborne blast effects. When he returned to base, his B-29 was dangerously radioactive. At first the air force planned to destroy it. However, in the end it was simply washed and quarantined for awhile.

Eatherly was examined by air force physicians, who told him he had not been harmed because he was inside the plane. Six months later he was discharged.

Shortly after discharge, Eatherly became moody, tense, and insecure. He began to feel dizzy, fatigued, and weak. In 1947, his wife miscarried and the fetus was found to be malformed. Mrs. Eatherly asked her physician if her husband's exposure to radiation could have had any damaging effects. After a special test, the physician told Eatherly that radiation exposure was a possible explanation for an unusually high number of abnormal spermatozoa. Claude filed a claim with the VA, which was denied.

The VA said that Eatherly's claims for physical and mental disability caused by "atomic operations" was an aberration. "Of all the men who were involved in the atomic operations in Hiroshima, Nagasaki and Bikini, only Eatherly has claimed physical or mental damage."

His condition worsened. He began to have blackouts and long periods of memory loss. He robbed a U.S. Post Office and was arrested, tried, and convicted. During the trial he complained that he had never felt right since his exposure to radiation in Bikini.

Reporters discovered that the man being tried had targeted the bomb dropped on Hiroshima. One newsman suggested that Eatherly had committed a crime so society would punish him for his crime against Hiroshima. Soon the story was national news, and Claude Eatherly was in the public eye.

He was an embarrassment to the air force because he was

complaining about radiation exposure, and the air force did not want to be accused of injuring one of its pilots. Eatherly was under psychiatric care at a VA hospital and was an outpatient during his trial. The air force asked the VA if Eatherly was mentally or physically impaired. The agency said he suffered from deep schizophrenic guilt because he had been instrumental in killing more than 100,000 Japanese. For fifteen months he was heavily drugged, receiving constant doses of Dilantin, Thorazine, Ritalin, and Benzedrine, as well as electric shock treatments and coma insulation therapy.

Finally, Eatherly was able to get out of the VA hospital. He spent the rest of his life preaching the dangers of nuclear testing and trying to organize a movement to ban nuclear weapons production. He died of lymphoma in 1978.

A good case can be made, I believe, that Claude Eatherly was mortally wounded when he was ordered to fly through an atomic cloud at Bikini.

Crossroads

> *Every precaution was taken to provide adequate protection to assure the safety of the military personnel who participated in the nuclear tests.*
>
> —Vice Admiral Robert R. Monroe
> Director, Defense Nuclear Agency

The 42,000 men who were en route to Crossroads had various thoughts about what they would experience. At least one of them feared that he would never see his parents again.

On May 18, 1946, Wayne Moore, an eighteen-year-old sailor aboard the U.S.S. *Saidor*, wrote his mother:

> We are on our way to Bikini Atoll that is the Cross-

> roads where the bomb is going to be dropped. They say this ship may be demobilized by the terrific combustion of the bomb, and they say the heat will be so great that our lives will be in danger. Momma, they told us that we may never come back. They gave us a party and all the liberty we wanted. Well, Momma, you may make $10,000 soon because you are the beneficiary of my G.I. insurance.

Jim Elliott was a healthy young farmer when he joined the navy. He was assigned to the U.S.S. *Arkansas*, one of the ships anchored in the Bikini lagoon during the two nuclear tests of Operation Crossroads. Before the first one, the crew of the *Arkansas* was transferred to another ship and taken twenty-one miles away from the blast area. The *Arkansas* was placed approximately six hundred twenty yards from the site of the detonation.

Two days after test Able, Elliott and other navy people returned to the *Arkansas*. They stayed only briefly because the ship was radioactive and judged "too hot" for occupancy. The men left the ship again, returning a couple of days later to crate up the test animals that had been left on board the vessel before the shot. Elliott was told that at least 20 percent of the animals died from radiation poisoning. The *Arkansas* sank during the subsequent Baker underwater test.

Elliott had other duties. He placed warning signs on ships that had survived the blast. One sign—KEEP CLEAR, DANGER, VERY RADIOACTIVE—was put on a submarine, the U.S.S. *Skate*. The *Skate*, in the front line of target ships, was still afloat, but had been severely damaged. The blast and heat turned the *Skate*'s superstructure into a gnarled mass. A few days after the test, the warning sign was removed and the *Skate*'s crew boarded the ship. The vessel would run but could not be submerged. The crew took it to sea to pass in review before the admiral's flagship.

Elliott had other tasks in the lagoon. He was a member of a salvage crew that raised parts of damaged ships from the bottom. The sailors were allowed to swim in the lagoon where the ships were anchored. Shortly after Elliott's first swim, he complained of nausea.

Elliott left Bikini Atoll aboard the U.S.S. *Clymer* for the United States. The *Clymer* stopped at Pearl Harbor. Between Hawaii and California, the crew was ordered to dump all food overboard because it was contaminated from radiation. During the rest of the trip, the crew subsisted on canned meat and hardtack. The men wondered how much of the contaminated food they had eaten before the dumping. They were warned by an officer not to discuss the incident with anyone.

Within eleven months after Crossroads, Elliott's weight had dropped from one hundred eighty-two to one hundred eighteen pounds. Today he suffers from internal bleeding, skin cancers, pains in his bones and joints, and dimming vision. He has tried to locate others who were at Crossroads with him, but so far he has found more widows than shipmates.

Among Elliott's mementos of his Crossroads experience is a certificate entitled "Grand Council Exclusive Order of Guinea Pigs," presented to him when the *Clymer* was en route to Hawaii.

Elliott has been denied service-connected disability by the Veterans Administration and at one VA hearing was accused of lying. A board member told him that he could not have packed test animals into crates after test Able because the Humane Society would have forbidden their use in radiation experiments.

Elliott is not alone searching for former naval test participants: the U.S. Navy Nuclear Test Personnel Review Department is having an incredibly difficult time locating the 135,000 men who participated in the seventeen-year program of atmospheric-explosion tests.

Guadalcanal to Nagasaki

A member of the occupational forces would have had to stand at ground zero naked for several consecutive days in order for him to be suffering any ill effects from the bombing.

—Lieutenant Colonel William McGee
Public Information Officer,
Defense Nuclear Agency

Sam Scione survived the bloody banzai charges of the Japanese on Guadalcanal, Tarawa, Saipan, and Okinawa. The young marine, a member of the elite Second Marine Division, was in some of the fiercest fighting of the entire Pacific campaign. Before he landed on Okinawa to deliver a knockout blow to Japan's last strategic Pacific island, Scione spent a nervous day below deck on the troop transport, fearful that his ship would be hit by a Kamikaze pilot.

Okinawa fell and the marines went back to Saipan, where they trained hard for another massive attack. Scione was told his division was going to assault the Japanese mainland. During training, news reached the marines that atomic bombs had been dropped on the Japanese cities of Hiroshima and Nagasaki. A few days later, they learned that Japan had surrendered. Scione's reaction:

> Not knowing the cruel effects of atomic bombing, we were as happy as monkeys in a banana tree. A few weeks later, we were ordered aboard a transport ship. Soon enough, we learned that our previously unknown destination was Nagasaki.
>
> When we sailed into Nagasaki harbor, we crowded to the port side of the ship and craned our necks for a view. We looked for human life—there was none. We saw total devastation. The major buildings were nothing but skeletons. We arrived at

> the dock and there was only one old Japanese man there. The rest of the population had fled to the mountains because they were told there would be atrocities.
>
> We spent the first couple of nights and days in a burned out factory. It rained hard, and I learned how fish must feel sleeping in water. Later we were moved to a schoolhouse.
>
> My particular duties were to disarm Japanese, place guards at key locations and patrol the city in a jeep. We never learned anything about radiation or the effects it might have on us. We went to ground zero many times and were never instructed not to go there.
>
> At ground zero I saw a phenomenon which I could not comprehend. I saw the shadow of a man on a brick wall with nothing else around and no man to make the shadow. I realize now that this shadow had to have been a human being who was fused to the wall at the time of the explosion of the atom bomb.

During the five months the marines were in Nagasaki, they drank the water and ate the local food.

Scione returned to the United States. In the fall of 1946, seven months after leaving Nagasaki, his hair began to fall out in patches and his body was covered with weeping sores. The following spring he was hospitalized at Camp Lejeune, North Carolina. His symptoms now included a chronic stomach disorder, dizziness, disorientation, and extreme fatigue. Unable to diagnose his illness, the Marine Corps placed him in a psychiatric ward. He stayed there until he was discharged from the service.

From 1947 to 1972, Scione visited a succession of physicians as his ailments became worse. In 1972, he had a complete relapse and was admitted to a VA hospital. At the end of four and one-half months, he was released from the hospital and declared totally disabled, but he had no medical diagnosis.

Scione has applied for service-connected disability three times, and like most atomic veterans, he has been denied.

Scione summarizes his feelings:

> I feel my problems are definitely radiation-related, and because of this I have been denied the opportunity to make a living and enjoy the fruits of life. After I raised my children, I wanted to grow old naturally, not grow old prematurely because I was exposed to radiation.
>
> Even though thousands of us survived combat, we have been dying slowly because of weapons made by our own government. The way it appears to me now is that our marine division, which could not be beaten or destroyed by the Japanese, is being destroyed by purposeful and deliberate lack of care by the very government we fought to protect.

In December 1979, the Defense Nuclear Agency said in a letter to the White House advisory staff, "The maximum dose which may have been received by any serviceman in either Nagasaki or Hiroshima in an absolutely worse case is less than one rem."

In April 1980, an article titled "National Archives Yield Secret Radiation Data" in the *Washington Post* reported:

> Two months after the atomic bomb exploded over Nagasaki, two government research teams found low-level radiation in the Japanese city . . . that was over ten times the radiation safety standard for the general population.
>
> The once secret reports are bound to increase the controversy that has developed over whether U.S. troops sent to Nagasaki in 1945 absorbed enough

radiation to have caused cancers and other diseases that appeared after twenty years or more.

The Year of the Animal

About 7,000 square miles of territory downwind [from Bravo] was so contaminated that survival might have depended upon prompt evacuation or upon taking shelter. During the actual test, of course, there were no persons in the area.

—Lewis Strauss, Chairman
Atomic Energy Commission,
Bravo Report, February 1955

On March 1, 1954, the United States exploded the first and the largest hydrogen bomb tested in the Pacific. Bravo was 17 megatons in size, large enough to obliterate all of Manhattan and substantial parts of Long Island and New Jersey.

Gene Curbow, an atomic veteran who was assigned to a unit that measured wind velocity and recorded weather conditions, remembers: "For weeks prior to the blast it was known that prevailing upper level troughs indicated that the winds were blowing in the direction of inhabited islands." The thermonuclear bomb was detonated despite the fact that the weather information was reported regularly by radio to the Joint Task Headquarters at Eniwetok. Curbow, who was on Rongerik Atoll, 140 miles east of Bikini, continues: "When the shot was exploded, the wind was blowing right at us. When the shock wave hit, all the pre-fabricated buildings were damaged in one way or another. Nearly all the windows were blown out."

The Atomic Energy Commission, aware of the possible health consequences of its mistake, released an elaborate and false report saying that no humans had been harmed by Bravo's fallout. A total of 239 Marshallese, 28 servicemen, and the crew of a Japanese tuna boat, the *Lucky Dragon,* were enveloped by a cloud of grayish-white gritty ash.

John Anjain, a magistrate on Rongelap Atoll, which is about 100 miles east of Bikini, where Bravo was detonated, remembers what happened:

> In early 1954 I was in Mujuro Atoll, five hundred miles south of Bikini, and a man who worked for the AEC stuck out the tip of his finger about a half-inch and said, "John, your life is just about that long." I asked him what he meant, and he explained that they were setting off a mighty bomb on Bikini soon. I asked him why my people were not being evacuated, and he explained that no word had come from Washington to move us.
>
> I went back to Rongelap and on the day of the explosion, I arose before dawn and thought I saw what appeared to be a sunrise, but it was in the west. The sight was beautiful with many colors, and I was surprised.
>
> A little while later, the sun rose in the east. Then some time later, something like smoke filled the entire sky, and shortly after that, a strong and warm wind like a typhoon swept across Rongelap. Then all of a sudden, we heard the great sound of the explosion. Some people began to cry with fright, because they thought another war was starting. Several hours later a grayish-white powder began to fall on our atoll. It fell on people, into the drinking water, and on the food. We did not know what it was, and many of the children played in the ashlike powder. You could see less than a half mile at the time.

The next day I inspected all the water catchments with the health aide and the school principal, and we saw that our water had turned yellow. I then warned the people not to drink the water and told them to drink only coconut milk.

Later, people began to get sick with vomiting, aches all over their bodies, eye irritations. Burns appeared on their skin. A general weakness and fatigue set in. After the second day, most of the people were unable to move around as usual.

On the evening of the second day, a seaplane arrived with two men who brought some strange machines. They stayed about twenty minutes and took some readings of the water catchments and soil, and then they left. They told us little, and we still did not know what had caused our sickness.

On the morning of the third day a navy destroyer came, and an officer told me, "John Anjain, you have to leave this island at once or you and your people will die." At this time, most of the people were feeling quite dizzy, and they were very weak. We were moved to Kwajalein, and we were very sick and in much pain. Our burns had started to bleed. Three doctors arrived from the States and made us bathe three times a day because they said our illnesses were of a new type and there was no medicine for us.

After moving from atoll to atoll, we were finally returned to Rongelap in 1957—three years after we left. We were told that there was a little bit of radiation left on the atoll, but it would not injure our health very much. We returned, but we had much fear.

After we had been back for a few months, many women began to have problems with childbearing.

On several occasions, women gave birth to creatures that did not resemble human beings: some of the creatures looked like monkeys, some like octopuses, and others like bunches of grapes. Nothing like this had ever happened before. We called 1957 the year of the animal because the newborn looked more like animals than humans. The people complained about these deformities, but the AEC doctors told us not to worry because "there was just a little radiation left on Rongelap."

In 1963, the thyroid problems started to occur. Many of my people had to have their thyroids removed, and others will have to take pills for the rest of their lives.

In 1969, the AEC took my son, Lekoj, and two other children to New York for their thyroid problems. In 1972, Lekoj became ill and was sent to Honolulu for blood transfusions. The AEC doctors told me he would be all right. My son was then transferred to Washington, D.C. I went there to see him and he appeared very, very sick. The next day he died from leukemia. It was the saddest day of my life.

After this incident I swore never to believe the AEC doctors again. I went to Japan with the members of the Congress of Micronesia to ask help from independent doctors. The Japanese doctors came to the Marshall Islands but were forced to leave by the governor of the trusteeship. They told us that we should never have returned to Rongelap in 1957. Now we know that it was a huge mistake to believe those who told us that it was safe.

At the present, the people of Rongelap are really frightened and angry. From the beginning of the bomb testing program we have been treated like animals in a scientific experiment.

And There Were Others

Two hundred eighty miles east of the Bikini Atoll is the atoll of Utirik. Margaret Ataddy was a child when Bravo exploded. She says:

> On the morning of the bomb I awoke and saw the western sky turn bright red. Later, I heard the explosions and felt the walls of my house shaking. The ground shook, too. The next day a mist fell on our island. In a few days all the people on our island began to get sick. Then the navy came and moved us to Kwajalein. We were placed in a roped-off enclosure which we could not leave. There was a guard who patrolled to make sure that we did not leave the enclosure.
>
> We came back to Utirik in June and ran out of the food and water the AEC supplied us. We had no choice but to eat our local foods and drink our catchment water.
>
> The AEC started sending a doctor to examine us, but his program has brought much grief to our people. He never tells us the truth about out health problems and treats us like children. He tells us he wants to help us, yet he examines only a few people. He never examined the children. He tells us it is all right to eat our food, but he eats the food on the AEC ship. Arrowroot, which is one of our major foods, has all but disappeared and is bitter and acrid tasting.
>
> I have had many female problems after the bomb, and I am only thirty-five. In 1968, I gave birth to a baby that had no skin—it was a monster. Thankfully, it was stillborn. I gave birth two years ago to something that looked like a placenta, and it died one day after it was born. All of the women here are afraid when they have their babies for fear of having problems from the poison! None of these problems

> occurred before the bomb. We are fearful that the radiation poisoning will stay with us the rest of our lives and our children's lives, and their children's lives.

There were ninety people living on Utirik in 1954. Thirty have died, thirty currently have cancer, and one-half the remaining population suffers from cataracts.

The Marshallese could have been warned that the radioactive cloud from Bravo was heading their way and told to seek shelter, but the AEC was silent until the fallout had been deposited on the occupied islands.

Dr. Rosalie Bertell, a Catholic nun, is the director of cancer research for the Ministry of Concern for Public Health in Buffalo, New York. She has specialized in researching the effects of radiation on the human body for more than ten years. Called "just another antinuclear torch bearer" by Lieutenant Colonel Hartman B. Mowery of the Defense Nuclear Agency, Dr. Bertell has warned: "Continued exposure to low-level ionizing radiation will destroy the integrity of the gene pool. Damage will appear mild in the offspring which survive—the most seriously damaged will die. However, the mildly damaged will be less able to cope with radiation and eventually the line of offspring will die out and produce no more viable children." It appears that the Marshallese are tragic examples of the truth of Dr. Bertell's warnings.

Ted Lombard, of Gorham, Maine, knows about the genetic effects of radiation exposure. He was exposed to raw plutonium and uranium dust during the Manhattan Project. He had four children, born after his exposure. All the children, now young adults and teenagers, are suffering from undiagnosed neuromuscular disorders and seizures. His eldest daughter, once a physical therapist, is confined to a wheelchair. Two grandchildren have recently developed digestive problems and blood disorders. Another son, born before Lombard's exposure, is in perfect health.

And There Were Others

NTS—The Nifty Fifties

We must not let anything interfere with these tests—nothing!

—Thomas Murray
AEC Commissioner, 1955

The years 1951–1955 will be remembered as the radiologically dirtiest in the history of nuclear testing in Nevada.

Lawrence Livermore Laboratory, formerly known as the University of California Radiation Laboratory at Livermore, came to the Nevada Test Site in 1953. The number of nuclear tests that year was increased to nine to allow the new laboratory to field test its theoretical concepts.

On April 11, 1953, Livermore's first atmospheric test occurred. It was code-named Ray, and a substantial yield was expected. The bomb exploded with all the force of a small firecracker. Observers saw neither a blast nor a flash, and Livermore's first attempt at an outdoor nuclear detonation failed to destroy the bomb's enclosure on top of a one-hundred-foot tower.

Fourteen days after the embarrassment of Ray, the Nevada Test Group had another opportunity to test a nuclear weapon. This time the planned shot, called Simon, exceeded its estimated yield by 25 percent and erupted with the explosive power of 52,000 tons of TNT. More than 3,000 troops in trenches were covered with thick layers of dust, and seven "volunteers" who were in a trench slightly over a mile from ground zero, received as much as 100 roentgens of exposure.

Three weeks later, another Livermore shot was fired, named Harry. Harry was even dirtier than Simon. People of St. George, Utah, disgustedly call the explosion "Dirty Harry." One AEC official said, "That first Livermore explosion caused one hell of a contamination problem both on and off the site."

Plastered

East, they [the atomic clouds] go over St. George, which always gets plastered.

—Lewis Strauss, Chairman,
Atomic Energy Commission

May 9, 1953, is indelibly etched in the memory of Elizabeth Catalan, who formerly lived in St. George, Utah. In the early 1950s, St. George, 110 air miles away from the Nevada Test Site, had a population of 4,500. Elizabeth Catalan knows the consequences of the town's location:

> My family came to St. George when I was four. My father went there to teach the sciences at the high school and college and later became the president of the college.
>
> Before the atomic tests began, the air force and representatives from the AEC came to town and held a meeting in the high-school auditorium. We were told that we were a vital part of the national defense effort, and though the test site was close, there was no danger.
>
> At first, the test site officials always gave us twenty-four hours' notice before a blast. Bomb watching became the new pastime. We arose in the predawn hours and drove to the west side of Utah Hill outside of town and waited in the eerie darkness.
>
> Once you have watched an atomic blast, you never forget it. The sight attacks all the senses. I remember the awe of it: the intense light searing the sky, the rumble of sound traveling through and above the ground, and most incredible of all, the cloud rearing higher and higher in the sky before it begins to fan out into a mushroom of overwhelming proportions.

As the testing passed into weeks, then months, then years, we became less interested in watching the sky. A sort of laziness developed among the officials who were supposed to notify us before a detonation. Shots were postponed, and no further announcements issued. Winds seemed to be the overriding factor. If the winds were blowing south toward Las Vegas or west toward California, the tests were delayed. On the other hand, when the winds blew east, the bombs were exploded. We were the "downwind residents," but we just didn't know it.

Over the years I recall many window rattlings in my bedroom and the glows in the sky, but one particular explosion will always haunt me.

At 5:05 a.m. on May 19, 1953, a brilliant flash preceded the dawn. We were still asleep when Harry was detonated from a three-hundred-foot steel tower. The tower was vaporized into tiny airborne particles of radioactive iron and steel mixed with vaporized equipment, soil particles, and ground debris. The mass rose rapidly skyward in a dark, ugly, roiling fireball.

Obviously, this nuclear device was different. It sounded different, and, instead of mushrooming, the fireball rose and spread quickly. Airplanes sampling the cloud discovered immediately that it contained dangerous radioactive residue.

Soon offsite readings also were high, and it was apparent to AEC officials that the people of St. George should be warned of the airborne menace heading their way. The AEC wrestled with the perplexing problem of alerting us downwind residents to the danger without causing undue panic or fear. Unsure how to handle this problem, the AEC officials for a time did nothing. They finally decided to contact local safety units and the radio station so that a general warning could be issued. The news was broadcast on radio that a nuclear device had been detonated, creating a cloud of debris, and although it was headed toward St. George, we were assured there was no danger. People were urged to stay indoors for two hours as a precaution until the cloud had passed. The announcement was repeated, and it closed with the message "There is no danger."

My family was at home that noon when my father called. He had been told about the cloud's path and wanted my mother to keep us children indoors. Since he had been assured there was no real cause for alarm, he continued his day's business, in and out of doors all afternoon. Looking out the kitchen window, my mother could see the cloud, looking like a large thunderhead, dark, and ominous, spreading across the sky as it approached.

As Harry's cloud passed overhead, the AEC monitor in St. George became disturbed. He sampled the milk from the local dairies and found a high radioactivity reading. This was not a local problem any more, for although the milk was collected in St. George, most of it was trucked in to Las Vegas for processing and distribution. Some of the milk undoubtedly went to the Nevada Test Site.

The townspeople were edgy. They had been cautioned about fallout before, but never had they seen such an ugly, thick, darkness overhead. The AEC was edgy, too. Panic had to be avoided because a scared small town could bring adverse publicity, reflecting on the nuclear weapons testing program.

The AEC monitor took a second set of readings

on the milk coming out of St. George that afternoon. He called the Nevada Test Group in Las Vegas, and three men left for St. George immediately. The morning milkings had already been trucked to Las Vegas. Clearly the AEC had to control the situation. The monitor in St. George and the AEC men consulted, but still did nothing.

After the two-hour danger period had passed, the AEC issued an "all clear," and St. George went back to normal. The cloud had passed over, and residents believed there had been no danger.

By evening St. George was a dangerously radioactive area. The average monitored air concentration of radioactivity was five times higher than any level ever encountered in an inhabited area within two hundred miles of the test site. And the radioactivity was not contained because contaminated milk was moving to Las Vegas. The AEC understood the problem, but defined it this way: what is the cost of adverse publicity to the nuclear testing program? To warn St. George of its danger and recall the contaminated milk might bring undue alarm. The AEC solved the problem by ignoring radiation readings and allowing the milk to be distributed.

The cloud from Harry continued to drift eastward, and it passed over other small towns and farmlands. The fallout dusted cars, lawns, houses, and people. Particles of radioactive metals and debris drifted to the freshly tilled soil, plants, and grazing pastures. "Dirty Harry" was now part of the local food chain, and its radionuclides would eventually come to rest on the tables of people. Contamination already was in the milk.

My father, outdoorsman and always robustly healthy, was one of the first of many of our townspeople to die of leukemia. He was forty-eight years old. My little sister died at age thirty, cause undetermined. Entire families in this Mormon community have fallen to cancer and other degenerative diseases. One of my father's friends, Elmer Pickett, buried eleven members of his family.

There have been other health problems in our family. Not one of us, including me, has not had some serious illness to learn to live with.

Grable—Not Betty

And the military displayed a complacency bordering on recklessness about the hazards of aboveground testing. Civilian officials and the media are rarely eager to confront the military with charges of having made mistakes—yet mistakes there have certainly been.

—David E. Lilienthal, Chairman
Atomic Energy Commission
1950

Harry was Livermore's first success in the nuclear arena. The 1953 continental series in Nevada provided an invaluable learning experience for the laboratory's youthful scientists. Still to come was the most exciting event of the 1953 tests, shot Grable, which saw the world's first atomic projectile fired from a 280 mm cannon. The new artillery piece, able to fire either a conventional round or an atomic projectile, was successful in its first and only atomic attempt. Intended to destroy otherwise invulnerable fortifications and turn back the massed advances of communist troops, the cannon later was moved to the Far East, where it was an effective psychological weapon that helped end the war. Samuel Cohn, involved in nuclear weapons design at the Rand Corporation, said in 1980 that "Grable was an antipersonnel device achieving its effect through prompt nuclear radiation. The biological effects of radiation were sufficiently well understood to allow anyone to make the deduction that Grable was an antipersonnel weapon."

Fifteen minutes before Grable's firing at Frenchman Flat, seventy-five military physicians knelt in a sandbagged open bunker twenty-five hundred yards from where the 15-kiloton projectile was to explode. The doctors prepared themselves as the moment of detonation approached. One of them remembers:

> We were told to keep our back to the blast during the actual detonation. As soon as we heard the explosion, we were to turn around and witness the fireball ascending into the sky. We were told to run to within fifty yards of ground zero after that and retrieve food, water, and munitions samples that had been placed there. After we collected the specimens, the material was to be sent to a laboratory for evaluation of radiation and thermal effects.

At precisely 8:30 a.m. on a clear desert day, the physician's experiences began:

> Following the countdown to "one" there was a brilliant flash that I saw with my back turned to the blast and with my hands covering my eyes. I even saw the bones in my fingers. I felt intense heat on the back of my neck. When I turned around and opened my eyes, I was partially blinded by a light many times brighter than the sun. I think I turned around too soon, because I was blinded temporarily by watching the glowing fireball. Within seconds, all of us, as we had been instructed, began running toward ground zero to collect our specimens. I went

> all the way, and because I loved to run and was faster than my companions, I was the first to arrive at the fifty-yard marker.

Why would trained physicians expose themselves to such radiation? "Believe it or not, we didn't know the danger of what we were doing," said the doctor. "No one told us."

The doctor will never know how much exposure he received because he was not even issued a film badge. His experience is typical of that of many military nuclear weapons test participants. However, the designers of the nuclear devices knew what they were detonating. These men usually watched the explosions from ten to twelve miles away, and they were always upwind from the blast. The military participants, under the control of the Defense Department, were sent rushing into dangerously contaminated areas shortly after a blast. The emphasis was on the elimination of fear, and participants were encouraged to have a "love affair" with the bomb.

Within ten years after the physician's rush to ground zero, he developed neuromuscular problems and dimming vision. Today he is totally paralyzed and partially blinded by advanced cataracts.

Hot Spots and the Unexpected

> *I want to know. I want to know if the atomic tests killed my mother.*
>
> —Tim Barker
> son of Susan Hayward

At the Nevada Test Site, 1954 was a quiet year. Nuclear testing had returned to the Pacific Proving Grounds. Devices in the megaton range could not be tested in Nevada. To the east of the continental testing area, in a place called Snow Canyon, producer Dick Powell assembled a cast of two hundred twenty from Hollywood to film *The Conqueror*. Among the stars were John Wayne, Susan Hayward, and Agnes Moorehead. In addition to the cast, three hundred extras, primarily Shivwits Indians, a band of Utah Paiutes, were hired to portray wandering Mongolians. Unwittingly, the production was filmed twelve miles from St. George, Utah, at one of the offsite radiological "hot spots."

During breaks in filming, John Wayne and his sons, Michael and Patrick, used a Geiger counter on prospecting outings nearby. Michael Wayne said afterward that when his father used the Geiger counter and the instrument clicked, the Waynes thought the areas they were in contained some kind of ore. The thought of radioactivity from fallout never occurred to them, since they had no knowledge of the nuclear cloud's path. The cast and crew spent three months on location in Snow Canyon. When they went back to Hollywood to finish filming in a studio, they took sixty tons of desert rock and sand with them. The rock and sand were used to cover a large set in order to maintain the film's scenic continuity.

A statistically incredible ninety-one members of the cast of two hundred and twenty have contracted cancer, and forty-eight are dead, including Wayne, Powell, Hayward, and Moorehead. Shivwits extras have problems too. Many have died, and survivors live with the consequences of radiation.

Tesla

Today's shot, gentlemen, will be a 1.2-kiloton device.
—Loudspeaker announcement
Nevada Test Site, March 1, 1955

Jim O'Connor was a nineteen-year-old corporal assigned to the 232nd Signal Support Company, part of the permanent army detachment at the Nevada Test Site. O'Connor's company set up hand-laid communications networks from observer trenches to portable field switchboards. The switchboards were linked to a teletype terminal that relayed immediate postshot conditions to an army command post located several miles from the blast area. O'Connor's wire team usually operated far forward of the trench lines from which the main body of the troops observed the blasts. Often the wire team was in a planned detonation area the evening before a test.

O'Connor, who has an excellent memory, recalls Tesla:

> Tesla was one of those little shots. We were told it was expected to yield slightly more than one kiloton. It was originally planned to go off on February 25 but was postponed.
>
> My team's location was twenty-five hundred yards, or about a mile and a half from the three-hundred-foot tower.
>
> My position was eight feet to the rear of the switchboard bunker. The bunker was eight feet long and five feet wide. It was covered by planks of wood with a double layer of sandbags on top. I drove a three-quarter-ton truck that carried wire and other equipment. During the shots, I parked the truck in a sloping depression. I knelt next to the vehicle when the device was fired. I also used the truck as an emergency vehicle if there was a call for it.
>
> The night of February 28, a Marine Corps captain, sergeant, and twenty-four men arrived at our location. The officer told my first sergeant his contingent had permission to proceed two hundred yards forward of us. I thought those guys were crazy, but who the hell was I to question the captain. I told them that if there were any problems I'd come

down to their position in my truck and help out. The captain then took his men forward and stopped the group about two hundred yards away. Those guys started digging their own trenches. You could hear the sergeant barking out orders telling his men what to do. I had seen two atomic explosions, and I felt those marines had no idea what was in store for them. I couldn't believe people would come out to the site and dig their own trenches. Our trenches were dug by the army engineers who used trench diggers and the trenches were six feet deep.

We spent the night out there awaiting word that the shot would be fired.

O'Connor was kneeling by his truck when Tesla was fired:

I was blown into the side of the truck. I was stunned and had a nosebleed, but managed to get to my feet and stagger out of the trench. The first thing I saw was that the vehicle had been knocked over and was leaning against one of the sides of the depression. The canvas top covering the cab was on fire. The bed of the truck was covered with sand and partially buried; the bags on top of the switchboard bunker were even burning.

About that time Joe came out of the bunker, coughing and wheezing, and fell on the ground next to me. During the whole time we were together I never heard Joe say a swear word, but he looked at me then and said, "Jim, I am never going in that fucking hole again!" I grabbed him by the arm and pulled him up and told him we had to get the truck out. We started throwing sand on the canopy to put out the fire. Suddenly, my first sergeant appeared and started yelling at us to go help the marines. Hell, I had forgotten about the marines! I was concerned about the truck and myself. I was woozy and kind of weak-kneed, but I didn't argue. I stopped what I was doing and ran toward the marines' position. Two or three other guys from my wire team were ahead of me, and we were all running fast.

As I approached the marines' position, I feared the worst. I didn't see any movement. All I saw was mass confusion and some people who were partially buried. I tried to run faster and made it to the first pair of hands I saw. Man, what a fucking mess! All those marines were trapped. Lots of sand had been thrown into their holes on top of them. They must have been lying down facing the bomb when the thing exploded.

I had to pull one marine from his hole. He was obviously in shock, as he just looked at me with a blank stare and moved his head from side to side, not saying a word. His helmet had been knocked off. We started pulling the others out. Some of them freed themselves, but there was mass confusion. They were disoriented and in a state of shock. Some of the marines began walking back toward the switchboard bunker, while others moved in the direction of ground zero and the service road. Several sat in their holes and didn't move.

I thought, What the hell has gone on here? Where is some medical aid for these people? I saw that the service road had been damaged by the blast and no rescue vehicles could get through. Finally we assembled the marines and led them away to a utility road. Some trucks came and took them off in the desert. I never did learn what happened to them, and I didn't ask.

O'Connor and the rest of his team returned to their area and began cleaning up the debris. They put out the canopy fire, but the truck was wedged in the depression.

Three hours later, O'Connor became nauseated and began to vomit. The next day, his nose bled for a long time and he developed a high fever. He was sent to the infirmary, but was returned to the field within twenty-four hours.

Why did the Tesla test cause such serious problems? Later that day, the Atomic Energy Commission held its regularly scheduled meeting—number 1063—in Washington. Commissioner Murray asked Chairman Strauss, "Lewis, do you have any more information on Tesla?" The chairman replied, "We saw flash results which appeared to be six times larger than estimated. I hope there will not be anything like that in connection with Turk" (the next scheduled shot). Commissioner Murray said, "The point is that it was four or six times larger than Livermore thought it would be, though Bradbury at Los Alamos guessed it higher."

No one at the meeting asked questions about the safety of people at the test site exposed to the blast.

Tesla, another Livermore experiment that exceeded the planned yield by a factor of at least six, demonstrated yet again why no human beings should have been involved in such unpredictable events. But O'Connor and thousands like him would feel the effects of more nuclear errors before atmospheric testing would end.

The Other View

We simply are unwilling to concede that 3,200 of every 10,000 test participants who die of cancer . . . are [not] now developing the diseases that normally accompany late middle or old age.

—Lieutenant Colonel Hartman B. Mowery
Infantry Biomedical Effects Department
Defense Nuclear Agency

For thirteen years, a civilian employee worked in the field for the Atomic Energy Commission. Currently employed by a nuclear contractor, he must remain anonymous. He and his associates signed agreements before obtaining their top-secret clearances. They were never to discuss their duties or work with anyone outside their top-secret environment. If they did, they were subject to a ten-thousand-dollar fine and/or ten years' imprisonment. Even his wife didn't know what this employee did after he left home for Nevada or the Pacific. He has since come to some specific conclusions about test procedures:

> Every time I saw you military troops leaving your trenches and marching or attacking toward ground zero, I thought the act was a clear demonstration of military thinking that was stupid as hell. If they wanted to see whether or not you would vomit or fall over, they could have done other things rather than put you in a contaminated area without protection. You asked me if I was in Nevada during the 1957 Priscilla test. Well, I will never forget Priscilla because I was caught in the fallout. After I retrieved my instruments near ground zero, I left the area immediately. I stayed in an instrument retrieval area for three minutes maximum—only long enough to get the thing, put it in a lead box, and hightail it out of there.
>
> On my way back to Camp Mercury, the bright day became as dark as night. The cloud from the explosion was directly overhead. All of a sudden it was raining white-gray ash. The fallout was everywhere, and I closed all the vents in my car. I still had my respirator device on, because I was in the critical inhalation area. We considered the area from the lip of the crater out to a six-mile radius as the critical

inhalation area—an area where military troops conducted their maneuvers frequently after a blast. I didn't intend to allow any of the residue to get inside my car. The fallout stayed with me a long time, and when I reached Mercury I had to drive my car to the decontamination center. My automobile was really hot and had to be washed twice a day for four days, and even then after the washing the tires were registering a high radioactivity reading.

The AEC always had an elaborate system for decontamination of both our vehicles and our bodies. After we returned to camp we were checked immediately by radiological-safety specialists who went over us completely with a very sensitive instrument—much more sensitive than a Geiger counter. As soon as the radiological check was complete, we were then scrubbed with stout wire brushes and special detergents while still in our protective clothing. After the scrubbing, we were hosed off. We then went to a second hosing station and were hosed off again. Then we removed our protective clothing. If it was still radioactive, it was burned and we received a new issue.

After all that, we had our nose and ears swabbed to see if there were any radioactive contaminants present. Then we submitted a twenty-four-hour urine sample that was tested for plutonium and other radioactive isotopes. The procedure for decontamination and monitoring of contamination levels was consistently thorough.

We were not allowed a whole-body gamma exposure that exceeded 3.9 roentgens during a thirteen-consecutive week period. If we happened to receive a higher dosage, we were sent home for a while on emergency leave. The ridiculous thing is that the military, who didn't wear protective clothing, were allowed nearly double the exposure of our maximum safe level.

My primary job in Nevada was to retrieve instruments, but I had another assignment: I was in charge of the dogs. Before the shots, I would strap the dogs to the ceilings and walls of partially concealed bunkers. Those that were not strapped to the walls and ceilings were chained to the floor. After the shot, I went into the bunker to see how the dogs had fared. We had a quick test. A psychologist who worked with me taught the dogs tricks. After a shot, we had the dogs do their tricks. If they could still remember a trick, we spared them. If they could not, then we knew right away that the animals had been damaged. Those who were damaged were destroyed right away and examined scientifically to determine the effects of heat, blast, or radiation damage. The other animals were put to sleep within three weeks and autopsies were performed. They were checked specifically for plutonium inhalation.

Now, I want you to know that as far as I am concerned, my superiors did everything possible to assure our safety, but it may not have been enough. Some years after I left the field, I became ill and had my cancerous bladder removed. My doctor and I tried to get a pathology lab to reduce my bladder to ash and check it for plutonium. I'll never know if it was done. The lab kept the organ, but never let me know what was done with it.

Yeah, I have been able to keep track of many of the others who were there with me. About twenty people who were there are either ill or dead. I am talking about only those who worked with me in the field. It is very shocking when you think about it.

Because I'm a conscientious person who believes our government, I decided to call the toll-free number set up by the Defense Nuclear Agency in 1977 to help people who were exposed to atmospheric testing. Since I wanted to be specific and factual, two of my friends and I researched all the shots we took part in—dates and everything. We even wrote down the dosimeter readings we remembered from various tests. It took us about three weeks to assemble all this information. Once I had it, I called the toll-free number. I couldn't believe what an idiot they had on the other end of the line. He impressed me as some fourteen-year-old who had been borrowed from a local high school to answer the phone. Obviously, he had no grasp at all of what we were talking about or the information I was trying to give him. He kept asking me over and over again, "When were you tested, when were you tested?" "Tested," I thought. "Tested for what—mumps, measles, chicken pox, IQ or bunions?" I tried to tell him the names of the tests I had been in, but he interrupted quickly to ask, "When were you tested?" I stared at the phone and my disgust grew. I hung up without giving the guy any information. I had wanted to tell him I had cancer, the names of the tests I had witnessed, and the readings that had been recorded. I wanted to help the government collect important information. Instead, what an insult! None of my friends who are sick called that number after I told them what had happened.

If the government really wanted information, why the hell couldn't they have put somebody on the phone who knew what questions to ask?

I don't think that anyone in government will ever admit that the country's nuclear weapons program was responsible for our ill health. In comparison to you military people, we were well protected, but in retrospect, all of us should have been wearing lead suits like the cloud samplers of the late fifties did.

I have one last thing to say: It's a damn good thing I wasn't in the military, because I probably would have spent my life in Leavenworth. If anyone had ordered me to go to the close proximity of ground zero after a blast without protective clothing, I would have shot the son of a bitch right through the head.

From the Arkansas *Post Dispatch* of June 4, 1980:

The United States Government may be involved in a scandal, the magnitude of which would make such things as rampant influence peddling in President Ulysses S. Grant's administration, the Teapot Dome scandal, Watergate and the Korean payoff scandal seem like child's play.

Thousands of U.S. veterans and civilians who participated in nuclear weapons testing eighteen to thirty-five years ago believe such a scandal has and is taking place.

8.

The Reunion

Radiation makes no friends; it only creates enemies.
—Jess Clark
Atomic Veteran

I first learned of Orville Kelly's fledgling atomic veteran organization in August, 1979, when I heard Patricia Broudy interviewed on a Los Angeles radio program. She told how her husband, a former marine major, had been exposed to radiation during shots Priscilla and Hood—the same tests I had taken part in. Major Charles Broudy died of cancer in 1977, and his widow said she believed his death was a result of his exposure at the Nevada Test Site. I phoned Mrs. Broudy after the program and she told me about Orville Kelly.

At the time, my own life was falling apart. For several years I had lived with neuromuscular problems that no physician had been able to diagnose. By 1979, those problems were becoming progressively more debilitating. A four-day stay at one of the country's foremost diagnostic clinics told me nothing. As far as the medical profession was concerned, I was in perfect health. But I knew something was wrong.

There was no apparent reason why I should be feeling so poorly. Before resigning my commission in 1964, I had completed ranger, airborne, and an abbreviated version of scuba-diving school—three of the most physically demanding training programs in any of the services. After my Marine Corps years, I stayed in shape, running two or three miles a day and frequently playing long hard sets of singles tennis.

When my neuromuscular problems became worse, I got in touch with a cousin who had family medical records. A four-generation search of those records turned up no evidence of neuromuscular disorders.

Many of the physicians who examined me asked if I had ever been exposed to toxic chemicals. The only toxic substances I had ever been exposed to were those at the Nevada Test Site, and I related that fact to the doctors. But they knew nothing of what I conveyed.

And my health was not my only problem. My marriage was failing, and in an effort to salvage it, I had sold my electronics business. I thought that if I spent more time with my wife of thirteen years our marriage would improve, but it didn't. Then, like any entrepreneur who no longer runs the business that has filled his working life, I was feeling quite depressed.

So there I was—forty-three years old, divorced, and no longer employed. But I was obsessed; determined to learn if other nuclear test veterans were having the same kinds of physical problems I was. Finding them, however, was a long, often frustrating task. I came across the Defense Nuclear Agency's toll-free number. When I telephoned, I naïvely asked how I might reach other veterans. The answer was polite but evasive: "We don't give out that information; we only collect data." I later learned that I was one of more than 46,000 callers at that point.

After talking to Mrs. Broudy, I got in touch with Orville Kelly in Burlington, Iowa—a place I had never heard of. He told me he and his wife had recently incorporated the National Association of Atomic Veterans, which they had founded in April 1979. The organization's purpose was to help veterans who had problems caused by their involvement in nuclear testing. Kelly also told me that he had cancer and that many

NAAV members were ill. When I asked if any had undiagnosable neuromuscular problems he said, "Oh my God, yes! It's not uncommon for them to see anywhere from ten to twelve doctors looking for diagnosis and treatment with no luck."

We talked about many other things that day. This forceful person whom I had never met made a strong impression on me. He was already quite an authority on the problems of atomic veterans, and he let me know that we could expect virtually no help, either medical or financial, from the government. The Veterans Administration, he said, was "the most insensitive of all."

He sent me an association newsletter. Reading it was difficult and painful. I didn't think of myself as a veteran but as a citizen soldier who had spent three years serving his country. I was reluctant to relive a period of my life that was over twenty years in the past. If my health problems were radiation related, I had no idea what I might do about them. I did, however, resolve to discover if my suspicions were correct.

Something Is Wrong Here

Fallout . . . I am worried.
—Major L. S. Stephenson, USMC
at the Nevada Test Site after shot Priscilla

I didn't know much about the Defense Nuclear Agency, successor to the Manhattan Project. During the 1960s, it was called the Defense Atomic Support Agency; early in 1971, its name was changed to the present one. A fact sheet the agency sent me was reassuring. As far as official Washington was concerned, I had little to worry about as a consequence of my exposure at the test site. The fact sheet also told me that part of the agency's mission was to help veterans. I decided to write describing my Priscilla experience. I especially wanted to learn if the fallout that had drifted down on us after the detonation, burning a hole in my uniform, was anything to be alarmed about.

My answer came on March 14, 1980. Although it was intended to reassure me, I became more concerned than ever. A Colonel William McGee signed the letter, which said in part:

> The Marines were in trenches 4,250 yards from ground zero. Our records indicate that there was no fallout in the trench area. However, the shock wave from the trench area raised a large amount of sand, dirt and debris which was *not* radioactive. It is entirely possible that you and your battalion commander mistook this dust for fallout. Records indicate that the Marines visited the display area for a short period of time and then exited. Thus it appears unlikely that inhalation of radioactive particles occurred. The low external exposures of the Marines as evidenced on the film badges, would seem to demonstrate the effectiveness of the radiological safety measures.

The fallout plot that McGee sent me showed trenches where the colonel described them, and the path of Priscilla's cloud. However, I had an official Marine Corps equipment display and trench-line diagram. Our trenches were thirty-five hundred yards—slightly less than two miles—from ground zero, not where Colonel McGee's diagram showed they were. There may have been trenches forty-two hundred fifty yards from ground zero, but we weren't in them. I remembered specifically and vividly that after we left the trenches Major Stephenson and I were in a rain of fallout—tiny particles of whitish-gray ash fell on his right shoulder and lapel and on my right sleeve, leaving a burn. He had said distinctly, "We are receiving fallout, and I am worried."

Colonel McGee was clearly wrong when he said the dust that blew into our trenches was not radioactive. Priscilla was tested at Frenchman Flat, a barren, dry lake bed some six square miles in size. There had been nine atmospheric nuclear tests there before my arrival, as well as many safety experiments—nuclear explosions in which there is no fireball. Obviously, the area was saturated with residual radiation. And McGee's comments about the effectiveness of the radiological-safety measures really amused me. I'll never forget the AEC field worker who came running up to us, pointing at his instrument and waving his arm frantically ordering us to get the hell out of the area.

Obviously, the field worker did not think too highly of our radiological-safety measures; otherwise, he would not have become so alarmed.

Here was I, an eyewitness, being told I had not seen or experienced what I knew absolutely to be true. Colonel McGee must have relied on accounts by people who had not been there. As soon as I read his letter, I resolved to find out if others were being replied to as I had been. Months passed, and I collected a great deal of material. I learned to use the Freedom of Information Act to pry loose buried documents, and I did a great deal of telephoning and corresponding.

While I was in the midst of this, I met Orville Kelly for the first time in Los Angeles in December 1979. Kelly, with his wife Wanda, and Pat Broudy with her attorney, Ronald Bakal, joined me for a press conference at the Greater Los Angeles Press Club. Kelly had positive news. He had just been awarded radiation-related, service-connected disability compensation by the Veterans Administration. The twelfth successful claimant, he had set a vital precedent: he was the first veteran to be awarded compensation without having exhibited symptoms while on active duty. I answered questions about my Nevada Test Site experiences. Afterward a reporter told me about Jim O'Connor, veteran of the 1955 Nevada tests, a local man who has a serious muscle disorder.

The next day, the Kellys and I held another press conference in San Diego. As Kelly told what it had been like to be a nuclear test participant, I watched the audience's reaction. Shock, horror, and disbelief were mirrored in their faces. As previously, we asked for help in finding others who had shared our experiences. A reporter for the *San Diego Union* came to me afterward and told me about two men who lived nearby, both of whom had bone deterioration problems. One had been a cloud sampler and the other a diver.

I talked later to the former diver, Charles Fleming, who told me his bones were "turning to powder." He had been at Eniwetok in 1951. His group's mission had been to dive in the lagoon and bring up instruments that measured the effects of underwater blasts. The divers usually did this within two weeks after an explosion, as soon as the water was no longer considered radioactive. Fleming had called the Defense Nuclear Agency to tell them what he had done and what was happening to him. The agency offered no help, even when he mentioned that he was the last survivor of his diving team.

> *Look to your health; and if you have it, praise God and value it next to a good conscience.*
>
> —Izaak Walton

Early 1980 was a particularly trying time. I kept looking for medical answers, going from one specialist to another. I was changing gradually from Tom Saffer into "the interesting case." I could find no physician in my part of California who had ever examined someone exposed to ionizing radiation from nuclear tests. None knew what to make of me.

I became more and more frustrated. One doctor said, "Tom, I've checked you for the five thousand known diseases, and you don't have any of them!" Another told me, "You'll just have to consider yourself cursed." It all boiled down to being told there was not much anybody could do. Whatever was happening to me evidently was beyond medicine's experience.

In desperation, I turned to the government for help and went to a VA hospital. After I waited for hours, an internist finally saw me. I didn't know it, but he'd been assigned to deal with a special class of atomic veterans. The Defense Nuclear Agency had identified a group that had received radiation exposure of twenty-five or more rems at nuclear tests and advised each by letter to have a physical. When I was being processed at the VA hospital, they asked me, "Did you get a letter from the Defense Nuclear Agency?" I had not received the letter in question, but, thinking they meant the letter from Colonel McGee about Priscilla, I said I had.

The VA doctor who examined me was arrogant and hostile at first. He glowered at me and snapped:

> This whole thing is a big waste of the taxpayers' money. I've been ordered to give you men physicals and write these time-consuming long reports. The files will end up in a government vault and gather dust. Nobody, including me, knows anything about the effects of radiation exposure. Japanese exposed during the war are still dying, and nobody knows how long that will last. It'll probably be another fifty years before we know about the effects of radiation, too late to do any of you veterans any good.

He checked me over thoroughly, nevertheless, and as he did

he mellowed. We had physician friends in common and he lived near me. When he finished, he said, "Well, you have problems but I don't think you have cancer."

I asked anxiously, "What kind of problems?"

"Well, I'd rather not say because I don't want to alarm you," he replied.

I began to lose my composure. "Doctor, I beg you to tell me what you suspect is wrong. I've been to nearly twenty doctors and not one has given me a diagnosis."

The VA doctor looked at me, sighed, and said, "I think you have multiple sclerosis, maybe caused by radiation, maybe not." He went on to tell me there was no prognosis and no cure.

I dressed and left, not really shocked or depressed. Most of all, I was relieved that someone finally had told me I was not imagining my symptoms.

Once you've been told you have an incurable disease, you have some but not many choices. One of mine was to explore alternative medicine, to discover if I could improve my health without resorting to conventional treatment, since there was none. My other choice was to make every effort to find other atomic veterans who might have symptoms like mine. As time went on, I would make considerable headway in both endeavors. The VA doctor was wrong. I did not have multiple sclerosis. As for atomic veterans, there were far more than I suspected, and many of them did indeed have symptoms like mine.

Nightmares

These . . . things I saw, and a great part of them I was.

—Virgil
Aeneid

Orville Kelly called one evening in February. He'd had a letter from a marine who had been at the Nevada Test Site in 1957, maybe at shot Hood. "I can't tell you all he wrote over the phone," Kelly said, "but I think you ought to get together."

That weekend I drove to Santa Barbara to see Israel Torres. A retired sergeant who had been awarded the Silver Star for heroism in Korea, he had been at Desert Rock with the Fourth Marine Provisional Atomic Exercise Brigade. Torres had difficulty moving around or talking. He wore leg, arm, and back braces. He had lost most of his teeth, all of his hair, and his sight was failing. He looked much older than forty-six.

He wanted to call me captain, even after I told him to call me Tom. As a career marine, that kind of respect had been drilled into him. However, I didn't want him to feel our session was one in which a noncom was being interrogated by an officer. Rather, we were two former servicemen comparing our experiences. And his had been much worse than mine.

This was when he told me the story that appears in chapter 2, about how his trench line had collapsed at shot Hood, two of his men had been missing afterward, and military radiation monitors had dismissed him with, "Man, you've had it." I showed him one of the products of my research, a July 7, 1957, Salt Lake City *Deseret News* story that read in part, "A unit of 2,000 marines who participated in the test entrenched about three miles from ground zero withstood the blast without harm."

Torres smiled. "Well Tom, that may be what that paper said, but that writer wasn't in my trench. I know differently."

I read on: "Seismographs at Cal Tech in Pasadena, California, recorded the blast one minute after detonation. Hood had the force of a large earthquake."

If that much force had been recorded four hundred miles

away, I told Torres, I was surprised more trenches hadn't caved in three miles from ground zero. Then I got more specific. "Israel," I asked, "have you any idea how much radiation you received? Have you ever tried to get your film badge reading?"

He had tried and gotten nowhere. "I wrote to the corps in November 1979, and asked for my reading," he said. "Others in the brigade had gotten theirs, and I was hopeful. The corps wrote back two months later, and I have their letter right here." He read from it: "While no individual record of radiation exposure at Hood is known to exist for you, the recorded doses for other members of Company 'E' ranged from 0.500 to 0.980 rem, gamma. As a point of comparison, this range of exposure may be compared with the 0.700 rem, gamma, dose received from a clinical X-ray at this time."

I added, "Israel, that's interesting, because every member of the brigade I know of has been told his film badge reading."

Could the fact that Torres may have received a lethal radiation dose have been the reason his was "not known to exist"?

Or, I said, something else might have happened. Many film badges at Hood were lost or destroyed. I'd been told that a unit from the Lexington, Kentucky, Depot was supposed to record badge readings. The unit never got to the Nevada Test Site or was understaffed. Marines were dragged in haphazardly to do the film badge dosimetry. The tent set up for them to work in was blown over, and badges scattered across the desert. If what I had been told was true, I said to Torres, his could have been one of the lost badges, ". . . or perhaps those of you who had high doses aren't supposed to know what your exposure was."

Torres asked me what my own exposure was. I told him it had been one of the highest recorded at the shot, 0.960 or nearly 1 rem, and that I had doubts about that. Dr. Karl Morgan was on the staff of the Oak Ridge National Laboratory during the 1950s and 1960s and spent considerable time at the test sites. He has said that film badge readings were inaccurate by as much as 1,000 percent.

I had brought along several other items I had turned up in my research. I showed Torres a clipping from the July 1957 issue of *Leatherneck*, the official Marine Corps magazine. It set the stage for other material I wanted Torres to see. Titled "The Biggest Shot," the *Leatherneck* article said: "Radiological safety teams were dispatched to ground zero [after Hood] to check for radioactivity. There was none." So much for the official version.

Then, another version of the story. I showed Torres a report prepared by a scientist who had studied the neutron dose at Hood. The report projected that the estimated neutron dose at 1,000 yards from ground zero after the Hood shot was "20,000 rads" (over 3,000 times our allowable maximum dosage).

Then I showed him *The Radiation Safety Monitor's Reference Handbook*, a publication dated February 1956. Used to instruct the military's radiation-safety officers, it said, "In an air burst the . . . neutrons reaching the earth . . . are enough to produce a lethal radiation dosage up to about seven hundred yards from ground zero." So much for the Marine Corps assertion that Hood produced *no* radioactivity. The government's own publications showed that radiation in fact was enormous in an area surrounding ground zero; an area in which marines were *ordered* to maneuver immediately after the shot.

My brief dissertation bewildered Torres, especially when I reminded him that his E company had gone to within four hundred yards of ground zero to establish a helicopter landing zone almost while Hood's echoes were still reverberating. "Why didn't they tell us, Tom," he asked. "Why didn't they tell us how contaminated it was out there?"

I told him that we had not been warned because they didn't want us to know; that the supposed value of the military's involvement in the tests would have been greatly lessened if the public and the participants knew the dangers. Then I got to the real point of my visit. I asked Torres to tell me the things he had written about in his letter to Orville Kelly, the things that had happened at the test site immediately after Hood's detonation, and after his unit got back to Camp Pendleton. He sipped from a glass of water and began his story:

> I kept vomiting off and on after the exercise. My vision was blurred and I was in one hell of a lot of pain. My private hell began as soon as we got back to Camp Pendleton. None of my superiors would talk to me about my two missing men. I never had a chance to look for them. They put me in the hospital because of my back pain and vision problems.
>
> I was having nightmares about my missing men and about something else horrible I'd seen out there in the desert after we'd been decontaminated and were in our trucks. We'd only gone a short way when one of my men said, "Jesus Christ, look at that!" I looked where he was pointing, and what I saw horrified me. There were people in a stockade—a chain-link fence with barbed wire on top of it. They looked like zombies, with deformed hands and faces. Their hair was falling out and their skin seemed to be peeling off. They were wearing blue denim trousers but no shirts. When we passed those people—there were ten or twelve—they tried to cover their faces with their hands. They looked more dead than alive, but they were alive! Good God, it was scary.
>
> While I was in the hospital I told my nurse what

I'd seen. She told me not to worry, she'd tell the doctor. The next day when he looked in on me, he said, "The nurse told me a most unusual story. What about those people you say you saw at the test site in Nevada?" I told the story again and he said, "That's quite a story. We'll talk about it later."

The next morning they wheeled my bed to a room off the ward. My doctor was there with a second one. They never told me who the other one was, but I think he was a psychiatrist. They asked me questions for more than three hours, trying to find out who was with me, and who could corroborate my story about the people I had seen. I gave them the names of some of the other marines who were with me in the truck. At the end, one of the doctors said, "You're imagining all this. What you say you saw simply could not and did not happen."

The next morning, three doctors questioned me. One said he was going to hypnotize me and that nothing bad would happen. He tried to hypnotize me but couldn't, and he really chewed me out for not cooperating.

A couple of nights later they woke me up and gave me a pill to "help you rest more comfortably." The next morning, they took me to the Balboa Naval Hospital in San Diego. Later that day, they strapped me in my bed and wheeled me to a room where there were four men. The only one I recognized was a corpsman from the hospital at Camp Pendleton. There were more questions. "Where were you born?" "What's your religion?" "What's your rank and serial number?" I was nervous and uncomfortable, but I answered all the questions.

Finally, one of them asked me what I'd seen at the

> test site, and I told the story of the people behind the chain-link fence again. They told me I imagined I saw those people. I said I was telling the truth, and offered to take a lie detector test. They ignored my offer and went on asking questions. One of them called me a liar, and forced a large pill down my throat. I was still strapped down and had to swallow it or choke. I must have been kept drugged for days, because I woke up back at Camp Pendleton in the hospital. The day I left to return to my unit a doctor told me not to repeat the "bizarre" story about the people I'd seen. He said if I did, he'd see to it I was thrown out of the corps.

Torres was glad to be out of the hospital, but he was in no shape to carry out the demanding job of a platoon sergeant. He was still groggy, nauseated much of the time, and had lost strength in his arms and legs. Back at Pendleton he became a loner, avoiding his fellow noncoms. He worried about his future and said nothing more about his two missing men or the people he had seen behind the wire enclosure.

What had he seen? No one who knows the full story has talked about it, and no documentation has surfaced. But Torres is not the only one to tell such a story about what he saw while he was at Camp Desert Rock.

After he got back to Camp Pendleton, his superiors couldn't decide what to do with Torres. Soon he was back in the hospital, complaining of dizziness, double vision, severe headaches, and muscle spasms. Released four months later, he was told his problems were psychological, not physical. Within two weeks he collapsed and was rushed to the base hospital for emergency back surgery. As soon as he was able, he rejoined his company for the third time in the year since he had been at shot Hood. He had been to sick call and in the hospital so often that a doctor told him he had better shape up or his rank would be frozen.

Alarmed at the possibility of never being promoted again, Torres stopped reporting to sick call and pushed himself to keep up with his company. A new regimental commander took over the Fifth Marines. He ordered the regiment to make a hundred-mile hike with full equipment. Torres remembers the grueling march:

> I didn't want to leave the Marine Corps. It was my whole life and had given me opportunities I never would have had as a civilian. To prove I was dedicated and physically fit, I made the hike with forty pounds of gear on my back. I was in considerable pain. The day after the hike I was back in the hospital with the same problems, only this time worse. I couldn't walk at all. My whole body was numb. I had more back surgery. While I was in the hospital, my company first sergeant came to see me and told me not to give up the fight. He said he knew I was in such bad shape because of the nuclear test, but that nobody would admit it.
>
> He told me the two men I had not seen since the trench cave-in had died of "complications." Their next of kin had been told they died during a training exercise. The Nevada Test Site had not been mentioned. The first sergeant presented me with the Boondocker Supreme Award for having finished the hundred-mile hike. His eyes misted as he did it, and I cried. It was the last award I ever got from the corps.

Torres was well on the way to becoming a shattered man. What his beloved corps had done to him meant he could no longer stay in it. He had been spending nearly 80 percent of his time on light duty at Camp Pendleton. In November 1963 he was told he was being recommended for a medical discharge and assured that release from active duty was not due to any intentional misconduct or willful neglect of duty. He was sent home on indefinite leave and, on February 1, 1964, permanently retired from the corps.

He could have accepted what happened had he been wounded in combat, for that would have meant his career had ended for a soldierly reason. As it was, he had been injured in a foolhardy field exercise, a fact the corps refused to admit. In the aftermath of that injury he had been ridiculed and treated cruelly. A new form of agony followed discharge. Torres had a predictably hard time adjusting to civilian life, and his health continued to get worse. The only advantage to being out of the corps was that he could keep trying to prove what he knew to be true without fearing reprimand or retaliation. He was more determined than ever to confirm what he had seen behind the wire enclosure, and to discover what had happened to his two men.

He wrote to his U.S. Representative, Democrat Richard T. Hanna of California, describing what he had seen and asking for a congressional investigation. A perfunctory reply came back, assuring him that staff would look into the matter. Torres never heard from Hanna's office again. He decided his efforts were useless and gave up—for a long time. Sixteen years later, he decided to renew his campaign to prove that his health problems were caused by radiation, that he had lost two men to the bomb, and that he had seen strange, mutilated people in a stockade after Hood. He still got nowhere.

I had listened quietly to Torres with growing amazement. Was what he said true? If he was not imagining these things, how was I going to corroborate his stories? I didn't know, but I resolved to try. We shook hands and I left, promising to keep in touch.

In April 1980, I went to the Marine Corps Historical Center in Washington, D.C., to study the unit diary reports of E company. After two days of looking at microfilm, I had traced the company roster from June 17, 1957, to February 1959. Although I read each daily report, I didn't discover any fatalities. I did learn that two men from E company had been in and out of the hospital for several months after shot Hood. Their revolving-door stays reminded me of Torres's. Finally, one was kept in the hospital until he was released from active duty and assigned to the Ninth Marine Corps Reserve District. Further research hit a dead end. I decided to stop trying to confirm the fatalities, but before I did I made one last phone call.

One of my former platoon members now lives in the Midwest. When he was a twenty-one-year-old PFC we knew him as an out-of-place young intellectual. When I reached him I asked, "Did you ever hear of any injuries during the Hood exercise?"

Without hesitating he answered, "Yeah, two marines were killed on impact."

I was taken aback at this sudden confirmation. "What?" I asked. "Are you sure?"

He said:

> Yes, I'm positive. They panicked when the thing went off and jumped up and tried to get out of their trench. This meant they were hit by the full force of the shock wave. The trench walls were collapsing and they were overwhelmed by rock, dirt, dust, heat, and the blinding light from the fireball. They died later. Lots of guys in the Fifth Marines knew about this.

Only a Memory Away

Doomsday is the eighth day of the week.

—Stanley Kunitz

One document that would clear up the confusion about what happened to the brigade at shot Hood is the after-action report. Challenged to produce it, the corps still has not done so, despite a three-year search. Either it was never written, or it was destroyed, or else it has been lost. I am puzzled by my discovery that there is no official report of the activities of the largest Marine Corps Atomic Exercise Brigade ever assembled. The three brigades that had been to the Nevada Test Site before ours produced such reports.

The brigade's recommendations after shot Hood do exist, however. In the absence of an after-action report, they provide some background for determining what happened and, more important, shed some light on just how misguided and uninformed the military was about nuclear testing and its role in it.

A major brigade recommendation was that future atomic field maneuvers involve "stockpiled"—that is, in the inventory—weapons instead of "the scientific testing of a nuclear device." *All* weapons detonated during the tests from 1945 to 1962 were experimental, quasi prototypes, not weapons being manufactured. Livermore Laboratory, which designed Hood, did not begin to stockpile weapons until late 1958.

What the brigade recommendation was implying, without coming out and actually saying so, was that there had been a number of unexpected problems after Hood and that thus it might be wiser in the future to use weapons whose results were more predictable.

This indicates that the corps may have failed to understand what was going on in nuclear weapons development. Since all the weapons exploded at the test sites were experiments, not demonstrations of already perfected weapons, the military could not expect to use them as occasions to develop tactics for a future nuclear war. That war presumably would be fought with stockpiled weapons, not experiments such as shot Diablo, which completely misfired.

The generals and Pentagon officials did not make the distinction. They insisted that troops take part in events that used the test site as an outdoor laboratory for experiments in which literally anything might happen. The AEC understood the risks, and was reluctant to have anyone other than its own trained, protected people involved in the tests. The nuclear scientific community opposed the military's remorseless determination to expose troops to radiation during experiments. All-powerful at the time, however, the military regularly overcame the scientists' objections.

Another of the Fourth Brigade's post-Hood recommendations was that all field-grade officers (majors and above) take part in future nuclear exercises.

At times the corps' nuclear dreams took on an almost *Dr. Strangelove* quality. One guts-and-glory general was especially enthusiastic at the prospect of using low-yield nuclear devices as tactical weapons. He wanted to have a 1-kiloton weapon detonated inside Camp Pendleton itself. Fortunately, the AEC turned down his request. Had the general had his way, people in Oceanside, California, the community next to the base, might well have shared the harrowing experiences of those living in St. George, Utah.

The seventeen-year nuclear weapons atmospheric testing program was a staggering example of man's inhumanity to man. The unwitting participants were fit and dedicated young servicemen—the nation's finest. They never dreamed they were being used in experiments that would result in untold physiological and psychological harm.

They were proud to wear the uniform and serve their country. They were placed at the test sites during a time when urgency to advance technology completely overshadowed moral responsibility. No one needed to take part in atmospheric testing. The effect of nuclear detonations on people and equipment could have been determined as well—better—by evaluating data gathered by instruments at the test sites in laboratories afterward. As Dr. Gerald Johnson has said, "It was an environment where no one should have been present except people who were trained and protected, people who were thoroughly schooled and who knew the potential danger of their assignment."

A military exercise may fail without serious consequences to the service involved. But what of participants whose lives are abruptly and permanently ruined because of a terrible accident, or worse, the incompetence and stupidity of those in charge? After shot Hood, Israel Torres did everything humanly possible to pull himself back together so he could continue his chosen career in the corps. The corps, which was responsible for his desperate situation, turned on him, reviled him, and in the end would have none of him. After all these years, a last turn of the screw was finally to crush Torres: in August 1980, he learned that he has leukemia. Taps for another career marine, sacrificed in the mindless quest for nuclear supremacy? No official has even admitted that his disease is radiation-related. As Torres says:

> I tried to make the Marine Corps my career, but the bomb changed all that. After I was given those pills in San Diego, almost everything went blank until one night years later, when I started having nightmares about those people I saw. Human beings treated like experimental animals. And I feel responsible for the death of those two boys. They were in my platoon and I led them into the trenches. The nightmares are horrible. Since the bomb I have been living a life of hell on earth.

I cannot prove it, but I am nearly certain that we members of the brigade were exposed to one of the early neutron bomb experiments. As Gladwin Hill in the July 6, 1957, *New York*

Times put it: "The device was not a weapon model but a nuclear assembly designed to try new development ideas."

I was able to corroborate the story Israel Torres told me about the two marines who may have died as a result of the Hood experiment by talking to my friend in the Midwest.

What about the other story? Was there indeed human experimentation at the Nevada Test Site during the atmospheric testing program as Torres says? Experimentation, that is, involving people other than the thousands of servicemen who were needlessly exposed to the effect of the bombs? Sadly, there is a strong indication that there may have been.

When he told me his story, Torres had no idea that another Nevada Test Site veteran had tried to bring about an investigation of a human-experimentation incident much like the one he had witnessed. Jim O'Connor, a California atomic veteran, was part of the permanent party at Camp Desert Rock during the mid-1950s. His nuclear human-experimentation experience was even more horrifying than Torres's.

The night before a large detonation in 1955, O'Connor told me, he saw people being put in a bunker several hundred yards closer to ground zero than his position. Immediately after the early-morning shot, O'Connor tried to get to the bunker. As he got close he smelled burning flesh. When he was within approximately fifty yards, he saw what he described as a human being writhing behind the bunker. The man was in terrible condition, bleeding from ears, nose, and mouth. He was trying to tear away wires attached to his head. O'Connor was horrified and started to leave, but, overcome by heat from the bomb, he partially collapsed.

Soon he was jerked upright by two men wearing protective radex clothing. They threw him into the back of a jeep and took him to the infirmary at Nellis Air Force Base. He, like Torres, described what he had seen and was given "calming" drugs. O'Connor returned to active duty three weeks later, and can remember little that happened during the rest of his time at Camp Desert Rock.

One thing he does remember, though, was that he was taken to an army camp after spending a few days in the infirmary at Nellis Air Force Base. O'Connor was assigned to a psychiatrist who showed strange movies to the young soldier. Jim recalls that each time he began to relate what he had seen at the bunker the physician would say, "It's time to see a movie, Jim." What movies! O'Connor states that first there would be a flash of a Disney character like Mickey Mouse, then Tojo, then Donald Duck, then Hitler, then someone's mother, followed by segments of the bombing of Hiroshima. O'Connor saw these movies every day for approximately ten days. Today he believes he was being deprogrammed.

Neither O'Connor nor Torres has been able to learn if what they saw were human, where the "people" came from, or why they were there. For years, O'Connor has bombarded authorities urging an investigation of what he saw. He has gotten absolutely nowhere, and the event remains a mystery. At one point, when he was pressing for an investigation by the army, O'Connor was told by Major Alan Skerker at the Pentagon, "Jim, we don't know what it may have been. We can neither confirm nor deny what you say you saw."

In the years since, O'Connor has more or less resigned himself to the fact that his mystery will never be resolved. He said recently that he wasn't going to talk about it any more, that people were beginning to look upon him as some kind of nut.

O'Connor and Torres have never met. The incidents each describes occurred two years apart. The two independent accounts do raise questions about the full extent of experimentation carried on at the Nevada Test Site. The weapons themselves were experiments. Servicemen sent there to witness the detonations were, in a sense, part of a monstrous military experiment, although that fact dawned on them only later. Animals—dogs, pigs, sheep, monkeys—were purposely exposed at the detonations. Is it possible there were wired-for-instrumentation humans?

The entire scope of what occurred at the Nevada Test Site probably will never be known. It is in the interest of those who were in charge to preserve the tightest security—if need be, forever.

Bob Alvarez and Howard Rosenberg have discovered and reported a National Aeronautics and Space Administration experiment involving terminally ill people. Nearly a hundred of them were exposed to high levels of radiation in chambers at Oak Ridge, Tennessee, between 1960 and 1974. Rosenberg says the patients were told they were being treated with radiation in hopes of improving their condition. In fact, the tests probably were carried out to discover how much radiation astronauts could absorb before becoming ill or nauseated. The project was financed jointly by NASA and the AEC.

Another experimentation study began in 1955. Dr. Eugene Saenger, chief of the radioisotope laboratory at the University of Cincinnati Medical Center, was in charge of a project in which eighty-seven cancer patients were given doses of as much as 250 rads (roentgens) of half-body and whole-body radiation during a sixty-minute period. The study was carried out in the name of "cancer research," but in 1960 the Defense Atomic Support Agency, predecessor to the Defense Nuclear Agency, awarded a $650,000 contract to the Cincinnati project, to determine the amounts of radiation a soldier could withstand before his combat effectiveness was impaired.

Countdown Zero

A Public Statement

You men . . . were victims of a stupid mistake made by stupid men.

—Dr. Karl Z. Morgan
Health Physicist

Early in 1980, I was invited by the National Committee for Radiation Victims to testify on behalf of atomic veterans at a public hearing to be held in Washington, D.C., that April. The group asked that I spell out our charges against the Defense Nuclear Agency and the Veterans Administration. The appearance was highly unusual for me. I had never spoken out against government agencies, and I approached the hearing with considerable trepidation. I actually feared government retaliation.

I had heard of people who had been threatened by the government because they criticized it for not adequately protecting them from radiation and for not telling them the truth about the potential danger of their radiation exposure. One veteran told me he had such an experience while on active duty. In the late 1970s, while a chief petty officer in the navy, Gene King began to have physical problems and he related them to his having taken part in a "nuclear experiment" off Christmas Island in the Pacific in 1962.

King said he was on an operating table in 1977 for a spinal block during a procedure to remove a growth in his colon when he became aware of three men standing off to his left. He could see only their legs and noted that they were wearing civilian clothes.

One of the men said, "Chief, how much money do you want—five thousand dollars, ten thousand, twenty-five thousand, fifty thousand?"

King tried to raise his head to look at the man, but one of the others moved to his side and held his head down.

The questioner repeated, "How much money do you want?"

King answered, "I don't want one damn cent! What I want is for you to admit that radiation caused the problems that are forcing me to retire early."

The unidentified man snapped, "That's a very poor attitude. Are you sure it isn't money you're after?"

King said angrily, "Hell no, I already told you all I want is the truth. I want an official admission that I'm a radiation victim."

There was a pause. Then, King says, the anonymous questioner blurted, "Well, we'll just have to kill him then."

At that point the physician exclaimed, "Not in my operating room you don't!"

The men left, and a shaken Gene King never learned who they were.

I also talked to Dr. John Gofman, who was threatened by the government. When Dr. Gofman agreed to become director of the biomedical department of the Lawrence Livermore Laboratory in 1963, he told the laboratory director, "I won't take the job unless I'm guaranteed I will have scientific freedom." The director assured him he would never be asked to compromise his scientific or medical ethics. He was assigned to investigate and report on the overall effects of radiation on humans.

Dr. Gofman completed the study in fall 1969 and reported his findings in a speech to the Institute of Electrical and Electronic Engineers. He told the audience his study showed that all forms of human cancer can be induced by radiation, that there is a linear-percentage cancer increase per unit of radiation exposure, and that children are far more susceptible to radiation-induced cancer than older people. He also reported that his study indicated that the cancer hazard from radiation was twenty-five times greater than he or anyone had previously suspected.

Dr. Gofman and his associates calculated that if everyone

in the country were exposed to the then federally listed permissible dose of radiation of 170 millirems (.170 rems) a year, there could be as many as thirty-two thousand more annual cancer cases. In other words, the smallest amount of low-level ionizing radiation not only could cause cancer but undoubtedly would.

Three weeks later Dr. Gofman delivered an expanded version of his speech at a congressional hearing in Washington. When he finished, a Joint Committee on Atomic Energy aide told him that the committee chairman, Representative Chet Holifield of California, wanted to see him.

Dr. Gofman describes the meeting:

> Art Tamplin [a Gofman associate at Livermore] and I were taken to a special security-cleared room where members of the committee were waiting. Art and I sat at a green table opposite Holifield, who asked, "What the hell do you guys think you are doing to the Atomic Energy Commission's program?"
>
> He then berated us at length. When he finished, one of the aides said, "Mr. Holifield, these are two highly respected scientists from Livermore." Holifield replied, "I don't give a damn who they are. They're going to have every little old lady in tennis shoes in this country up in arms against the AEC program."
>
> I tried to explain that the AEC had sponsored the study and that I was sure our research was sound. The congressman leaned over, looked me in the eye, and said, "Listen, there have been lots of guys before you who tried to interfere with the AEC program. We got them, and *we'll get you!*"
>
> I knew then that the AEC's claim that it wanted to know the truth about radiation was completely

phony and that Holifield had become a creature of those he supposedly was regulating.

Within two years, John Gofman's research funds had been cut off and his staff assigned to other projects. He left Livermore in 1972 and returned to his professorship at the University of California at Berkeley.

Another incident was on my mind as I was about to testify. A friend had told me about a reporter who wrote an uncomplimentary story about the Defense Nuclear Agency. The story said that the agency claimed that part of its mission was to investigate each atmospheric test, assess the radiation dose received by each military participant, and provide information to veterans to use in Veterans Administration claim proceedings. It went on to quote a public information officer at the agency: "These guys, the veterans, are getting old enough so that they are just getting sick from being on the good old earth. Somebody has convinced them to blame all their illnesses on radiation."

After the story was published, the reporter called the spokesman and asked if he was upset over it. The alleged reply: "I don't get upset, I just get even."

The incidents I had personal knowledge of, coupled with the government's generally hostile attitude whenever someone cast doubts on the wisdom of the atmospheric testing program, caused me to reflect long and hard before I testified. The evening before the hearing, I met Utah people who lived downwind from the Nevada Test Site, uranium miners, Marshallese, men and women who had worked at the Nevada Test Site, fellow atomic test veterans, and men who had been ordered to Hiroshima and Nagasaki to clean up and restore order after the bombs were dropped. I will never forget the experience. There were hundreds of us, all radiation casualties, representing thousands of other radiation victims. I certainly found myself among my peers.

There had been speculation as to whether the government knew that the Hiroshima and Nagasaki cleanup veterans had been exposed to harmful radiation. This speculation ended when someone read aloud a story from a 1945 Los Angeles *Examiner*, quoting Dr. Harold Jacobson of the Oak Ridge Laboratory. The day after the first bomb was dropped, he had said:

> Any Japanese who tries to ascertain the extent of the damage caused by the atomic bomb in Hiroshima is committing suicide. The terrific force of the explosion irradiates every piece of matter in the area. Investigators in a contaminated area will become infected with secondary radiation which breaks up the red corpuscles in the blood. People will die much the same way leukemia victims do.

On Saturday, April 12, I was the third person to testify. While waiting for my turn I listened to Elizabeth Catalan and Preston Truman tell the sad stories of deaths and illnesses in their families. Both lived downwind from the Nevada Test Site as children.

Now it was my turn. I was introduced by the chairman, Harvard professor Everett Mendlesohn. I sat behind a small table covered with microphones and tried to see the audience through the glare of television lights. I knew the hearings were being broadcast live by public radio, and I wondered exactly who would be listening.

I spent the first few minutes telling about my experiences at the Priscilla and Hood shots, and then I briefly described my current physical problems. I explained that atomic veterans had had no government help and told about Defense Nuclear Agency and Veterans Administration hostility toward us. I said that, despite two congressional hearings dealing with our exposure at the test sites, nothing positive had happened.

After eight or nine minutes, I came to the part of my presentation that I hoped would have the greatest impact. I had a letter to Orville Kelly from Dr. Irwin Bross, director of the Biostatistics Laboratory at the Roswell Park Memorial Institute in Buffalo, an authority on the health effects of ionizing radiation. I said, "Is it any wonder atomic veterans are upset, why we feel we are used, and why we are angered by the abuses we suffer? We have asked ourselves and others many, many times why this stonewalling and coverup is occurring, and I think we finally have at least a partial answer." Then I read from Dr. Bross's letter:

> As you probably know, it is in the record that President Eisenhower made a decision in 1955 setting a policy of deliberately confusing the public on the hazards of fallout and ionizing radiation exposure. The cornerstone of the policy was official sanction for the myth that low-level ionizing radiation was harmless. This myth has been official policy now for twenty-five years and is still the theme of the LiBassi Report [*Report of the Interagency Task Force on the Health Effects of Ionizing Radiation*, June 1979]. From firsthand experience with how this report was produced, I believe that it was deliberately fabricated with the express purpose of blocking compensation claims for the victims of low-level radiation. It is a false and fraudulent imitation of a scientific document. It is now being used for its intended purpose. This means you are not up against a difference of opinion, or even ignorance of radiation effects. Basically, you are up against the full force and majesty of the United States government and of the scientific establishment supported by this government. It is sad indeed that the harmless myth which has served to protect weapons testing programs is

> now being used to balance the federal budget, by denying fair compensation claims to the veterans and others exposed to low-level radiation.

Dr. Bross's statement—my "bombshell"—caused a noticeable stir in the audience. People had been silent, but now there were gasps and whispers. I finished with my own thoughts. I concluded:

> The injustice continues. It is long past the time to reverse the injustice. There is not one atomic veteran who does not love his country or who would not put on the uniform again to defend it. But we men who should have been decorated for our valor in doing what we were forced to do are dying as rejected and forgotten persons. We are the living and dying examples of the effects of nuclear testing and exposure to low-level ionizing radiation. Unfortunately, time is not on our side, because one day our voices will be stilled and quieted by our deaths. We cannot reverse what happened; we only pray and insist that it never happen again. What has become of this nation that extolls humanitarianism as a way of life? The situation of the atomic veteran is indeed tragic; it is a national disgrace.

When I finished I went to a small room near the stage. I was sipping a soft drink when someone handed me a calling card and said a visitor wanted to see me. I read the name and title and saw the man was a special assistant to the general counsel of the Veterans Administration. I thought, "Uh-oh, here it comes. The VA's after me already, and here I just finished my speech. They sure didn't waste any time." I expected to be confronted by an angry official who would lash into me because I had criticized the agency. But after we shook hands, he surprised me.

"Tom," he said, "I'm Timothy Craig, and Max [Max Cleland, then administrator of the Veterans Administration] asked me to tell you he's sorry he couldn't be here today. I must tell you I understand the frustration you atomic veterans feel. Frankly, I don't think our agency is the right group to be reviewing radiation claims because we don't know enough about them."

"Then who should review the claims?" I asked.

"Some independent professionals who are familiar with the medical aspects of radiation exposure. What you need is a change in legislation to create an independent review group. If I were you, I'd approach the Senate Committee on Veterans' Affairs and try to bring about the change. I think Senator Cranston would be willing to listen."

I'd been listening carefully. "I'm glad you feel this way," I said. "The way the system works now the entire burden of proof is on the veteran, and it's practically impossible for us to prove that our problems were caused by exposure to radiation. All we can do is present the facts of our test participation and that we were in a hazardous area. The VA then decides whether there's a probability a disease was a result of the exposure. So far, you've said we could never have been harmed. Ninety-eight percent of our claims have been rejected."

"Yes, I know," Craig replied, "but I can't change that. Your organization needs congressional help."

We talked for a while longer and Craig left. I was surprised that a Veterans Administration staff member would admit that the agency's system was basically wrong, and that if atomic veterans wanted help it would have to come from somewhere else. In the meantime, nearly two thousand more claims would be denied, causing painful deprivation and needless suffering.

While I was at the hearings, I tried to talk to all the nearly one hundred atomic veterans who were there. Their stories were sadly similar—exposure, illness, and denial. Most of these men were my age or younger. Many told of the outright arrogance they encountered at VA hospitals. The mere mention of radiation-induced illness meant you were either told you were "crazy" or asked to leave.

One of the most pathetic stories was from a man who had been an airborne photographer during Crossroads. He was sent up to take pictures of the mushroom and spent hours flying around it as it rose into the troposphere. His camera was well protected, but he wore only a flight suit. Over the years his health had deteriorated. He could no longer speak. He sat in a wheelchair; his head hung to one side and he could raise his arm only with great effort. A woman friend, who was taking care of him, said he was a "diagnostic dilemma." She said he had dizziness and equilibrium problems, could not stand, and had lost his voice the previous year. When they found the Defense Nuclear Agency's toll-free number, she called and told the agency about the strange neuromuscular disorders that were turning her friend into a vegetable. Within a week, the agency sent a team to evaluate his condition.

"You know what they did?" the woman said. "They gave him an *IQ test* and left. But they found he wasn't a blithering idiot. His IQ was one hundred and thirty-two!"

One of the people who made a strong impression on me at the hearing was Dr. Edward A. Martell, a radiochemist at the National Center for Atmospheric Research in Boulder, Colorado. He is especially knowledgeable about atmospheric radioactivity and radioactive fallout. In the 1950s, Dr. Martell was on the staff of the Armed Forces Special Weapons Project. He said:

> We see cell damage expressed in various chronic ailments—premature aging, nerve cell damage, diseases of old age, paralysis, and loss of faculties. I never realized until I talked to many of the victims here

> how many remarkably related delayed effects they seem to exhibit.
>
> With regard to my own experience, I didn't get exceptional exposure—only a few rads from the Castle Bravo series. I have developed all the symptoms of multiple sclerosis. Now if this were an isolated case, let's say it could be completely unrelated. But I strongly suspect a thorough examination of all the various nerve disorders and delayed effects experienced by many of the exposed individuals, expressed in a variety of nerve disorders—loss of faculty, loss of hearing, loss of sight, partial paralysis, temporary blindness—these symptoms are all associated with the expected delayed effects of penetrating radiation.

The three days these radiation victims spent together was a deeply moving experience. Many realized for the first time, as I did, that there are thousands of people who are victims of nuclear events.

On Monday morning I went with a delegation that met with executive-branch representatives at the White House. We had high expectations. There to hear us were a member of the Interagency Task Force and a Justice Department official. They were apathetic, and it was obvious they were doing nothing more than paying us bureaucratic lip service. Toward the end of the meeting, an American Indian read a statement that had taken her weeks to write. Her husband, a uranium miner, could not come to Washington with her because he was seriously ill. I was appalled when the bureaucrats rose and departed without an apology, leaving her reading her statement to a room full of radiation victim delegates. I thought, "Never in my life have I seen such rudeness and insensitivity, and to think my tax dollars keep these guys employed."

I left the conference feeling heavily burdened. I had learned that there were hundreds if not thousands like me, who shared my experience and my ailments. I was not encouraged to know that in that gathering there were many with neuromuscular disorders. I knew that if the government ever did conduct a study, it likely would be only of cancers that could result from radiation exposure. The Atomic Bomb Casualty Commission never mentioned or studied neuromuscular disorders among the Japanese, and its report is the scientific community's model for subsequent inquiries. I learned afterward, however, that the Soviets had documented many forms of neuromuscular disorder that occurred after a huge nuclear explosion in an underground radioactive waste storage area, irradiating tens of thousands.

From Washington I went to New York to visit the staff of "60 Minutes." I had called Palmer Williams, the senior producer, from Washington to urge the program to dig into the problems of atomic veterans. After considerable conversation, he invited me to come to the studio.

When I arrived, I met a sympathetic producer, Joe Wershba, who had been at the Nevada Test Site in 1952 filming the atmospheric tests for CBS. We were joined by Williams, Harry Reasoner, and Morley Safer. I laid out the issues and the government's attitude toward us. As I talked, we watched a documentary about Paul Cooper, Jim O'Connor, and people who lived downwind from the Nevada Test Site. I made the point that "60 Minutes" should not try to prove that our problems were radiation-related but should stress what happened at the test sites, interview Orville Kelly and others, and bring in a Defense Nuclear Agency spokesman. Wershba seemed interested. I couldn't judge Safer's reaction. Wershba was a gracious host afterward, showing me around the studio and introducing me to the commentators and producers. In a way, my story surprised them. Williams said, "You look so healthy, we should play tennis this weekend." I told him I would like nothing more than to play tennis, but that he probably would beat me easily because of my severe joint problems. "It's great to be told you look well," I said, "but what's happening to me is going on where nobody can see it—in my cells."

Two weeks later, "60 Minutes" began filming a segment about atomic veterans. A crew went to Iowa City, Iowa, to see Kelly, who was then in the hospital again. The program was broadcast on September 28, 1980. It was well done, with a single exception: Vice Admiral R. R. Monroe, director of the Defense Nuclear Agency, presented an unrebutted "chalk talk" claiming that no more than a dozen of the two hundred thousand veterans who were at the test sites could have contracted cancer from the "low levels" of radiation they encountered.

Dr. Glyn Caldwell, of the Center for Disease Control, should have had air time. The findings of his study were released in the October 3, 1980 issue of the *Journal of the American Medical Association.* Nine leukemias [the only cancer studied] were discovered among 2,595 shot Smoky participants. That was nearly three times the 3.5 cases expected among a population of that size and age group. Two weeks later, "60 Minutes" read part of a letter from Dr. Tim Lee Carter on the air. Congressman Carter criticized the program for ignoring the only epidemiological study ever made of atomic veterans.

I went back to Washington in June for more research and inquiries. I wanted to talk to the officer in charge of the Marine Corps Nuclear Test Personnel Review Board to try to discover what the corps was doing about contacting former marines who had taken part in nuclear tests.

Before I went to Marine Corps Headquarters, I stopped at the office of the Citizens' Radiation Hearings to read transcripts. I was especially taken with an interview done by Ken Marshall, a Crossroads atomic veteran. He had asked Dr. Karl Z. Morgan, who had been at Bikini, why men had been sent on board contaminated ships so soon after the explosion. Dr. Morgan replied:

> You men at Bikini were victims of a stupid mistake made by stupid men, but all the tests after Crossroads were deliberately planned and conceived experiments with servicemen used as test samples to see how much they could take physically and psychologically.

I found that to be quite an admission from someone who had an important role in the test program.

Later, when I went to Marine Corps Headquarters, I talked to a captain who became keenly interested when I told him I had been at shot Hood. He told me what I already knew: that the corps had never been able to find the brigade's after-action report. Since I was an officer in the brigade, might I have seen it or did I know where a copy might be? He said he had called the brigade commander, General Tschirgi, who had retired several years previously, and asked about the report. The general could tell him nothing, he said.

The report is a critical factor in a numbers game the military has been playing with atomic veterans. When the corps asked General Tschirgi about it, he told me later, they said, "We desperately need it to prepare for a congressional hearing. Lots of marines are complaining that their illnesses are linked to those tests." The hearings were in January and February 1978. Testifying, the corps said there were only 1,706 marines at Hood. Representative Carter pressed a marine major at the hearings on the matter.

> MAJOR: Sir . . . although the press release indicated 2,100; the *after-action report* [emphasis supplied] indicates there were 1,706.

CARTER: Are you pretty sure of that?
MAJOR: Yes sir, I am.

The major should have not said he was sure, because he was wrong. On July 11, 1957, Camp Pendleton's base newspaper, the *Pendleton Scout*, said: "There were 2,100 marines in the test." And on July 5, 1957, the AEC Office of Test Information—always scrupulously accurate—said: "2,100 marines immediately launched an assault on an imaginary enemy after today's shot." The major must have gotten his number from the Marine Corps Historical Center, which keeps records of marine units dating back to the 1700s. The center can *identify* only 1,706 men who partcipated in the Hood test. A staff member says, "We have no idea who the other three hundred and ninety-four were." A major discrepancy could occur in identifying the number of atomic veterans if each service revised its figures downward. The Defense Nuclear Agency first said there were 250,000 military test participants. More recently, it has said there were 195,956. Its policy seems to be that if it cannot positively identify a veteran by name, then he wasn't there. I have talked to many widows who say their husbands told them they were at a particular test, yet no record of their participation exists. One begins to wonder about the mysterious St. Louis record center fire in 1973, in which thousands of service records were destroyed. And then there is the elusive after-action report, which no one can produce and the corps claims to be looking for. Somehow, the major was able to quote from it at the 1978 hearings.

The captain with whom I talked also claimed there is no record of the marines who were present at shot Priscilla. A few hours before it, we were told we were there as "observers," which may account for the fact that the corps kept no permanent record of our presence. When I asked the captain if he knew of any marine fatalities at any of the shots he seemed surprised, saying, "No, I haven't heard of any, have you?" I did not answer but changed the subject.

The day after I visited Marine Corps Headquarters, I went to the Defense Nuclear Agency to look at a declassified document. While there, I spent three hours with Dr. Edward Still, a veterinarian and head of the Biomedical Effects Department. He had spent three years during the 1960s at Camp Parks in California. Sheep were exposed there to as much as 500 rems an hour of cobalt 60 radiation. Such a dose would ordinarily kill a sheep or a man within two weeks to two months. Most of the irradiated sheep at Camp Parks died by the thirtieth day. I had wondered how a veterinarian who took part in radiation experiments with sheep could suddenly become an authority on the effects of low-level radiation on humans. But Dr. Still had made public statements that no serviceman or civilian involved in atmospheric testing ever received a harmful dose of radiation.

Dr. Still's claims brought to mind what Dr. Edward Martell said about Defense Nuclear Agency information statements:

> What does the Defense Nuclear Agency do? They take film badge records, which are a measure of penetrating radiation, and they discuss the small degree of effect expected in the way of cancers and leukemias. Now most cancers and leukemias are caused by internal emitters—alpha contaminants, beta emitters. And so, the best way of deceiving all of you about the effects of radiation is to talk about the effects of one class of radiation when you are measuring the other. The agency's fact sheet is a masterpiece of misleading statements about the serious effects of radiation of various types of carcinogens that you people were exposed to.

Dr. Still also had made statements of how troop movements and film badge readings had been re-created. These re-creations showed, he said, that nearly all test participants had received radiation doses of no more than .5 rem. I knew that the Defense Nuclear Agency contractor which reconstructed troop movements and radiation exposure was Science Applications, Inc., known in the industry as SAI.

SAI is a $150-million-a-year Department of Defense contractor involved in the development of advanced design technology for strategic weapons systems and in nuclear weapons analysis support for the Ballistics Missile Defense Systems Command. SAI thus is a *big* defense contractor, beholden to the military for its very existence and certainly for its future. It is highly unlikely to bite the hand that feeds it by making reports that reflect negatively on the Defense Nuclear Agency or any aspect of the nuclear weapons program, including nuclear testing.

Most atomic veterans aren't paranoiac—I know I'm not. Yet sometimes we do get the feeling we're playing against a stacked deck. That thought ran through my mind that day in Washington. The then-secretary of defense was Harold Brown, former director of Livermore Laboratories. One of the devices his laboratory had created, Hood, was being evaluated for radiation effects by an organization that indirectly reported to, and certainly needed to have the good will of—yes—Harold Brown.

Back to Dr. Still: I had no intention of debating him and I certainly didn't want to quarrel with him. I hoped to ask him specific questions that might help me improve my own health and perhaps learn some things I could pass along to other atomic veterans. I was in enemy territory, however, and I knew it.

I told him about my Priscilla experience and asked if I might not have inhaled some radioactive dust. The dust was not of a size I could inhale, he said. Yet I remembered reading an AEC report that went into detail about the fine granulated sand at Frenchman Lake that created problems when bombs were detonated. What if I had yawned when I was three hundred yards from ground zero, or opened my mouth wide while talking? I asked. Would that have meant a mouthful of radioactive isotopes?

"Highly unlikely," according to Dr. Still.

Well then, what if radioactive material had gotten into my body through my ear canals? After all, AEC people had daily ear and nose swabs to check for contaminants.

"But they were in contaminated areas," said Dr. Still.

"So were we after Priscilla," I told him.

"How can you be sure?"

"Because an AEC field man with an instrument in his hand came rushing up and ordered us to leave."

Dr. Still tried to cut matters short by repeating the party line. "Nobody ever received enough prompt radiation to cause any harm."

I wanted to know what "enough" was.

Dr. Still took out a cigarette, tapped it on his desk a few times, and continued with the party line. "The Nuclear Regulatory Commission has established a five-rem maximum allowable exposure for its workers, and your exposure was much less than that. If you have had extensive x-rays in your lifetime, they will cause more damage than your exposure at the test site."

The x-ray/test-site-radiation-exposure analogy is an ancient one, used for years by nuclear apologists to reassure worried people. The analogy skips quickly around a proven scientific fact: *there is no known safe level of ionizing radiation.*

I got absolutely nowhere with Dr. Still. As we were winding up our discussion, he seemed to be trying to calm me (perhaps I had lost my temper just a bit) with the government's traditional get-rid-of-the-problem pacifier: a promised study. The Defense Nuclear Agency was going to fund a National Science Foundation study of veterans' test site radiation. I didn't ask when, but Dr. Still volunteered it would

begin as soon as participant atmospheric tests had been ide tified which warranted further study. "Identified by Scienc Applications, Inc.," I thought to myself. I said nothing and w parted. I went back to the public affairs office to try to mak sense of the report I had come to study.

9.

Countdown Zero

Countdown n. The act or process of counting backward aloud to indicate the time elapsing before an imminent deadline that will initiate an event or operation.
—The New American Heritage Dictionary

I had been hunched over a desk in the Defense Nuclear Agency's public affairs office—possibly the worst place to be, especially for an atomic veteran—just before I got the news. I had called Lew Golinker at the National Veterans' Law Center for help in clearing up a point. He seemed strained and distressed. I asked why.

"It's getting so I'm afraid to pick up the phone any more. Always bad news. Two weeks ago it was Harry Copolla [a Nagasaki cleanup marine veteran], and today's news was even worse. Orville Kelly died. Wanda called two hours ago."

("While I was talking to the unctuous Dr. Still," I thought.)

"She said the funeral is Saturday," Golinker went on.

"Lew, this is sad news," I said. "I'll call you tomorrow and we can work out going to the funeral together."

"How ironic," I thought—to learn about Orville's dying when I was at the Death's Nuclear Agency, as he always called it. He had trouble deciding which was the more inhuman, the Veterans Administration or the Defense Nuclear Agency.

Dr. Still, who did not see me, bounded into the next room.

"Did you hear? Did you hear?" he burbled to a secretary. "We had a shot today at the Nevada Test Site!"

He was beaming, and I thought, "This fellow is really sick. He thinks there's no harm when you blow one off underground, which of course is not true."

He questioned the secretary. "Have you made the press release?"

When I walked into the room, he straightened up. "Doctor," I said, "I'm sure people in St. George, Utah, will be happy to hear the news that another gift of radioactivity is on the way."

He bristled. "Oh, no, we don't have that problem any more."

"Well, I have a problem," I said. "One of my best friends, Orville Kelly, died this afternoon, and I have to leave here now."

I left the room and headed for the lobby. When I was a short way down the hall, I heard the secretary on the phone. "Is the director still here? Be sure and tell him Mr. Kelly died today."

The Defense Nuclear Agency had every right to be relieved, for it would no longer have to deal with one of its most outspoken critics. It would soon learn, however, that there were plenty of critics out there to carry on what Kelly had begun.

Orville's funeral was on June 28. Many people were there to pay tribute to him. He was buried with full military honors. A friend, Deanna Edwards, sang a song she had written for him: "You're Only a Memory Away." Thousands had been touched by Kelly. When he spoke, no matter what the size of the audience—twenty or a hundred thousand—people heard a simple, honest, hopeful, and supportive message. He taught each and every one of us to live one day at a time, and to make each day count. Wanda put it best:

Orville was my closest friend. I could listen to him talk for hours. He was the most incredible person I have ever known. I've never looked at life the same way since Kelly taught me the importance of a day. He changed my thoughts and attitudes toward life and people. He will always live in our hearts. I will dedicate my life to continuing Orville's work in the association.

The Nuclear Defense

We are not in the health effects business, we are in the business of defense.

—Defense Nuclear Agency

June 28, my birthday, was not a time for celebration. Orville Kelly was buried that day, and we knew what had killed him. His death certificate read, "Death was caused by: Nuclear Radiation Induced Lymphoma." Twenty-three years before, to the day, I had been facing the new dawn in the Nevada desert, waiting out the countdown before shot Diablo. I remembered that birthday, too, because I later determined the trench line I was in was heavily contaminated with residual radiation. When two army captains rushed up to my work detail two days before the shot, while we were clearing sand out of the trenches, I suspected something was wrong. Their concern, and their peremptory order to put on masks, told me that. They knew what I did not know: those trenches were saturated with radiation from previous shots. My party should have been ordered out of the trenches immediately, but like the people of St. George, Utah, we were never warned. The officers were part of the permanent military party at Camp Desert Rock, which meant they knew about shot Wilson, detonated the day I arrived at the camp. I had not seen or been aware of the early morning test.

The day Wilson exploded, there were only light surface winds. The nuclear cloud did not dissipate as expected. Instead, the stem dragged at a low altitude and tilted slightly north of due west. Observers had to be evacuated from the control center. When the Reynolds Electric and Engineering Company carried out its radiological survey mission, which had been delayed for several hours because of heavy contamination, the team got readings of 100 rads (roentgens) at an altitude of twenty-five feet. The bottom of the stem continued to amble west, passing directly over the trenches used for shot Diablo. I referred to different maps and overlaid them. My party had been digging at a place that had received heavy fallout from a 10-kiloton explosion.

When I found this out, I tried to reach the marines who had been in the work party. The Defense Nuclear Agency blocked my effort. Its letter said, "The Government is not required to undertake an unusual action such as this. We would not consider serving as a conduit for a mass mailing." Would letters to the thirty-three marines in my work party have constituted a "mass mailing"?

When I called on Dr. Edward Still at the Defense Nuclear Agency, I told him I had been in touch with thirty marines who had been at shots Priscilla and Hood. Ten had died of cancer, I said, and only two were healthy. "There is no significance in that small number," he sniffed. "Then help me reach all twenty-one hundred who were at shot Hood, and I'll give you a full report on their present health," I said. He refused. Later I was told at the agency, "We are not in the health effects business, we are in the business of defense."

Countdown Zero

The Cornerstone

> *Most exposures to Department of Defense personnel [servicemen] during the tests were quite low—averaging about half a rem.*
>
> —William H. Taft IV
> General Counsel
> Department of Defense

The cornerstone upon which the Defense Nuclear Agency supports its radiation claims is the film badge that was worn by some nuclear test participants. Before 1957, everyone at the test sites was not badged. During the early 1950s, a single badge was issued per platoon, or a single badge per busload of troops. Film badges were a gamma film pack consisting of two layers of unexposed special film showing through a 1½ x 1½-inch opening in the badge itself. When gamma rays caused ionization, the film darkened. Later, it was developed and the darkening measured. This information was then converted to exposure units expressed in rems. After a nuclear shot, the film was supposed to be developed under carefully controlled time and temperature conditions.

When men were scattered across the desert and only one wore a badge, re-creating average exposure for all was virtually impossible. Nevertheless, the Defense Nuclear Agency maintains that average exposure for military participants was .5 rem. The calculation has become part of the official record, regardless of its accuracy, and there is no way to correct the record.

Another flaw in the use of Defense Nuclear Agency film badge assumptions is that most badges were covered by part of a uniform during detonation. Also, in most cases, men wore the badges on the front of their bodies while in a trench, and turned their backs to the detonation. This meant that gamma rays had to pass through a human body before reaching the badge. Thus readings were diminished. Finally, badges were worn at the time of the tests and not developed and assessed until sometime later, occasionally in a flimsy tent in the scorching desert—hardly a controlled condition.

A comparison of film badge readings with readings from more sophisticated instruments would demonstrate film badge inaccuracy. On April 25, 1953, Navy Captain Robert A. Hinners volunteered to record the effect of a 50-kiloton detonation from a trench slightly over a mile from ground zero. He carried a high-range radiation survey meter, capable of measuring gamma radiation five hundred times higher than instruments used by military field radiological safety units. In addition, Captain Hinners wore three film badges—one inside his steel helmet, one inside his left breast pocket, and one clipped inside his hip pocket.

Eight seconds after detonation, Captain Hinners took a reading from the meter. It was exactly 100 rems. The meter readings varied from 100 rems to 40 rems during the approximately two minutes he stayed in the trench. His film badge readings were: head, 12 rems; chest, 12.11 rems; hip, 17.12 rems. The average radiation recorded by the badges was 14.07 rems, only an eighth of the survey meter's readings.

There may be another reason the Defense Nuclear Agency maintains average exposure was only .5 (one-half) rem. In the absence of film badge information, the agency may have relied on radiation readings recorded by the survey meter used at the time by military radiological field survey units. The primary instrument used by these units during the 1950s was called the AN/PDR 27. Its maximum radiation-scale range was 500 millirems per hour, or .5 rem.

The Veterans Administration

What is the extent of the term "disability" and who is to be the judge of it?

—John Dickinson
Constitutional Convention
August 27, 1787

On June 15, 1979, the Defense Nuclear Agency and the Veterans Administration signed a memorandum of understanding to "formalize and improve existing procedures to ensure the most complete investigation of veterans's ionizing radiation claims." In fact, the agreement made denying atomic veteran claims easier. The Defense Nuclear Agency tells the Veterans Administration the "probable exposures" of a petitioning veteran at a test site. This provides the Veterans Administration with a factual pretext to deny the claim. It does this, making statements such as, "Your recorded or estimated exposure was 'X,' which is considerably less than the safe level established by the Nuclear Regulatory Commission, 5 rems for workers exposed to radiation. The causation has not been established; therefore, service connection is denied." Or, the agency may say, "Your disease is not one of the selected diseases that could be caused by high doses of radiation exposure. Therefore, your claim is denied."

The Defense Nuclear Agency or the Veterans Administration has not taken the moral issue into account—that a serviceman was exposed to a deadly carcinogen without his knowledge or consent. What most veterans who file claims do not realize is that there may be a conspiracy to deny their claims. Speaking at a seminar, Dr. Rosalie Bertell discussed illnesses that can result from radiation exposure. She used the complaints of atomic veterans as examples, and explained the attitude of the insensitive Veterans Administration. When she had finished, a man from the audience asked to see her. He introduced himself as someone who had served on a Veterans Administration regional review board. The man said he had reviewed atomic veteran claims but was powerless to approve them. He said an internal memorandum established a policy that a claim be denied automatically if a veteran had been exposed more than fifteen years before the date of his claim. For a claim filed in 1980, a veteran was thus denied unless exposure occurred after 1965, and all atomic veterans were exposed prior to 1965. He also told Dr. Bertell that a claim for benefits because of a genetic disorder in an atomic veteran's child would not even be considered. The man said he felt these mandates added up to a travesty of justice and that he was considering resigning.

Thomas Mancuso, professor of occupational medicine at the University of Pittsburgh, is a pioneer in industrial cancer research. Although the government cut off funds for his study of the effects of radiation on nuclear workers at the Hanford Nuclear Reservation, he was able to obtain private backing and complete it. The government was not pleased when he found that low levels of ionizing radiation definitely cause cancer, and that the cancer risk from this type of radiation is at least ten times higher than previously suspected.

At the 1980 radiation hearings in Washington, Dr. Mancuso said, "The veterans were exposed and exposed and exposed and they never . . . never had any measurements of internal radiation."

Dr. Mancuso told Orville Kelly what he thought of the Veterans Administration in a letter in 1978:

> What I believe had occurred in the veterans' claims procedure is the application of an older concept which was generated many years ago in the design of the claim form. This form was predicated on the immediate observable cause-and-effect relationship, for injuries and for certain types of illnesses. The

> introduction of weapons testing marked the introduction of another type of soldier exposure; the exposure to ionizing radiation, which the soldiers cannot see, smell or feel and whose effects most often occur after a great many years. Similarly, soldiers exposed to chemicals either in peace or war may sustain long-term delayed cancer effects. These are usually referred to as the "silent killers."
>
> The point being made is that the long-term delayed effects such as cancer from radiation were not recognized in the drafting of the specific criteria for a veteran in the filing of a compensation claim.
>
> Consequently, the veteran claim system itself, by its very nature, has a built-in barrier against the recognition of long-term effects which occur many years later, because these cancer effects cannot become manifest within the short time period between the first exposure and termination of service or the year after termination of service. This recognition is even more difficult for cancers which occur within the body itself, the internal type of cancers.

Dr. Mancuso's point is logical, even obvious. The Veterans Administration, established in 1930 to deal with battlefield casualties and easily traced service-connected disabilities, has absolutely refused to adapt its hidebound policies and procedures to the realities of the nuclear age. It will not even entertain the thought that there is a new kind of veteran—the atomic veteran—whose service to his country has resulted in wounds that cannot be treated by first aid or conventional hospital care. Indeed, the wounds may not even become apparent until years after they were inflicted, and then in ways that baffle the most sophisticated medical practitioners. Dr. Mancuso again:

> Since the illness occurs several decades later, there is no way to establish a link to prior medical records as required by the form because these records could not exist. Therefore it is unreasonable to deny a compensation claim because there is no medical record during the specified period when it relates to cancer or leukemia due to ionizing radiation.

A Veterans Administration official has expressed the proposition about as bluntly as it can be expressed: "Not until our backs are really pressed against a wall do we even begin to consider latent somatic effects."

Dr. Irwin Bross, of the Roswell Park Memorial Institute, has a theory about the obstacles confronting atomic veterans when they deal with the government. He expressed it in a speech to the American Statistical Association in Houston on August 13, 1980:

> Atomic veterans are victims of a technogenic disease. Techno—"technology"; genic—"caused by." Thus, a technogenic disease is caused by technology.
>
> Science and facts tend to support contentions of atomic veterans, but the political and economic clout of those determined to protect their vested interest is on the other [side]. . . .
>
> The federal agencies play a rough and dirty game. They don't really want to debate us; they want to destroy us. . . .
>
> Someone high up in government has given orders that the goal of a balanced federal budget must not be jeopardized by the payout of large sums in compensation for radiation claims.
>
> The implicit assignment in the Veterans Administration claims procedure has biased the decision against the veteran in order to hold down the pay-

ment for compensation. Thus, nearly all of the veterans have been denied service-connection. In practice, therefore, the "benefit of the doubt" has been pre-empted by the agency making the decision. It is morally disgraceful to cheat the veterans in this manner. This issue should be debated on the real moral grounds and not on spurious statistical grounds.

The Berkeley Physicians

The loss of even one human life or the malformation of even one baby . . . should be of concern to all of us.

—John F. Kennedy
Address to the nation announcing the end of U.S. atmospheric testing, July 1963

At about the time I was seeing a neurologist at the University of California, two young physicians were completing reports that represented nearly two years of work. Dr. Susan Lambert and Dr. Henry Vyner, both of Berkeley, had volunteered to study physiological and psychological disorders among atomic veterans. The National Association of Atomic Veterans had asked the Center for Disease Control to expand its study of shot Smoky veterans to include all atomic veterans, but the center was not able to do that. Efforts to persuade the Veterans Administration to undertake a medical study went nowhere. Dr. Lambert and Dr. Vyner were responsive.

When I talked to them, they suggested I consult the same doctor who had diagnosed Jim O'Connor's neuromuscular problem. It seemed we had at last found a neurologist in southern California who could deal with veterans of the Nevada Test Site. O'Connor, a former professional race driver, had been struggling with a mysterious muscle disorder much as I had. He had seen twelve doctors, with no satisfaction. Finally, in desperation, he wrote to a relative at the Harvard Medical School, who recommended a local man specializing in collagen diseases (abnormalities in the connective tissue). O'Connor saw him, and after many tests was diagnosed as having a malfunction of the muscles caused by unusual enzyme changes in the blood. In time, it usually renders the muscles useless.

Encouraged by doctors Lambert and Vyner, I saw the same neurologist. On my third visit, he gave me a tensilon test. I had a positive reaction, and he told me I had myasthenia gravis—an incurable, abnormal muscular weakness. I did not have multiple sclerosis, as the Veterans Administration doctor had told me earlier. Suddenly there were two atomic veterans living in the same area who had been exposed to radiation at the Nevada Test Site, who were diagnosed as having muscle diseases.

To confirm this diagnosis, I decided to go to a University of California medical center to see a physician others considered the "neurologists' neurologist." He was an authority on myasthenia gravis and was on the board of the Myasthenia Gravis Foundation. I had more tests. The last time I saw him, he said:

> You have a neuromuscular disorder. I don't concur with the doctor who diagnosed myasthenia gravis, but our tests show a definite abnormality.
>
> I don't know what caused your condition or how far it will progress. There is no treatment, and I cannot tell you if it will ever regress. We will just have to watch you. If you reach a point where you can't function, we have plenty of beds here at the hospital.

> Just don't ask me to get involved in this radiation controversy, because I won't. Consider yourself and the others from the test site who are ill as the few who sacrificed yourselves for the many who were spared.

Then he asked, "Would you tell me where I can get copies of those photographs you showed me? [the Priscilla and Hood explosions]. I think the colors are beautiful, and I want to put them on my office wall."

I thought, "Good Lord, here I've spent weeks trying to educate this man about the health effects of radiation exposure by telling him what happened to me. He tells me I have practically no hope and charges me a big fee, but he's more interested in getting some nuclear explosion pictures. What the hell has happened to the medical profession? I sure wish my father [for many years a highly respected country doctor in Middleburg, Virginia] was still alive."

After this shocking encounter, I resolved never to see another physician. I was especially angered by the doctor's remark that I was among "the few who were sacrificed." I always suspected I had been used in some covert experiment without my knowledge, but I believed in my heart it was the Marine Corps' gung-ho delusion that caused mistakes that needlessly endangered our lives. After all, the commandant himself, in 1952, said that well-trained, highly disciplined marines could withstand the effects of nuclear weapons detonated practically in their faces and continue to function.

Being "sacrificed" was a different matter altogether. If I had been injured in Korea or even in Vietnam fighting for some ostensibly national cause, I could have accepted that. You joined the marines, after all, to fight and if necessary die for your country. But to be destroyed by an insidious killer because some eager, myopic hawks wanted to play with nuclear firecrackers was a different matter altogether, and more than I could bear.

I remembered the time in 1980 when Patricia Broudy had been on a panel on PBS television in Los Ageles. Two other members of the panel were a retired general and a colonel still on active duty whose specialty was civil defense.

"What good was served when three hundred thousand men were ordered to participate in atomic weapons testing where many have died and others are dying currently as a result of their exposure to radiation?" Mrs. Broudy asked. Both the general and the colonel avoided the question by turning the discussion in other directions. She persisted, finally demanding, "Would one of you gentlemen please answer my question?"

"Yes, I guess we should," the colonel said. "The experiments were invaluable. We learned so much from them." After the session, he walked over to her and put his arm around her. "I'm truly sorry you lost your husband," he said. "I just wanted you to know all of us have benefited from those tests. They were worthwhile, and the men who died were not sacrificed in vain."

Mrs. Broudy pulled away, looked scornfully at the colonel and shot back, "Well, I'm sure there are lots of widows and men with cancer who will be happy to hear that." She stalked away, leaving the colonel with his mouth agape.

Dr. Lambert and Dr. Vyner decided to study atomic veterans because of the persuasiveness of three men: Orville Kelly, Crossroads participant Jess Clark, and myself. Clark put his case to them at a meeting in spring 1980:

> Ten years ago, atomic veterans were satisfied if they got treatment and some sort of disability benefits. We didn't fully understand our problems. We thought they probably were the result of accidents or carelessness. This group of veterans was scattered, confused, made up of sick people suffering

from cancer, mainly. They didn't expect to live long.

Today, we're dealing with survivors, veterans with disabling diseases that are not cancer-related, besides those who have cancer. All of them are aware that there was guinea-pig–type testing. They know that there were coverups, and that in many instances their problems have been swept under the rug. Many of these veterans are destitute, because they have lost their jobs. Many have lost their homes and possessions. In some cases, families have been broken up and proud people forced to live on welfare. Veterans Administration claims are routinely denied.

No one in the medical profession has studied or tried to provide relief to this outcast group. We won't get relief without a medical study. I know it's asking a lot of you, but if you look I think you'll find a syndrome here. As physicians, you can perhaps save thousands from dying prematurely. We desperately need your help.

Clark obsessed was a difficult man to resist. Dr. Vyner began a pilot study, selecting twelve California veterans to evaluate. He chose men who had not known each other before the study began. It was not intended to be epidemiological. Dr. Vyner decided to evaluate the group's psychological problems. In sixteen months he finished a paper, "The Psychological Effects of Ionizing Radiation." Some of its conclusions:

Eleven of the twelve men studied have had a virtually identical psychological response to ionizing radiation. The similarity of this response amongst these eleven men has been so striking that it appears to comprise a syndrome—which I have tentatively named Radiation Response Syndrome

> (RRS). The syndrome is a collection of adverse psychological responses to ionizing radiation that have been demonstrated amongst atomic veterans.
>
> Radiation Response Syndrome is marked by a veteran's preoccupation with his physical illness, and a virtual obsession with (1) piecing together the circumstances of his own involvement in the nuclear tests, (2) proving that radiation caused his illness, (3) sometimes having to prove that he is actually ill in the first place, and (4) convincing the Veterans Administration and his family, friends, and greater society that all of the above is true.

Vyner's analysis of RRS also touched upon "identity conflict." A veteran who once saw himself as healthy, patriotic, a successful father and husband, begins to believe he is unhealthy, unpatriotic, and unable to support his family.

Veterans with RRS, according to Vyner, develop a "remarkably similar world view," which includes "anger at the government based on the belief that the government knowingly placed them in a dangerous situation and now is refusing to accept responsibility" and "guilt over their anger with the government."

Many atomic veterans' problems have previously been discounted because these veterans demonstrated what Vyner called "undiagnosable symptoms." But, he suggests, "reasonably good evidence indicates that these symptoms may be the expression of previously unrecognized diseases caused by ionizing radiation." His conclusions:

> It appears that the atomic veterans are developing a whole spectrum of heretofore unrecognized health problems. The central problem is that they have contracted an illness that is not only misunderstood, but is probably beyond complete comprehension. As a result, they have developed psychological

problems and have been unable to obtain adequate medical care.

Dr. Lambert spent a year examining atomic veterans, listing their symptoms and listening to their stories. These men, it seemed, had one common adversary—the Veterans Administration. Her own anger surprised her, to the extent that she listed her thoughts in a paper:

> The Veterans Administration has clearly shown itself to be an irresponsible government agency that grossly falls short of a minimal workers' compensation system.
>
> In an attempt to exercise their rights for medical care and benefits in compensation for their work in the Armed Forces, nuclear veterans have filed disability and death claims with the VA. In the face of disabilities that include eight different types of cancer, bone and muscle diseases, cardiovascular diseases, sterility and blindness, the VA has denied ninety-eight percent of the veteran's claims.
>
> The VA employs any one of four different arguments to deny a veteran's claim: (1) Issue of causation; (2) Disease not known to be caused by radiation; (3) Inadequate dose of radiation, and (4) You weren't at the test site.
>
> The VA placing the burden of proof on the atomic veteran is asking him to do the scientifically impossible.
>
> The medical focus of the scientific and lay communities on the adverse effects secondary to ionizing radiation is on cancer. However, there are other problems such as cataracts, atherosclerosis and genetic effects to be considered. To refer only to cancer deaths not only ignores morbidity data on cancer, but it totally disregards the quality of life so

insidiously impaired by noncancerous diseases.

Why should the atomic veteran receive medical aid and subsequent compensation? The answer is simple: it is the only decent, ethical thing to do. The testing program was ostensibly to improve the U.S. nuclear weapons capability; having military personnel present was human experimentation. These men were put through simulated combat maneuvers to test the psychological and military responses of the human organism to the nuclear stressor.

In addition to the human experimentation, the government had substantial evidence in the 1950s and 1960s of the adverse health effects secondary to radiation. For over twenty-five years this information has been available to the scientific community and to the government.

It is ironic that this nation in forty years has gone from splitting the atom to producing nuclear weapons of a capacity equivalent to twenty million tons of TNT, and yet we cannot demonstrate the maturity and the decency to compensate those men who suffer the consequences of such a technological feat. The VA shamelessly denies claims in the face of men who lived by and acted upon that very substrate that this country holds dear—patriotism. The VA is a sleeping giant—it is the second largest agency in government and it does nothing to benefit those who need the agency's help most. The VA is a monolith of archaic administrative machinery that has little understanding of human suffering.

On April 10, 1980, the National Veterans' Law Center in Washington, D.C., filed suit against the Veterans Administration on behalf of several atomic veterans. In *Gott* v. *Cleland* (Max Cleland was then the VA administrator) the plaintiffs challenged the rules presently used by the Veterans Administration in evaluating atomic veterans' claims. The rules were promulgated after the Defense Nuclear Agency and the Veterans Administration decided what they should be. The atomic veteran plaintiffs argued that the rules had gone into effect without allowing the public—atomic veterans, scientists, and others who might be affected or who might contribute to the rule-making process—to be heard. This procedure, they claimed, was a violation of federal law. In September 1981, a U.S. District Court in Washington, D.C., agreed, invalidating the rules and ordering the two agencies to comply with rule-making law should they decide to promulgate rules affecting atomic veteran claims in the future.

Congress has paid some but not much attention to the problems of atomic veterans. Again, the deck appears to be stacked. Many representatives and senators are retired military officers, or are in the active reserves. This means they depend on military pay to supplement their incomes, and may be reluctant to criticize the services as a consequence.

Also, the nuclear lobby in Washington is extremely powerful and well financed. As one retired representative put it, "To ignore that lobby is to commit political suicide." The present administration gives almost blank-check support to the military; headlines regularly proclaim this or that monstrous military buildup. With political currents running so strongly in the military's favor, Congress is less likely to approve legislation that appears to restrict or reprimand the defense establishment.

The bill that would most directly benefit atomic veterans is H.R. 1733, sponsored in the 97th Congress by Representative Norman Y. Mineta, Democrat of San Jose, California. Mineta's bill was originally sponsored in the previous Congress by Representative Tim Lee Carter, but it got nowhere. It provides:

> . . . and such veteran suffers from any disability or disease caused by or attributable to exposure to atomic or nuclear radiation during such service, such disability or disease shall be considered to have been incurred in or aggravated by such service, notwithstanding that there is no record of such disability or disease during the period of service and that such disability or disease did not become manifest within one year from the date of separation of such veteran from such service.

H.R. 1733 deals with several atomic veteran roadblocks, and would be of considerable benefit to atomic veterans if enacted. However, it seems destined for the legislative graveyard instead. The House Veterans' Affairs Committee does not seem disposed even to schedule hearings on it.

Another piece of legislation of marginal benefit to atomic veterans miraculously became law. It is less significant as legislation than as an innocuous measure which provoked a paranoid diatribe of opposition from the Department of Defense—evidence, if any were needed, that the military establishment will go to any length to deny atomic veterans what they rightfully deserve.

California's Senator Alan Cranston tacked his amendment onto a routine bill providing medical care for Vietnam veterans exposed to Agent Orange and other herbicides. Senator Cranston's amendment went a logical step further and included atomic veterans after he considered a written plea from Wanda Kelly, executive director of the National Association of Atomic Veterans. Her letter to Cranston, supported by fourteen case histories, had outlined the lack of medical assistance for atomic veterans.

The wrath of the Department of Defense was awesome. Its general counsel, William H. Taft IV, wrote a letter opposing the amended bill and predicting that its passage apparently would mean the end of civilization as we know it. According to Taft, the bill

> . . . creates the unmistakable impression that exposure to low-level ionizing radiation is a significant health hazard when available scientific and medical evidence simply does not support that contention. This mistaken impression has the potential to be seriously damaging to every aspect of the Department of Defense's nuclear weapons and nuclear propulsion programs. The legislation could adversely affect our relations with our European allies, impact upon the nuclear power industry, and raise questions regarding the use of radioactive substances in medical diagnosis and treatment.

Notwithstanding the Defense Department's vision of Armageddon, Congress enacted the legislation.

An article in the magazine *Science* of May 22, 1981, supports the nongovernment view of low-level radiation. Physicists William Loewe and Edward Mendelsohn used a computer to reconstruct the radiation exposure of the Japanese at Hiroshima and Nagasaki. They conclude that most of the cancer caused by the bombs was from low-linear-energy-transfer gamma rays. Their report strongly suggests that low-level ionizing radiation is much more lethal than anyone had suspected. If the findings of Loewe and Mendelsohn hold up (and their data has been validated by the Oak Ridge National Laboratory) then there is a totally explainable reason why so many atomic veterans exposed to supposedly low-level gamma radiation are ill.

If a study were conducted limited to veterans who went close to ground zero shortly after a nuclear detonation, the morbidity/mortality incidence likely would be alarming.

These men were the ones who were exposed to air heavily laden with dust from the bomb's explosion. The probability of inhalation of the dust is significant.

To Tell the Truth

The people themselves must take the initiative to see that they will never again be led to slaughter. To expect protection from their government is folly.

—Albert Einstein

Although there have been many studies of what constitutes a safe level of radiation exposure, the exact level remains in dispute. Atomic veterans are innocent hostages, imprisoned in a no man's land of controversy among military and nonmilitary technicians. Our radiation exposure should not be calculated by those who played death games with us. We can get an honest count only from a neutral public health agency.

One of the greatest injustices ever inflicted on a class of Americans—the trashing of atomic veterans—will end only with a uniform compensation law for radiation victims. The law must wipe away the archaic standards that now allow the routine denial of radiation claims.

The nation's military budget is becoming a trillion-dollar mushroom, yet there is not a penny in it for victims of military technology. During the 1950s and 1960s, billions were spent to perfect more lethal nuclear weapons and try them on us. The Defense Department and the Atomic Energy Commission knew—and their knowledge is a matter of record,—that these monsters would harm the guinea pigs. Even so, these agencies married horror and its victims.

Atomic veterans ask only that our government look us in

the eye and come clean with us. We did our duty when we were told to. We served in the valleys of the nuclear shadows of death—Hiroshima, Nagasaki, Bikini, Eniwetok, Desert Rock. The only products the military manufactures are veterans and casualties. It is inhuman to experiment with these products, play games with them, and then deny that they exist. Among radiation victims, only atomic veterans are still beating at the door. Japanese and Marshallese have been given medical help, and in some instances they have been compensated for damages. Those harmed by the nuclear accident at Three Mile Island in Pennsylvania have won a $25-million judgment against the utility that operates the plant.

Atomic veterans are the only class of citizens who were exposed to the effects of ionizing radiation from nuclear weapons tests who have *not* been recognized as radiation victims. When veterans have used the judicial process to seek restitution, the cases have been dismissed because federal judges are bound by the Feres Doctrine, which prohibits servicemen from suing the government for abuses or injury incurred while on active duty. Former nuclear weapons test participants have been denied due process of law.

However, on November 9, 1981, a major breakthrough occurred that has given new hope to all atomic veterans, widows, and families. The U.S. Ninth Circuit Court of Appeals in San Francisco ruled in a 3–0 decision that Patricia Broudy will be allowed to argue the issue of "Post Discharge Failure to Warn" before a jury.

Mrs. Broudy's attorney, Ronald Bakal, delivered a compelling argument in which he contended that the late Charles Broudy was never warned of the potentially harmful effects of his radiation exposure when he was discharged in 1960. Bakal contends that the government knew the possible health consequences and that if Broudy had been warned of those consequences his cancer might have been detected in its early stages and his life might thereby have been prolonged.

In another case, on November 3, 1981, the U.S. Third Circuit Court of Appeals in New Jersey ruled that Stanley Jaffee did not have the right to seek damages from military and civilian officials responsible for the nuclear tests.

Jaffee is a Nevada Test Site veteran who developed inoperable breast cancer, which he claims resulted from his exposure to radiation when he was ordered to stand unprotected in the desert and watch an atomic explosion.

Although Jaffee lost the decision by an 8–2 vote, one of the dissenting judges, John J. Gibbons, called the ruling "affirmatively evil." Judge Gibbons elaborated:

> That any judicial tribunal in the world, in the last fifth of this dismal century, would choose to place a class of persons outside the protection against human rights violations . . . is surprising.
>
> That it should be an American court that would allow this to happen will dismay persons the world over who are concerned with human rights.

The truth must come home to the American people. Now, there is only numbed public ignorance. It exists because few citizens understand the lethal dangers of radiation. The United States has some thirty thousand nuclear weapons sleeping in arsenals, standing at attention on missile launching pads, dozing in the bellies of bombers, and crouched in the dark bowels of submarines. They are the greatest threat to the survival of the human race in its history, but they are not the only nuclear threat.

Few of us are aware of the silent winter, the final human winter, a chill season of reckoning being brought by the residual fallout of the experiments that flung us around like rag dolls in the Nevada trenches. Fallout from those tests lingers up there, still killing people. Diffused plutonium has a halflife of twenty-four thousand years. It keeps falling, drizzling its deadly isotopes into our food chain. A chip of plutonium the size of a dime, sufficiently fragmented, can kill millions.

Nuclear wastes from weapons production during the seventeen-year atmospheric testing program are still with us. And much more nuclear waste exists than that from the manufacture of these prototype weapons. Nuclear weapons have been turned out at an accelerated pace in the years since. Eighty percent of all nuclear waste comes from weapons production. Its storage and disposal, if disposal is possible, are ominous problems. Currently, some seventy-five million gallons of nuclear waste are stored.

"Stored" is a euphemism. The waste's malignant radiation continues irreversibly for tens of thousands of years. Within thirty to forty years, the lethal stuff eats its way through any container so far devised and begins to leak. If it leaks on the surface, it poisons the ground and the atmosphere. When it is buried and leaks, it seeps into the vast aquifer that is the source of most of our water. The food chain cannot escape the venom of nuclear waste. Neither can marine life, if waste is disposed of by sinking it in the sea.

And then there are nuclear waste explosions, whose possibility the government denies. Governments are sometimes deceitful. A supposedly "safe" nuclear disposal dump in the Soviet Union blew up in 1957. The Russians might as well have fought a war. Perhaps as many as sixty thousand people perished, according to the U.S. Central Intelligence Agency. Mysterious diseases are ravaging the survivors, and a vast area of Russia has become a bleak nuclear desert.

If the nuclear treadmill is not stopped, every American is well on the way to becoming a nuclear veteran. As civilians, they will not even be able to beg the arrogant stonehearts at the Veterans Administration for help and be turned away, as we have been.

Researching *Countdown Zero*, I discovered things I could

hardly believe and did not want to believe. Sometimes I imagined myself now confronting my earlier self, twenty-two-year-old Lieutenant Thomas Saffer, about to march into that trench and brace himself for shot Priscilla. I would say some things to that starry-eyed Virginia Military Institute graduate that nobody was there to say to me.

I would tell him that his school's ancient honor code was a dead letter when the bomb went off. "Never lie, never cheat, never steal," it says. We were lied to about the bomb. We were cheated out of a normal life. We had our lives stolen from us by a useless nuclear experiment. Oh, I would have told him about all the hideous things that were about to happen. He probably would have cursed me as an ancient, silly Jeremiah.

Then I would have gone with him, thirty minutes later, to a devastated place where three hundred carcinogens in thirty-six different forms were poisoning the air he breathed. He would point to his film badge reassuringly and smile. I would tell him that the lethal radiation seeping into his insides was a hundred times as intense as that lying badge recorded. He'd probably have gone on smiling, for the dangers I was warning about are unseen, and unfelt, contrasted to the blinding light, intense heat and crushing force of the bomb. Why fear what you cannot hear, see, or feel?

And then I'd have told him that years later, brought to his knees by nameless, ravaging maladies, he would turn for help to those who'd ordered him into the trench. They'll sneer and laugh when they see you, I'd say, and tell you yours was a noble sacrifice, crawling into that trench. They'll tell you to get lost. What happened to you was almost nothing. It was only something we call a half rem, they'll say. Besides, we're not sure we believe you were even there that day. Quit bothering us.

Unbelievable and terrifyingly un-American, but what happened happened, and is still happening—to a young Lieutenant Saffer and now to an older and wiser author Saffer.

During my search for the truth I would be totally shocked and appalled by the hostile comments of those whom I thought were in the business of assisting atomic veterans. I would not know where to turn next. But then, when things appeared the darkest, I would be befriended by a man who had encountered the same things. But he fought back and won. He would give me hope and purpose when the government's attitude, my illness, and the absence of medical answers had thrown me into deep depression.

And then my friend, whom I had come to admire as much as any man I had ever known, would die. And I would stand by his casket the day of his funeral.

Then I would promise the spirit of my friend that I would complete what had become so significantly important to both of us. I would tell his spirit that I would not fail him. The story of the atomic veteran would be told the way he intended it to be. I would not stop until I wrote the final words of *Countdown Zero*.

Epilogue

Orville Kelly and I started this book in Burlington, Iowa, and Newport Beach, California, in November 1979, and I completed it in Washington, D.C., in October 1981.

I began the work as an inquisitive person who had nothing more to work with than some horrifying recollections and a title and a few pages of manuscript from a man who always wanted to write his third book entitled *Countdown Zero*. Orville Kelly chose the title, but the residue from nuclear weapons claimed him before he could write the book.

At times I felt I had embarked upon an impossible task, but one discovery begat another, and slowly the pieces of the puzzle began to come together. The facts I uncovered were often staggering and at times frightening.

As long as I live I shall never forget the expression on Dr. Gerald Johnson's face when I told him what happened to us in the trenches when the Hood shot was detonated. He registered disbelief and horror, and for the first time, I think, he realized that the military had ordered real human beings into those trenches when he was detonating the explosions in Nevada in 1957. But Johnson and I recognized that neither of us was supposed to know what the other was doing at the test site. Dr. Johnson has, since his nuclear weapons testing days, made official attempts to stop the arms race. He was the personal representative of Harold Brown at SALT II and is currently working on a plan to have the inventories of the world nuclear arsenals cut in half.

Gerry Johnson and I are but two veterans of nuclear testing who were eyewitnesses to the horrible destructive power of nuclear weapons. Now, twenty-four years after our Nevada Test Site experiences, we agree that if this bull-headed nuclear march to potential oblivion is not stopped, the consequences could lead to the end of civilization as we know it.

The atomic veteran story is important in one way, because people must be warned that any of them could easily become atomic veterans if the dedication to maintaining nuclear weapons supremacy remains unchecked.

However, we cannot change the past; we can only learn from it. And, to my knowledge, never has such blatant disregard for human life been allowed to continue unchecked for so long a period. During the writing of this book, eight of the men I interviewed died; their average age was 46.6 years. To the end, with but one exception, all eight were denied assistance by the Veterans Administration.

In my estimation, atomic veterans as a population are experiencing a mortality/morbidity rate three to five times that of the general population.

The solution to the tragedy of the casualties of the nuclear age is far from resolved, and perhaps the atomic veterans were not sacrificed in vain. They shall continue to be the living and dying examples of the victims of a technology that outgrew the moral responsibility of the participants. I hope Americans will be outraged enough to assure that the tragedy of the atomic veterans and their civilian counterparts will never be repeated. It is sad to see that so many Americans have become victims of government technology.

—T.H.S.

Epilogue

From *The New York Times*, February 8, 1982:

> Sacramento, Calif., Feb. 7 (UPI)—A former Army medic, breaking 25 years of silence, said today that he was ordered to enter false data to hide the fact that soldiers at four atomic tests in 1956 and 1957 were exposed to dangerously high levels of radiation.
>
> The former medic, Van R. Brandon, said the top secret medical group he had been in kept two sets of ledgers to record radiation readings from film badges worn by soldiers at the Yucca Flat, Nev., test site. . . .
>
> "We were instructed to keep two sets of books," Mr. Brandon said. "One set was to show that no one received an exposure above the approved dosimeter reading.
>
> "The other set of books was to show what the actual reading was. That set of books was brought in in a locked briefcase attached to a man's wrist by a set of handcuffs every morning," he said.

On February 9, 1982, the Department of Energy, the successor to the Atomic Energy Commission, denied all of Brandon's allegations.

Appendix

Roll Call

Taps

Mike Esperanza—cancer
Charles Broudy—cancer
Bill Starbuck—cancer
Orville Kelly—cancer
John Loveridge—cancer
Paul Cooper—leukemia
Carl Mautte—leukemia
Patrick Stout—leukemia
Claude Eatherley—cancer
Wayne Moore—perished in a fire
John Wayne—cancer
Susan Hayward—cancer
Agnes Moorehead—cancer
Dick Powell—cancer
Elizabeth Catalan's family: father—cancer,
  sister—unknown cause
Charles Fleming—unknown cause
James Kleinschmidt—cancer

Delayed Radiation Illness

Israel Torres—tumors, leukemia
Charles Trent—cancer
Jack Fisher—loss of one eye, left leg amputated
Donald Coe—leukemia
James Elliott—totally disabled
Sam Scione—totally disabled
Ted Lombard—totally disabled
Physician at shot Grable—totally disabled
Jim O'Connor—totally disabled
Former AEC field worker—cancer

How to Make a Freedom of Information Act Request:

Every citizen of the United States is entitled to obtain declassified documents from federal agencies. Further, requests may be made to have classified documents declassified.

The Center for National Security Studies, 122 Maryland Avenue N.E., Washington, D.C., 20002, publishes two guides:

Using the Freedom of Information Act: A Step by Step Guide

The 1981 Editon of Litigation Under the Federal Freedom of Information Act and Privacy Act

Source for Defense Nuclear Agency Reports:

Address: Washington, D.C. 20305

1. The Fact Sheet—toll-free number: (800) 336-3068
2. DNA reports of nuclear tests where military participants were present may be obtained from:

National Technical Information Service
5825 Port Royal Road
Springfield, Virginia 22161
Attn: Order Department

In order to obtain the reports you should have the reporting agency's file number, obtainable from the DNA computerized listing of published reports. Some of the reports are maintained in public and university libraries throughout the United States.

Atomic Veterans Organizations:

The National Association of Atomic Veterans
1109 Franklin Street
Burlington, Iowa 52501
Phone: (319) 753-6112
Director: Wanda Kelly

Australian Nuclear Veterans Association
P.O. Box 145
Moorooka, Queensland, 4105
Australia
Attn: Pat Creevy

Civilian Organizations:

National Committee for Radiation Victims
317 Pennsylvania Ave., SE
Washington, D.C. 20003
Director: Karen Wilson

Citizens' Call for Utah
3046 East 7145 South
Salt Lake City, Utah 24121
Director: Elizabeth Catalan

Nevada Test Site Radiation Victims Association
953 E. Sahara, Suite E 15A
Las Vegas, Nevada 89114
President: Bennie F. Levy

Legal Assistance:

The National Veterans' Law Center
Washington College of Law
Massachusetts and Nebraska Avenue N.W.
Washington, D.C. 20016
Director: Lewis Milford
Phone: (202) 686-2741

Medical Assistance:

Susan Lambert, M.D.
Henry Vyner, M.D.
Radiation Research Institute
2288 Fulton Street, Suite 306
Berkeley, California 94704
Phone: (415) 848-8056

Political Assistance:

Your U.S. representatives and senators have offices in your state or district and in Washington, D.C. Consult your local library for the *Congressional Directory Committees of the 97th Congress* which has a complete listing of all elected representatives and their committees.

Senate:

The Senate Veteran Affairs Committee
Alan K. Simpson, Wyoming, Chairman
Jonathan R. Steinberg, chief counsel
United States Senate
Washington, D.C. 20510

Smoky participants: 3,225
Contacted: 2,595

Results:

Leukemia Cell Type	*Cases Observed*	*Cases Expected*
All types	9	3.5
Acute myelocytic	4	1.1
Chronic myelocytic	3	0.7
Hairy cell	1	0
AML and CML	7	1.8

Nuclear Detonations

Total world number and yield of nuclear detonations through 1962:

Cumulative Total: 441
Cumulative Yield: 255,705 kilotons or 18,265 Hiroshimas

Total world number and yield of nuclear detonations through 1975:

Cumulative Total: 801
Cumulative Yield: 325,045 kilotons or 23,218 Hiroshimas

Countries that participated in atmospheric nuclear testing: United States, U.S.S.R., United Kingdom, France, Peoples Republic of China, India.

Source: *Health Physics*, Pergamon Press, Northern Ireland, July 1977

Number of Nuclear Weapons in World Arsenal:	
United States	30,200
U.S.S.R.	21,000
France	498
United Kingdom	364
China	194
India	Unknown

Source: *World Military and Social Expenditures 1980*, by Ruth Leger Sivard

Veterans Instructions for Filing Disability Claim

Contact your closest regional Veterans Administration office and obtain two forms:

1. Veterans application for compensation or pension, Form 21-526.
2. Standard Form 180

Procedure:

Form 21-526 is the form used for information pertaining to your case. Form 180 is the form used to request your military personnel and medical records. Locations of the record center for each branch of the service are found on the back of this form.

In Section II of Form 180, it is suggested you state:

"I request a copy of my entire military record, including all service medical records and other documents relating to my military service. In addition, I wish to obtain a record of my radiation exposure that may be contained in my military records or in records maintained by agencies that are affiliated with the Department of Defense."

In Section IV of Form 180, you should state:

"Claim for veteran's benefits."

You should obtain the following information:

a. The dates and location of the nuclear tests where you were present.

b. The operation or test shot code names.
c. The number of tests in which you were a participant.
d. The name of the organization to which you were assigned; your branch of service and your rank and serial number at the time of the test.
e. The duty station from which you were sent to the test site.
f. A detailed description of your activities during the entire period of participation as best you can recall, to include:
1. How far you were from ground zero or surface zero during each explosion.
2. Your position during the detonation (trench, ship, under cover, in the open, closed vehicle, plane, etc.).
3. Did you move to or toward ground zero or surface zero after the detonation? If so, how soon and how close to the detonation point did you proceed?
4. How long you remained in the vicinity of the explosion and after advancing to the close proximity of the detonation point.
5. What were the conditions around you?
   a. Wind changes
   b. Fallout
   c. Heavy dust, dirt or debris
g. Whether a film badge was issued and worn.
h. Names of other military personnel who were with you at the time of participation.
i. Complete clinical records of all medical care received during or after service tenure. Include all tissue blocks, slides, or other pathology samples. Keep *one* set yourself. Send a set via certified mail or have your physican and/or hospital send this vital information by certified mail.
j. Attempt to obtain from physicians, nuclear physicists and/or health physicists letters to support your

claim that your illness was caused by exposure to ionizing radiation.

Assistance in obtaining information to support your data for disability claim:

1. Dates and places of tests:
   a. National Association of Atomic Veterans
   b. Defense Nuclear Agency
2. Individual maneuvers at test sites:
   Project coordinators—National Association of Atomic Veterans
3. Military radiation exposure, alternate source:
   Reynolds Electrical and Engineering Company (REECO)
   P.O. Box 14100
   Las Vegas, Nevada
4. "Procedures for Adjudication of Ionizing Radiation Claims" This is a VA publication that delineates VA procedures that are used in judging a veteran's radiation claim. These forms may be obtained from the National Association of Atomic Veterans.

Procedural and Appellate Rights of the Veteran as published by the Veterans Administration:

Representation: You may be represented, without charge, by an accredited representative of a veterans organization or other service organization recognized by the Administrator of Veterans Affairs, or you may employ an attorney to assist you with your claim. Typical examples of counsel who may be available include attorneys in private practice or legal aid services. The services of a recognized attorney are subject to a maximum fee limitation of $10, set forth in 38 U.S.C 3404(c).

New Evidence: You may submit additional evidence to strengthen your claim. It is in your interest to send us any new evidence as promptly as possible. We will carefully consider it and let you know whether it changes our decision.

Personal Hearing: If you desire a personal hearing to present evidence or argument on any point of importance in your claim, notify this office and we will arrange a time and place for the hearing. You may bring witnesses if you desire and their testimony will be entered in the record. The VA will furnish the hearing room, provide hearing officials, and prepare the transcript of the proceedings. The VA cannot pay any other expenses of the hearing, since a personal hearing is not required.

Appeal: You may appeal our decision to the Board of Veterans Appeals at any time within one year from the date of this letter if you believe the decision is not in accord with the law and facts now of record. You can start the appeal process by filing a Notice of Disagreement. You may do this by writing a letter to this office stating that you wish to appeal. If more than one benefit is involved, you should identify the benefit or benefits for which you are appealing. If you decide to appeal, we will advise you further as to your procedural rights as your claim progresses through the several stages of the appeal process.

Glossary

Radiation: A Brief Explanation

The type of radiation emitted from nuclear explosions is called ionizing radiation. Ionizing radiation includes: x-rays, gamma rays, alpha, beta, and neutron radiation, natural background radiation, medical x-rays, and that emitted in all phases of the nuclear fuel cycle from mining and milling to waste storage. Ionizing radiations which are hazardous to the human body fall into two categories: 1) *external* radiation which originates from a radioactive source or material outside the body, and 2) *internal* radiation which results when a radioactive material is deposited inside the body through inhalation, ingestion, and/or breaks in the skin.

When radiation enters the body, one of four events may occur:

1) it may pass through the cell without causing any damage;
2) it may damage the cell, but the damage may be repaired;
3) it may damage the cell, but the cell may divide before being repaired;
4) it may kill the cell.

Internally deposited radioactive material is extremely hazardous since it produces constant radiation exposure until it is removed from the body by excretion or decay. The half-life of a radionuclide refers to the time necessary for one half of a given amount of it to decay.

The most common measurements of human radiation are rads and rems. Both refer to the amount of radiation absorbed by the body, but the rem is a more precise measurement of biological damage. Because the rem is an inconveniently large unit for radiation protection purposes, doses are often expressed in millirems (mrem). One rem equals 1000 millirems.

Compiled from: "Basic Radiological Safety Training Manual," prepared by Radiological Safety Division, Reynolds Electrical and Engineering Co., Inc., February, 1959, and "Radiation Health Information Packet," prepared by Environmental Policy Institute, 317 Pennsylvania Avenue, S.E., Washington, D.C. 20003.

Where and what types of radioactive elements attack the human body:

Bone	*Half-life*
Barium 140	13 days
Phosphorous 32	14 days
Promethium 147	2 years
Plutonium 239	24,000 years
Radium 226	1,620 years
Ruthenium 106	1 year
Strontium 90	28 years
Yitrium 90	2 years
Zinc 65	245 days
Liver	
Cobalt 60	5 years
Lungs	
Krypton 85	10 years
Radon 222	38 days
Plutonium 239	24,000 years
Uranium 233	162,000 years

Muscle	
Cesium 137	30 years
Potassium 42	12 hours
Ovaries and Testes	
Barium 140	13 days
Cesium 137	30 years
Cobalt 60	5 years
Iodine 131	8 days
Krypton 85	10 years
Potassium 42	12 hours
Plutonium 239	24,000 years
Ruthenium 106	1 year
Zinc 65	245 days
Skin	
Sulfur 35	87 days
Thyroid	
Iodine 131	8 days

Source: Corbet P. Stewart, *Toxicology Mechanisms and Analytical Methods*, Academic Press, 1962

Definition of Terms:

airburst — A nuclear weapon exploded at an altitude of more than 500 feet.

alpha particle — A helium nucleus, consisting of two protons and two neutrons, with a double positive charge.

atom — The smallest particle of an element.

atomic cloud — An all-inclusive term for the mixture of hot gases, smoke, dust, and other particulate matter from the bomb itself and from the environment, which is carried aloft in conjunction with the rising ball of fire produced by the detonation of a nuclear/atomic weapon.

beta particle A charge particle emitted from the nucleus of an atom and having a mass and charge equal in magnitude to those of the electron.

dosimeter An individual dosage-indicating device—more specifically, a direct-reading quartz-fiber electroscope sensitive to gamma radiation and about the size of a fountain pen. Otherwise known as a pocket dosimeter, a pocket electroscope, or a quartz-fiber dosimeter.

fallout The process or phenomenon of the fall back to the earth's surface of particles contaminated with radioactive material from the nuclear cloud. The term is also applied in a collective sense to the contaminated particulate matter itself.

film badge A small packet containing photographic film which is used to obtain individual radiation dosage readings. Readings are primarily of gamma radiation.

fission The process whereby the nucleus of a particular heavy element

	splits into (generally) two nuclei of lighter elements, with the release of substantial amounts of energy. The most important fissionable materials are uranium 235 and plutonium 239.
fusion	The process whereby the nuclei of light elements, especially those of the isotopes of hydrogen, namely, deuterium and tritium, combine to form the nucleus of a heavier element with the release of substantial amounts of energy.
gamma rays	High frequency (short wave) electromagnetic radiation emitted by some radioactive nuclei. These rays differ from other magnetic radiations primarily in that they result from transformations within the nuclei of atoms rather than from the electrons outside the nucleus as in the case of x-rays. These rays move at the speed of light.
Geiger counter	A low-dose-rate, high-sensitivity detector of beta and gama radiations. It may be either a lightweight portable detector or a laboratory instrument. Also known as a Geiger-Müller counter.
genetic effect of radiation	Inheritable changes, chiefly mutations, produced by the absorption of ionizing radiations.
ground zero	The point on the surface of the

land or water vertically below or above the center of a burst of a nuclear weapon.

half-life The period of time it takes for the radioactivity of any amount of the element to be reduced by half, i.e., The half-life of strontium 90 is twenty-eight years. Starting with one pound of strontium 90, in twenty-eight years there will be one half pound of radioactive material, in twenty-eight more years there will be one quarter pound, etc.

hydrogen bomb A term sometimes applied to nuclear weapons in which part of the explosive energy is obtained from nuclear fusion (or thermonuclear) reactions.

kiloton The energy of a nuclear explosion which is equivalent to that produced by the explosion of 1 kiloton (i.e., 1,000 tons) of TNT.

megaton An explosive force equal to 1,000,000 tons of TNT, or 1,000 kilotons.

neutron Elementary nuclear particle with a mass approximately the same as that of a hydrogen atom and electrically neutral. Neutrons attack the central nervous system causing immediate nausea, diarrhea, and convulsions. Depending on the dose, some victims die within hours, while for others, death comes sixty to ninety days later with respiratory failure, delirium, or coma. Those not killed would be prone to leukemia or other cancers in later years.

Nevada Test Site (NTS) — A 1,350-square-mile area in southern Nevada about 65 miles northwest of Las Vegas.

nuclear radiation — Particulate and electromagnetic radiation emitted from atomic nuclei in various nuclear processes. From a weapons standpoint the important nuclear radiations are alpha and beta particles, gamma rays, and neutrons. All nuclear radiations are ionizing radiations.

rad — A unit of absorbed dose of radiation; it represents the absorption of 100 ergs of nuclear (or ionizing) radiation per gram of the absorbing material or tissue.

radiation sickness — A syndrome chracterized by nausea, vomiting, diarrhea, and psychic depression, following exposure to appreciable doses of ionizing radiation.

rem — a unit of biological dose of radiation; the acronym derives from "roentgen equivalent man."

shock wave — A continuously propagated pressure pulse (or wave) in the surrounding medium which may be air, water, or earth, initiated by the expansion of the hot gases produced in an explosion.

thermonuclear device — A hydrogen bomb in which very high temperatures are induced by a fission reaction to bring about the fusion of light nuclei to form the nucleus of a heavier atom, thus releasing a large amount of energy and producing fewer radioactive isotopes (fission products).

weapons effects — A nuclear detonation conducted for the purpose of testing a nuclear device intended for a specific type of weapon system.

yield — The total effective energy released in a nuclear (or atomic) explosion. It is usually expressed in terms of the equivalent tonnage of TNT required to produce the same energy release in an explosion. The total energy yield is manifested as nuclear radiation, thermal radiation, and shock (and blast) energy, the actual distribution being dependent upon the medium in which the explosion occurs (primarily and also upon the type of weapon and the time after detonation).

Notes

Specific citations are not given for material obtained by Thomas H. Saffer during the course of confidential interviews with individuals who were involved in the atmospheric nuclear weapons testing program.

Abbreviations: AEC = Atomic Energy Commission
UCRL = University of California Radiation Laboratory

Chapter 1

page **19**
Voice: Shaun Carberry, "Atomic Testing Ends in Sickness and Death," *Enlisted Times*, 5/79, p.6.
page **20**
Priscilla: "Administrative Plan 1-57, Desert Rock VII, Marine Corps," 5/15/57; "Test Director's Report on Operation Plumbbob," UCRL, 11/15/57.
page **24**
Mission: "Exercise Desert Rock VII and VIII, 1956–1957, Final Report of Operations, U.S. Army."
page **25**
Mission: TSgt. R. A. Suhosky, "Biggest Shot," *Leatherneck*, 9/57, p.31.
Tschirgi: Biographical Information, Marine Corps Historical Center.
Order: "Brigade Order 003121.2," 5/27/57.
page **26**
Mission: "Exercise Desert Rock VII and VIII, 1956–1957, Final Report of Operations, U.S. Army."

page 27

Clean Weapons: AEC Meeting No. 1265, 2/11/57; J. W. Finney, "Clean Bomb Development," *New York Times*, 6/25/57.

Nevada Test Site: AEC, "Location of Proving Ground for Atomic Weapons," 12/13/50; *Washington Post*, 12/19/78.

Concern: *Time*, 6/3/57.

page 28

Fallout: "The Effects of High-Yield Nuclear Explosions," statement by Lewis L. Strauss, chairman AEC, 2/55; Message to JCS from Gruenther, Paris, France, 3/55; Message to Gruenther from JCS, 3/11/55; AEC Meeting No. 1062, 2/23/55.

page 29

Threats: Thomas H. Saffer interview, 4/13/80.

Advance Party: THS interview, 5/20/80

page 30

AEC quarters: AEC, "Continental Atomic Tests—Background Information for Observers," Summer 1957.

page 31

Nevada Test Site: AEC, "Location . . ." 12/13/50; Memo to Brig. Gen. K. E. Fields, Dir. Div. of Military Application, from Shields Warren, M.D., Dir. Div. of Biology and Medicine, AEC, Appendix F, 3/25/52.

Troop placement: Letter to Chief, Armed Forces Special Weapons Project, from Commandant of the Marine Corps, 10/1/52.

Troop responsibility: Letter to Dir. AEC Div. of Military Application, from Chief of Armed Forces Special Weapons Project, 10/15/52; AEC Meeting No. 794, 12/23/52; *Infantry School Quarterly*, 10/55, p. 13.

page 34

Participants: "Exercise Desert Rock VII and VIII, 1956-1957, Final Report of Operations, U.S. Army, Annex E—Actual Participation from All Sources, Observers-Troops-Projects"; "Effects of Radiation on Human Health," hearings before the Subcommittee on Health and the Environment of the Committee on Interstate and Foreign Commerce, House of Representatives, 95th Congress, 2nd Session, 1/25/78.

pages 37–39

Handouts: "Operation Plumbbob, Nevada Test Site, May–October 1957, Field Radiological Defense Operations, Civil Effects Test Group, Appendix D."

page 41

Trenches: "Administrative Plan 1-57, Desert Rock VII, Marine

Corps," 5/29/57;" Exercise Desert Rock VII and VIII, 1956–1957, Final Report of Operations, U.S. Army."

Balloon: "Test Director's Report on Operation Plumbbob," UCRL, 11/15/57, p. 53.

Animals: Shirley McGreal, "Monkeys Go to War," *Mainstream*, Winter 1981, pp. 20-22.

page **45**

Priscilla: "Exercise Desert Rock VII and VIII . . ."; Letter, Wieler, 7/17/57.

pages **51–52**

Helicopters: "Operation Plumbbob On-Site Rad-Safety Report—OTO-57-2," Reynolds Electrical and Engineering Co., Inc., Health and Safety Division, 9/57.

Fallout: "You Go to Desert Rock," *Armed Forces Talk*, 9/19/52; "Operation Plumbbob On-Site . . ."

Chapter 2

page **55**

Arming Party: "Test Director's Operation Plan, Operation Plumbbob," 4/1/57, p. 126.

page **59**

Diablo; Loudon S. Wainwright, "The Heroic Disarming of Diablo," Life, 8/22/57.

page **60**

Fallout: Dan Noyes et al., "Operation Wigwam," *New West*, 12/1/80, p. 27; "The Forgotten Guinea Pigs," A Report on Health Effects of Low-Level Radiation Sustained as a Result of the Nuclear Weapons Testing Program Conducted by the U.S. Government, for use of the Committee on Interstate and Foreign Commerce, U.S. House of Representatives and Its Subcommittee on Oversight and Investigation, 96th Congress, 2nd Session, 8/80.

pages **61–62**

Teller: William Manchester, *The Glory and the Dream: A Narrative History of America, 1932–1972* (Little, Brown and Co., 1975), pp. 699–701; "The Day After Trinity," documentary film, 1981.

USSR test: Daniel M. Wilkes, "Lawrence and Livermore," *Newsline* (Lawrence Livermore Laboratory, University of California, Fall 1978).

pages **63–64**

Teller: Alice Kimball Smith and Charles Weiner, *Robert Oppen-*

heimer, Letters and Recollections (Harvard University Press, 1980), p. 285; Manchester, *The Glory . . .*

McMahon: David E. Lilienthal, *Journals of David E. Lilienthal: Atomic Energy Years 1945–1950* (Harper & Row, 1964), pp. 388–92.

Harold Brown: Wilkes, *Newsline*, 1978.

page 65

Livermore Laboratory: "Lawrence Livermore Laboratory," 8/78; "Lawrence Livermore Laboratory Background and Current Research" (Lawrence Livermore Laboratory, University of California, Feb. 1980).

page 66

Fallout: AEC Meeting No. 1265, 2/11/57; AEC "Radiation Annex to Public Information and Education Plan for Operation Plumbbob," 5/15/57; "Paul Jacobs and the Nuclear Gang," documentary film, 1979.

Clean weapons: "Ike Says This About 'Clean' Bomb," *U.S. News and World Report*, 7/5/57.

pages 67–68

New procedure: "Test Director's Report on Operation Plumbbob," UCRL, 11/15/57.

Brigade at Hood: Nevada Test Organization, Office of Test Information, Release no. OTI-57-NN, 6/28/57.

page 69

Trench locations: "Exercise Desert Rock VII and VIII, 1956–1957, Final Report of Operations, U.S. Army."

Coulomb A: "Announced United States Nuclear Tests July 1945 through December 1979" (Dept. of Energy, 1/80).

Moratorium: Tod Ensign and Michael Uhl, *G.I. Guinea Pigs* (Playboy Press, 1980).

page 72

Arming Hood: "Test Director's Report on Operation Plumbbob," UCRL, 11/15/57.

page 74

Effects: *Las Vegas Sun*, 7/6/57; *Brownsville Herald*, 7/5/57.

page 75

Delay: "Veterans' Claims for Disabilities from Nuclear Weapons Testing," hearing before the Committee on Veterans' Affairs, U.S. Senate, 96th Congress, 6/20/79, p. 57.

page 76

Echo Company: "Veterans' Claims . . ."

Torres: THS interview; "The Israel Torres Story," *Atomic Veterans Newsletter*, Spring 1980.

page 79

Survey Team: "Operation Plumbbob On-Site Rad-Safety Report, OTO-57-2," Reynolds Electrical and Engineering Co., Inc., Radiological Safety Division, U.S. AEC, 9/57.

Altitude: Robert Considine, "Most Powerful A-Blast Set Off at Nevada Site," *Deseret News—Salt Lake Telegram*, 7/5/57.

pages 81–82

Sherker and Putnam: "Effects of Radiation on Human Health," hearings before the Subcommittee on Health and the Environment of the Committee on Interstate and Foreign Commerce, U.S. House of Representatives, 95th Congress, 2nd Session, January 24, 25, 26, February 8, 9, 14, 28, 1978, pp. 316, 1089.

Neutron: "Test Director's Report on Operation Plumbbob," UCRL, 11/15/57.

pages 83–84

Neutron: Letter to THS from Lt. Col. William J. McGee, U.S. Army, Freedom of Information Officer, 7/7/80.

Operations Order: "Test Director's Report on Operation Plumbbob . . ."

Epigraph: AEC Meeting No. 1062, 2/23/55.

page 85

Hardtack: "Operation Hardtack, Eniwetok Proving Ground, March–August 1958, Final Report," prepared by Commander Task Group 7.3.

Chapter 3

page 87

Epigraph: "A Lonesome GI, Eniwetok Atoll," excerpt from a poem written in 1956, author unknown.

page 94

Marshall Atoll: "Marshall Islands—A Chronology 1944–1978," Micronesia Support Committee.

page 95

Relocation: Giff Johnson, "Marshall Islands: The Radioactive Trust," *New Pacific Magazine*, Nov.–Dec. 1980.

Planning Test: AEC, Meeting No. 1308, 10/22/57.

page 96

Hardtack I: "Announced United States Nuclear Tests July 1945 through December 1979" (Dept. of Energy, 1/80).

page 99
Security: *Atomic Times*, 4/13/56.
page 116
Ball of flame: "Announced Nuclear . . ."
Fitzpatrick: *Sacramento Bee*, 6/27/80.
page 120
Fisher: Letter to OEK from Jack Fisher.

Chapter 4

page 143
Feres: Feres v. United States, 340 U.S. Code 135, 95L ed 152, 71 S CT 153.

Chapter 5

page 152
Cooper: Nancy Cooper, "The Paul Cooper Story," *Atomic Veterans Newsletter*, Spring 1980.
Bones: Howard Rosenberg, *Atomic Soldiers* (Beacon Press, 1980).
Uniform: Frank W. Martin, "Paul Cooper was the Army's Nuclear Guinea Pig," *People*, 8/1/77.
page 154
Pekarsky: George Raine, *Salt Lake City Tribune*, 4/7/77.
page 155
Carter: Raine, *Salt Lake City* . . .
page 156
Cosgriff: Raine, *Salt Lake City* . . .
page 161
Jones: "Effects of Radiation on Human Health," hearings before the Subcommittee on Health and the Environment of the Committee on Interstate and Foreign Commerce, U.S. House of Representatives, 95th Congress, 2nd Session, January 24, 25, 26, February 8, 9, 14, 28, 1978.
page 167
Testimony: Transcript of testimony given by OEK before Veterans Administration Regional Board, Des Moines, Iowa, 4/3/79.
page 175
Pilgrims on the path: "VA Nuclear Test Claims Appear Low," *U.S. Medicine*, 12/1/80.

Chapter 6

page 178
Resolution of inquiry: George Raine, *Salt Lake City Tribune*, 9/1/77.

page 179
Records: "Studies of Participants in Nuclear Tests, Annual Report for the Period September 1, 1979–August 31, 1980," prepared by C. Dennis Robinette for the National Academy of Sciences-National Research Council, Washington, D.C.; Shaun Carberry, "Atomic Testing Ends in Sickness and Death," *Enlisted Times*, 5/79, p. 6.

page 194
AP report: "A-Test Veterans to Receive More Aid," *Los Angeles Times*, 6/21/79.

Chapter 7

page 203
Mautte: Letter to Carl V. Mautte from L. J. Piccirillo, Adjudication Officer Veterans Administration, Hartford, Conn., 11/19/79.

page 204
Stout: "Reassessing the Health Threat of Radiation," *Medical World News*, 4/13/70, p. 23.

page 205
Eatherly at Hiroshima: Robert E. Light, *National Guardian*, 3/27/61.

page 207
Epigraph: "60 Minutes," CBS television network, 9/28/80.
Reactions: "Operation Crossroads, the Official Pictorial Record," Office of the Historian Joint Task Force One (Wm. H. Wise and Co., 1946).

page 208
Moore: Letter from Wayne Moore to his mother, 5/18/46.

page 212
Radiation: Letter to Norman Solomon from Ellen L. Goldstein, 12/18/79.

pages 213–14
Epigraph: "The Effects of High-Yield Nuclear Explosions," statement by Lewis L. Strauss, chairman AEC, 2/55.
Bravo Fallout: "Marshall Islands—A Chronology 1944–1978," Micronesia Support Committee.

Marshallese: Giff Johnson, "Marshall Islands: The Radioactive Trust," *The New Pacific Magazine*, November–December 1980.

page **216**

Anjain: "Proceedings of the National Citizens' Hearings for Radiation Victims," Washington, D.C., 4/12/80.

page **217**

Ataddy: Glenn Alcalay, "Marshall Islands Field Report, March 4–April 7, 1981.

page **218**

Torch bearer: Letter to Sen. William L. Armstrong from Lt. Col. Hartman B. Mowery, DNA, 11/29/79.

Other son: "Veterans' Claims for Disabilities from Nuclear Weapons Testing," hearing before the Committee on Veterans' Affairs, U.S. Senate, 96th Congress, 6/20/79.

page **219**

Epigraph: AEC Meeting No. 1062, 2/23/55.

Increase in tests: "Veterans' Claims . . ."

page **223**

St. George Radiation: "The Forgotten Guinea Pigs," A Report on Health Effects of Low-Level Radiation Sustained as a Result of the Nuclear Weapons Testing Program Conducted by the U.S. Government, for use of the Committee on Interstate and Foreign Commerce, U.S. House of Representatives and its Subcommittee on Oversight and Investigation, 96th Congress, 2nd Session, 8/80.

pages **224–25**

Epigraph: David E. Lilienthal, *Atomic Energy: A New Start* (Harper & Row, 1980), p. 29.

Grable: T. R. Fehrenback, *This Kind of War* (Macmillan Company, 1963), p. 641; S. T. Cohen, "Enhanced Radiation Warheads: Setting the Record Straight," *Strategic Review*, Winter 1978; THS interview.

pages **226–27**

Film stars: Statement by Tim Barker, "The Cancer Connection," KABC-TV, Los Angeles, 1981; Karen Jackovich and Mark Sennet, "New Controversy over John Wayne's Death—Did A-Bomb Tests Give Him and Other Stars Cancer?" *People*, 11/10/80, pp. 42-47.

page **231**

Telsa: AEC Meeting No. 1063, 3/1/55; Letter to Sen. William L. Armstrong . . .

Notes

Chapter 8

page **239**
Fact sheet: "Defense Nuclear Agency Fact Sheet," Public Affairs Office, Washington, D.C.

page **240**
Priscilla: Letter to THS from Lt. Col. William J. McGee, U.S. Army, Freedom of Information Officer, 7/7/80.

page **241**
Tests at Frenchman Flat: Letter to THS from David G. Jackson, Freedom of Information, Dept. of Energy, Nevada Test Operations office, 7/18/80.

page **247**
Neutrons: Frank von Hippel, "Induced Surface Radioactivity from Nuclear Explosions Just Above the Earth's Surface, A Preliminary Draft," 1/23/80; Hdqtrs. Task Group 7.2, Joint Task Force Seven, "Radiological Safety Monitor's Reference Handbook," 2/56.

page **255**
Bomb: Todd Ensign and Michael Uhl, *G.I. Guinea Pigs* (Playboy Press, 1980), p. 76.

page **259**
Radiation Tests: Howard Rosenberg, "How Much Radiation Can an Astronaut Withstand? NASA Used Dwayne Sexton to Find Out—Informed Consent," *Mother Jones*, Sept./Oct. 1981; Richard Ballantine and Joel Griffiths, *Silent Slaughter* (Henry Regnery Co., 1972).

page **270**
Russia: AEC, "Remote After Effects of Radiation Damage," translation of Russian data, 1972.

page **271**
Smoky: Glyn Caldwell, M.D. et al., "Leukemia Among Participants in Military Maneuvers at a Nuclear Bomb Test—A Preliminary Report," *Journal American Medical Association*, vol. 244; Letter to Morley Safer, "60 Minutes," from Congressman Tim Lee Carter, 9/30/81.

page **273**
Test participants: "Nuclear Test Participants by Service" (Defense Nuclear Agency, 1980).

page **274**
Animals: Marilee Strong, "Dispute Over What Those Animal N-

Tests Results Mean," *Livermore–Pleasanton Valley Times*, 8/7/80.

Chapter 9

page 282

Wilson: "Analysis of Radiation Exposure for Task Force Warrior, Shot Smoky, Exercise Desert Rock VII-VIII, Operation Plumbbob," prepared by Science Applications, Inc., for DNA, 5/31/79; "After Action Report, U.S. Army, Technical Service Chiefs, Operation Plumbbob, Camp Desert Rock VII and VIII, Annex G"; "Operation Plumbbob On-Site Rad-Safety Report—OTO-57-2," Reynolds Electrical and Engineering Co., Inc., Health and Safety Div. 9/57; "Operation Plumbbob Off-Site Rad-Safety Report—OTO-57-3," 11/12/58; Letter to THS from Lt. Col. William McGee, 3/14/80.

page 283

Epigraph: Letter to G. V. (Sonny) Montgomery, Chairman of the Committee on Veterans' Affairs, House of Representatives, from William H. Taft, IV, General Counsel DOD, 9/4/81.

Film badges: "Basic Radiological Safety Training Manual," Reynolds Electrical and Engineering Co., Inc., Radiological Safety Div., 2/79.

page 284

Film badges: "Report of Participation in Selected Volunteer Program of Desert Rock V-7," 4/25/53.

Radiation gauge: "Radiological Defense, An Introduction to Instruments for Military Use," vol. IV, prepared by Armed Forces Special Weapons Project, 1/50.

page 285

Claims: "Joint Dept. of Defense and VA Memo of Understanding on Investigation of Ionizing Radiation Injury Claims from Veteran Atmospheric Nuclear Weapons Tests Participants," 6/15/79.

page 286

Mancuso: "Proceedings of the National Citizens' Hearings for Radiation Victims," Washington, D.C. 4/12/80.

page 288

VA official: George Raine, *Salt Lake City Tribune*, 4/7/77.

page 289

Bross: Irwin Bross, "What Is Fair Compensation for Veterans Exposed to Fallout from Nuclear Weapons Tests?" American Statistical Association, Houston, Texas, 8/13/80.

page 293
Jess Clark: Letter to Lew Golinker, Natl. Vet. Law Center, from Jess Clark, 9/4/80.
page 296
Lambert: Susan Lambert, M.D., "The Veterans Administration: A Theoretical Workers' Compensation That Fails the Atomic Veteran," 3/12/81.
page 297
Gott v. Cleland: *Gott v. Cleland,* U.S. District Court for the District of Columbia, Civil Action 80-906, Washington, D.C., 4/10/80.
page 298
Cranston: *Congressional Record*, Senate, 6/15/81.
page 299
Taft: Letter to G. V. (Sonny) Montgomery . . .
Legislation: *Congressional Record*, Senate, 10/16/81.
Loewe and Mendelsohn: Eliot Marshall, "New A-Bomb Studies Alter Radiation Estimates," *Science*, vol. 212, 5/22/81.
page 302
Gibbons: *Las Vegas Sun*, 11/7/81.
Halflife: Helen Caldicott, *Nuclear Madness*, (Autumn Press, 1978), p. 5.
page 303
Russian disaster: "The Kyshtym Disaster," produced by Jeanne Solomon, "60 Minutes," CBS-TV network, 8/2/81.

Additional References

Armed Forces Special Weapons Project. "Radiological Defense, An Introduction to Radiological Instruments for Military Use." Vol. 4, January 1950.

Atomic Energy Commission. "Atomic Test Effects in the Nevada Test Site Region." January 1955.

_____. "Civil Effects Test Group Continental Tests, Operation Plumbbob, Nevada Test Site." June 25, 1957.

_____. "Information for Participants in Federal Civil Defense Administration in Operation Plumbbob." December 3, 1956.

_____. "Joint AEC-DOD Public Information Plan for Operation Plumbbob." May 2, 1957.

_____. "Nevada Test Site Information Handbook." March 10, 1957.

_____. "Public Information Plan for Operation Plumbbob." February 12, 1957.

_____. "Troop Participation in Continental Tests," November 22, 1957.

_____. Meeting No. 677. April 1, 1952.

_____. Meeting No. 865. May 21, 1953.

_____. Meeting No. 1313. November 6, 1957.

Bertell, Dr. Rosalie. Affadavit presented before Veterans Administration Board of Appeals in Washington D.C., September 11, 1979.

_____. Letter to Don Hewitt, producer, CBS News, "60 Minutes." October 10, 1980.

"Camp Desert Rock—Information Book," U.S. Army. 1957.

"The Day After Trinity," Documentary Film produced by John Else for Public Television station KTEH, San Jose, California, 1981.

Department of the Army. "Atomic Battlefield." *The Big Picture*, April 14, 1958.

Department of Defense. "The Effects of Nuclear Weapons." Published by the U.S. Atomic Energy Commission, June 1957.

"Discussion of Radiological Hazards Associated with a Continental Test Site for Atomic Bombs," Minutes of a meeting held at the Los Alamos Scientific Laboratory, Los Alamos, New Mexico, August 1, 1950.

"Exercise Desert Rock V—Marine Corps Report." Headquarters 2nd Marine Corps Provisional Atomic Exercise Brigade, Camp Pendleton, California, May 19, 1953.

Favish, Allan. "Radiation Injury and the Atomic Veteran." *Hastings Law Journal*, XXXII (March 1981).

Hersey, John. *Hiroshima*. New York: Bantam Books, 1959.

Hill, Gladwin. "Atom Test Rips Blockhouse." *New York Times*, June 25, 1957.

Hugghe, Patrick, and Konigsberg, David. "Grim Legacy of Nuclear Testing." *New York Times Magazine*, April 22, 1979.

Additional References

Jablon, Seymour. "The Origin and Findings of the Atomic Bomb Casualty Commission." *Nuclear Safety*, XIV (November 1973).

Johnson, Giff. "Another Nuclear Cover-Up." *New Pacific Magazine*, vol. 6. no. 2.

Joint Chiefs of Staff. Memorandum to the Director of Military Application, Atomic Energy Commission, March 20, 1967.

_____. "Radioactivity Aspects of Atomic Warfare." October 11, 1956.

Joint Task Force 1. Memorandum from Commander to the President, August 5, 1946.

McCarthy, Shirley. "VA Defends Policies, Not A-Bomb Victims." *Washington Post*, August 4, 1980.

"Marines Await A-Blast." *Las Vegas Review-Journal*, June 25, 1957.

"Measurement of the Residual Radiation Intensity at the Hiroshima and Nagasaki Atomic Bomb Sites." Naval Medical Research Institute, Naval Medical Center, Bethesda, Maryland, April 16, 1946.

"Medical Aspects of Atomic Explosions." Artillery and Guided Missile School, July 1953.

Miller, Judith, and Miller, Mark. "Cancergate: America's Nuclear Whitewash," *Swank*, August 1980.

Morgan, Karl Z. "Cancer and Low-Level Ionizing Radiation." Lecture at the Fourth International Summer School on Radiation Protection, Dubrovnik, Yugoslavia, August 21—September 1, 1979.

National Academy of Sciences. "Study of Participants at Tests of Nuclear Weapons." Paper presented at the 28th Annual Scientific Meeting, Radiation Research Society, New Orleans, Louisiana, July 1-5, 1980.

"Nevada Test Site Road and Facility Map." Prepared by Holmes and Narver, Inc., for the U.S. Department of Energy.

"Nuclear Armaments, An Interview with Daniel Ellsberg." *Conservation Press*, Berkeley, California, Spring 1980.

"Operation Plumbbob, Civil Effects Test Group." Office of Technical Services, Department of Commerce, Washington D.C., August 17, 1960.

Pincus, Walter. "National Archives Yield Secret Radiation Data." *Washington Post*, April 13, 1980.

Pinsky, Mark Alan. "The Legacy." *Critical Mass Journal*, vol. 6, May 1980.

Pollock, Richard. "The Guinea Pig Brigade." *Critical Mass Journal*, vol. 5, August 1979.

"Report of Exercise Desert Rock VI—Marine Corps, 3rd Marine Corps Provisional Atomic Exercise Brigade." March 1955.

"Report of the Interagency Task Force on Compensation for Radiation-Related Illnesses: Phase I." February 1, 1980.

Southwick, Rodney L., Assistant Director DIS. Memorandum to Brigadier General A. D. Starbird, DMA, April 15, 1957.

Storke, Brigadier General H P. Memorandum to Each Member of the Camp Desert Rock Command, June 2, 1952.

Taylor, General Maxwell D. Memorandum to the Secretary of Defense re Operation Plumbbob (formerly Pilgrim), March 8, 1957.

Vyner, Henry M. "The Psychological Effects of Ionizing Radiation." Radiation Research Institute, Berkeley, California.

"Were You There?" *Parade*, June 1977.

Index

Index

Index

Index